I0733330

ALSO BY MARIA V. SNYDER

CHRONICLES OF IXIA / STUDY SERIES

Poison Study

The Study of Poisons

Magic Study

The Study of Magic

Fire Study

The Study of Fire (forthcoming)

Shadow Study

Night Study

Dawn Study

The Study Chronicles: Tales of Ixia & Sitia

CHRONICLES OF IXIA / GLASS SERIES

Storm Glass

Sea Glass

Spy Glass

THE ARCHIVES OF THE INVISIBLE SWORD SERIES

The Eyes of Tamburah

The City of Zirdai

The King of Koraha

THE SENTINELS OF THE GALAXY SERIES

Navigating the Stars

Chasing the Shadows

Defending the Galaxy

HEALER SERIES

Touch of Power

Scent of Magic

Taste of Darkness

INSIDER SERIES

Inside Out

Outside In

OTHER BOOKS

Up to the Challenge

(A Collection of SF & Fantasy Short Stories)

Storm Watcher

(A Middle Grade Novel)

Discover more titles by Maria V. Snyder at www.MariaVSnyder.com

THE STUDY OF MAGIC

MARIA V. SNYDER

The Study of Magic / Maria V. Snyder

Cover design by Joy Kenney

Interior Art by Dema Harb

Maps by Martyna Kuklis

Published by Maria V. Snyder

Paperback ISBN 9781946381248

Hardcover ISBN 9781946381255

Digital ISBN 9781946381231

To Amy Kaplan. You reached out to me all those years ago, and I'm so grateful that you've become my friend. Here's to many more weekend hijinks, writing retreats, and tea!

And to Kitty (a.k.a Valek the Bug Assassin) for keeping my lap warm during all those late night writing sessions. I forgive you for deleting page 214 when you decided to snooze on my keyboard.

THE TERRITORY OF IXIA & THE CLANS OF SITIA

Designed by Martyna Kuklis

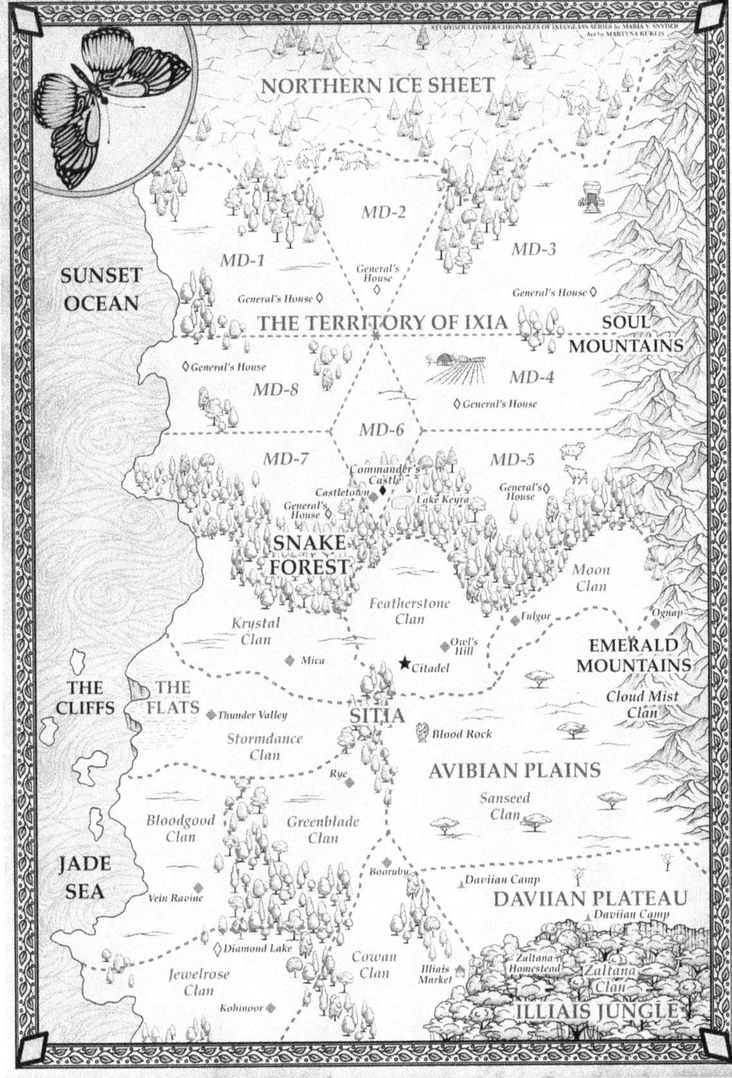

THE COMMANDER'S CASTLE COMPLEX
Designed by Martyna Kuklis

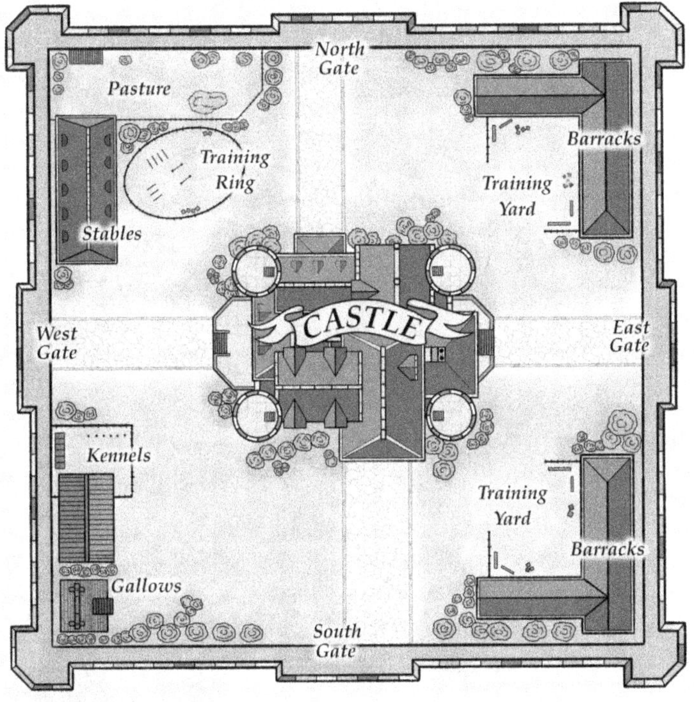

THE MAGICIAN'S KEEP
Designed by Martyna Kuklis

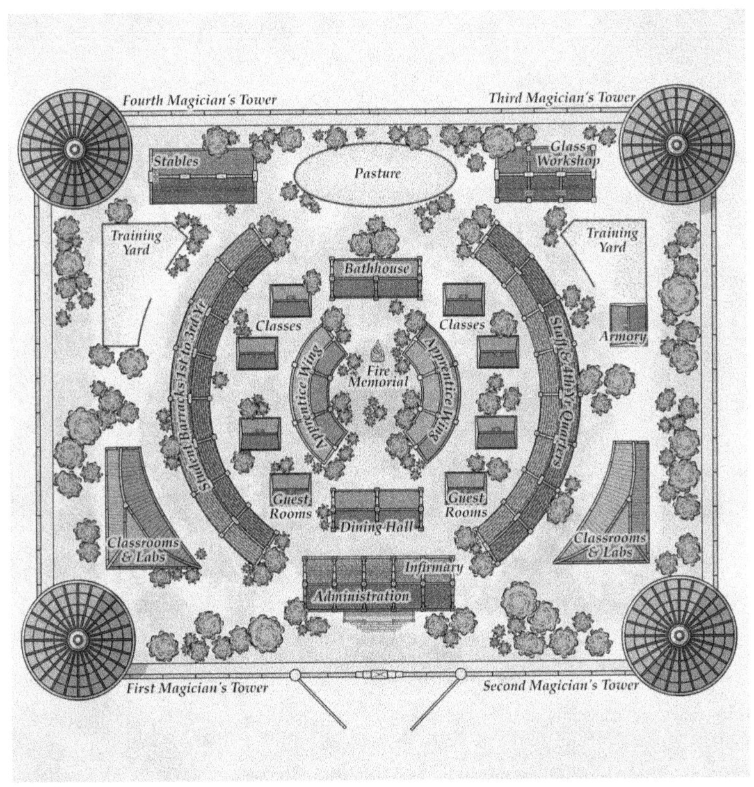

THE CITADEL

Designed by Martyna Kuklis

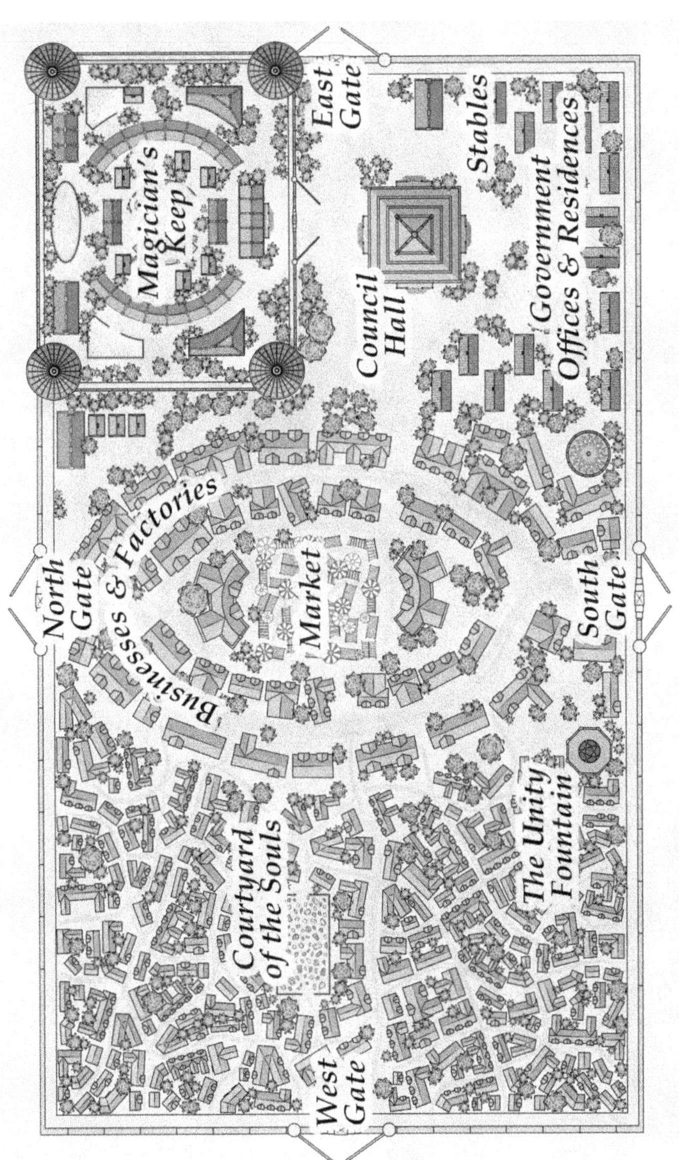

CHAPTER 1

The oversized manor house sat like a fat cow amid the brown fields. Rows of dried-out wheat stalks stubbled the ground, providing no cover for Valek. He and Ziva Moon camped in the small woods nearby, waiting for darkness. A chilly wind blew from the west. It rattled the dead leaves and smelled of rain.

Valek studied the crude map Ziva had drawn on the cold, hard ground. She'd marked all the entrances, windows, and the best route to Ruby, her daughter's, room. A path that would reduce the risk of Valek encountering anyone, especially her ex-husband, Dothan. Not that Valek couldn't handle the powerful magician, but this was a classic snatch and dash operation. It worked best without any witnesses.

"I should go with you," Ziva said. "You're a stranger. Ruby will be scared." She tucked her long brown hair behind an ear. Where it stayed for three seconds before the wind pushed it back into her pretty face.

It was a bad idea for so many reasons. "You need to stay here. If Dothan catches you, I'll have to save you and then there'll be no chance of rescuing your daughter because he'll be on alert. Don't worry, Ruby won't even wake up until she's in your arms." Thank fate, or the four-year-old child was bound to make enough noise to rouse the household.

"Is sleeping juice safe for kids?"

Mothers. Valek suppressed a sigh. "Yes. It's just a small dose. You should focus on your plans for after you have your daughter. Do you know where you're going to stay?"

"My mother—"

"No. That'll be the first place Dothan looks."

"I've a cousin in—"

"No relatives or friends."

"I could return to—"

"No previous addresses."

"Maybe Fulgor—"

"No cities in the Moon Clan's lands."

She huffed. "I am a magician, too. I can use my illusion magic to hide from Dothan."

"Are you strong enough to keep up your disguise every single time you're in public?"

"I won't need—"

"He's wealthy and well connected. He'll hire people to search for you in all the obvious places. You can never let your guard down."

"So, I'm supposed to pick a random clan and city in Sitia?"

"Yes. And I'd suggest even at your new location, you wear a disguise. It doesn't have to be magical."

He gave her a moment to collect her thoughts. When they had rode north from Delip in the Cloud Mist Clan's lands, Valek tried to discuss all these logistics with her, but she was so focused on getting her daughter, she refused to consider an after. Once he rescued Ruby, all hell would break loose, and she wouldn't have time to make these important decisions.

Valek had promised Ziva a favor when she'd helped him escape not only the jail in Nubium, but the noose. And she had aided him in stopping Tam, an infamous assassin, from killing Yelena.

"How will you support yourself? Do you have any money saved?" he asked.

"I…have the salary I earned as a guard."

He waited, but she didn't continue. "Did you like working at the jail?"

"No. It was horrible. I only did it so I could make friends with the other guards and maybe convince them to help me get Ruby back. When you were dragged in, it was the perfect opportunity for me."

"Is there any other job that you're qualified for?"

She stared at him. "Job?"

Clearly she had not thought anything through. He considered Sitia. The country was divided into eleven clans and, while most people lived in the land of the clan they were born in, it wasn't unusual for them to move to another. "Do you have any association with Thunder Valley, the capital of the Stormdance Clan lands?"

"No."

"Great. That's your new home. Once you arrive, go to twenty-five Squall Lane and tell them you're part of Valek's protection program. The password is waterspout. They'll get you and Ruby settled in a new place and find you a job."

"But that's so far away."

He bit back a groan of frustration. Valek had hoped to put Ziva and Ruby on their horse and send them on their way. But if he did that, they'd probably be captured right away. The Commander would be annoyed at Valek's delay in returning to Ixia, but he couldn't do a poor job even if it added two weeks to his trip. To avoid that, he'd send them to one of his safe houses.

Part of his duties as Ixia's Chief of Security was to keep an eye on the country of Sitia, their neighbor. One of the ways he kept track of the political climate in Sitia was by sending members of his corps to collect intelligence. These agents lived in safe houses that Valek frequently used when he was traveling in Sitia. Twenty-five Squall Lane was one such house.

When darkness settled over the valley, Valek watched until all the lantern lights in the manor house extinguished. Then he remained by their small fire for a couple more hours, ensuring that the occupants inside had enough time for their slumber to deepen. Patience was critical in his line of work. Hours and hours of preparation would often be followed by a short burst of activity.

Ziva paced around their campsite, burning off her nervous energy. Before he left, he gave her a list of instructions.

"Once the horses are ready to go, wait for us," he said. "Do not approach the house. Understand?"

She bit her lip but nodded.

Careful not to trod on any crunchy broken stalks, Valek headed toward the house. The half-moon cast just enough light to reveal the path. His outfit comprised of a simple midnight-blue tunic and pants, Hidden in the various folds of the fabric were darts filled with sleeping potion, a set of lock picks, and his daggers. His broadsword was too long and cumbersome for this type of operation. It was sheathed on his horse's saddle along with his pack.

When he reached the house, he looped around to the back door and picked the lock. It sprung easily. Entering the kitchen, he closed it behind him but left it unlocked for a quick getaway. He stopped and listened for any sounds of movement. It was dark and quiet. The fire in the hearth had been banked for the evening, but the smell of roasted meat lingered on the air, making his stomach grumble. Travel rations were a poor substitute for a home-cooked meal.

Following Ziva's instructions, he crept through the house. His heart kept a steady pace despite the situation. This was familiar territory for him; working as an assassin all those years ago had inured him to the danger. However, he kept alert. He might be confident but he wasn't stupid.

Ruby's room was at the end of the hallway on the second floor. To avoid any creaky stairs, Valek shimmied up the banister. The door next to Ruby's was ajar—her nursemaid's quarters. Pausing by the gap, he listened to the woman's steady breathing. Then he entered Ruby's room.

Dolls lined the shelves and a pile of stuffed animals sat in the corner. Her small bed was low to the ground. The blankets were rumpled, but there was no sign of Ruby. Valek searched the rest of the room. No luck. Had someone tipped Dothan off?

The girl's pillow was dented, and a faint warmth lingered on the sheets. Remembering the nursemaid's open door, Valek checked, hoping the girl sought comfort from her nanny. The woman slept alone. Biting back a curse, Valek retreated.

The household staff and farm hands all slept on the third floor. Would the girl go to one of them? There was another possibility, but Valek was loath to consider it.

At the other end of the long hall stood a set of grand double doors. Dothan's room. As Valek approached, he noticed they hadn't been closed properly. He peered through the small gap. Sure enough, Ruby slept curled up next to her father. Also on the bed was a puppy. It stared quizzically at the door.

He had seconds before all hell broke loose.

CHAPTER 2

Valek yanked out a handful of darts filled with sleeping potion, but he had to widen the crack in the doors to get a good shot. As soon as he moved it, the puppy bounded off the bed with an excited yip.

Dothan sprang out of bed with a dagger in his big hand. "Ruby, get behind me," he ordered his daughter.

The girl scampered behind her father. So much for a quick snatch and dash. Valek had hoped to avoid any additional trauma for the little girl.

He flicked his hands out to show Dothan he was unarmed. The gesture was an attempt to distract the man as Valek launched two darts. The one aimed at Dothan's throat stopped in mid-air as the man's magic swelled. The dart dropped to the floor. Now the power pressed against Valek's skin. Good thing Valek remained immune to magic's effect. He wondered what defensive countermeasures the magician was attempting.

Reluctant to draw his knife, Valek waited for Dothan to make the next move. The puppy who had been sniffing Valek's boots staggered and flopped to the floor.

"He killed Pawl!" Ruby cried, darting to the dog.

"Ruby, don't." Her father tried to grab her arm, but she slipped past.

Ruby sat down inches from Valek. She scooped Pawl into her lap. Hugging him tight, she bawled.

"No. Please." Dothan's voice shook with anguish. He carefully placed his weapon on the bed. "Please don't hurt her."

The raw grief on Dothan's square face was not the reaction Valek expected. Or rather, not the response Ziva had warned him about. Valek crouched down to the girl's eye level. "Pawl's not dead, Ruby. He's sleeping."

She glared at him. "He's not waking up."

"He won't for a while, but he will."

"Why did you sleep my dog?" she demanded.

"I planned to sleep you all and take you to your mother," Valek said.

Ruby squeaked in protest and scooted back toward her father with Pawl still clutched to her chest.

Interesting. The thud of heavy boots sounded behind him. Valek stood and whirled in time to see Ziva charging down the hallway. So much for her staying with the horses.

"What are you waiting for?" she demanded. "Grab her and let's go!"

"There's been a...complication," Valek said tilting his head toward Dothan.

Ziva looked at her ex-husband, whose expression hardened into a scowl. "Ziva, you know the courts have awarded me custody for a good reason. Your rules—"

"Shut up." She turned to Valek. "It's not complicated. You're an assassin. Assassinate him."

Ah. He wondered if she'd hoped this exact scenario would play out tonight and Valek would be forced to kill the man.

When he didn't move, she added, "You owe me a favor."

"I do." Valek considered.

Ruby had returned to hiding behind her father. The girl was

clearly not happy to see her mother, but it could be due to bad stories told to her by Dothan. The man remained quiet. He hadn't threatened or bargained or begged for his life. Only that one plea for his daughter.

Losing patience, Ziva charged toward Ruby. Magic swelled and she slowed, then struggled to advance as if fighting through a fierce gale. The power pushed her back until she was pinned to the wall.

"Valek," Ziva puffed. "I saved…your life. You owe…me…my daughter."

A strangled cry came from Dothan at the mention of Valek's name.

"Except, it appears she doesn't want to go with you," Valek said.

"She's four. That bastard's…been lying to her—"

"Then why is *Ruby* pushing you away?" Valek asked.

"She…can't. She's *four*."

"Apparently, she can." Valek remembered Yelena's comment about using magic without knowing she'd pulled power. She had called it her survival instinct. Perhaps this situation was similar. Although, if the girl was that scared…he shuddered. Promise or not, Ruby's welfare came first.

"Can you ask Ruby to release Ziva?" Valek asked Dothan.

"Ruby, honey. Let your mother go."

"I don't wanna."

But then the girl huffed, and Ziva sagged as the magic disappeared.

"Since this is a case of one's word against another…" Valek placed two darts on the palm of his hand, showing them to Ruby's parents. "These are loaded with a truth serum. One prick each and we can settle this matter."

"There's nothing *to* settle," Ziva said, crossing her arms over her chest. "You owe me."

"And I will still owe you a favor, but I'm not putting a child at risk."

"At risk! I'm her mother."

"Then act like one, Ziva," Dothan said. He pushed up his sleeve, exposing his forearm. "Go ahead."

There was his answer. Instead of pricking Dothan, he sent the dart into Ziva's neck. She cried out in shocked betrayal as she plucked it from her skin.

"I'm reporting you to the…" She wobbled. "The…" Ziva slumped to the ground.

"Did you sleep her, too?" Ruby asked.

"Yes."

"Truth serum?" Dothan raised an eyebrow.

"I wish. It would make my life so much easier." Well, he had his goo-goo juice, but that could be unreliable.

"Did Ziva really save your life?"

"Yes."

"That's an act of treason in Sitia. She could be hung."

"Which is why I'm taking her with me." Valek pulled Ziva over his shoulder. "I'm sorry to disturb your sleep." As he carried her through the house, he braced for Dothan to raise the alarm and call for his farm hands to give chase. Only silence followed him outside.

The horses were tied to a nearby tree. Valek secured Ziva to her saddle, then mounted his horse. He clucked his tongue and headed north to Lapeer. It was a mid-sized town close to the Ixian border.

What a mess the night turned out to be. Valek had fallen for what Janco had called the "damsel-in-distress" trick. He'd believed her about her ex-husband without investigating further, while it deserved to be taken seriously, he should have confirmed the facts.

Why hadn't he asked more questions? It could have been due to being grateful for Ziva's help and for saving his life. Or due to the emotional whirlwind of saving Yelena from an assassin. Or because he'd fallen in love for the first time in his life.

What had Tam said about him? *You've lost your edge. Gone soft.*

Perhaps he had.

He'd promised Fourth Magician Irys Jewelrose that he would give Yelena a year to learn how to control and use her magic without him as a distraction. Plus, she needed to become acclimated with her new home. With Yelena safe in Sitia, Valek should be focusing his full attention on his work for Commander Ambrose in Ixia. He tucked all the messy emotions that had sprung from his heart over the last three seasons back into their dark little corner.

They arrived in Lapeer an hour before dawn, and he brought Ziva to his safe house. The town wasn't technically big enough to warrant a safe house, but with its proximity to Ixia, it was a prime location to spot refugees crossing the border.

After dumping her on the couch, Valek groomed the horses and told his agents they could either sell the animals or keep them. Then he dozed on an armchair while waiting for Ziva to wake.

She stirred a few hours later. Sitting up in alarm, she scanned the room. "Where's Ruby?"

"With her father. Why did you lie to me about Dothan?" he asked with his coldest tone; the one that had criminals confessing.

But her alarm turned to anger. "I saved you. You *owe* me."

He gestured around the room. "This is me repaying the favor. If I'd left you, you would have been arrested. Now answer my question."

"He took her away from me! Said I was a bad mother."

"Apparently, the courts agreed."

"He's powerful. Of course, they agreed."

"Apparently, Ruby agrees."

"She's *four*. And *apparently* too attached to her father. If she stays with him, she's going to grow up to be just. Like. Him. The child needs discipline. Order. A strict schedule. Rules. Because Dothan and I both have magic, Ruby's going to be a master magician, and she will need *my* guidance on the use of her powers. Dothan is too soft. He bought her a puppy! How can she be a ruthless leader with his guidance?"

Valek would be impressed that she managed to keep her beliefs hidden from him for so long, but instead a heavy weight settled deep in his chest. The Commander always said power corrupted, and here was yet another variation on its effects.

"Now you know why Ruby needs me," Ziva said. "We can try again. Maybe next season? By then, Dothan—"

"No. Our relationship ends now. You have two choices, Ziva. One, you disappear. My agents will help you relocate to another city in exchange for your promise to stay away from your daughter. Two, you stay. In that case, my agents will deliver you to Dothan's door all wrapped up with a pretty bow, so he can decide what crime you'll be arrested for."

"How about you let me go, and I won't say a word to the authorities about *you* or your *agents*?" Ziva countered.

Since she had no idea of her current location, it was an empty threat. "You want a third choice? All right. How about I deal with you right now and my agents will bury your body?"

Ziva's face drained of color. Finally, the woman was afraid of him.

"Consider this, Ziva. It's clear you've lost Ruby's affection. She will continue pushing you away and no one, except me, can stop her. What's your choice?"

"I'll disappear." Her tone was borderline begrudging.

"And?"

"I promise to stay away from Ruby."

Valek suppressed a sigh. Ziva's words didn't match the calculation in her gaze. "Good choice. *I'm* going to hold you to that promise." He made eye contact with her, driving his point home. "And good luck. Perhaps you'll use your obvious determination to find a purpose for your own life."

He left the room and explained to his agents what he needed them to do. "Once she arrives in her new town, have our local spies keep an eye on her. If she leaves, send me a message."

"Yes, sir."

Not the best solution. Her fear of him would fade, and she might try to go after her daughter again. However, he truly hoped Ziva would find her own way. If not… Well, Valek would deal with her.

He left the house—and Ziva—behind and hurried to reach the Snake Forest before full daylight. Not that he was worried about the Ixian patrols in the forest, but he didn't want any Sitians to recognize him and give chase.

On a map, the Snake Forest resembled its name. It was a narrow strip of green, undulating from east to west. The forest was part of the Territory of Ixia, and a hundred feet past the edge of the forest was the official Sitian border. The Commander had the trees and bushes cleared so no one could sneak in. Which didn't work. At all.

The cold air flowing through the trees held a crisp pine scent with an earthy hint of moisture. It was the first day of the warming season and the dark clouds to the west promised rain. Valek avoided the patrols by pure habit, so he surprised the soldier on duty at Military District 5's station. The poor woman jumped about a foot in the air, then she peered at Valek as if not quite sure she believed his identity. Too tired to care, he checked on Onyx. The station didn't have a stable—no need as all the patrols were done on foot—but the black stallion grazed nearby. A long lead line was tied to his harness.

The station's captain came around the building. He was

broad-chested and muscular. "We've been exercising him for you, sir."

"Thank you."

"We didn't have any grain for him, so we took turns riding him to town to buy him feed and some supplies." The man pulled an apple from his pocket. Using his knife, he cut slices. Onyx raised his head at the sound and trotted over. The captain fed the horse. "He's really quiet in the forest, sir. Knows where to put his hooves. Too bad we don't have more horses like him. We could cover more ground and chase down fugitives faster."

Only the Commander, his advisers, generals, and high-ranking officers, rode horses to travel. Mostly because horses were expensive to keep and train, and the Commander believed that the money would be better spent on the people. However, using horses for border patrols wouldn't require too many extra resources.

"That's a good point, Captain. I'll look into it."

The man brightened in surprise. Valek didn't think it was that much of a compliment, but then he remembered this station had been under General Brazell's jurisdiction. And the general had been ignoring his soldiers and diverting funds from the army to build his illegal Criollo factory.

If Valek hadn't been so tired, he would have noticed the run-down station and worn uniforms on the patrol.

Calculating the cost of feed—he'd been away for fourteen days—Valek handed the captain a couple gold coins. "For the supplies."

"Oh, no, sir. You don't—"

"I do. Now, what's the gossip?" Valek led the man inside as he listened to the rumors. The border patrols were always the last to get the latest news and, by the time it reached them, the information tended to be either exaggerated, garbled, or outright incorrect. Valek helped clear a few things up but couldn't answer the question of who the Commander planned to appoint as the new general of MD-5. No surprise that was the captain's biggest concern.

Exhausted, Valek eventually collapsed onto a cot in the back room to sleep for a few hours.

∼

Onyx was saddled and waiting for Valek when he woke. He thanked the captain and headed to MD-5's manor house. The man was right about the horse. Even at a fast pace through a carpet of dead leaves, Onyx's hooves failed to make any crunching sounds. Valek hadn't noticed it on the trip down to the station house; he'd been too worried about Yelena to pay attention.

Not long after he'd left the station, sheets of rain swept in with a cold blast of wind. Valek pulled his cloak tighter around his shoulders. Good thing he didn't need to camp overnight in the storm as he arrived at the manor right before nightfall.

When Valek and Onyx reached the stable, Adviser Dema waited for him. He'd been spotted on the road, and, of course, Commander Ambrose demanded to see him right away.

"Now?" he asked her.

Her long black hair had been pulled into a bun. She wore the standard adviser's uniform—black shirt with two red diamonds stitched onto the collar, black pants, and boots. "Now."

By that point, the rain had soaked through to his skin and there were puddles of water in his boots. At least Onyx was in good hands. Back in his home, the stable boys descended with warm towels, combs, and fresh hay. Lucky bugger.

As Valek trudged after his colleague through the large U-shaped manor house, he longed for a hot bath and dry clothes. They arrived and Dema waited until Valek entered the room before dashing off to…well, he'd no idea. The lanterns had been lit in the Commander's office, which had been Brazell's before the general was arrested and incarcerated. The yellow glow did not give off any warmth, neither did the Commander's cold gaze as it swept over Valek's bedraggled appearance.

Valek shivered.

"Sit down," he ordered.

He perched on the edge of the plush chair facing the massive wooden desk. The Commander stood and went to a sideboard. He poured a couple drinks and handed one to Valek before resettling behind the desk. Valek took a grateful sip. The whiskey burned down his throat and warmed his stomach.

The Commander had regained a bit of the weight that he'd lost, but that hard edge he'd acquired since his ordeal lurked in his gold almond-shaped eyes. More gray streaked his bristle short black hair, even though the man was only forty-one-years-old.

"Report," the Commander ordered.

Valek recounted his pursuit of Tam, also known as Tame-quintin, the assassin that had taken Yelena's order of execution with the intent of carrying it out. The order the Commander had signed because magicians were illegal in Ixia; any mage caught in Ixia was hanged. Valek also included in his report the details of his capture.

"A magician named Ziva Moon helped me escape from prison in exchange for a favor. She also accompanied me to Delip, a city in the Cloud Mist Clan, where we caught up to Tam. With her aid, I was able to trap and kill Tam," Valek said.

"And the favor?" the Commander asked.

Reluctant to detail the family drama, Valek said, "Taken care of."

The Commander quirked an eyebrow but said nothing as he sipped his drink. After an uncomfortable silence, he asked, "What happened to Yelena's order of execution?"

Ah. "Ziva Moon put it into my saddlebags. I'm assuming it's still there."

"Still won't touch it?"

"Not unless it's to burn it, sir."

The Commander huffed in either amusement or annoyance, it was hard to tell. "You didn't miss much while you were gone, Valek. I've uncovered a few more people involved in Brazell and Mogkan's plot to overthrow me and have arrested them. I also decided to promote Colonel Ute from MD-3 to general of MD-5. Her service record is stellar, and she's impressed me over the years."

"Are Generals Tesso and Hazal still here?" Valek asked.

"No. I sent them home. Both are rather opinionated, and I want Ute to run her Military District as she sees fit." Ambrose smiled wryly. "Plus, I don't want her turning into... What did you call the other generals?"

The Commander knew *exactly* what Valek had called them. He never forgot anything. Even though he was being teased, Valek was happy to see Ambrose relax a bit.

"Old windbags," Valek supplied.

He snapped his fingers. "That's it! Does she provide enough fresh blood for you?"

Another jab. "Yes, sir."

"Good. You are to take a couple soldiers and deliver the promotion to her. Then escort her here."

That was unusual. Normally, the Commander sent the papers to the district's general to notify the person of a promotion. "Are you expecting trouble?"

"Possibly. This is the first time since the takeover that I've promoted someone to general. The other seven have been together a long time, and they are probably expecting me to have a meeting and consult them on the new general. It would be a courtesy and generate good will toward the newest member. Except, I'm in no mood to play nice. Not when one of *my* generals tried to usurp me. Plus, the old windbags would want to promote another old windbag."

Ah yes. The good-old-boy network.

The Commander took a drink as he gazed into the distance for a moment. Then he returned his attention to Valek. "By sending you to officially present the paperwork, I'm letting all the generals know I'm serious. If I send the orders to General Franis, he might hang on to it in order to delay things and perhaps demand that a meeting is called. Either way, he'll have all the generals in an uproar in no time. He might still try to slow you down."

Valek smiled without humor. "He can try. We'll also be traveling through MD-4. Do I need to worry about General Tesso?"

"You will leave in the morning, and, by the time the rumors circulate, you'll be in MD-3." The Commander paused. "Take an extra horse for Ute just in case Franis refuses to give her one. He'll probably send a message to Tesso. Be careful on the way back. Even though you outrank the generals, they're unhappy with you at the moment."

"They've never been happy with me."

"That's on me. Since you tried to assassinate me before the takeover, they've never fully trusted you. They campaigned long and hard for you to be ranked below them. I refused."

"That's a long time to hold a grudge."

"It is. And they all have an army of loyal soldiers, so you should prepare for some trouble."

"I always do."

"Good. Stop by to collect the paperwork before you leave."

"Yes, sir."

"Dismissed."

Valek downed the rest of his drink and left. Since he was already soaked and it was still raining, he headed to the barracks to recruit a couple soldiers. The Commander considered, *in the morning* to be *dawn*. And Valek desperately needed a good night's sleep.

The rain drummed on the roof of the wooden barracks. The flames flickered inside the lanterns as the cold wind blew through the gaps in the walls. The soldiers not on duty either huddled around burn barrels or were wrapped in heavy cloaks and playing cards. A few slept on the bunks.

Valek hoped Captain Ari wasn't on duty. While the Commander's elite unit was filled with top-notched individuals, Valek preferred to travel with a familiar person. Plus, Ari had proven to be intelligent, dependable, and more than qualified, and Ari would know who else would be right for the mission.

He found Ari playing cards in the farthest building. Valek was surprised to see his partner, Janco, sitting next to him. Janco had been skewered by a sword about a month ago while fighting to save the Commander. Valek thought the man would still be off the duty roster. However, Janco was wrapped up in a blanket and looked pale. Perhaps he remained on bed rest.

Ari jumped to attention when he spotted Valek. He scowled at the others until they surged to their feet.

"At ease," Valek said. "Captains, a word?"

The three of them found a quiet corner.

"Yelena?" Ari asked immediately. A worried crinkle rose between his pale-blue eyes. Ari had been the one to discover Tam wasn't a member of Brazell's army and had figured out when the assassin left, giving Valek enough time to catch up.

"Safe," Valek said.

Both men relaxed. They were beyond friends with Yelena. Probably in the realm of family.

"Phew," Janco said. "That was an agonizing two weeks."

"And Tam?" Ari asked.

"Dead."

"Good."

"Ari, I've been assigned another mission and need some backup. Do you know how to ride a horse?"

"Yes, sir."

"Do you know anyone who is qualified to go with us?"

"Me!" Janco raised his hand.

"Aren't you still recovering?"

"No. I'm healed. One hundred percent good to go. And I was practically raised on a horse."

Valek looked at Ari.

"The medic released him for duty," Ari said.

That didn't help. "Riding long hours is hard on the body, Janco. Are you sure your stomach and back muscles can handle the motion?"

"Yep!"

Valek jabbed Janco directly on his injury.

Janco jumped back in surprise. "What was that for?"

"Any pain?" He studied Janco's expression.

"No."

"We might run into trouble, and you might need to fight multiple opponents."

Janco's dark eyes lit up. "Promise?"

Suppressing a sigh, Valek turned to Ari. "I'm asking *you*, not the medic, if he's cleared for duty."

"Janco on a bad day is still better than these other soldiers on their good days."

Janco puffed out his chest and beamed.

"You know a yes would have sufficed," Valek grumbled.

"I know."

"All right. Meet me at the stables at dawn."

"Dawn," Janco cried. He wrapped his arms around his stomach and hunched over in mock pain. "I'm not feeling so good."

Shaking his head, Valek left the men to prepare for the trip. After a quick stop to talk to the Stable Master, he hurried to the baths for that long awaited hot soak.

Thirty minutes before dawn, the Commander handed Valek the official promotion papers for Colonel Ute. The scroll was sealed and wrapped in wax paper to keep it dry. Valek looked forward to handing it to Ute. Much of his job dealt with criminals, liars, murderers, death, and blood; it was a nice change of pace to bring someone joy.

"I've removed Yelena's execution order from your saddlebags," the Commander said. "It's in a secure location. You don't need to worry about anyone else finding the order and targeting her. As long as she remains in Sitia, she's safe."

The apprehension that had settled in his chest like a bad cold dissipated. "Thank you, sir."

"Make this a quick trip, Valek. I'm ready to go home."

"Yes, sir."

As Valek strode to the stables, he considered his home. He'd lived in the castle for the last sixteen years, but the thought of returning to his suite of rooms without Yelena held no appeal. While she had lived in his quarters, they'd been colleagues simply sharing a space. They discussed cases, talked about fighting techniques, and other odd topics that had come up during their days. Nothing exciting nor romantic, but he treasured their time together, and had rushed back every night to work in his apartment instead of his office just because Yelena would be curled up on the couch reading.

Keeping busy would be the key to surviving these next eleven months without Yelena. Perhaps he should request the time off well in advance, so the Commander had ample time to prepare for when Valek was away. He had never asked for a day off since they'd met. He hadn't a reason.

A sudden sobering thought occurred to him. What if, after a

year, Yelena no longer wished to be with him? What if she met someone else? They had a mere week together as a couple, it wouldn't be a surprise if her feelings changed. Just the thought of her rejection caused a painful contraction right where he'd stuffed his emotions. Best not to dwell on *what ifs*. Especially ones he had no control over.

The black sky lightened slowly, as if being scrubbed away layer by layer. Happy that the rain had stopped, Valek avoided the puddles at the entrance to the stables.

Onyx and three horses stood in the center aisle. They were saddled and ready to go as requested.

"…truly think I'm allergic to dawn," Janco said to his partner as they arrived. He sneezed. Probably to prove his point. Or perhaps due to the dust-laced air. An unavoidable aspect of a building full of horses, straw, and grain.

Janco's sleepy expression dropped when he spotted the horses. "Ooohhh, she's a beaut!" He went over to the liver-colored chestnut horse with big brown eyes and a glossy black mane. She cocked a long ear as he ran his hand down her neck, withers, and legs, checking for hot spots. "What's her name?"

"Lovey," the Stable Master said, joining them. "And this one is Hugh."

Hugh was a big and sturdy dappled gray. His mane and long tail were charcoal colored. Even his eyes were a dark gray.

"The other is Clover the Clever, she's the smartest in the stable and has the smoothest gait. We call her Clover for short. Are they dark enough for you?"

Clover the Clever was a bay with a reddish-brown coat. Her mane and tail had been braided.

"Yes, thanks," Valek said.

"Why does their color matter?" Janco asked.

Ari answered. "We're riding north where everything is still in the grips of the cold weather. A light-colored horse will not blend in as well. And I'm guessing we want to blend in."

"We do. Well, as much as we can riding horses in Ixia," Valek said.

"Clover will be best for our new general to ride. She'll demonstrate the quality of MD-5's breeding and training program," the Stable Master said with a smirk.

Ari and Janco glanced at Valek. "New general?"

It never ceased to amaze Valek how quickly gossip traveled through the staff. If only his spy network was as efficient. Hopefully the rumors only mentioned the reason for his trip and not their destination. "I'll brief you on the way. Secure your gear. We don't have time to waste."

The captains filled the saddlebags with their supplies and strapped their swords onto the saddles for quick and easy access. Each also had a backpack with a bedroll attached. The spartan travel shelters along the route were uncomfortable, and the thin mats would be welcome after a full day of riding.

Ari mounted Hugh, while Janco hopped onto Lovey's back. Clover's reins were tied to Onyx's saddle. With Valek in the lead, they headed north. General Franis's manor house was in the south-eastern section of MD-3, and close to the border with MD-4. It was near the foothills of the Soul Mountains, close to the various entrances of the diamond mines that crisscrossed the long mountain chain. Mines that Franis oversaw, ensuring the onsite supervisors followed the Commander's safety protocols. Mine collapses, gas explosions, and workers getting lost and dying in the tunnels were a thing of the past. The chain still produced diamonds, although not as many as in the past, and they were all shipped to the Commander who either gifted them to hard workers or sold them.

The trip would take approximately five and a half days on horseback. The route Valek decided to take would, thankfully, be far to the east of General Tesso's manor house and near the rolling foothills.

Valek briefed Ari and Janco about the mission during their

first stop to rest and feed the horses around noon. A blanket of clouds sealed the sky, transforming the landscape into a stark world filled with hues of gray. Water rushed from a nearby spring and snaked through the still frozen ground. Ice crunched on the stream's banks, but the horses didn't seem to mind the brisk temperature as they ducked their heads to drink.

"Why would the generals expect to be consulted?" Ari asked. He chewed on a stick, claiming it was beef jerky. "We're never asked about our colleagues before they're promoted."

"Many of the generals have been with the Commander since he made the decision to takeover Ixia. They worked with him and his family in the diamond mines and trained him how to fight and strategize. They didn't work their way up through the ranks like you and Janco, so they have a different relationship."

"I'm not sure you can say Janco *worked*," Ari teased.

"Hey!" Janco glowered at his partner. "Every one of my promotions was earned with blood, sweat, and tears." He smirked. "The tears of my *opponents*, that is!"

Ari groaned. Before they could start bickering, Valek told them to mount up.

They were still within the borders of MD-5 when the light began to fade and they reached the first travel shelter. The small rectangular shaped building's roof extended over the stalls for the horses. The ad-hoc stable had some bales of straw and buckets.

After they rubbed down the horses and filled the buckets with water and grain, they trod inside as darkness settled. The horses had excellent night vision, but Valek didn't want to exhaust them by riding more than eight hours each day. Better for them to save their energy for the trip back. The one-room shelter contained two rows of four wooden bunk beds and a hearth. The place was empty.

Ari piled firewood on the stones and set it alight. They boiled some water for tea.

Janco gnawed on a stick of jerky. "*Pah*," he spat. "I'm already sick of travel rations. Will we have time for a hot meal at the general's house?"

"I expect that we'll be there for a few days to give the Colonel time to pack and say goodbye. The general will probably have a congratulatory dinner for her," Valek said. "Unless he's not happy about the promotion."

"And then?"

"We won't linger over the goodbyes."

Janco laughed. "In that case, there won't be a *good* in goodbye."

He certainly had a unique way of looking at life. And it struck Valek that he didn't know much about either man's past. "How did you and Ari meet?"

"I'm surprised you haven't read our files," Ari said.

He had. They were filled with dry facts and dates. "You were both assigned to the same unit when you were promoted to the Commander's garrison, but that doesn't tell me *how* your friendship formed."

"Ho, boy," Janco said. "That story will take *all* night."

"No, it won't," Ari countered.

"Yes, it will. Because it's more than us meeting at the castle complex. It goes back to before. To why we joined the army and what happened along the way."

"Valek doesn't want to hear all that."

"What else is there to do?" Janco looked at Valek.

While he suspected the story would be a rambling account with lots of tangents and details he didn't need to hear, Janco had a point. There was nothing else to do.

"Go ahead," he said.

Janco rubbed his hands together as glee shone in his eyes. Valek already regretted encouraging him and the man hadn't said a word yet.

"When I was eleven, two major things happened that shaped

my life," Janco said. "My father was lost at sea, and the Commander took over Ixia."

CHAPTER 3

*E*leven? Janco was starting his story at the age of eleven. Ari rubbed a big hand over his face and gave Valek a this-is-all-your-fault look.

Janco ignored Ari and continued. "As a result of my father's death, we moved from the coast of MD-7 to my uncle's farm in the middle of nowhere. Oh wait, I think the tiny village in central MD-7 had a name… Boring Ville? Or was it Yawn Town? The only improvement from coastal living was the lack of sand. Sand is an evil substance. Let me tell you just how evil. One time—"

"Stay on topic," Ari warned.

"Oh. Right. Where was I?"

"Yawn Town."

"Right. The place was surrounded with crops as far as the eye could see. Bored to a point that one more conversation about green beans would literally cause my head to explode, I began an earnest career in getting away with things."

"Things?" Valek asked.

"Yup. Anything. Stealing, swearing, sabotaging, refusing, arguing, shirking any and all responsibility. Anything. The goal was not to get caught, but if I was…" He shrugged. "The punishments didn't stop me or slow me down. Just encouraged me to be smarter. And then the Commander's Code of Behavior arrived in town, and I had an entire new list of things to get away with."

"Except murder," Ari said as he added another log to the fire. Sparks flew into the air.

"Oh yes. Of course not murder or harming another person. I'd never do that. Well, I would defend myself if someone attacked me, but I wouldn't instigate. One time, my annoying cousins stuffed—"

"No one cares about your cousins," Ari said.

Janco pouted.

"Do you have siblings?" Valek asked.

"No." He sounded horrified. "Thank fate. My mother said I was a difficult baby."

"Still are," Ari muttered.

"Cute. Anyway, over the next seven years I became a frequent visitor of the local jail. My mother would bail me out. But while I was in there, I made friends with Anders, a man who was serving a twenty-year sentence for burglary and assault with a deadly weapon. He claimed it wasn't him and that he'd been framed."

Valek huffed. Everyone incarcerated claimed they were innocent.

"I freely admitted my guilt and bragged about it. But to meet someone who was so sincere and so miserable…" Janco rubbed the scar that crossed from his right temple to where the bottom half of his right ear used to be. "And so convincing. I stopped my getting away with things and switched to breaking Anders out of jail."

"How old were you?" Valek asked. This hadn't been in Janco's file.

"Seventeen. I learned how to pick the complicated cell locks, figured out the best time to avoid the guards, forged the paperwork so Anders could relocate to MD-2, and packed him a travel bag. When the time came, I slipped past all five guards and unlocked Anders' cell door. We were almost free when an alarm was raised. Next thing I knew, we were surrounded. Anders grabbed me, pulled a knife, aimed it at my throat, and threatened to kill me if they didn't let us go. I thought he was pretending. The guards let us escape the jail. Once outside, I thought he'd release me, but I'll never forget what he said." Emotion gripped his voice and Janco paused. His flippant attitude gone, he stared at the fire, seeing into his past.

Valek exchanged a glance with Ari. Should they change the subject? Ari shook his head.

"Anders said, 'Thanks for the help, kid. It's amazing how someone so smart could be so stupid. I can't leave you behind and I'm not taking you with me, so goodbye.'" Janco rubbed his neck. "He moved to slit my throat. I moved to get free. All I remember is standing over his prone form with his knife in my hand and my blood dripping on him. Instead of slitting my throat, he'd sliced half my ear off. He was arrested and sentenced to another twenty years. By the time I recovered from the injury, I was eighteen years old. As an official adult, I was given the choice to be sentenced to ten years in prison for my part in the escape attempt or to sign up for the Commander's army for ten years. That was an easy choice. I figured the army had to be more interesting than sitting in a cell for ten years."

Interesting. The Code of Behavior had strict sentencing for each crime. No deviations. No negotiations. No leniency for a first offense. It didn't matter who you were or who you knew, everyone received the exact same punishment. Clearly, Janco's judge didn't agree with the Code of Behavior. In this case, neither did Valek. In fact, there were a number of cases over the years where Valek held the opposite opinion of the Commander regarding the code. Valek would never have met and fell in love with Yelena if he didn't circumvent the Commander's harshest sentence.

"How much time in the army do you have left?" Valek asked Janco.

"One year!"

"Are you planning to find another job?"

"Hell no. My army career is *finally* getting interesting. These past three seasons have been a blast. I can't wait to see what's next."

Rogue magicians, plotting generals, poisonings, and black-market dealers weren't what Valek would consider a blast, but he also appreciated a challenge.

"You almost died," Ari reminded him.

Janco *pished*.

"Basic training must have been boring," Valek said.

"It was. I started out as a private last class, or so it felt. I could either have fooled around and tried getting away with things again, or I could go all in. I found out pretty quick that I loved winning sparring matches. After that, there was no turning back. So, I went all in, practicing eight hours a day. I climbed the ranks and fought everyone until there was no one left at the MD-7 garrison who could beat me." He grinned.

"Even the garrison's Weapons Master?" Valek asked.

"Not even him. I received my promotion to lieutenant and transferred to the Commander's castle soon after I bested him."

"Now we're *finally* getting to the good part," Ari said.

"Ha ha," Janco deadpanned.

"How long did it take for you to reach lieutenant?" Valek asked.

"Seven years."

That was remarkable. Most soldiers weren't offered the chance to go from a non-commissioned rank to an officer during their entire careers.

"My first unit in the Commander's garrison focused on teaching us special skills. We were all new and, on the first day, we were given a list of skills to choose from. I picked scouting. Sneaking around in the woods sounded fun and better than being in charge of supplies or guarding the treasury. *Yawn*! Then our captain wanted to test our fighting abilities. I naturally challenged the most impressive opponent in order to show off my superior techniques."

"Naturally," Ari said.

"You challenged Ari," Valek said.

"Yup. Do you want to guess who won?"

Valek considered the two men. Ari had strength and speed. Janco was also fast, but he was more flexible. "It would depend on the weapon. If you fought with swords, you would win. If you fought hand to hand, Ari would win."

Janco looked at Ari. "I should have picked swords. The big lout knocked me unconscious!"

"You wouldn't concede the match," Ari said in his defense. "Nor would you for the next five, nine, dozen…who knows how many more matches. Annoying. And to my increasing irritation I had also picked scouting."

"What about my irritation?" Janco asked. "Paired up with the most boring and serious man in the world, who I couldn't best!"

"And still can't," Ari shot back. He looked at Valek. "Even with swords."

Now that was impressive. "Noted."

"It's just a matter of time," Janco muttered.

"What changed your attitudes about each other?" Valek asked them.

"Janco's tenacity. He doesn't know how to quit. We once tracked an enemy for days because of him. Didn't matter that, once we caught up, our enemy turned out to be an elk and he wouldn't shoot it for dinner, he still considered it a win."

"*She* could have had elk puppies waiting at home for her," Janco interjected.

"Calves. They're called calves."

"Details." Janco waved it away.

"And that brings me to my other point, his view on life is completely different than mine. I see dinner after a grueling six-day hunt and he sees a family," Ari said. "Plus, out of all the people in our unit, no one else could touch his skills. If I aim to be the best, then I need to have the second best by my side."

"Ha! You wish," Janco said.

"I know." Ari sobered. "He's the brother I wish I had."

For the first time since Valek had known Janco, the man appeared stunned. He opened and closed his mouth several times, but no sounds escaped.

Ari ignored him. "I grew up in MD-4. I'm the youngest of three boys. The runt of the litter." He smiled, but then it faded. "My father and brothers were soldiers for the King's army. I was twelve when the growing resistance arrived in our town. Since I was much younger than my brothers and they were well known as soldiers, they asked me to attend Ambrose's somewhat secret meeting and report back. Honored and excited about spying, I agreed."

Valek sensed where Ari's story was headed, but he kept quiet.

"Except, Ambrose's speech made sense. He was well spoken and obviously intelligent. Every point he raised matched what I'd been thinking about the monarchy. The corruption. The greed. My father and brothers would never be promoted since they had no connections in the upper ranks. They didn't even earn a living wage. We all lived together, scrimping even though my father worked two jobs. And yet..."

Now it was Ari's turn to stare into the flames. "Yet, when I told them about what Ambrose planned, what he intended to fix, they rejected his ideas. Claimed he was just another charlatan; duping idiots like me. What did I know? I was twelve. But I couldn't dismiss his ideology so easily. Ambrose moved on to the next city, but he left a group behind to continue recruiting supporters. Without telling my family, I started helping the resistance in my town. Small things like delivering messages or tipping them off about raids."

"How long before your family found out?" Valek asked.

"Not until after the Commander successfully took over Ixia. I was thirteen, and my father and brothers were given the choice to switch sides. They were offered double their salaries. My brothers could have afforded to live on their own, get married, have children. I couldn't believe it when they stubbornly remained loyal to the monarchy. I argued with them, but all that did was get me disowned. They were arrested and incarcerated for a few years before being assigned menial public works jobs. They considered themselves heroes."

"Thirteen is rather young to be on your own," Valek said, remembering when he'd been disowned at the same age. At least, Valek had a purpose. A goal.

"I would have been living on the streets, scrounging to survive if the King had been in charge. But the Commander kept his promises. His people found homes for all the kids on the streets. And since I helped with the resistance, I was adopted by Ohin, the captain of the patrol."

"A good man with no sense of humor," Janco added. "None. We don't get along. That shouldn't be a surprise."

It wasn't.

"While most people were still reeling from the change in politics, the change in everyday life, and having to readjust biases that had been based on bloodlines and wealth, Ohin understood the ample opportunities the Commander's military offered to everyone. He started training me right away," Ari said. "I enlisted as soon as I turned eighteen and worked my way through the ranks. Unlike Janco, it took me two years longer to get promoted to the Commander's garrison."

"That's because single-minded determination doesn't work," Janco said. "You'd think it would, but it leaves no room for imagination and invention. Again, Ohin is a great man, and his fighting technique is textbook. So textbook that it's predicable. I had to work on Ari to embrace the crazy. Took me forever just to get him to crack a smile."

"If I had no imagination, how did I manage to beat you all those times?" Ari asked.

"I didn't say you didn't have it. It was buried under all that rule-following seriousness. Choked by the conviction that this job is too important to have any fun. My antics were what brought out your wild side that you needed to win."

"Or those textbook techniques actually work, especially against an opponent who didn't bother to read the textbook."

"Textbook, shmeck-book," Janco said. "When we started working together, Ari quoted rules and regulations to me all the time. And, yeah, sometimes following a certain protocol worked, but I began to suspect that deep down there was more to Ari than a boring grunt. I've since discovered he's the brother I didn't know I needed."

Valek was glad these two found each other. He had a few other agents who clicked and worked well together, but it was rare for two people to sync so well and balance each other out— one's weakness was another's strength. Was it like that with him and Yelena? He'd like to think so, but they'd only had such a short time together.

"Okay, so we spilled our guts, what about you?" Janco asked.

Surprised, Valek asked, "Me? Everyone knows my story."

"Worked as the Commander's assassin and killed the King and the entire royal family. Yeah, but no one knows what drove you to become an assassin."

"I look good in black," Valek joked.

Only Ambrose and Yelena knew his full backstory. Knew about the King's men killing his three older brothers and setting him on the path of vengeance. How he enrolled in the School of Night and Shadows to learn the art of assassination. How Valek had been hired to target Ambrose and failed, becoming his loyal second instead. It wasn't something he liked to talk about, and Ari and Janco weren't officially assigned to his corps. Even though he was hoping they'd become part of a team that would eventually become his seconds, they were currently unaware of his plans.

The silence stretched. Apparently, the joke wouldn't be enough. And he did owe them something in return for their stories.

"You both compared your relationship to brothers. My story started with my brothers. Like Ari, I was the youngest and I was also disowned." He gave them a watered-down version of the events that led him to the Commander, skipping some details.

Eventually, the fire died down and they each spread their bedrolls on a lower bunk. Valek didn't set a watch. They were still in MD-5, and he thought the chances of being ambushed were low. As he drifted off to sleep, he realized Janco had been right. Their stories had taken longer than anticipated.

They encountered no problems the next day, however by the end of the third day, Valek noticed Janco sat stiffly on Lovey, no longer moving easily with her. His face was pale and drawn, and he hadn't joked or teased the night before. Valek suspected Janco's injury didn't like the jarring gait of the horses. They had crossed into MD-4 that afternoon and had increased their pace. Valek would need both men to be at their best.

"Change of plans," he told them. "We're overnighting in Pelator instead of in a shelter."

"Isn't that risky?" Ari asked. "Word might get back to General Tesso."

"He's bound to find out regardless. We need fresh feed for the horses, and I need a hot meal and a soft bed."

Ari glanced at Janco, who clutched his reins as if they alone kept him from toppling from his horse. Then he flashed Valek a grateful smile.

"There's an inn that is frequented by the Commander's officers, so they have a stable." The innkeeper was one of Valek's agents and could be trusted to keep their visit quiet.

They reached Pelator an hour after sunset. The town, if he could call it that, had four main east-west streets and six north-south roads. Most of the citizens worked in extracting ore from the mountains and houses outnumbered businesses. The single inn, The Spot, sat at the northern edge of town.

Myzel, the innkeeper, heard the horses and came outside. She took one whiff, and said, "You're not stinking up my inn. Go to the bathhouse and I'll take care of your horses."

"Sweet lady," Janco snarked when they were well away. But it was half-hearted, and he seemed eager to follow her orders.

At the bathhouse, Janco stripped off his cloak and uniform in no time. He sank into the hot water with a sigh of contentment. Valek studied the purple scars on Janco's stomach and back, looking for signs of infection. None. His muscles were either still healing or stiff from not being used for so long. Not ideal.

Back at the inn, Myzel's staff had set out bowls of hot stew, bread, and tankards of ale. A feast. Janco groaned in pleasure.

After dinner, Ari and Janco went up to their rooms while Valek had a chat with Myzel. Around fifty years old, she was one of his more experienced agents. The combination of her kind face and friendly demeanor made people instantly trust her, spilling all their secrets. Handy for a spy.

"What's the gossip?" he asked.

"All the buzz is about the shake-up down in MD-5. Has General Brazell really been arrested?"

Valek gave her the short version of Brazell's plot to overthrow the Commander.

"That explains the rumors that the Commander is planning to replace all the generals and that he's sent you out hunting magicians."

"Did that make anyone in Pelator nervous?"

"No. The people who live here are law-abiding. It's the travelers that are far more interesting."

"Oh?"

"I had a caravan come through here a couple days ago. They were delivering wool to MD-3."

"Isn't it too early for wool?" Valek asked. Sheep were usually sheared at the end of the warm season, which was four months away.

"Yes, but I searched the wagons, and they were full of skeins that needed to be dyed."

"Did you inspect the wagons? Some have false bottoms for hidden storage."

"I didn't get a chance. One of the merchants must have spotted me snooping around and sent a guard to watch the merchandise."

Which wasn't unusual for a caravan. Except wool wasn't high on the list of stolen goods. It was odd, but not overly concerning. The wool could have been left over from last year. "Keep an eye out for more caravans and let me know if you find anything."

"Yes, sir. Anything else?"

"Do you have any pain powder?"

"For that poor young man of yours?"

"Yes."

"You should leave him here to recover. We've a couple capable people in the local patrol who could take his place."

"Capable enough to beat you?" he asked.

"Well, now, let's not get too excited." Myzel gave him a sly smile.

He laughed. "That's what I thought. Besides, if I leave him here, he'll drive you crazy. And I'm not ready for you to retire. You're too valuable."

"Then why did I get assigned to this speck on the map?"

"Because Boaz was transferred here."

Myzel blushed. "How did you…"

He waited. Would she deny her feelings for the patrol captain? It'd been obvious to Valek when they'd all worked on a case in MD-1. The patrolman had been promoted after that successful mission. And, like all newly minted patrol captains in Ixia, he had been sent to a speck on the map to prove he could run a patrol station before he could be assigned to a larger city.

"Yes, well…" She cleared her throat. "I'll go get that powder." Rummaging around her kitchen cabinets, she found a pouch and gave it to Valek along with a spoon. "Mix a teaspoon with some hot water as needed for pain. There's a kettle in the hearth."

"Thank you, Myzel. And just so you know, this speck is on a vital travel route, and I wouldn't trust anyone else to watch over it."

Her cheeks reddened again. Adorable.

Valek poured a cup of hot water before heading upstairs. Even though Ari and Janco had their own rooms, they were together. Valek paused outside the half-opened door. Although they spoke in low tones, it sounded as if they were arguing.

"…going to be left behind," Ari said. "Why didn't you say something?"

"I felt fine. Who knew riding a horse could hurt so much?" Janco argued.

"When's the last time you rode?"

Valek entered, Ari sprang from the chair, but Janco didn't

move from the bed. He lay on his side and his tragic expression told Valek he expected to be removed from the mission.

Setting the cup on the nightstand, Valek spooned powder into the water and stirred until it dissolved. "Drink all of this," he ordered Janco, waiting until the man downed the entire contents. Janco grimaced at the bitter flavor but didn't complain. A miracle.

"Did you get that from your agent, Myzel?" Ari asked.

"Why do you think she's one of my corps?"

"She didn't ask for our papers."

"Maybe she recognized me."

"She wasn't scared of you, and she treated you like an equal. Only your corps members do that."

"Good point." Valek handed the pouch to Ari. "Give him one spoonful mixed in hot water when the pain gets bad."

Ari looked stricken. "Sir?"

"I don't trust him to take it when he needs it. You know him best, so you can oversee his pain management."

"But, the mission—"

"We leave at dawn. I hope you sleep better tonight, Janco." Valek left.

Janco bounded down the stairs the next morning despite his claim to be allergic to dawn. The good night's sleep and pain powder had done their jobs. They ate a quick breakfast, thanked Myzel for her hospitality and the fresh supplies, and headed north.

They reached General Franis's manor house by mid-afternoon on the sixth day of their journey. Stopping at the stables first to see to the care of their horses, Valek spoke with the MD-3 Stable Master. If the tall man wondered about the extra horse, he didn't say anything. Soon after, one of the boys bolted for the main building, probably to warn the general of their arrival.

When the horses had been settled, Ari said, "We'll stay in the barracks. They're a good place to pick up on the local chatter."

"But we expect to be invited to any fancy meals or celebrations," Janco chimed in. "I'm a great dancer."

"Of course you are." Ari humored him.

"Really. My mother taught me." He beamed.

Valek bid them goodbye with instructions to find him if they heard anything concerning.

"What's your definition of concerning?" Janco asked.

Ari waved Valek away. "I got this."

"I'm serious. Valek might be looking for something that we wouldn't know is concerning because we haven't been trained as one of his agents."

Valek paused. Janco had a point. "In this case, it won't be anything subtle. Would you like to train to be in my corps?"

"We'd rather train to become your seconds," Ari said.

"No one has said that you can't challenge me if you're in my corps."

The Commander had urged Valek to find a second in command and so Valek had issued a challenge. If anyone could beat him in a fight, they'd earn the right to the job.

"But we don't want to be assigned to some remote town, working undercover. We want to continue working with you."

"Ah. I'll see what I can do."

Valek considered their request as he headed to the manor. Their desires were in line with what he wanted, but would it be unfair to the other people who hoped to become his second? He'd be working besides his second or seconds on a day-to-day basis. It'd be better if he actually liked and respected them.

General Franis met him at the grand entrance. Not a good sign. The general's manor was built the same in all the Military

Districts. A four-story brick building shaped like a square U with three equal sides.

"Valek, it's a pleasure to see you," Franis said, shaking his hand. "What brings you here?"

"I'm here at the Commander's request." Valek glanced at Franis's advisers, who hovered at the edges.

"Of course. Come on in." Franis dismissed his aides and led Valek into the main foyer.

While the manors were all structured the same, each general had decorated them to their own styles. Each organized them differently as well. At age forty-five, Franis was the youngest of the generals and his aesthetic had a modern feel with sharp-edged geometrical artwork in bright colors, granite topped tables, and minimal decorations, adding to the drafty chill of the air.

They climbed to the second floor. Franis's black hair was military short, but the top was a bit longer and styled. Tall and lean, he still had his youthful good looks. He wore a general's uniform, which consisted of black pants and a black jacket with gold buttons. Each Military District had been assigned a color and purple was MD-3's. Over Franis's left breast were five embroidered purple diamonds.

When they entered the general's office, Franis took off his jacket and hung it on a hook just inside the door. Underneath he wore a black shirt that had small purple diamonds stitched onto his collar—five on each side. His office's decoration matched the rest of the house, except glass topped Franis's desk.

"Would you like a drink?" Franis asked, gesturing to his sideboard filled with bottles.

Valek would love a drink. "No, thank you." He needed to stay sharp.

"Have a seat." Franis settled behind his desk. Files and stacks of papers had been neatly arranged on the surface, with a cleared area in the middle for him to work. "Is this regarding the unpleasantness in MD-5? I'd no idea Brazell was plotting with a southern magician. He had joined Ambrose's resistance later and wasn't one of the original members."

Valek thought it interesting that Franis was distancing himself from Brazell. As for his involvement, they'd found no evidence that any of the other generals were involved. Not yet.

"It is regarding the unpleasantness. The Commander has promoted your Colonel Ute to general of MD-5, and I'm here to deliver her papers personally." He watched Franis's expression closely.

Shock blanked the man's face for a moment before he visibly collected his wits. "Ah, that's…fast. Why the rush? Is it a temporary assignment until she proves herself or we find another who is more…suited?"

Valek noted he used the word *suited* and not *qualified*. "The Commander has made up his mind. Where can I find Colonel Ute?"

"Ah. She's…ah. On assignment, I think."

"Think? She's your highest ranked officer. Wouldn't you know?"

"She works with my advisers. Let me…" He stood and pulled on a cord near the window. "I'll find out. In the meantime, please make yourself comfortable. Ah, here's Jasia. Please escort Adviser Valek to one of our guest suites so he can rest up after his long journey."

"Yes, sir," the young woman said.

She wore a page's uniform, but she bore a striking resemblance to the general. One of his two daughters?

"Adviser? This way." She swept a hand out, indicating that Valek should precede her.

Valek debated if he should go or remain here until he learned the location of Colonel Ute from Franis. He outranked the general, but it would generate more ill will if he reminded the man of his rank. In the end, he thought he'd get more cooperation if he went along with the fake hospitality. Besides, he had other avenues available.

He followed Jasia to a well-appointed suite of rooms. Thinking of Ari and Janco sharing a bunk bed in the barracks, he smiled at the lavish accommodations.

"Is there anything I can get for you? Tea and biscuits? Or something else from the kitchens?" she asked. "Our chef is one of the finest in Ixia."

"No, thank you. Do you know where I can find Colonel Ute?"

Jasia probably knew more about what went on in the household than her father.

"Her office is on the ground floor, east wing. She splits her time between here and the garrison, which isn't far. If she's not here, you can find her there. Are you going to be inspecting the base?"

"If I have the time. Thank you, Jasia."

She flashed him a smile. "If you need anything, pull that cord and someone will come to assist you." She left.

Valek inspected the long rope of fabric that hung from the ceiling. The cords hadn't been part of the original design, and the Commander wouldn't be happy to know Franis had installed them. They had been used by the King. The Commander required his people to be self-sufficient and to avoid excesses. It had been years since the Commander had visited all the Military Districts. Perhaps it was time for another trip.

Setting his pack on the bed, Valek changed from his adviser's uniform into a standard sergeant's uniform with purple diamonds. He grabbed the papers for Ute and hurried to the east wing.

The door was ajar, and voices sounded inside. Valek paused to listen.

"...say why I needed to leave this afternoon?" a woman asked.

"No, sir, but it's urgent."

"Captain Wells—"

"The general has ordered *you* to personally handle it, sir."

"I guess I ought to be honored. Okay, Lieutenant, please tell the general I'll leave within the hour."

"Yes, sir." A man rushed from the office but stopped short when he spotted Valek. "Is there something I can help you with, Sergeant?"

"I've a message for the colonel."

The man bristled and straightened. "All messages are supposed to come through the proper channels."

"Oh, I assure you, Lieutenant. This is as proper as it gets." Valek stepped closer and lowered his voice. "A *direct* channel." He gave him a knowing nod like the man should know what he was referring to. Would the man's ego allow him to ask more questions? Valek guessed not.

"Of course. Carry on, Sergeant."

"Yes, sir!" He snapped and entered the office.

Colonel Ute stood in the middle of the room. Her hands were on her hips and her posture radiated disproval. "A direct channel? Care to explain, Sergeant?"

He moved closer. Ute's uniform was similar to Franis's, except she had four diamonds stitched on her unbuttoned jacket. She'd pulled her honey-colored hair into a bun, but a few tendrils had escaped and curled around her oval face. Golden eyes flecked with brown stared at him, as if daring him to lie to her. A formidable woman in her mid-thirties, she was an excellent choice for general.

"It's a message from the Commander."

She relaxed when she recognized him. "Adviser Valek, why are you in disguise?"

"Because I suspected the general would send you away on

some distant mission, and I wanted to intercept you before you could leave. Am I right?"

"I've been ordered go to an outpost near the border of MD-2 and the Northern Ice Pack."

Valek laughed. That was about as far away as one could get from the manor house while still being in MD-3.

"I'm glad you find it amusing. It's cold and icy near the NIP, even in the hot season and it's where we transfer all the problem soldiers. The only explanation is that I somehow pissed off the General. He knows how much I hate the cold." She shuddered.

"Would the climate in MD-5 be more to your liking?" Valek asked.

Her gaze sharpened. "It would. Why?"

Valek pulled out the scroll and handed it her. "Because you've been promoted to general of MD-5."

Stunned, she stared at him. "Are you serious?"

"Open it."

Breaking the wax seal, she unrolled the parchment. Her eyes widened as she read the official missive. When she glanced up, disbelief warred with elation. "Me?"

"You." He enjoyed watching her reaction. "Do you accept the assignment?"

"I've a choice?"

"Of course. You can refuse the promotion. It'll be a difficult posting due to the recent activities in MD-5. Frankly, it's a mess and will take seasons to sort out. The other generals won't be happy they weren't consulted. You saw what General Franis did, ordering you to the farthest reaches of MD-3 just to buy him some time to contact the others."

"He ordered me to leave right away. I should be pack—"

"As a general, you don't answer to anyone except the Commander."

"And you. But you never seem to use that privilege."

"It's very rare, but I've used it. Do you need more time to think about it?"

"No. I accept." She grinned. "I like a challenge."

"Then let me be the first to congratulate you, General Ute." He shook her hand. "The Commander has asked me to escort you to your new posting. When would you like to leave for MD-5, General?"

"General Ute." She marveled. "Not sure I'll ever get used to the title. I thought it would never happen. We heard about MD-5, but there are so many qualified colonels in the Territory of Ixia."

"There are. However, the Commander chose *you*. He has faith in *you*. Remember that when the other generals are pushing back, claiming you're not the best candidate."

She sobered. "Do you have faith in me?"

"I do. And don't hesitate to ask for help or advice from me or the Commander. It's not a sign of weakness or a sign that you can't do your job. You have a hard road ahead of you, General. Use your resources. We're on your side."

"Thank you." She pulled in a deep breath and looked around her office. "I'll need four days to pack and tie up a few loose ends. And say goodbye."

"Do you have a family, General?"

"No. Like you, I'm married to my job."

He wanted to correct her, to tell her he had Yelena. Yet here he stood in MD-3 and Yelena was far to the south in Sitia, living a separate life.

"Shall we inform General Franis of your decision?"

Ute squared her shoulders. "We shall."

"Then let's stop by the guest quarters, I've something for you."

Back at his rooms, Valek changed into his adviser's uniform. He dug into his pack and pulled out the general's jacket with five green diamonds stitched onto it.

"I had to guess your size." He handed it to her.

"What if I had said no?"

"It would have remained in my pack getting even more wrinkled."

She laughed.

To say General Franis was not happy about Valek finding and delivering Ute her promotion was an understatement. He demanded to see the paperwork and studied it for a long while. Then he placed it on his desk.

"I'm sorry Ute, but I can't accept this as authentic. The Commander has recently been compromised by Brazell. He was trapped in a magical coma for days and was being influenced by magic for months. According to generals Tesso and Hazal, he wasn't completely recovered. Therefore, he's not in his right mind to make big decisions like this. We're going to discuss the situation. Don't worry, you'll still be one of the top candidates under consideration. In the meantime, I believe I ordered you to the NIP outpost."

Poor Ute just gaped at Franis with a crushed expression. She started to remove her general's jacket.

Valek put a hand on her shoulder, stopping her. "I assure you the Commander is fully recovered and not in the mood for these games, General Franis."

"Games? This from the man who is supposed to be keeping the Commander safe? Where were you when Brazell and his pet magician targeted the Commander? How could you allow that to happen? Perhaps you are in league with them?"

Valek admired the General's efforts to undermine his integrity. "I'm not going to explain nor defend my actions to you. The Commander will brief you on the incident when he is ready."

"Not good enough. I'm not releasing Colonel Ute until I've talked with the Commander."

"It's not up to you. In fact, by refusing the Commander's orders, you're committing treason. Unlike you, I obey the Commander's orders and will escort General Ute to MD-5."

"You're in *my* district, Valek. You're outnumbered."

If he had a gold coin for every time someone had told him he was outnumbered, Valek would be a very rich man. He waited for Ute to respond. This was her first challenge. Would she cave to Franis's demands or assert her rights?

"You no longer have any authority over me, General Franis," Ute said. "I'm leaving immediately. Please have my personal effects packed and sent to MD-5." She turned on her heel and left.

Valek silently celebrated as he followed her from the room. He caught up to her in the hallway.

"Now what?" she asked. Her hands were shaking.

"We'll grab my knapsack and then swing by your rooms so you can pack a travel bag."

"I can pack while you—"

"No. We stay together."

"Do you really think—"

"Yes." He hurried to the guest quarters. Time wasn't on their side. Good thing Valek had never unpacked. He grabbed his bag and they headed to her suite on the ground floor.

"I would have liked to say goodbye, and thank a few people," she said.

"You can come back to visit." When she gave him a dubious look, he added, "Eventually."

She impressed him by how fast she gathered her belongings.

"I'm getting a raise," she said. "I'll buy what I need."

They rushed to the barracks to pick up Ari and Janco. Halfway there, Valek spotted armed soldiers. They had formed a defensive ring around the stables.

CHAPTER 4

"Do we need the horses?" Ari asked. "It'll take longer to get to MD-5, but we won't have to fight our way through a dozen soldiers to get to the stables."

Valek and Ute had reached the barracks without being seen. So far, they were safe, but it wouldn't last long.

"You outrank them," Janco gestured to them. "Can't you just order them to stand down?"

"They're loyal to General Franis," Ute said. "As far as they're concerned, I'm impersonating an officer and Valek is my accomplice."

"Then let's fight," Janco said with a gleam in his eyes.

"There's only four of us," Ari said.

"So? We can handle multiple opponents."

"I'm not injuring our own people," Valek said. "They're only following orders."

"We could do a merry chase," Janco said.

"Do I even want to ask?" Valek looked at Ari.

But the big man looked thoughtful. "It could work."

With no other good options, Valek and Ute headed straight toward the group of people guarding the stables. As soon as they were recognized, the soldiers pulled their weapons. As expected, ordering the soldiers to step aside resulted in a refusal, followed by a demand that Valek and Ute surrender.

In response, Valek and Ute took off running for the forest nearby. The soldiers gave chase. Valek didn't know how merry it was, but they managed to draw the guards away from the stables. He hoped Ari and Janco would be able to execute their part of the plan.

When they reached the woods, Ute said, "Follow me. I know this area very well."

"Yes, General."

Ute laughed somewhat hysterically. "This is not what I imagined would happen after I'd been promoted."

At least she wasn't out of breath. However, the leafless trees provided minimal coverage and the dead leaves and icy puddles created quite a racket underfoot. Valek had no idea how they would lose their pursuers. A dozen or more soldiers pounded behind them, calling out their position.

The sun hung low in the sky, casting long, thin shadows. They might be able to disappear in the dark, if they didn't run right into a trunk. He considered climbing a tree, but not while they were still visible.

Ute grabbed his arm, pulling him sharply to the right. The ground sloped down into a rocky area. They'd reached the edge of the foothills. Another sharp right and they ran along a gulley which deepened, blocking them from view. While happy to be out of sight, Valek worried they'd get trapped. Ute increased the pace and suddenly, the gulley's walls disappeared as if a giant hand had knocked them down.

"Avalanche," Ute said, panting. "This way. Hurry."

They climbed up along the avalanche's path, keeping low.

Skirting big boulders and squeezing through narrow openings, they entered a maze of debris.

"There was…a…village here," Ute said, heading to a pile of timbers.

Underneath the pile was a space just big enough to slither through. Valek realized it had once been a house when Ute opened a hidden door in the floor and gestured him inside.

When he hesitated, she said, "No one remembers this place. The avalanche happened before most of them were born."

Valek dropped into the dark hole and moved aside to give Ute room. She pulled the door and set it back over the opening. The darkness was instant. If they were found in here, there would be no escape.

He explored the space with his hands. The small square room was about five feet wide and had dirt walls. He found nothing but exposed roots. "Storage room?" he whispered to Ute.

"No. A shelter. Every house had one. This area is prone to avalanches and the residents would hide in them until the roaring stopped. Except, the one that destroyed the town came in the middle of the night and killed everyone." There was a long pause. "I was just out of basic training when my unit was sent to help recover the bodies."

Tough assignment for a newbie. At least the cold air and snow would have considerably slowed the rate of decomposition.

With nothing to do but wait, Valek sat down and leaned his back against the wall. As his sweat-soaked shirt turned to ice in the damp shelter, Valek wished he'd kept a few items from his pack. He'd given it and his cloak to Ari and Janco, so he could run unencumbered.

It didn't take long for the muffled shouts to filter through the wood. Valek remained relaxed and considered his options should they be discovered and arrested. Unfortunately, he was well acquainted with the configuration of the jail cells in the generals' manor houses. He had sewn a hidden set of lock picks into the hem of his shirt. If they were found during a search, then he would have to rely on Janco's jailbreaking skills. A scary thought. Or Ari and Janco could return to MD-5 and report Valek's predicament to the Commander. Ambrose would either be amused or angry. Valek would bet money on the Commander being angry at him for not avoiding capture.

The voices died down, but Valek wasn't about to make the mistake of leaving his hiding place too early. Many times, when his prey had gone to ground, he'd lain in wait for them to become impatient or confident that he'd moved on and he'd nab them. Fun stuff. Despite the cold seeping into his bones, he figured they had a couple hours to kill.

"What exactly happened in MD-5?" Ute asked in a whisper. "I don't trust the rumors. Usually, they have a kernel of truth, but there's always more to the story."

Valek explained about how Brazell and Mogkan had used Criollo to breakdown the Commander's will so they could use magic to influence him. He detailed the rescue and the fallout.

"This Criollo sounds like a powerful drug. What's to stop someone else from manufacturing it?"

"The factory and all the Criollo were burned. The few people who know the recipe have been arrested. The main ingredient comes from Sitia and it's illegal to import. The border patrols will be extra diligent in searching for Criollo's seed pods. Plus, it smells delicious when manufactured. That was part of its appeal. It tasted good."

"Did you eat any?"

"Yes. But magic doesn't work on me."

"Right." She was silent for a few minutes. Probably processing all the information Valek had provided. "Just how much of a mess is MD-5?"

"Brazell spent most of his budget building the Criollo

factory. Finding money to pay for salaries and supplies and the million other things needed to run a military district before the next year's stipend arrives is going to be tricky."

"I suspect I'll be cursing Brazell's name many times per day."

Valek chuckled. "Think of the bright side."

"There's a bright side? Do tell!"

"You can blame everything on Brazell."

Ute laughed. "I think I'll make a big plaque with the words, 'It's all Brazell's fault,' embossed on it and hang it in my office."

"That's the spirit."

Frozen to his core, Valek unfurled. His muscles protested the motion. Hard running followed by a few hours of inactivity wasn't a good combination for his body. Ute had fared better since she had her heavy general's jacket to ward off the chill.

The darkness remained the same when Ute lifted the trap door. It took a moment for their eyes to adjust. A thin sliver of moonlight illuminated the narrow opening under the timbers.

"I'll go first," Valek whispered. He pulled his knife before lying on his stomach and sliding under the gap. Once clear, he hopped to his feet and braced for an attack. Nothing happened. He waited several minutes more before sounding the all clear.

Ute joined him. She dusted off her uniform.

Valek glanced at the sky. Clouds skittered across the moon, temporarily dimming the light. "We're in luck."

"What do you mean?" she asked.

"We would be too visible in full moonlight, but those clouds will help create shadows to hide us in the forest while still allowing enough light to find a safe path."

"Is this what you do for the Commander? Creep around in the dark?" Her teasing tone mixed with an undercurrent of dismay.

"While creeping in the dark is one of my skills, I also stalk prey, set ambushes, work undercover, climb walls, and am a master of disguise."

"Good to know."

Ute led the way through the foothills. Their rendezvous location with Ari and Janco was north of the manor house. In order to stay warm, Valek kept a fast pace. The wind blowing from the west didn't help.

They encountered a couple of Franis's patrols and used those deep shadows to avoid detection. The run-ins slowed their progress. By the time they reached the meeting point, there were only a few hours left until dawn. Valek almost staggered in relief when he spotted Ari, Janco, and the four horses waiting in a small clearing.

"What took you so long?" Janco asked. "I'm frozen solid."

Valek didn't bother to reply. He pulled his cloak from his pack and wrapped it around his body. In between bouts of shivering, he asked Ari, "Any trouble?"

"The Stable Master wasn't inclined to help us. But I changed his mind."

"Oh?"

"The poor guy had an unfortunate encounter with Ari's fist." Janco *tsked*. "What a klutz."

Valek raised an eyebrow.

"Other than a headache when he wakes up, he'll be fine," Ari assured him.

Ah. "Mount up," Valek ordered and hoped his stiff and frozen legs would cooperate. He managed to sit astride Onyx, but it wasn't pretty.

"South?" Janco asked as he settled on Lovey.

"No. General Franis is bound to have all those roads blocked. Unfortunately, we're taking the long way. Northwest toward MD-2 and then south."

"Won't that bring us closer to General Tesso's house?" Ari asked.

"Yes, it will."

"At least if we're caught by Tesso, it'll be warmer," Janco muttered.

"See?" Valek said to Ute. "There's a bright side to everything."

She laughed. "I'll add that to my plaque."

Valek hated to push the horses after only a half day of rest, but they needed to be well away from the manor house before they could stop for longer than the brief breaks to feed and water the horses.

The sun rose behind them as they headed northwest and it wasn't until the sun set that Valek thought they'd gone far enough. They halted at the next travel shelter, and, after taking care of the horses, they built a huge fire in the hearth and crowded around it. Conversation was limited to one-word replies, usually about passing or sharing food.

Everyone was clearly exhausted, but Valek had to set a watch. "I'll take the first shift," he said. "Then Ari and Janco."

"And I'll take the last," Ute said. When he looked at her, she added, "I've plenty of experience on watch. You don't get to become a general without doing a ton of grunt work."

"See, Janco?" Ari asked. "All those hours of grunt work that you complain about might just get you promoted."

"Still won't stop me from complaining."

Ari shrugged. "Worth a try."

"All right," Valek said. "We'll do three-hour shifts. That way everyone gets at least eight hours of sleep, and it'll give the horses ample time to recover.

Valek pulled on his hat and gloves before wrapping his cloak around him. He did a perimeter check and scouted the road from the southeast—the direction their pursuers would use. Everything remained quiet and still. He returned to the horses in their mini stable. They dozed fitfully and he trusted their sensitive hearing.

He sat on the stack of straw bales in the corner and, thankfully, out of the wind. To stay awake, he thought of Yelena, wondering where she was and what she was doing.

Yelena and Fourth Magician Irys Jewelrose had taken the children Mogkan had kidnapped from Sitia with them. They planned to find the kids' families. However, the magician had locked up their memories prior to their kidnapping, so it would be a difficult task.

Adding to the complication were all the children Mogkan had reduced to mindless vessels so he could steal their magic, enhancing his own. Those unfortunate victims remained in MD-5 and their families would not have a happy ending. Anger coursed through Valek over not knowing this beast was in Ixia for the last fourteen years, and for not killing Mogkan as soon as he confirmed he was a magician.

It would probably take seasons for Yelena and Irys to figure out which child belonged to which family. As one of the children kidnapped, Yelena would eventually discover her own family. Mogkan had mentioned Yelena's connection to the Zaltana Clan. They lived in the Illiais Jungle, which was at the southern end of Sitia—as far away as a person could get from Ixia. Yelena liked to climb into the treetops. Perhaps that was another clue to her heritage.

Hopefully, Yelena would end up at the Magician's Keep—a school that taught young magicians how to control and use their magic. The school was located in the Citadel, and they officially started classes at the beginning of the cooling season. The Citadel was only a two-and-a-half days' ride from the Commander's castle. It was the capital of Sitia, and where the Sitian Council held their sessions.

It didn't matter where Yelena was located. Valek planned to be with her exactly one year after she left Ixia. By waiting a year, he would have fulfilled his promise to Irys to not be a distraction.

Valek checked the perimeter every thirty minutes or so to keep warm and for peace of mind. When his shift ended, he went inside to wake Ari. He, Janco and Ute had opted not to sleep on the bunks. Instead, they had spread their bedrolls right next to the hearth. Already awake for his shift, Ari fed a few logs to the fire. It blazed merrily, beckoning Valek closer.

Ari gestured to his bedroll. "Use mine."

"Thanks." Valek pulled off his boots but kept his cloak on. By the time Ari left the shelter, he was fast asleep.

The morning dawned clear and bright. Ute boiled water for tea and Janco fed the horses. All had been quiet during the night—the good news. Valek calculated their location and estimated it would take them seven days to reach MD-5's manor house—the bad news. They would have to stop for supplies, as they hadn't wanted to burden the horses with the extra weight of feed bags during their escape.

Word would eventually reach Franis and Tesso as they traveled south. There was no avoiding it. Instead of worrying about the generals' responses, Valek concentrated on making it difficult for anyone to find them. Having traveled all over Ixia on missions for the Commander, both before and after the takeover, Valek was very familiar with the landscape.

As they journeyed, Valek bypassed the main roads, and overnighted in little used travel shelters. They stopped in small towns where Valek had assigned agents who could purchase supplies for them.

On the second day after leaving Franis' manor, they crossed

into MD-4, and on the fourth day, a few hours past noon, they encountered a caravan of eight wagons. It was unusual since most merchants avoided riding over the rutted, bumpy secondary routes. But they exchanged a friendly hello with the drivers, and all went on their merry way. Except, Valek couldn't stop wondering why they weren't on the main roads.

"Oh no. He's got that look," Janco said.

"What look?" Ari asked.

"The one where someone is about to get into trouble."

Valek glanced at Janco.

"Not me. I haven't had to take the pain powder in days."

"Something's not right about that caravan," Valek said. "I'm going to circle back and see what they're transporting."

"In broad daylight?"

"If I get the chance. If not, then when they stop for the night." He turned to Ute. "This road will take you to our next shelter. I'll meet up with you there."

"You need backup. Commander's orders," Ari said. "We always travel in pairs."

Except Valek rarely worked with a partner. *And look how that turned out in Sitia.*

"I'm quiet," Janco said.

"We both are," Ari added. "Comes with being a scout."

"All right. Janco, you're with me."

"Yes, sir." Janco wisely kept from gloating.

"How long do we wait for you?" Ari asked.

"If we're not at the shelter by morning, keep heading southeast. You'll run into the main north-south route and that'll take you into MD-5."

Ari and Ute exchanged a glance that clearly meant they wouldn't be following his orders.

"It's imperative that General Ute reaches the Commander," Valek said. "I doubt we'll have any trouble that we can't handle."

Their expressions didn't change, and Valek didn't have time

to argue. He spurred Onyx into a gallop and Lovey followed right behind. Valek estimated how much distance the caravan would have traveled by now. They couldn't cover as much ground as a horse carrying a single rider.

When Valek thought they were getting close, he eased Onyx into a trot until he caught a glimpse of the last wagon, then he slowed to a walk. Hopefully none of the drivers would turn around. Plus, the noise of the wagon wheels rumbling, in addition to the jingle of harnesses and clip clopping of hooves, should cover any sound Onyx and Lovey made.

Unfortunately, the caravan did not stop to water or feed their horses. Valek and Janco followed them until they reached a travel shelter a few hours after sunset. Hanging back, Valek and Janco guided their horses into the forest and dismounted.

"We'll have to wait until they settle in and are asleep for the night," Valek said.

"If they don't post a guard, we could check the wagons while they're eating their dinner," Janco suggested.

Tempting. Valek didn't want to waste too much time on this side jaunt. After they cared for Lovey and Onyx, Valek and Janco crept closer to the shelter. Janco's near-silent progress over half-frozen ground, debris, and fallen limbs surprised Valek. Although it shouldn't have. The captain had proven his skills when they'd implemented the fugitive exercise in the Snake Forest. Yelena had been their mock escapee, and she had impressed the hell out of Valek when she covered her bright red uniform with green leaves and then proceeded to climb into the treetops to avoid detection. Ari and Janco had tracked her despite her cunning. If Valek hadn't distracted them, they would have found her.

Finding a comfortable and not too damp spot to wait, they watched the activity. The drivers rubbed down the horses, who munched from feed bags. Buckets were filled with water and set nearby. One man tested the tarps covering the beds of the wagons, ensuring they remained secure and keeping whatever was inside dry. Or perhaps just keeping it from blowing away.

After the chores were finished, everyone went inside the building. Janco, who'd been lounging against a tree, raised an eyebrow. Even though his expression was a clear communication, if Valek planned to keep working with Ari and Janco, he'd have to teach them his corps' signals. Valek shook his head and motioned to wait. One of the drivers might have forgotten something. When no one appeared after thirty minutes and voices drifted from the building, Valek pointed at the first four wagons and then at Janco.

He gave a thumbs up and melted into the shadows. Valek counted to ten before he approached the second set of four. Lifting the tarp, he exposed a pile of burlap sacks—the universal carry all. They were tied closed with twine. He loosened the knot on one and peeked inside. Skeins of wool.

If these were the same merchants that traveled through Pelator, why would they head east instead of north? All the dyeing and wool processing happened in MD-3. Unless a new business had set up shop in MD-4, which would be legal but might upset their neighbors in MD-3. That might explain the early shipping and surreptitious route.

Checking the next three wagons, Valek found the same cargo. Janco appeared next to him.

"By the amount of wool I found, there are lots of cold sheeps around," Janco whispered.

"Sheep is plural."

"Then what's the singular? Shoop?"

"Sheep is also singular."

"That can't be right. There's a horse and horses. Cow and cows. Goat and goats."

Janco continued to list all the farm animals, but Valek stopped listening. He considered the wagons. The wheels had sounded as if they'd carried a heavier burden than skeins of wool. Ducking down, Valek looked underneath the bed of one. It was hard to tell in the darkness, but the bottom of the wagon appeared deeper than the sides.

"Keep watch," he told Janco. Valek pulled the tarp half off and climbed into the bed. He shifted the burlap bags to the side, exposing a row of wooden boxes. Ah, the real cargo.

He counted. Seven rows of five boxes equaled thirty-five. The square-shaped containers were about a foot wide and unremarkable. Lifting one, he strained with the unexpected weight and size. Not square, but more of a rectangle, extending about three feet. Odd. The lid came off without trouble, revealing a stack of dark brown blocks inside. Bricks?

Valek picked up one block. Its surface was greasy and softer than expected. Once he held it up in the moonlight, the smell reached him. A cold dread rolled through his stomach as he recognized it.

Criollo.

CHAPTER 5

Cursing under his breath, Valek replaced the box, smoothed out the burlap sacks, retied the twine, and secured the tarp. The sudden desire to set it all on fire pulsed in his chest. Would this drug haunt him for the rest of his life?

"Something wrong?" Janco asked.

"There are boxes under the wool. Check those first four wagons to see if they have them too, then meet me back at the horses."

"Yes, sir." Janco disappeared.

Valek inspected the last three, but they were empty. Questions without answers swirled in his head. Where were they going? Who sent them?

Janco waited by the horses. "All four had those boxes. What's in them?"

"Criollo."

"Holy snow cats! That's…" Words failed him, but only for a moment. "Bad. Really bad. Terrible!"

"I'm aware."

"What are we going to do?"

"*You* are going to catch up with Ari and General Ute and get to MD-5 as fast as possible." He held up a hand, stopping Janco's protest. "The Commander needs to know about this. He needs to discover if this shipment was sent before or after Brazell was arrested. And if there are more caravans out here. Hopefully, Brazell kept good records of the shipments and they weren't destroyed when they burned the factory down."

"And you?"

"I'm following that wagon to its destination."

Janco's brows puckered in concern. "Will you send a message to the Commander once you get there?"

"Either that, or I'll destroy the Criollo before I return." When Janco's pinched expression failed to smooth, he added, "Don't worry about me. Worry about getting the general to the manor house without being delayed."

"Yes, sir." Janco mounted Lovey and saluted. "Safe hunting."

"Thanks."

Valek waited until Lovey was out of sight before he ate a quick meal and then returned to watching the caravan. Firelight flickered inside the travel shelter, and a warm yellow glow lit the windows. He spread his bedroll on a hidden spot that had a good view. It would be another frosty night. Eventually, one of the drivers came outside to guard the wagons. During the long night, they took turns on duty.

Two more nights of the same routine and, by the third evening, Valek was ready to put on a disguise and join the caravan in the shelter, claiming to be a fellow traveler. Instead, he suffered another bitter night on his bedroll, catching only a few hours of sleep.

By the end of day four, they had traveled well into the northwestern corner of MD-4. Another day's travel would bring them to the Six-Pointed Star—it was the place where the borders of six Military Districts all converged. When the Commander took over Ixia, he drew a big diamond around the castle on the map then he marked the eight Military

Districts, ignoring natural borders like rivers, mountains, and forests.

The caravan turned southeast instead and reached MD-4's garrison. Valek hung back and watched as the wagons were admitted into the military base.

He gaped as they trundled through the gates as if expected. More questions bubbled. Did someone intend to use the Criollo to gain control of the entire garrison? Was General Tesso involved?

It was too vital to waste time speculating. He needed to get inside. Scanning the walls and seeking toe holds, he— Laughed. The lack of sleep had dulled his senses. If anyone had full access to one of the Commander's bases, it was Valek.

He spurred Onyx, heading toward the gate at a gallop. The guards spotted him and stood in front of the wooden barriers with their hands on the hilts of their swords.

Their lieutenant stepped from the guard house. Everyone tensed as Onyx approached. Valek slowed his horse and halted next to the lieutenant.

"Who are you? And what's the nature of your visit?" the lieutenant asked.

"That caravan that just came through. Who approved the delivery?"

"That information is confidential. I believe I asked you a question."

"You asked me two." Valek opened his cloak. Weapons were drawn. The sharp blades flashed in the moonlight. Slowly, he revealed the two red diamonds stitched onto the collar of his uniform. "I'm Adviser Valek, and I need to know about that caravan."

Uncertain, the lieutenant squinted at Valek, then glanced at Onyx. "Can you join me in the guardhouse while I send for my supervisor?"

Valek dismounted and tied Onyx's reins to the gatepost. "As

long as you also send one of your people to keep an eye on that caravan. I want to know where they unload their cargo."

"Yes, sir."

"Make it fast, Lieutenant."

"Yes, sir."

With the lieutenant watching his every move, Valek waited in the guardhouse. At least it was warm. Impatience thrummed through his veins. He really needed to visit the garrisons more often. Perhaps when the Commander toured the military districts, they could stop at the bases as well.

Finally, a disheveled captain arrived. His hair was sleep matted on one side. "What is the emergency, Lieutenant? And it better involve blood, dismemberment, or fire or I'm going to—"

"Captain Silas, I assure you the matter is urgent," Valek said, glad he recognized the man from a previous visit.

The captain turned to him and paused. He straightened and ran a meaty hand through his hair. "Adviser Valek, my apologies, I didn't see you there. What's the trouble?"

Valek explained about following the wagons. "They're carrying illegal goods."

"Lieutenant, where was that caravan headed?" Silas asked.

"To the pantry, sir. I sent Sergeant Gia to ensure they don't deviate from their destination."

So, the man did know. "Who ordered the delivery?"

The lieutenant glanced at the captain, who gestured for him to get on with it. "I...I don't know, sir. They had the proper paperwork and I...just didn't look at the signature."

At least he was honest.

"They arrived late at night with weapons, and you didn't *look?*" Anger sharpened Silas's tone.

"They should still have their papers with them," Valek said, stopping the dressing down before it could start. "Let's go." He strode through the gates and headed for the pantry in the northeast corner. Lanterns blazed from lampposts that marked the main roads. Even though the garrisons had been built by the old Kings of Ixia, they appeared as though the Commander had commissioned them because they all had a similar layout and shared the same spartan aesthetic.

Valek's first undercover assignment as an assassin had been working as a stable boy for two and half seasons in Icefaren's garrison. During that time, he had learned the location of every structure, every pathway, and every shadow. He could pick every lock and climb every building. When the soldiers who killed Valek's brothers were assassinated behind locked doors, no one had any clue that the culprit was the fifteen-year-old stable boy.

"What do you intend to do?" Silas asked, hurrying to keep up. "Should I contact my boss, Major Bridget? Or perhaps wake the colonel?"

"Not yet." Valek didn't want to tip either of them off, just in case one of them had arranged for the delivery.

When they neared the pantry, Valek slowed. The wagons had been parked outside the kitchen's storeroom. The lantern light didn't quite reach this area, but the moonlight illuminated the activity. The burlap sacks from two wagons had been tossed to the ground and the drivers were hauling the wooden boxes inside, disappearing down the steps to the storage room underground. One man—presumably the leader—stood nearby, watching the activity.

A person detached from a shadow and approached them. "They have been here this entire time, sir," she said to Silas.

"Thank you, Sergeant Gia. Can you fetch me a bullseye lantern?"

"Yes, sir." She dashed off.

"You have a plan?" Valek asked.

"We need to inspect their paperwork. There's not enough light for my eyes to see the small print. What do you want to do once we learn who ordered the illegal merchandise?"

A good question. Valek's first impulse was to remove the boxes and burn them in a big bonfire. Yet, the name on the papers might not be the person responsible for the delivery. It'd be best to hide and wait to see who arrived to check the pantry. But he couldn't trust anyone in the garrison. Not even Silas, who could be pretending to be going along with Valek because he knew his name wasn't on the documents. Good thing he always had two agents working undercover in all the garrisons. He'd check in with them later.

"Nothing yet. Let's see what we find out first." Valek hedged.

Sergeant Gia returned with the lantern. She handed it to the captain.

"Thank you, Sergeant. You may return to your post."

"Yes, sir."

"You want to take the lead?" Silas asked.

"No."

Captain Silas ran his hand through his hair again, squared his shoulders, and strode to the man standing next to the lead wagon. Valek assumed a bored expression and followed.

"Excuse me," Silas said. "What are you doing here?"

"Unloading cargo, sir."

"What are you delivering?"

The merchant shrugged and gestured to the pantry. "Probably ingredients or something. I've no idea. I just transport it."

"Where are your papers?"

He fished into his pocket and removed a folded parchment. "Here ya go."

Silas set the lantern on the seat of the wagon and opened the shutter. A beam of light illuminated the paper.

While he read, Valek said to the man, "Rather late for a delivery."

"I know, but we've a schedule to keep."

"Oh? Where are you headed?"

The man pointed his long chin at the burlap sacks. "They're full of wool for the clothing factory in MD-3."

Valek watched the unloading for a moment. "I can get you some extra helpers so you're not here all night."

"That's okay. We're almost done."

"Just the two wagons?"

"Yeah."

Valek stilled. There had been three empty wagons. Did that mean they had already delivered Criollo to other locations? And where were the last three going? He refrained from asking the man. Too many questions would raise his suspicions.

"Everything looks good," Captain Silas said, handing the papers back to the man. He tucked them into his pocket.

Valek followed Silas. When they were out of sight, Silas stopped. "General Brazell signed the papers."

"And who ordered the delivery?"

"No one. It's a gift from General Brazell. According to the papers, he sent what he calls 'the brandy dessert, as promised' to Generals Tesso and Franis. One wagon to the manor house and two to the garrison in each district." Silas paused. "Does that make sense to you?"

Valek recalled the Commander's brandy meeting, where each general brought a bottle of their finest brandy to share. When it had been Brazell's turn, he sent around a square of Criollo filled with strawberry brandy. It'd been well received, and Brazell offered to send the recipe to the other generals. None of them knew Criollo was used to break down a person's will so they become very susceptible to magical suggestions. The Commander had ordered everyone who did know about Criollo's abilities to keep it a secret.

"Some. There are three empty wagons. I assume the cargo of one of them went to Tesso's manor, but what happened to the other two?"

"Perhaps the garrison in MD-5." Silas suggested.

That didn't make sense. Brazell wouldn't want to influence his own soldiers. They were already loyal to him.

But they weren't loyal to Mogkan. The magician hadn't been upset when he'd thought Brazell was dead and had mentioned finding another way to takeover Ixia right before Valek killed him. It was possible that Mogkan sent the wagons before he'd died.

Valek considered. Even with traveling during the cold season, the caravan would have delivered the Criollo weeks ago. Unless this was the last one to go out. Or the tail end of the deliveries.

The thought of all the soldiers in Ixia ingesting Criollo caused panic to simmer in Valek's chest. What if Sitian magicians sensed the army was compromised and decide to attack? "Did the papers indicate when they started their journey?"

"I didn't see a date."

Valek needed more information.

"How would you like to proceed, sir?" Silas asked.

"Arrest all the drivers. Confiscate the boxes and don't let a soul near them. Bring the leader to me in the interrogation room."

"Yes, sir."

The leader of the caravan sat across the table from Valek. He eyed the red diamonds stitched onto Valek's collar and scowled. "This better be quick, I've a schedule—"

"To keep. I'm aware." Valek studied the man.

He wore the standard brown trader uniform of a simple tunic and pants with calf-high boots. Straggly gray hair matched his unkempt beard. His long, narrow face was weathered and lined with wrinkles. To give the man credit, he didn't squirm or drop his gaze under Valek's scrutiny.

"What is your name?" Valek asked.

He huffed. "Roth. What's this all about?"

"The substance in those boxes you just delivered is illegal."

"Oh, come on. It's some kind of dessert from General Brazell."

Despite what he'd claimed earlier, Roth did know the contents. "Are you aware Brazell was arrested for treason."

"Well, yeah, I've heard the rumors. But the adviser said the delivery was approved by the Commander." Roth shrugged. "As long as the paperwork is legit, I don't ask questions. I just do my job, transporting cargo from point A to point B in an endless loop."

Valek kept his expression neutral despite getting a few good bits of information, including the caravan was sent after Brazell's arrest. "Which adviser?"

"Ah, the lady." Roth pulled at his beard. "What's her name… Tall with long dark hair?"

Sounded like Adviser Dema, but that was impossible. If Valek was wrong about Dema's devotion to the Commander, he'd quit his job because of sheer incompetence. "Where did you get this particular cargo?"

"There's a warehouse near the foothills of the Soul Mountains. The workers loaded it up and off we went."

"Where exactly is this warehouse?"

"Straight east of that factory that just burned down."

"You have three empty wagons. Where else did you deliver the boxes?"

Another huff. "Two wagons to MD-5's garrison. One to General Tesso's manor house. And before you ask, the remaining three were going to MD-3. One to General Franis's house and two for the garrison. Plus, the wool. Unless that's illegal, too?"

Valek ignored the jab. Whoever sent the wagons was targeting MD-5 as well. Was that because Brazell was no longer in charge? Had someone decided to continue with the plot Mogkan and Brazell started? Valek thought they had uncovered all the conspirators. Perhaps Mogkan had his own accomplices, people who were unknown to Brazell.

"Have you delivered those boxes to any other garrison or manor house?" Valek asked.

"No."

"Are there other caravans transporting them?"

"I dunno."

Valek waited.

Roth crossed his arms but didn't show any signs that he'd lied. "Can I go now?"

"No. You and your team will stay here until I can determine the degree of your involvement."

Hopping to his feet, Roth said, "We followed orders and didn't do anything wrong. You can't lock us in jail."

"I can. However, you'll remain as guests in the barracks until this matter is resolved. If you try to leave without permission or become too troublesome, then your accommodations will change. And not for the better." Valek stood and strode to the door.

The two guards that had accompanied Roth waited outside to escort the trader back.

"Adviser Alea," Roth called.

Valek turned around.

"That's her name. The adviser who hired us."

"Thank you."

As soon as Valek entered Captain Silas's office, the man put his hands up, stopping him. "I'm out. This is too big for my rank. Colonel Laban requests your presence in their office A-sap."

"Are you in trouble?" Valek asked.

"Time will tell." He handed Valek Roth's papers.

"I'll let them know you've been very helpful."

"I appreciate that."

Valek's thoughts whirled as he headed to the colonel's office suite. Just like Colonel Ute, Laban split their time between the garrison and the General's house. Valek would have preferred not to get Laban involved, but it was too late. Laban had probably already sent a messenger to Tesso, alerting the general about Valek's presence. At least it would take a couple days for Tesso to get the message.

Two guards were stationed on either side of Laban's door.

"Go on in," the guard said. "The colonel is expecting you."

Lovely. Valek rapped his knuckles on the wood as a courtesy before entering the spacious room. A large oval-shaped conference table took up the left side, a sitting area with four couches and four armchairs had been arranged in front of a massive fireplace on the right side. Back near the far wall, Colonel Laban stood behind their desk. And sitting in an oversized armchair in front of it was General Tesso.

Valek bit back a curse. General Tesso's presence just transformed the situation with the Criollo from bad to worse. At least he shouldn't know about the incident in MD-3 with Ute.

"Ah, there you are," Tesso said in a clipped tone as Valek drew closer. "We were just discussing you."

Valek noted Laban's stiff posture, indicating their irritation. Tesso's dour expression also didn't bode well for this meeting.

When Valek remained quiet, Tesso added, "We wondered why you didn't feel it necessary to alert the garrison's commander of your presence and your claims against a trade caravan."

There were several concerning words in that sentence. "Because it wasn't necessary to wake the colonel for a situation that I'm quite capable of handling," Valek said.

"You can't just come in here and order my people about," Laban said.

"I can. They're my people, too."

"Look, Valek," Tesso said. "After the debacle with Brazell and the Commander, your reputation isn't exactly stellar right now.

And to add to it, you're accusing a trade caravan of transporting illegal goods. Since when is a dessert considered illegal?"

"Regardless of my reputation, I'm under no obligation to explain my actions to you or anyone else besides the Commander."

Tesso laughed without humor. "The Commander who you are sworn to protect? The one you allowed to be captured and almost killed? The one you abandoned soon after to pursue some assassin in Sitia? *That* Commander?"

The general must have learned of Valek's mission to save Yelena before he left MD-5. He wondered how he found out so fast. Had the Commander shared the information? Regardless, Valek failed to rise to the bait. Instead, he gave the general his flat killer stare. He'd love to assassinate the man and put Laban in charge.

Tesso was unimpressed. "Well, *that* Commander is not yet recovered from his ordeal. He's making hasty, emotional, and illogical decisions and you're not considered reliable anymore. In fact, what are you even doing here? You should be by the Commander's side, ensuring no one else can harm him, and not going on foolish errands for him. Let alone this side jaunt, chasing after nothing."

Ah. So, Tesso did know about Ute. Again, the news had traveled much faster than it normally would, which was concerning. However, the general was not *all* wrong. Valek should be with the Commander.

"Your opinions have been noted, General," Valek said. "If you're finished expressing them, I've work to do." Valek stepped to leave.

"Where's Colonel Ute?" Tesso demanded.

"*General* Ute should be at her manor house in MD-5 by now." Valek hoped.

"Not for long. The generals are discussing this hasty promotion along with your failure in keeping the Commander safe.

We plan to present a number of actionable items to the Commander."

"Good luck with that," Valek said and headed for the door.

"I wouldn't be so flippant if I were you," Tesso called after him. "You could lose your job or be arrested and hung for treason."

Or I could move to Sitia and be with Yelena and not have to deal with any of you anymore. Tempting. Very tempting.

Well aware that the general would countermand all Valek's orders, he hurried through the garrison. Valek had the rank to override the General, but that would put the soldiers like Captain Silas in a difficult position.

One of Valek's undercover agents worked in the kitchen. Pale pink light crept over the black sky, so he hoped to find Nowles prepping for breakfast. The slight man stood at a counter chopping green peppers with a precision and speed that either spoke of years of practice or hinted at Nowles's extra training with knives. Valek would have to remind him to tone it down or it might blow his cover.

Catching Nowles's gaze, Valek signaled.

Soon after, Nowles joined Valek in the hallway behind the vast kitchen.

"Better make it quick, boss," Nowles said. "Busy time, and my absence will be noticed."

Valek explained about the boxes that had been delivered the night before.

"Oh yeah, the head chef is ecstatic about the contents. She's been told to serve it only to the higher ranked officers and no one else. Must be expensive."

Interesting and completely opposite of the Commander's orders regarding his army. He required that everyone be treated equally and to have access to the same services and benefits no matter their rank. "It's a drug called Criollo. You can't let anyone ingest it. I want you to steal every box, every bit of it, and burn it."

Nowles gaped at him. "I'd have more success if you ordered me to fly."

"I'm serious."

"So am I! Chef Rae is already guarding it like a dog with a new bone."

"Have Tila help you."

"Still not enough. Can you send me a few more agents?"

"No time."

Nowles wiped his hands on his apron. "How bad is it if they eat it?"

"It's not lethal, but it can be addictive. And..." And it took time to work. Valek drew in a deep, calming breath. Although his instincts screamed at him to destroy it immediately, it wasn't dire. Plus, there needed to be a magician in the garrison to take advantage of the drug's effects.

That possibility stopped Valek. Had Mogkan created his own network of undercover magicians in all the Ixian garrisons and manor houses? A frightening thought.

"And?" Nowles prompted, pulling Valek out of his spiral.

"If the officers eat some, it'll be fine. Just take care of it tonight."

"The op might blow our covers."

"That's fine. Return to the castle, I'll assign two new agents."

"And if we're caught?"

"I'll send a rescue team."

"I'd say it's been a pleasure to see you, but I know you can spot a liar."

Valek smiled. "Get back to work."

"Yes, sir." Muttering under his breath, Nowles dashed away.

While Valek would have loved to find the guest quarters and

a soft bed to spend the day in, he needed to leave the garrison before Tesso sent soldiers to arrest him. He had left Onyx at the gate, but he doubted his horse was still there.

On his way to the stables, Captain Silas intercepted him. "The drivers have been given permission to leave with their wagons and cargo."

Not a surprise. "And the explanation?" This ought to be good.

"It seems there has been a misunderstanding. A certain…" He cleared his throat. "High level adviser has panicked and is causing problems over nothing. Overcompensating for his incompetence, this adviser is jumping at shadows and no longer fit for the job."

Valek laughed, giving extra points to the general for his creativity. Then he sobered. "In my experience, shadows can be quite deadly."

Silas gave him a sly smile. "They're also good at hiding secret activities."

Valek stilled. "For example?"

"Let's say there are three wagons carrying a dangerous and illegal substance that also happens to be heavy. Deep in the shadows, one can empty the containers holding this material and fill them with…oh, let's say rocks, just in case the drivers are allowed to continue on their journey."

"And the boxes in the pantry?"

"Alas, not enough time, but the substance that was collected will be properly disposed of. In the shadows of course."

"Of course. Captain Silas, I think you're due for a promotion and reassignment. I don't think the people at this garrison appreciate your talents as much as I do."

"Thank you, Adviser Valek."

"It might take a few months for the paperwork to go through, since I'm overcompensating for my incompetence."

"Now, now. I never said *you* were the high level adviser."

Smooth. Perhaps he should recruit Silas for his corps.

Valek found Onyx in the stables. His saddle, pack, and the tack had been removed and hung on the wall in his stall. The big black horse's coat gleamed as if he'd been recently groomed. All good, except the stall's door was secured with a large padlock.

While glad Onyx had been taken care of, Valek worried about the delay that would be caused by picking the lock and then saddling his horse. Nothing to do about it, except to get a move on.

As the sky lightened, Valek worked at a fast pace. Unfortunately, it wasn't fast enough.

"Hey," a booming voice called. "You're not allowed in here."

Valek finished tightening Onyx's girth straps, then faced the Stable Master. "I don't need permission."

"General Tesso—"

"Has no authority over me."

"But he has authority over *me*."

"So do I," Valek said in a cold tone. "And authority over the General."

"Yeah." The man drew the word out. "But once you leave with your horse, I'll be in trouble regardless."

Good point. "How are you planning on stopping me?"

"Well, I was hoping you'd just leave the stables. That way I followed my orders to keep you from getting your horse. See? I'm sure you can work out another way to depart the garrison."

Valek crossed his arms as if thinking about it, drumming his fingers on his right sleeve. "Okay, sounds fair." He held out his hand. "Deal?"

Relieved, the Stable Master grasped it. "Ouch." He jerked it away. "What was that?"

"The answer to both our problems," Valek said, tucking the

used dart into his left sleeve. It only took that one awful time, when he mixed up the empty darts with the full ones, for him to develop a system of keeping track.

The man wobbled and then slumped to the ground as the sleeping potion took effect.

By the time Valek finished getting Onyx ready, the day shift was awake, and the garrison hummed with activity. Did General Tesso really expect the Stable Master to stop Valek, or was the man a diversion? Interesting that none of the stable boys had reported to work yet. Was there a unit of soldiers lying in wait for him? And did Valek really have a choice? It was hard enough to sneak out on his own. Almost impossible with a horse. Unless…

Valek stared at the sleeping Stable Master as an idea formed. Pulling clothes off an unconscious person was awkward, difficult, and time consuming. However, Valek managed to change into the Stable Master's uniform. It stank like sour milk and Valek had to tighten the belt.

He gathered Onyx's reins and walked beside the horse as they left the stables. Striding with purpose and confidence, Valek headed toward the gate. He tried to keep Onyx between him and everyone else in case someone actually looked at him and not at the uniform. The requirement that everyone who lived in Ixia wear a uniform indicating their job was both a bane and a boon to Valek.

This time, it appeared to be working. No one stopped him or called a halt. Valek strode up to the gate and reached his first obstacle.

The lieutenant from last night stood in front of the gate with his arms crossed. "Nice disguise, but I've orders not to let you leave, sir."

Valek sighed for many reasons. First, the man didn't have his weapon drawn. Big mistake. Second, the ring of soldiers behind him also did not have their weapons out. Third, there was no one behind Valek. Fourth, no archers. Who trained these people? Did they just expect him to give up?

Since sneaking out was no longer an option, Valek mounted Onyx, turned him around and took off. Shouts followed. Valek waited a few seconds, then spun Onyx back toward the gate.

The shocked expressions of the guards, who had spread out in their pursuit with the faster ones in front, was comical. Valek charged them. Not many people were willing to block a two-thousand-pound animal running straight at them at full speed. Instead, they scattered, diving out of the way. Fun.

Onyx reached the gate and Valek held his breath. Would the horse balk at jumping over it? Heck of a time to find out. Without breaking his stride, Onyx launched, sailed over the barrier, and landed with a slight stumble. Valek grabbed his mane to keep his balance as Onyx righted and galloped away from the garrison.

Valek imagined General Tesso telling the other generals that a man without guilt wouldn't have run. More evidence for his campaign to get Valek fired. He didn't care what the generals thought. If Valek didn't destroy the remaining Criollo, the Commander would kill him.

Which meant he needed to go to Tesso's manor and confiscate the Criollo. Had the general warned his people at the house about Valek? Normally, he'd march right in and take what he needed. No questions asked. However, if the general said Valek wasn't to be trusted or should be arrested, then the direct approach wouldn't work. Valek would have to sneak in and contact his agents. Together, they'd have to steal and then dispose of the Criollo. Time consuming and difficult, but not as hard as swiping it from a garrison.

At least, Valek wouldn't have a general countermanding his

orders when he confiscated the Criollo from MD-5's garrison. By then, he hoped to know who had sent those wagons and where else the cargo had been delivered.

Engrossed in his thoughts, Valek didn't notice the three other riders heading for him until Onyx slowed. He groaned when he recognized Ari, Janco, and General Ute. If they truly wanted to be a part of his team, they needed to follow his orders. Both men looked properly terrified of Valek's reaction. Good.

When he reached the group, Ute held her hand up. "I take full responsibility."

Valek bit back a growl. "What happened?"

"When we reached the border of MD-4, it was guarded by soldiers. Captain Ari's idea to scout ahead saved us from an ambush. We headed west to test a few more roads leading south, but all have been blocked. The new plan was to travel into MD-6 and then turn south, but Captain Janco found Onyx's tracks and I decided we should attempt to rendezvous with you."

"How did he know they were Onyx's?" Valek asked her.

"It seems that horses' hooves are not all identical."

Valek glanced at Janco. The captain fought to keep his serious expression as a smirk twitched his lips.

"The border guards indicated that General Franis was able to get a message about us to General Tesso," Ari said. "We didn't think we had the...clout to get through their barriers."

And Valek learned another lesson in not jumping to conclusions. They had avoided trouble and found him. Their skills as scouts certainly proved to be an asset to the mission. "You did the right thing," he said to the trio. "And now you can help me run an errand before we head to MD-5."

"Uh, what about the border patrols?" Janco asked.

"Don't worry, I've plenty of clout," Valek said, patting the side of Onyx's neck.

Janco leaned close to Ari and whispered, "I think his definition of clout is different than yours."

Valek raised an eyebrow.

Janco straightened. "What is the errand, sir?"

"Did you find out where that caravan went?" Ari asked.

A team effort to distract him. Nice. "I did, I'll fill you in on the way."

"To where?" Ute asked.

"General Tesso's manor house."

Janco made a strangled sound. Everyone looked at him. "Of course, we're going to the manor house," he said. "I'd forgotten we were invited to high tea with the General." He patted his pockets. "Hmm, I must have misplaced my invitation."

"Please don't tell me this is a typical mission for you," Janco whispered to Valek as they crouched in a dark shadow. "If so, I really have to consider if I want to continue hero worshipping you or not."

"Consider it a test of your patience," Valek replied.

"You assume too much," Ari said. "Janco doesn't have any patience."

"Are they always this chatty during a mission?" Ute asked.

He had no idea. "Let's stay focused." Valek detailed the plan to everyone again.

They waited until late into the night. When the occupants of the manor house were deep asleep, Valek signaled, and they broke into pairs to head in different directions. Ari and Valek toward the manor's pantry, and Janco accompanied Ute to the stables.

Sneaking into the house reminded Valek of when he and Yelena had broken in to Brazell's. They'd hunted for the source of Mogkan's extra power, hoping it would free the Commander from his magical control. The horrors they'd discovered still haunted him. Mogkan had siphoned the souls from the children he'd kidnapped from Sitia to amplify his power.

Yelena had impressed Valek by not running away screaming when she entered the place where she'd been tortured and raped as Brazell's son, Reyad, and Mogkan tried to steal her soul. Her inner strength and courage amazed him. A sharp pang squeezed his heart over the reminder of her absence.

Ari followed him on silent feet. They reached the kitchen without encountering anyone. Warmth embraced them as they entered. The fires in the ovens had been banked, but the sweet aroma of apple pie still scented the air. They had a four-hour window of opportunity between when the cleaning crew finished for the day and the pastry chef woke to start baking.

Jars had already been filled with Criollo and set on the shelves within reach of the dessert chef. Ari collected them while Valek swiped a bottle of whiskey and shoved it into his pocket. Then he unlocked the door to the pantry. The locks popped easily. Too bad the hinges squeaked as he pulled it open. He and Ari froze.

If he had the time to do this properly, he would have spent a few days learning all the quirks of the kitchen and staff so there would be no surprises.

When no candlelight shone under the door of the chef's quarters, Valek and Ari entered. The shelves in the main room were loaded with sacks of flour, grain, rice, and other staples. In the far corner were the stairs that led down to the cold storage. Valek took the lantern that hung nearby and lit it. Ari mimed shutting the pantry door and pointed to his ear.

Should they risk another squeak or leave it open? If the door was discovered ajar in the morning, it would cause an immediate investigation. Valek motioned to close it and braced for the noise.

Ari examined the hinges for a moment then set the jars on a

shelf. He lifted the door slightly before pulling it closed without a sound. Impressive.

He picked up the jars and joined Valek at the top of the stairs. He whispered, "I learned that trick from Janco."

Figured. Valek shook his head and continued into the cellar. The boxes of Criollo had been stacked along the left side. Smoked meat hung from hooks along the right side and wheels of cheese had been piled underneath. At the far end was a set of stone stairs that led up to the outside. While Ari counted boxes, Valek hurried up them. At the top of the steps was a set of metal doors that could only be opened from the inside. A large padlock kept them clamped together.

The lock proved to be more complicated to open than Valek expected. Was Tesso worried about people stealing food? Once he removed it, he pushed opened the doors. On the other side, Janco grabbed them and pulled them wide.

In the weak moonlight, Valek spotted Lovey hitched to a wagon. "Any trouble?" he asked.

"Nope."

"Good. Let's hurry."

The three of them loaded the boxes and jars of Criollo into the wagon. When they'd taken every bit, Janco jumped into the driver's seat, while Valek and Ari sat in the back.

This was the most dangerous part of the mission. An exposed target, the three of them scanned the area for guards. They glanced at the windows, seeking people peering out who might raise an alarm. They hoped no one would spot the wooden wagon or hear it creaking over the cobblestones.

No one breathed until they reached the woods east of the manor house. Ute waited for them with the rest of the horses.

"Is it just me or did that seem too easy?" Janco asked.

"It was too easy," Valek said. "It's been a number of years since the Commander and I have visited the manors and garrisons in Ixia. When I'm there, I test their defenses."

"How does that help?" Ari asked.

"They're informed that there will be a test. Even knowing to be extra vigilant, I usually get through. After I bypass their defenses, they pay more attention when I hold extra training sessions. It appears that they're long overdue for a refresher course."

"Yeah, but, you're *Valek*. The best of the best couldn't stop you." Janco said.

"I'm cocky, but not that cocky. Everyone gets caught eventually." Valek still made mistakes. His capture in Sitia was one recent example.

"It's a good thing they're out of practice or we'd have been chased tonight, and you might have gotten stuck in the garrison," Janco said.

"Well, I don't teach them *all* my tricks."

"Nice."

Valek, Ute, and Ari mounted their horses and Janco followed them south. They stopped before a bend in the road would expose them to the border guards. Ari melted into the forest around them to scout ahead.

When Ari returned, he reported, "There are six soldiers waiting in ambush at the border, three on each side of the road. You're right, they need a refresher."

"What would you do differently?" Valek asked.

"I would have them lying in wait right about a hundred yards before this bend and not at the border."

"It doesn't matter where they are," Janco said. "We're not getting this wagon past them." He fingered the hilt of his sword. "I could do with a little exercise after all this sneaking around."

"We're not smuggling the wagon passed them," Valek said. "Unhitch Lovey."

"Oh." Janco hurried to unhook all the straps, and then he saddled her.

Once he finished, he and Ari mounted and walked their

horses into the forest on the left side of the road. Ute mounted Clever and took Onyx into the right side. When they were in position, Valek took a swig of the whiskey he'd swiped from Tesso's kitchen before pouring it over the boxes. Then he set the wagon on fire, signaling the others to move away.

Valek ran to catch up to Ute. He joined her just as the flames reached the whiskey. A loud *whoomph* sounded, rattling the trees. The invisible energy wave that followed pushed on Valek's shoulders. They waited. Seconds after the explosion, six figures raced up the road toward the burning wagon.

They urged their horses onto the path, joined Ari and Janco, and trotted into MD-5.

"Now, *that's* clout," Janco said.

Valek and Ute reported to the Commander right after they settled the horses in the stables. It was late, but the Commander was still in what would soon be General Ute's office. They stood in front of the desk and took turns recounting all their adventures. The Commander listened without interrupting or reacting, which Valek had learned was a sign of anger. The Commander hadn't so much as twitched—another dangerous indicator. And his knuckles slowly turned white during the report.

When they were finished, the Commander dismissed Ute, telling her to get some rest and that they would start working on the transition in the morning. His pleasant, welcoming tone, gave her no indication of his fury. After all, it wasn't her fault the generals had behaved so badly. Not Valek's either, but he braced for the fire to reach the proverbial whiskey.

"I don't care how many people you need, find all of that damn Criollo and destroy it." His tone was ice cold. "Then find whoever is responsible for shipping it and kill them. *All* of them."

Whoomph.

"I've also changed my mind regarding Brazell," the Commander said. "Let's drag him to the castle and hang him. We'll invite all the generals to watch. They can see what a real hasty, emotional, and illogical decision looks like. And let's see if they still consider me not in my right mind to make big decisions."

Valek went to the sideboard and poured them both a drink. He set the Commander's glass on the desk before settling in a chair. "I've a better idea."

"Do tell."

"While it's very tempting, instead of hanging Brazell, we visit all the generals and garrisons. We haven't done it in years, and they need to see you being you."

"I want to go home, Valek. Not go on a parade. I'm in no mood to play nice."

"It's going to take me a while to find out who sent the Criollo and if there are more caravans. Once Ute is settled, which shouldn't take long, you can go home, and we'll start our tour in the beginning of the warm season."

The Commander sipped his brandy. "She's a good choice, isn't she?"

"An excellent choice."

"I'll consider a tour. In the meantime, I need to demonstrate my displeasure with Tesso and Franis."

"I'm sure you can think of something devious."

After a moment, he said, "I'm going to hit them where it hurts."

"Oh?" Valek raised an eyebrow. "Below the belt?"

"No. It'll be right on the money."

Ah, the money belt. "General Ute will appreciate the extra funds to get MD-5 back in shape."

"Precisely." The Commander relaxed back in his chair.

They discussed a few more things until Valek could no longer stifle his yawns.

"Go get a bath and go to bed, you look exhausted." The Commander sniffed. "You stink of smoke."

Valek laughed, downed his whiskey, and headed for the door where he turned and said, "I missed you, too."

Ambrose's chuckle followed him into the corridor. Before heading to the baths, Valek sent messages to all his agents working in the garrisons and manor houses, instructing them to hunt down every last bit of Criollo and destroy it. Remembering how the Commander had kept some in his suite to eat at night, Valek listed a number of places they should check.

After a glorious soak and a decadently long sleep, Valek went to Mogkan's office to continue sorting through his mess and to search for information on the Criollo shipping. Except, if Mogkan had been hiding some of his activities from Brazell, the information Valek needed wouldn't be here. It'd be hidden somewhere Brazell wouldn't accidentally find it. Like the room Mogkan had chained his victims. A person had needed a strength beyond the physical to go inside there when it had been occupied. Even with the place cleaned up, he was reluctant to go back.

He gazed around the room. Sometimes the best hiding places were in plain sight. And there were plenty of potential spots right here. He'd start with the office and go from there. A part of him recognized that he was procrastinating, but another part didn't care.

Ari and Janco arrived in the afternoon to report.

"We found the warehouse that trader described," Ari said. "No one was there, and it was empty."

"Did they see you coming?" Valek asked.

Offended, Janco huffed. "No. We went in stealth mode. We even surprised the fat mice that had been living on the Criollo crumbs."

"We checked for hidden caches, paperwork, and for a door to a lower level. Nothing," Ari said. "The structure is basically a barn."

"Thoughts?" Valek asked.

"They might have been tipped off by a co-conspirator about our interest," Ari said. "The foothills of the Soul Mountains are also quite close, and they're filled with caves and abandoned mines. Easy to find a place big enough to store a bunch of boxes."

"And almost impossible to find," Janco said. "Yet..." He rubbed the scar bisecting his right ear.

When he didn't say anything else, Valek prompted, "Yet?"

"If they're inside a cave, we can't track them unless there's dirt. And even then, the dirt eventually dwindles. However, if we find the entrance, we can wait and see if anyone comes out or goes in."

"But we didn't see any wagon tracks going east. They headed north, northwest and west. The perpetrators may have finished with their deliveries and left to carry out the next step in their plan," Ari said. "In that case, we should check all the manor houses and garrisons."

"What about MD-5's base?" Janco asked. "We can do another midnight raid. Maybe this one will actually be a challenge." His eyes gleamed as he bounced on the balls of his feet.

"General Ute sent a squad up there to take care of it. Her first order."

Janco deflated. "Oh well. Good for her. If the other generals don't eat her for breakfast, she'll make a good general."

"What do you need us to do now?" Ari asked.

Valek gestured to the piles and cabinets. "Pick a spot and

start searching. I'm looking for any mention of the Criollo factory, warehouse, and magic. Names, dates, deeds. Anything."

Janco eyed the overflowing conference table. "I'd rather search the caves."

"If you find any evidence they were using them, then you can go back to check them."

"This is not what I imagined you spent your time doing," Janco grumbled as he pulled a chair up to the table.

"You thought all I did was midnight raids, smash and grabs, and stopping assassination attempts?"

"Yeah."

"That's about ten percent of my job. The other ninety percent is sitting, reading, watching, collecting information, anticipating, guarding, and waiting. Lots of waiting."

Janco shuffled through a few folders. "I'm already bored, and I haven't even started."

Ari picked one of the corner cabinets and sorted through the contents. They worked in companionable silence—something Valek thought would be impossible with Janco in a room. Although... Valek considered. The captain might just be talented enough to appear as if he was working when, in fact, he was fast asleep.

Adviser Dema arrived close to dinner time. "I checked through all the information we've collected, but I didn't find any mention of an Adviser Alea."

Too bad, but Valek hadn't thought it'd be that easy.

"However," Dema continued. "I did find payments to Mogkan's team."

"Team?"

"Don't get too excited. I couldn't find any names or even how many people were part of this team. Perhaps Mogkan had a record of them?" She looked around at the messy piles. "Do you want some help with the search?"

"Doesn't the Commander need you?" Valek asked.

"Not tonight. He's working with General Ute."

Janco jumped to his feet. "You can tackle the table and I'll get us some grub."

Valek clamped down on a protest. Dema's attention to details would be useful and his stomach agreed with Janco. They needed food.

They worked late into the night and all the next day. Dema assisted in their search when she had free time. After each pile was assessed, it was moved to the hallway.

In the middle of the third day, a loud bang sounded followed by a string of curses. Janco crawled from underneath the table clutching a stack of folders. "I found something!"

"Is it about Alea? Or Mogkan's team?" Valek asked.

"No." Janco set the folder on the table. "It's a delivery list for the Criollo factory."

Valek scanned the pages, noting the mention of the deliveries of Criollo to the Commander's castle. They matched his recollections. Then he spotted a schedule of transports to the other Military Districts. Except, the first two shipments had been sent to only the manor houses. While the third had included stops at all the garrisons with a resupply dropped off at the manors. Valek stilled. That meant—

"What's wrong?" Ari asked.

"Mogkan's been sending Criollo to the generals."

"We already know that," Janco said.

"The caravan we encountered wasn't the first one. The generals have been receiving shipments since the middle of the cold season. Which means—"

"They've been eating it all along," Ari said.

"And if Alea is a magician..." Frustration choked off his words. Why did he think burning down the Criollo factory would neutralize the threat? It was like a weed and had spread as weeds do.

"If Alea is a magician, the generals are vulnerable to her influence," Ari finished. "Do you think that's why General Tesso was so...resistant to your efforts? And why General Franis behaved so badly over General Ute's promotion?"

"The generals never liked me, but, normally, they are more... subtle," Valek said. He considered. "It's possible, but that would mean there's a magician for each general. There's no way one person could control them all from a distance."

"Unless Alea has her very own magical ring of horror to boost her range," Janco said, spinning his finger in the air.

"That's a terrible thought," Ari said.

"What's worse?" Janco asked. "Seven magicians in Ixia, targeting each of the generals, or a single really powerful one?"

CHAPTER 7

Thinking of Mogkan, Valek replied, "One powerful magician is worse than seven with lesser powers. In either case, I need to alert my corps about the danger. Perhaps one of them will discover something useful."

"Do you have agents in the barracks at the Commander's castle?" Janco asked.

"Worried one of them is going to report you for sleeping through the morning meetings?" Ari asked.

"No," Janco shot back a little too quickly. "I'm just curious. We all know about your network of spies. How extensive is it?"

"That information is classified," Valek said. "And we have a problem to solve."

"What to do about the generals," Ari said.

"Yes. What would you suggest?"

Janco rubbed a hand through his goatee. "Why do anything? Won't the effects of the Criollo wear off eventually?"

"As long as there isn't any more Criollo. We don't know how much the factory produced before it was destroyed," Valek said.

"We could visit each general and you could track the magic

to the source and capture the magician. Ha!" Janco pumped his fist in the air.

Not a bad idea. Yet that assumed the magician was nearby. Then Valek remembered what General Tesso had said about the generals discussing the situation with the Commander and Valek.

"Or we wait until all the generals are in one place and see what happens," Valek said and told them about Tesso's comment.

"Won't that be too dangerous?" Ari asked. "What if there are seven magicians and they all come together?"

"We'll be one step ahead of them," Valek said. Ari and Janco failed to look reassured. "It'll be similar to the time we knew there was a threat to the Sitian Delegation. Remember? We discussed all the ways a person could target the talks and we planned for each. In the end, we stopped the assassination attempt."

"Except, Yelena almost died," Ari said.

True. And he had been completely powerless, unable to do a damn thing to help her. Dreadful.

"What's next?" Ari asked.

"We keep searching. There's still Mogkan's suite, his laboratory, and where he chained his victims."

Janco groaned. "I was afraid you'd say that." He rubbed his stomach. "I think I'd rather be stabbed again than go near there."

"If it helps, I don't think there's much in *that* room." He hoped. "I'll check it while you and Ari search his suite."

"My hero," Janco said.

A damp funk tainted the air in the two lower levels of the East Wing. Valek, Ari, and Janco each held a lantern to push back the darkness. Still not enough light. Valek stopped at every wall sconce and lit it. The windows had all been covered with bricks. Another thing to add to General Ute's long to-do list.

"We should set fire to this place," Janco suggested. "Give it a good cleanse."

The ground floor had housed Reyad's rooms, labs, and office, which had already been searched and cleared. The room of horrors, used by both men, was located at the end of the hallway. The floor above had been Mogkan's domain.

Ari and Janco climbed the stairs to Mogkan's suite, while Valek continued down the corridor. Blood and other bodily fluids had soaked into the stone floor, permanently staining it. Ari and Janco had fought ten guards in this narrow space to reach the victims. Janco had been skewered with a sword, but due to their efforts, Fourth Magician Irys Jewelrose had been able to get through and steal Mogkan's extra power source from him. It had been the turning point. Without their valiant efforts, Mogkan would have won. Brazell would be the new commander and Valek would be dead. He yanked his thoughts away from listing who else would be dead.

Instead, he focused on the now empty room where the children had been chained to the floor. Children wasn't exactly the right term. There had been some older teens and a few young adults. However, all the victims had been tortured until nothing remained but a shell. Rendered mindless, they ate and breathed and their hearts beat, but nothing else. Now freed, they would be cared for until they died.

With dread dragging at his heels, Valek entered. The metal drain in the center of the ground reflected the lantern light. The floor had been cleaned and scoured; the chains removed. The painted lines, linking each person, had faded with the scrubbing, but the design was still visible. The scent of cleaning fluid mixed with a fetid odor of feces. Bile rolled in his stomach. A heavy presence pushed on his shoulders and squeezed his chest. Magic?

He spun in a slow circle, seeking a direction. Was there a magician nearby or was it just a lingering residue? Irys had said the power generated by the victims had been immense. They had been arranged so they formed a shape similar to a wagon wheel to augment their power. They all had the ability to use magic, but Mogkan stole their will and had siphoned their energy. He had tried to do the same to Yelena, but her will had been stronger.

A pang of longing and worry brushed his heart. He hoped her strength and intelligence would keep her safe in Sitia. Logically, he knew she could protect herself. After all, she survived this horror, she could survive anything. But the heart tended to ignore logic and his arms ached to hold her.

Not able to pinpoint the source of his unease, Valek searched for a hidden door or a loose brick that might indicate a hiding place. Nothing. He checked twice and then bolted.

He joined Ari and Janco in the living room of Mogkan's apartment. "Find anything?"

"Nothing significant yet," Ari said. "You?"

"I found the desire to kill Mogkan again. He died too quick."

"Agreed."

"I almost lost the contents of my stomach." Janco handed him a book. "I read his journal. It details what he and Reyad did to those poor children and rates them by effectiveness. Let me save you from some nightmares, there's no information we can use."

They worked in sickened silence for the next few hours. Valek was about to call a fresh air break, and suggest they go cuddle some puppies, when Ari pulled a ledger from a hidden drawer in Mogkan's desk.

Valek scanned the pages. Excitement built and rushed

through his veins. "It's an account of everything regarding the Criollo factory. This is what I hoped to find."

"Does it mention Alea?" Ari asked.

"Yes. She's on top of a list with an asterisk next to her name, indicating she is the leader of Mogkan's Beta Team. The rest of the members are also named along with their abilities."

"Magical abilities?" Janco looked queasy.

"Yes. There's seven magicians total and Alea. Her skills are not listed, unless she doesn't have any. She was the one who distributed the Criollo after Mogkan died."

"That leaves one magician for each general," Janco said.

"Looks like we were right about Mogkan targeting the generals. I guess he was worried they wouldn't accept him as the new commander."

"But why is the Beta Team still going through with the plan?" Ari asked.

Good question. "Perhaps the team believes they can use the recent upheaval with the Commander and Brazell to turn the generals against me. With me out of the way, the team has a better chance of assassinating the Commander. With the generals on Beta Team's side, they won't protest the coup or send their soldiers to attack the team."

"If we didn't encounter that caravan, we might have never known about the danger," Janco said. "Talk about luck."

"Or good timing." Ari's broad face creased in concentration. "Word will eventually get to Alea and the others that we know about the Criollo. Do you think they'll give up? Go back to Sitia?"

"It's possible," Valek said. "But I'd rather they stay in Ixia so I can kill them. Seven less problems in the world."

Janco glanced at Valek's face and took a step back. "We have their names. Can we arrest them?"

Valek handed him the book. "Do you recognize any of the names?"

Janco flipped through the pages. "Uh. No. But this list..." He shuddered, then read aloud, "The ability to move objects, the ability to read minds, the ability to set fires...and it seems they all can do some kind of freaky mental communication with each other. That's just...unfair! How are we supposed to fight them?"

"If they're going to proceed with their plans, then we have the element of surprise."

"Won't they know we know?" Ari asked.

"They know I found the third Criollo shipment. I'll spread a little disinformation, saying we stopped the delivery, and the threat has been neutralized. Hopefully, they'll take that as a sign that we didn't figure out they were targeting the generals and continue with their plans, walking right into our trap."

"But our trap has mundane things like blades and swords. While they can set us on fire from a distance." Janco tapped his finger on the journal. "And once the gig is up, they'll all know about it in an instant."

"Then let's ensure *the gig* is never up," Valek said.

"You want me to do what?" the Commander demanded.

Even though they were in MD-5, they still continued with their nightly meetings. They were sitting in the living area of the lavish guest suite that the Commander had moved into after he'd woken from his magical coma. General Ute was in the process of cleaning out Brazell's wing, giving away all his heavy dark furniture and replacing it with bright colors and practical furniture with elegant designs.

Valek sipped his whiskey, waiting for the outburst to subside. The Commander really didn't need him to repeat his request.

"Why would I invite the generals to my castle, when the last thing I wish to do is deal with them?"

"For damage control, and to set a trap," Valek said, then explained about the discovery of Alea and the seven magicians in Ixia, and the targeting of the generals.

The Commander drained his brandy, stood, refilled his glass, downed it, filled it again and sat heavily on the couch. "Can you assure me that you'll kill all seven of the vile creatures?"

"You know I can't, but I'm going to try my hardest."

"This is precisely why I hate magicians. They're power hungry, greedy, manipulative and—"

"Would you include Yelena in that assessment?"

"Not yet. She's still new. After a while, all that power warps their thinking and all they want is more and more."

"We've had military officers who've abused their power. No magic required."

The Commander harrumphed.

"And then there are the master magicians in Sitia. If they all turned into ravenous creatures, then why haven't the four of them attacked us? Why work for a mutually beneficial trade treaty with Ixia? Why help us fight Brazell and Mogkan?" Valek asked mildly.

"Would you please stop countering my rant with logic. I'm not in the mood to be logical."

"Clearly."

Another annoyed huff, but the Commander soon relaxed back into the cushions and sipped his drink. Perhaps the brandy had taken the edge off his anger. "At least if all the generals are together, I won't have to visit their districts."

Valek wanted to argue, but he knew when to pick his battles.

"Find out if Brazell knew about this Beta team of Mogkan's, and if he has any additional information to share. He'll be traveling with us to the castle," the Commander said.

"Is that wise?"

Ambrose stiffened.

Valek rushed to explain. "This Beta Team might attack us to free Brazell."

"Are you saying we can't handle an attack?"

Oh no. Valek chose his words with care. "We can handle a physical attack. I'm more worried about a magical one. I don't know how long the Criollo lasts. You might still be vulnerable." That didn't go over any better.

The Commander's expression turned to stone. "Then it will be a good test. And if it doesn't work, it'll put my mind at ease."

And if it does, Valek and the Commander's unit would not only have to fight seven magicians, but the Commander as well. Lovely.

After the meeting, Valek headed to the jail cells in the underground level of the manor house. Brazell was the only occupant. He'd been incarcerated for approximately sixty days.

When Valek approached the cell, Brazell sat up. He'd been lying on a pallet of straw, which was much cleaner than the bedding Valek had been provided with during his short stay in the same accommodations. In fact, Valek had ensured the man was treated humanely and all his basic needs were met.

Blinking and shielding his eyes from the lantern's light, Brazell asked in a rough, disused voice, "Who's there?"

"An upstart, conniving, sneaky thief."

"Ah, Valek. You don't forget much, do you?"

"You're not the first to call me names."

"Nor the last, I'm sure." Brazell stood and moved closer to the bars. He wore the plain red gown that was given to all prisoners. The clothing was rumpled, but clean. He had lost some weight, and his gray hair had grown.

"What are you doing here?" he asked.

"We've been going through all your files. You made payments to Mogkan's Beta Team. Do you know who the members of this team were?"

"I think they worked with the Criollo."

"The manufacturing team?"

"I don't know. He handled everything regarding the factory. That team arrived later, though, after the factory was up and running, so they might have been extra security."

Valek studied his gaunt face for signs of deceit. Finding none, he asked, "Do you know who Alea is?"

"If she worked at the factory, I might have met her during one of my visits, but I don't remember anyone with that name."

"Did you know Mogkan was sending Criollo to the other generals?"

Anger creased his forehead. "I told him not to bother. After the brandy meeting, it was clear the generals were on my side."

Remembering the meeting, Valek doubted it. At least four of them held opposite opinions of Brazell's. Mogkan had been at that meeting and probably read their thoughts. "You do realize that Mogkan didn't follow your orders; that he had his own agenda?"

"I knew he wanted to attack Sitia. After I secured Ixia, that was his next move."

"I found evidence that he wanted both Ixia and Sitia, and you were just going to be a figurehead. Probably until your usefulness wore out; then he'd kill you."

Brazell scoffed. "No way that would have worked. I didn't eat any of the Criollo."

"That helps reduce a person's resistance to magic, but he didn't need it for you. You were together most of the time and he was a powerful magician. Using magic over a short distance doesn't require as much energy."

"No. *I'm* the reason he was powerful, and I could have removed his source at any time."

Classic denial. Plus, it had been clever of Mogkan to ensure that Brazell believed he was in charge.

"Then why did Mogkan hire seven other magicians? Why did he send the other seven generals three shipments of Criollo?"

It took a few heartbeats for Brazell to absorb his words and make the connections. Then he slammed his hands on the bars. "That bastard! He was going to turn the generals against me!"

A genuine reaction, which answered whether Brazell knew about the Beta Team. He did not.

"You can thank me and Yelena," Valek said.

"For what?"

"For preventing you from becoming a dead puppet. At least in here, you still have your soul."

Valek sprinted to the stables. Thank fate they were finally leaving MD-5 and returning home. They had been living at the manor for a full season and then some. It was the first day of the warm season and the sun hadn't crested the Soul Mountains yet. But today promised to be glorious.

Even the Stable Master's scowl couldn't ruin Valek's mood. The man stood next to Onyx, but the horse wasn't saddled and ready like the others.

"You can't take this one," the Stable Master jabbed his thumb at Onyx. "He's one of ours."

"Not anymore." Valek didn't bother with niceties. "Saddle him and two others. I'll send you replacement horses when we return to the castle."

The man gaped at him. "What do you need the other two for?"

"That's not your concern. Your concern is getting all the

horses saddled and ready by the time the Commander wishes to leave."

Valek left the stables and checked on the Commander's elite squad. The fifty soldiers needed to be extra vigilant. Ari and Janco had left yesterday to scout the route. However, if they encountered an ambush, Valek wanted Ari and Janco to be able to get on the horses and escort the Commander and the four advisers to safety. That was *if* the Commander allowed it. The stubborn man was more likely to stay and fight.

The plan was based on the hope that Ari and Janco would uncover an ambush before they all stumbled right into the middle of it. And they'd have time to prepare to defend themselves.

The horses were all ready when the Commander and the rest of his advisers joined the travel party. The Commander peered at the assembled soldiers with a frown. No doubt wishing for a smaller escort, though Valek would have liked another fifty. Brazell soon followed, guarded by two soldiers. His hands had been shackled behind his back. A cloak had been thrown over his shoulders to ward off the morning chill, and he'd been given a pair of boots to wear. The guards also carried a gag in case Brazell decided to preach, and extra manacles and chains to secure the prisoner at night. Probably overkill, but Valek was determined to deliver Brazell to the Commander's dungeon.

The Commander mounted his horse, signaling the start of the journey, and they all headed west at a fast walk. Valek had argued for a quicker pace. The soldiers could easily maintain a jog for hours, but the Commander vetoed the idea out of concern for Brazell, who wouldn't be able to sustain the pace.

While the Commander and the advisers stayed in the middle of the group, Valek urged Onyx to the front, keeping alert for any signs of danger. On occasion, he would loop around to the back and check for anyone following them. Onyx enjoyed the bursts of speed and would glance back at Valek in disappointment when he slowed down.

They stopped at dusk to set up camp for the night and to feed and water the horses. After Valek ensured all was well, he donned his all-black sneak suit and slipped into the forest. There was just enough moonlight to pick out the shapes of the trees and budding underbrush.

Moving with a lithe and soundless grace, Valek circled the camp, avoiding the guards posted to keep watch. The day's warmth still clung to the loamy scented air. But without clouds in the sky, the comfortable temperature wouldn't last long. When Valek completed each circuit, he ranged further out until he was satisfied no one lurked nearby. Now to test Ari and Janco.

Scouts typically checked the route for each day before the party left. Then they would return to the start, confirming the route remained safe. Once the party was in motion, they stayed a few hours ahead of the main group. It meant Ari and Janco would cover twice the ground or more than the rest of the travelers. Overall, the system worked well.

Ari and Janco would overnight close to the camp—when the risk of an ambush was the highest—just in case they were needed. When the distance away from the tents seemed right, he shuffled his boots slightly and lightly brushed a few dead leaves still clinging to a bush's branches. They rustled with the contact. Back in silent mode, he kept going before making more noise. He repeated this a few more times.

Nothing happened. Valek wondered if he had miscalculated until a large shadow loomed to his left. He reached for his knife but was tackled from behind. Landing face down on the ground, Valek's breath *whooshed* from his lungs as a weight settled on his back. His arms were yanked behind him and secured. Impressive.

"Gotcha," Janco said in an exultant whisper. "Now to see who's been tailing us all day." He rolled Valek over. "Ah, hell."

"Who is it?" the large shadow with Ari's voice asked.

"Not the person we'd hoped." Janco removed the cuffs and helped Valek to his feet.

Valek spat dirt out of his mouth as he gasped for breath.

Ari's teeth flashed. "Still a good catch. I bet we just passed one of Valek's infamous tests."

Janco chuckled. "Yup, he fell for our distract and tackle maneuver."

At least they were in good spirits, despite being tracked all day. When Valek recovered, he asked about it.

"An unknown person has been shadowing us," Ari reported. "They're good, too, keeping just far enough away that we can't spot them. Or get a good read on them."

"Frustrating," Janco added.

"How did you discover they were there?" Valek asked.

"Janco's been feeling itchy all day."

"Twitchy." Janco corrected.

"There's a difference?" Valek asked.

"Yes. Twitchy feels like there are invisible bugs crawling over my skin. Itchy is when there are real bugs on me." He flicked a black speck off his arm. "I really miss the colder weather."

"Says the man who whined that his frozen toes were going to fall off."

In other words, it was just a feeling. Valek didn't think the men were prone to an overactive imagination. Well…not Ari. And the big man was taking Janco's claims seriously. So, either the shadow's skills exceeded Ari and Janco's or… One or more of the seven magicians lurked nearby.

Images of magicians attacking the camp flashed in his head. Now who had the overactive imagination? Valek suppressed the desire to race back to protect the Commander. Instead, he walked in a slow circle around Ari and Janco, focusing on the weight of the air around him. When magic was directed at him, it pressed against his skin. If the shadow used magic to hide, Valek would sense it, but it wouldn't work on him. The benefit of being immune.

About three quarters of the way around, the air thickened and clung. Valek stopped. A silhouette stood a dozen yards away.

Behind him, Ari cursed. "They're standing right there."

"Where? I don't see them." Janco said, despite the fact the person was in his direct line of sight.

Valek, however stood between Ari and the silhouette. His immunity must be blocking the magic from affecting Ari. The magician had been using power to influence Ari's and Janco's perceptions. And if they could do that, they could read their minds as well. Valek muttered his own curse. The gig was definitely up.

"Bees!" Janco yelled.

Valek glanced at him.

He waved his arms wildly. "A swarm! Run!" Janco raced off.

By the time Valek returned his attention to the silhouette, it was gone. Valek took off, hoping to catch up. The magician tried to hide using magic, but that only gave Valek a direction of where they had gone to ground. Eventually, they stopped hiding. Instead, they wove through the dark forest at such a quick clip that Valek wondered if it was possible to have magical night vision.

The chase lengthened, heading south. Valek worried he was being led away from the camp on purpose. Were the other magicians attacking right now?

When the silhouette halted and turned to face him, Valek pulled his dagger and slowed down, approaching with care as he sought others who might be hiding nearby.

"Persistent, aren't you," said a female voice. She wore a one-piece black suit, similar to Valek's. Except for slits for her eyes, the hood covered her entire face. "You know it's not illegal to be in the forest."

"But it is illegal for a magician to be in Ixia. What are you doing here?" he asked.

"Gathering information. Your friends were very helpful. I know you're the big bad assassin and all, but do you really think you can counter eight magicians if we decide to attack you at one time?"

Ah. Alea had powers. Was this her? "Seven," Valek corrected. "You let me get too close, Alea."

She flinched. Gotcha.

"I know who you are," he continued, trying to throw her off balance. "I know all about you."

Alea laughed. "Cocky to the last. Did you ever consider that I might have wanted you to get close? That I might have the upper hand? No, of course not." She raised her hand. With her fingers spread wide and her palm facing him, she thrust it forward. "Break!"

Valek braced for the rush of power. The magical command wouldn't work on him, but it might knock him off his feet. Instead, a loud crack sounded above him. A tree branch fell right on top of him. The impact smashed him into oblivion.

Spikes of pain stabbed deep into his head, waking Valek. Garbled voices sounded nearby. A heavy weight pressed on his shoulders and back, pinning him to the ground. He hoped that was the reason he couldn't move. Breathing required much more effort than normal. At least, he was still breathing. Bright side.

He opened his eyes. The sun had risen and Janco was squatting in front of him.

Janco jumped to his feet. "Hey! He's awake!"

Shouts exploded in Valek's ear, sending waves of agony through his skull. Valek groaned.

"Better hurry," Janco called. "He doesn't look good."

"Everyone, grab an end," Ari instructed from…somewhere. "Lift up on the count of three. One. Two."

Janco crouched down. "Sorry, boss. This is gonna hurt." He grabbed Valek under the arms.

"Three!"

The weight lifted and Janco yanked him forward. The man was right. Pain blazed and raced through his body, consuming him. Passing out brought sweet relief.

The next time he woke, he was on his back with a blanket over him. Voices buzzed in his ears. Ari and Janco must have gone back to the camp to recruit helpers to lift the branch. With effort, he managed to separate the voices.

"We'll make camp here. I want this area secured," the Commander ordered.

Valek groaned. The entire camp had come. At least the Commander was safe. *For now.* That thought pounded in his head along with the pain. He'd been an idiot and had completely underestimated his opponent. Valek had made more mistakes in these last couple seasons than in the last dozen years. Was it due to falling in love with Yelena? He'd let his emotions free and now they ran wild, compromising his ability to deal with dangerous situations.

He needed to stay focused. But first he needed to sit up. The muscles along his back, shoulders and upper arms ignited with fire. Now he needed to throw up.

After he ejected all the bile in his stomach, a cool hand touched his forehead. Pain battled with nausea for a moment before his guts settled.

"You should lie down. You have a severe concussion," the person attached to the hand said.

He squinted at her. Cylvia, the squad's medic, stared calmly back.

"But—"

"Unlike you, everyone's fine. There wasn't an attack on the camp."

"But—"

"We're keeping vigilant." She handed him a cup. "Drink this so I can stitch up that gash on your head and examine you."

Valek raised an eyebrow. Even that small gesture caused his head to ache.

"It's to help dull the pain. Unless you'd rather—"

Downing the liquid, he wiped his lips. "I'm not that brave."

"I'd laugh, but I'm too worried about how many broken bones I'm going to find."

A sobering thought. Valek sank back onto the bed roll someone—probably Janco—had laid him on. The massive branch remained in place at the base of the tree. Cylvia threaded a needle with sutures. A few feet beyond her, Ari and Janco tried to appear as if they weren't hovering.

"Shouldn't you be scouting the route?" he asked them.

"The Commander ordered us to stay here," Ari said. "Said it was safer for everyone to stay together."

Good point. "Janco, go walk around camp, see if anything makes you twitchy."

"Oh. That's an excellent idea," Janco said.

Valek glanced at Cylvia. "Maybe my concussion isn't so severe?"

"Uh huh."

"Come on, Ari," Janco said.

"Why do I have to go?"

"Partners stick together no matter what."

They both looked at Valek.

"You need a partner," Ari said to Valek. "Rushing off without backup was really stupid. You're lucky you're not dead." They left.

Valek couldn't argue with him about rushing off. But he had a partner. Too bad she was in Sitia.

Cylvia cleaned the wound on the top of his head. He'd taken a direct hit. She stitched the skin together and Valek tried not to pass out. His vision blurred with each stab of the needle. And he avoided contemplating what it'd feel like if he hadn't downed that drink. It took forever.

"Hold still. It's a large gash. If you'd kept your hair short, this would be much easier," she said. After an eternity, she sat back on her heels. "Done. You'll need to see a medic in seven to ten days to get the stitches removed. Now, for the fun part."

"Why do I get the sense that your idea of fun isn't going to match mine?"

"Do you even know what fun is?" she countered.

His thoughts went immediately to Yelena. "I…"

"Thought so. Please sit up."

He bit back a groan and sat. At least this time his stomach didn't heave. Progress. Cylvia crouched behind him. Her fingers probed the base of his skull, traced his spine, pushed on his shoulder blades, then jabbed into his ribs. Each touch hurt like she was pressing on very sore muscles.

She lifted his shirt and whistled. "Very colorful bruising. Looks like a child's watercolor painting." Then she came around and repeated the process, trailing down his neck, testing his clavicle, ribs, and examining his skin. "Any sharp, stabbing pain?"

"Not sharp or stabbing."

"Good."

"My pain is good?"

"Yes. It means no broken bones. Which, considering the size of that branch, I'm surprised. Looks like your head took the brunt of the impact. Good thing you have a hard head." She gave him a wry smile. "Symptoms of a concussion are dizziness, headaches, inability to focus, nausea, and a lack of coordination."

"So, you're saying my dancing days are over?"

"Another symptom is thinking your jokes are funny."

"Ouch."

She set a pouch down next to him. "This is pain powder, your new best friend. Keep it with you at all times, you might have symptoms for a couple weeks, maybe a month or more."

Valek groaned. He didn't have time to be injured.

Cylvia packed up her kit. "You should rest, but I know you won't. If you feel like you're going to pass out, please lie down so you don't crack your head open. You used up most of my sutures."

"Your concern is heartwarming."

"You don't get any sympathy when you don't listen to medical advice." With that, she grabbed her bag and left.

He shouldn't get any sympathy as this was his own stupid fault, but he wasn't planning on wallowing in his misery. Instead, he gathered his energy, shoved the pouch of pain powder into his pocket, and stood. The forest spun around him. The ground undulated under his boots. Valek staggered to a nearby tree and held on. When the world stopped moving, he straightened and scanned the camp. A few tents had been wedged between trees. Not an ideal location, and probably a significant detour from their planned route, adding at least a day to their trip. The Commander wasn't going to be happy.

Janco was taking his new job seriously. The captain walked the perimeter, stopping every few feet to spread his arms wide for a few moments before moving on. Ari scowled into the woods as if daring anyone to attack his partner. Valek headed toward them, angling so he'd catch up with a minimum of steps because each of his strides increased the thudding in his head by an order of magnitude.

"Feel anything?" Valek asked.

"Nope, but we still have half the camp to test," Janco said.

"Even after you finish the sweep, I want you to let me know anytime you feel twitchy. Understand?"

"Yes, sir."

"And when we get moving again, I want both of you on horses."

"We're not scouting?" Ari asked.

"No. I want you close for the rest of the trip."

"Yes, sir."

Valek headed toward the Commander's tent. The man sat on a log next to it, sipping tea and talking with Adviser Dema. When they spotted him, they stopped.

"What are you doing?" The Commander asked.

"Uh, reporting in, sir."

"Valek, you look like death warmed over. No, I take that back. It would be an insult to those who do look like death warmed over."

Dema covered her grin with her mug.

"That bad?"

"Yes." The Commander gestured to a nearby tent. "Go lie down. It's an *order*. We'll continue our journey in the morning, and you can make your report when we're home."

Over the next four days, Valek and the soldiers remained on high alert for any signs of an ambush. Valek gripped Onyx's reins in white-knuckled fingers. Every step the horse took reminded him of his injuries. He was recovering a little bit each day, but not as fast as he'd like. Well, to be honest he'd love to find a magical healer right about now. Or have Fourth Magician Irys Jewelrose come for a visit. As a master magician, she could perform all the different abilities. He'd memorized all of them when he was hunting the King—who had master level powers—but he wondered if magicians kept a few of their talents a secret. It made perfect sense if they did.

He replayed the encounter with Alea in his mind. She had claimed to be gathering information. Valek hoped that meant the others weren't nearby. Janco had become twitchy several times during the first two days after Valek's injury. Each time, Valek had homed in on the direction of the magic and the four of them—Ari, Janco, and Dema, Valek's temporary partner—had spurred their horses through the forest, chasing Alea.

She'd stop using her magic as soon as the thunder of the sixteen hooves rolled through the trees, but Valek hadn't expected to catch her. No. He wanted to keep her at a distance. To let Alea know every time she used magic, she'd be a target. It seemed to work, as Janco hadn't felt twitchy for the rest of the trip.

After six days on the road, they reached the Commander's castle complex around midafternoon. Valek would have whooped with joy if drawing a deep breath didn't hurt. Instead, he silently celebrated as they entered the eastern gate.

"Captains," the Commander called to Ari and Janco.

They straightened and gave him their full attention. "Sir?"

"See to the horses and make sure the prisoner is safely ensconced in my dungeon."

"Yes, sir," they said in unison, then glanced at Valek in concern.

Both of those tasks would normally be Valek's. And while he was glad the Commander trusted them enough to assign Ari and Janco the jobs, Valek turned to protest.

"Go see the medic, Valek, and then take the night off. We'll meet in the morning."

"Death warmed over?"

"You're getting there, but all that racing through the woods couldn't have been beneficial."

"Permission to take a bath first, sir?"

"Granted. I'm sure Medic Channa would appreciate it."

Valek grabbed his pack and trudged into the castle. What he really wished to do was to collapse in his own bed and sleep for a year, but he dutifully headed to the baths. When Valek peeled off his uniform and looked into the mirror, he finally understood why everyone treated him as if he stood at death's door.

Purple, black, and green bruises covered the right half of his face. Scabbed over cuts lined his cheek and neck. Normally pale, his skin practically glowed in the dark. His brow was furrowed with pain. With great reluctance, he turned so his back was reflected in another mirror.

He laughed. Cylvia was being kind in describing it as a child's watercolor. The mottled crimson, violet, and olive that stained his skin resembled something a dog had killed, chewed, swallowed, and vomited onto his back.

Valek eased into the hot water, which soothed some of the throbbing in his muscles. The rest protested the motion with sharper complaints. Despite the all-over body ache, he eventually dozed.

A sound woke him and he surged to his feet ready to fight. Medic Channa stood there with her arms crossed.

"I was planning on coming to see you," he said, as all his injuries flared to life.

"I know. The Commander told me to expect you."

Dripping wet, he waited.

"He also said you were stopping here first, and I knew once you hit that hot water, I'd be waiting all night." She glanced at the window. Blackness painted the glass. "Let me examine you quick, so we can both get to bed."

Channa poked and prodded much like Cylvia had. Amazingly, there were three places on his upper body that didn't hurt. Progress.

"You've had a number of close calls, Valek, but this one is the closest. I'd tell you to rest for at least a week but know it's pointless."

Right now, the thought of staying in bed an entire week sounded just fine. "In this case, you could order me."

"I could. How about a promise? That if you feel dizzy, light-headed, or can't keep your balance, you will go to bed."

A good compromise. "I promise."

"I'll be checking on you these next couple days," she said before leaving.

Valek toweled dry and changed into a cleanish uniform. While he'd love to head straight to bed, he needed to inform the manager of his corps, Kenda, about the threat. They'd have to update the security protocols of the castle's guards to keep alert for signs that magic was in use. There were only a few noticeable clues, but it was better than nothing.

Even at this late hour, Kenda was in her office. Despite keeping track of his vast network of spies and a million other details, her desk was neat and organized. She was instrumental in their success.

She stood up when he entered, took one look at him, and said, "What the hell happened to you?" Kenda was also frank.

"I was attacked."

"By what? A pack of snow cats?"

"A tree."

Sinking in her chair, she covered her mouth, but couldn't hide the shine in her eyes. "Looks like the tree won."

"Ha. Ha." Valek explained what happened and briefed her on the threat of Alea and the other magicians. "I haven't had time to consider all the implications yet, but I'm going to assume they know we were planning to ambush them here."

"Well, that explains why I'm getting reports from our agents that the generals have been acting out of character. These magicians must already be influencing them."

"Then we really need to get them all here. At least to detox them from the Criollo."

"Should we send our people to provide extra security for the generals?"

"That's a good idea." He rubbed his forehead. Thinking hurt. "We have time to figure out how to find and kill the magicians. One problem at a time."

"That would be ideal, but we've been dealing with another problem since you left."

CHAPTER 8

"Another problem?" Valek asked, even though he really didn't want to know.

"Yes. Do you want to hear it tonight?"

"Not really."

Kenda ignored him. "This problem goes back to the middle of the cold season. Remember that woman you sent to me? Calls herself Captain Star?"

Yes, he did. Star oversaw a vast network of criminals. A network, Valek hoped to destroy. "Did she escape?"

"I wish." Kenda pinched her finger and thumb until they were almost touching. "I'm *this* close to sending her up to the Northern Ice Pack and feeding her to the snow cats."

"Is she not cooperating?"

"She won't shut up!"

Confused, Valek rubbed his aching head. "Isn't that a good thing? Star has information we need to uproot the rest of her organization."

"She's not divulging that information. Oh no, Star's strangely resistant to goo-goo juice. Instead, she complains about everything, she's nasty to everyone, and she gets very creative when she's bored."

"Have you tried other ways to persuade her to reveal her secrets?"

"A few. She hates being isolated the most, but it's only been a few months. She's strong enough to resist for a much longer time."

"Has she revealed anything important?"

"She did tell us that someone named Kangom hired her to kidnap Yelena on the way to MD-5. He's the same man who wanted to ruin the Southern Delegation's visit by poisoning the cognac. I don't have any intel on this Kangom."

"Kangom is Mogkan's Sitian name. And he's dead. Did Star say why Mogkan wanted Yelena captured? Yelena was heading right to him. In fact, she was locked in a guest room for most of her stay."

"Star said that Kangom…er…Mogkan, thought Yelena was an unnecessary complication and he wanted her secured in a remote location to keep you in line." Kenda raised an eyebrow. "Now why would he think *that* would work?" She smirked.

"No comment."

"Uh huh."

The qualities he admired most about Kenda, like her keen intuition and intelligence, were also the same ones that annoyed him the most when she used them against him. "How much information and evidence do we have on Star?"

Kenda pulled a thick file from a neat stack on her desk and handed it to Valek. "It's all in here."

"All right, I'll read through all this and think about how to deal with her. In the meantime, send our agents to watch over the generals. Have them confirm with our people in the manor houses that all the Criollo has been destroyed. Also tell them to determine if there has been anyone who joined the generals' retinues recently. A new adviser or officer."

"How recently?"

"Since the beginning of the cold season."

"Will do."

As much as he wanted to read through the file on Star, Valek had no energy. He trudged to his suite, entered the dusty living room, tossed the dossier onto his desk, climbed the steps to his room, and collapsed onto his bed fully clothed.

Ahhh. Nothing like being in your own bed after a long absence. He kicked off his boots and pulled the covers up. It would be perfect, except Yelena wasn't with him. A new ache joined the others. This one pulsed in his heart.

The next morning, he headed to the Commander's office. It was located in a room adjacent to the throne room. Unfortunately, it was at the far end, and Valek had to weave through the masses of desks and the dozens of officers and advisers who worked in the large space. Besides the noise assaulting his ears, a few people wanted to welcome him home. The smart ones took one look at his face and quickly moved out of his way.

By the time he reached the Commander's office, his headache had gone from throbbing to pounding. Lovely. Four guards bracketed the door. Double the normal amount. *Good.* He knocked. A faint 'come in' sounded, and Valek entered.

The Commander glanced out the window. The sun was high in the sky, but not at its apex.

"It's technically still morning." Valek eased into the chair in front of the desk, which was neat and organized. The black snow cat sculpture he'd carved for the Commander glinted in the sunlight. It was the sole decoration in the entire office.

"You slept through breakfast."

Valek straightened. "Sorry, sir. Have you eaten? Should I send for a meal?"

"No need. Kenda anticipated you would require extra sleep and tasted my breakfast. She said she would fill in until you train another food taster."

His reaction swung between being grateful and impressed. With Kenda risking her life, Valek had more motivation to train a taster than usual. He tended to procrastinate when it was his job. It *should* be part of his duties. After all, he was the most qualified. Except, not lately. Forgetting such an important task was another misstep.

"Do you need another day off?" the Commander asked when the silence lengthened.

"I probably do, but I don't have time." He detailed his encounter with Alea and summed up the reports from his agents. "It sounds like the other magicians are with the generals already."

"And if we invite them all here, we'll have eight magicians in one place. Can you and your network handle eight?"

"I believe so." Valek hedged. There were too many factors to consider for his aching head. He hoped a foolproof plan would arise once he felt better.

"Believe so? This is too critical for belief."

It was. He rubbed his head. "I have full confidence in my network. In myself."

"What about visiting each general and finding their magician? Dealing with them one on one?"

"It would probably work for the first general we visit. After that, the other magicians will be warned that we're hunting them and be ready. We need the generals here. I'll figure out how to counter the magicians."

"All right, I'll write the orders this afternoon. When do you want them here? The northern generals will need at least ten days of travel time."

Plus, the ten days for the orders to reach them. Valek considered. "Day thirty of the warm season. That will give them two days to get ready."

"Which they will all complain about."

"Even if you gave them a week, they'd still complain."

"All right, Valek, the orders will be ready in a couple hours."

"The messengers will be members of my corps. Kenda suggested providing extra security for the generals."

"That's a good idea, but we also need to increase the security for the castle complex. Do you have enough personnel?"

"I'll check with Kenda. If not, I'll pull some from the field."

"Good. You're dismissed."

"Yes, sir."

Valek headed to Kenda's office, hoping to catch her before she left to taste the Commander's lunch. He encountered her in the hallway right outside her door.

"Make it quick," she said.

"Thank you for covering for me this morning, but I'll taste the Commander's food going forward."

She poked him in the ribs. Fire ignited and ringed his chest. He sucked in a breath.

"You're barely able to stand. If Alea magically influences one of the cooks to poison the Commander's tea, your body is in no condition to fight off the effects." She cocked her head to the side. Her straight, shoulder-length, brown hair covered half her face. "Besides, I taught you everything you know about tasting poisons."

True. She'd joined his corps when she grew bored as a kitchen worker. Adept with all sizes of knives, she also had a vast knowledge of poisons, which she happily shared. With average brown hair, eyes, and looks, she blended in with any situation. Kenda had even managed to fool Valek a few times.

"But I'm not willing to risk your life," he said. She was far too valuable.

"Then you know what to do."

"You *do* know, I'm the one in charge."

"Yes, sir. Is there anything else?"

"The Commander is sending orders out in two hours, and we need messengers."

"Already assigned."

"We'll need extra security in the castle."

"Already in place."

"*This* is why I can't lose you."

"Then you better start training the next taster."

He growled and she laughed. Actually laughed. Then she gave him a jaunty salute before leaving.

His to-do list was a mile long, but Kenda's comment about Alea influencing the cook reminded him of the immediate danger. Except for him, anyone in the castle could be targeted and manipulated. Valek could sense when magic was in use, but he couldn't be everywhere. However he could stay close to the Commander in case Alea targets him.

Valek returned to his suite to grab the file on Star before stopping in his office to pick up the execution list.

Dust coated every surface, reminding him that he had fired his housekeeper, Margg, before he'd left for MD-5 and hadn't assigned another to take her place. A minor inconvenience that shouldn't be too difficult to rectify. Then again... It took him forever to trust her and she'd eventually abused her position. Perhaps he could dust and mop? He glanced around at the piles of books on the floor and conference table, the mountains of reports leaning precariously; the collection of carving rocks and candles littered everywhere. Perhaps not. He'd just have to ensure he was in the room when the new housekeeper cleaned.

Grabbing what he needed, he returned to the Commander's office.

The Commander was writing out the orders. His lunch tray remained on his desk. "Something wrong?"

"I realized I needed to be nearby in case Alea tries to influence you. If she does, I'll be able to sense the magic and stop her."

"You plan to stay with me all day?" His expression was neutral.

"Yes, and at night I'll—"

"No."

"I brought work with me, and—"

"No. The reason Brazell used the Criollo was to break down my will. I can assure you my will is quite strong, and I will not tolerate a babysitter." His voice had gone ice cold.

Valek ignored the warning tone and the Commander's use of the word *babysitter*. "Mogkan was in MD-5, trying to reach you from a distance. Alea could be inside the castle."

"Then I expect you to find her and not sit here with me all day. Consider it an order. Dismissed."

He hesitated, but then turned to leave.

"And don't let me find you camped outside my door," the Commander said.

"Yes, sir."

The throne room bustled with activity and noise. Valek could commandeer a desk from one of the officers or advisers who worked here. Technically, he wouldn't be right outside the Commander's office, but he'd still be nearby. And when the Commander saw him there... Valek sighed. It wouldn't be pretty.

The clammer of voices and his hunger finally drove Valek away. He hadn't eaten since...no idea. After grabbing a meat pie and a carafe of water from the kitchen—another overly loud place—he trudged to his office and collapsed into his well-loved chair.

Eating still hurt, but the food helped revive him and he considered his immediate problem: How to find Alea before her friends arrived? Valek dug into his travel pack and pulled out

Mogkan's journal. He read through the list of magicians and their talents.

Like them all, Alea could mentally communicate and influence thoughts. Then there was her ability to break a tree branch. Was that considered moving an object? Possibility. However, she'd waited until he was underneath it. He had jumped over several logs on the ground as he had chased her. Why not raise one of them to trip him? Perhaps she didn't have enough power to lift something that heavy. Far easier to break a branch and let it fall.

Then there was Janco. Had he sensed Alea's magic? Or was she not strong enough to influence him and Ari at the same time? No. They both couldn't see her until Valek blocked her magic for Ari.

His head throbbed. All this speculation wasn't helping. Valek needed to talk it out like he used to do with Yelena. He missed her more than he'd expected. She had woven into the fabric of his life so innocuously that he hadn't noticed it until she was gone, leaving him tattered and lonely.

Gah. He was being maudlin. Valek had others to help him brainstorm. Even though exhaustion pressed on his injuries, he roused his remaining energy and wrote a message. Then hunted down one of the pages who delivered messages within the castle complex. He handed the note to the boy and returned to his office. His extra bedroll was covered with dust, but he spread it out on the floor and promptly laid down.

A knock on his office door woke him two hours later. The nap had cleared his head and revived him somewhat. Still not at full strength, but at least the pity party was over. For now. He unlocked the door and let Ari and Janco inside.

Janco stared at him. "You look…uh…better?"

"Are you asking me or telling me?"

"Uh… Look, boss, I'm really sorry for freaking out in the

woods. I should have known bees don't fly at night and certainly not during the warm season."

"Not your fault, Janco."

"You wanted to scc us?" Ari asked, stopping his partner from voicing a protest.

"Yes. Have a seat." Valek settled behind the desk. "What happened when I took off after Alea in the forest?"

"That was Alea?" Janco asked with a groan. "That means there are *eight* of them now."

"Yes. That's about all I found out before she attacked me."

"It's more than we had before," Ari remarked. "I wasn't sure who to chase after at first. You both took off in opposite directions, but we're trained to never leave our partners, so I went after Janco. He didn't get far before the magic wore off. Or she stopped sending it. Then we tracked you and heard the branch crash in the distance. By the time we found you, the mag—Alea was gone. The limb was too heavy for us to lift. We ran back to camp, woke the Commander, and you know the rest."

"Thank you for rescuing me."

"Part of the job," Ari demurred.

"Not a damsel-in-distress, but I'm sure I can embellish the story a bit." Janco grinned.

"When you saw the bees, what did you feel?" Valek asked.

Janco's smile died. "Panicked. They were crawling all over me."

"Did they sting you?"

"Well, no 'cause they were imaginary."

"But you felt them crawling."

"Oh! Well, yeah. I guess that was me being twitchy."

"Have you ever felt twitchy when you were around Yelena?" he asked.

"Why do you— *Oh.*" Janco's gaze grew distant. "Not really. Well, at the end there, after she had her...epiphany about fighting and was hard to beat. I'd get this..." He rubbed his forearms. "Tingle." He shrugged. "I just thought it was me. The expectation of a good fight usually gives me goosebumps."

"What about when the Sitians visited?"

"Ah. Fourth Magician gives me the creeps. I know she's a nice magician, but…" He shuddered and then turned to Ari. "Remember that time we were practicing in the storeroom?"

"We practiced there hundreds of times."

"When the Sitians were in the castle, and we had that strange, intense conversation as if we were solving all the world's problems?"

"Yeah, I was agreeing with you. That almost never happens."

Janco ignored the comment. "I wanted to stop, but I couldn't. Not quite the creeps, but definitely weird."

"And what about at Brazell's manor house? When you fought your way to the room with the victims?"

Another shudder shook him. "Everything about that manor house gave me the creeps. But I was focused on fighting, I didn't notice anything else but block, block, dodge, stab, stab, duck, and repeat."

Ari grabbed Janco's arm. "The door."

"What door?"

"When we reached the end of the hall and Fourth Magician opened the door to that room. You flinched or something, and the guy you were fighting stabbed you." He turned to Valek. "Do you think Janco is sensitive to magic? Is that the reason for his twitching? I thought it was just his intuition and experience."

"I do, but I don't know how reliable it is. We need to experiment, but we don't have the time or resources right now. However, I'm ordering you both not to tell anyone."

"But Alea must know," Ari said. "Doesn't she read thoughts?"

"Yes, but neither of you would have been thinking about that. Just that Janco was feeling twitchy. Plus, I'm hoping she takes that knowledge to her grave."

"Why not tell people?" Janco asked.

"Think about it," Valek said. "Ari, don't help him."

The big man chuckled.

"I could be a target," he said, not looking at all upset by the revelation. "Alea might think I'll expose her and kill me. But I can still be affected by magic. So, I'm not much of a threat."

"You're enough of a threat for a high-stakes operation like the one Alea is trying to pull off. If it wasn't for you, I wouldn't have thought to search for magic that night," Valek said.

Ari grew serious. "We'll be extra vigilant."

"Are you still interested in being a part of my team?" Valek asked.

"We are." Ari straightened.

"All right. I don't want you sleeping in the barracks anymore. There are a couple empty bedrooms in the hexagon where my corps live. There's also a small suite that has two bedrooms and a common area."

"We'll take the suite," Ari said without consulting Janco.

Not a surprise. "Okay. Once we deal with the magicians, I'll start your training."

"Sneaky spy stuff?" Janco asked.

"Yes."

"Woo hoo!"

"And how are we going to deal with the magicians?" Ari asked.

"I'm still working it out." Then it hit him. Valek wouldn't be able to brainstorm with them. "Unfortunately, I can't tell you my plans."

"Why not?" Janco pouted.

"Because Alea will learn about them from our thoughts," Ari said.

"Yes, she knows both of you are working with me. I'll have to work with people who are unknown to her."

"But we can still help. Right?" Janco asked.

"Yes, you'll probably receive orders without explanations.

You'll have to follow them without question or thinking about it too much. Can you do that?"

They both agreed, but neither appeared happy about it. Valek didn't blame them, he wasn't pleased about the situation either.

"Report to Kenda. Her office is on the first floor of the hexagon. She'll give you the keys to the suite so you can move in right away. Also ask Kenda for a copy of the manual on silent communication. You need to learn and memorize the signals. It's the first lesson all my spies are required to master."

"What about Major Granten, our squad leader?" Ari asked.

"I'll send him your transfer paperwork."

Ari leaned forward, suddenly intense. "Can we still challenge you?"

Ah, he hadn't given up his goal of beating Valek in a fight and becoming his second-in-command. Ari had also threatened to promote Janco to be third-in-command.

"Of course." Valek looked forward to sparring them again.

"Ooohhh, let's challenge him now," Janco said. "One good jab to his ribs, and—"

"No. That wouldn't be fair." Ari crossed his massive arms.

"Who says it has to be fair?" Janco looked at Valek. "Right? There are no real rules, are there?"

"Nothing written down, but I can refuse a challenge."

"*We* won't issue a challenge unless it's a fair fight," Ari declared.

Ignoring Ari's comment, Janco asked, "Would you refuse if I challenged you right now?"

"Yes. These challenges are staged where everyone can witness them. No one would accept you as my second-in-command if I fought you while injured. You'd have the title, but not the respect or loyalty or cooperation of the other soldiers, my network, the Commander, the—"

"I get it," Janco said. "And I wasn't going to challenge you. I was just curious."

"Cat, Janco. Remember the cat," Ari said.

Janco grinned. "I still have four lives left."

Valek knew not to ask for an explanation or they'd be here all night. Instead, he dismissed them. They had helped in reminding him to be very careful who he confided in. The only mind Alea couldn't read was his, but he suspected she wouldn't read the minds of every single person in the castle. Too time consuming, and it would drain her energy. He had no doubt that she was already somewhere inside the castle complex.

It was easy enough to get inside without magic. All she needed was a uniform for one of the invisible members of the household, like a housekeeper or kitchen server, to blend in. Valek had done it countless times. Too bad he couldn't send Janco to go around the barracks, kitchen, and castle to see if anyone made him twitchy. He needed someone who was good at reading people but was relatively unknown.

Valek considered his corps, the advisers, the officers, but thought most of them would be...too obvious. Needing to move, he prowled around his cluttered office. He picked up one of the gray rocks he transformed into his sculptures. Perhaps a session in his carving studio would help him focus. But he wouldn't be able to tolerate the noise of the grinding wheel.

Setting the rock down, he spotted Sven's dagger. Grief filled his heart. Sven had died working undercover, attempting to stop the black market dealers. Valek planned to give the black blade to his son, Adrik, when he graduated from spy training. Valek smiled, thinking of Ari and Janco learning with a bunch of younger— Trevar!

Sven's best baiter was also training to become a part of Valek's corps. Trevar had an uncanny ability to read people and had hooked many customers for Sven's fake black market shop. He'd be perfect.

As he wrote the message requesting Trevar's presence, Valek thought of someone else who could help and wrote a second note.

~

Trevar arrived soon after. He paused in the doorway when he spotted Valek's bruised face but didn't comment. Instead, he said, "I hope this meeting is what I've been waiting for." His blue eyes flashed with excitement.

Valek led him to his desk and gestured for Trevar to sit down. "What have you been waiting for?"

"A mission. A challenge. Graduation. Take your pick. I'm bored stiff."

"You've only been in training for six months. You need a year at least."

Trevar sagged in his seat and ran a hand through his sandy-blond hair. "But it's all…repetition. Day in and day out. The. Same. Thing."

"There's a reason for that."

"Yeah, yeah. Muscle memory and being able to react automatically while under stress. It's no longer a challenge."

"I can confer with your teachers and see about accelerating your training."

"But I *know* everything."

Valek laughed. "Really? Wow, I'm impressed. I don't even know everything. If I did, I wouldn't be this bruised." He gently touched his cheek.

"Sorry, I'm just bored."

"So you said." Perhaps having Ari and Janco to train with would make it more interesting for Trevar. "How about a mission?"

Trevar sat up. All the angst disappeared from his handsome face. "Yes! I'll do anything! Please!"

Valek explained what he needed Trevar to do.

The poor guy deflated. "Be friendly with the newbies? How is that important?"

"It's very important. You have all the uniforms?"

"Yeah, we've been training on how to blend in. You want me to just chat people up?"

"Yes. Start with the kitchen staff and then housekeeping, pages, and the guards."

He perked up a bit. "The guards are more of a challenge. They get very cliquish and are generally suspicious of everyone. What about the soldiers in the barracks?"

"I've someone else in mind for outside the rest of the complex."

"What is the purpose of doing this? What am I trying to learn?"

"You'll know when it happens."

"Is this a joke?"

"No."

"All right. I'll go talk to people." He stood to leave.

"Make sure you turn on your charm, Trevar. Be genuine, think good thoughts, and don't make anyone suspicious."

Trevar paused as the seriousness of the situation finally sank in. "Will do."

"What happened to your face?" Maren asked.

"Hello, nice to see you, too," Valek replied.

She grunted. "Does your new facial tattoo mean you have a new second-in-command?"

"Yes. I'll be training Mr. Tree Branch when he arrives from the forest."

"Ahh." Unsure about the joke, she looked around his office.

"Is there a reason you wanted to see me?" A hopeful note had crept into her voice.

"Yes, but first tell me why you're so annoyed."

"Sorry, sir. It's nothing."

He waited.

"Just…feeling left out. Ari and Janco got to go with you to MD-5 and… I don't know. I kinda thought we were a team, which is silly because all we did was workout together. Well, we had that one mission." She grinned a Janco grin—all teeth and glee. "Nothing like a successful smash and grab to bring people closer." Then she sobered. "Maybe I should try to get a transfer into the Commander's elite guard."

"They're no longer with that unit. Ari and Janco have agreed to train with my corps."

"Really? I thought Ari wanted to be your second."

"He does. He's just taking another route to get there."

She eyed him. Her long blond hair was pulled back into a braid. Tall and athletic, she was deadly with a bo staff.

"My offer still stands," he said. Maren had impressed him with her fighting skills when she had challenged him, so much so that he'd offered her a spot in his corps.

"Really?"

"Really."

"I'll think about it."

"Good. In the meantime, I know you like to welcome the new female recruits and offer to help them get settled. Has there been anyone new lately?"

"How new?"

"In the last six days."

She mulled it over. "Several came in with the platoon from MD-3. They are not new to being soldiers, but new to the complex."

And a perfect cover for Alea. Platoons from other military districts frequently came for extra training. The Snake Forest was unique, as it was not only the biggest forest in Ixia, but it was along the southern border. If war broke out between Ixia and Sitia, all the Commander's soldiers needed to know how to fight in the woods.

"Have you talked to any of them?"

"No. Just seen them around the barracks."

From what he'd learned from Ziva Moon, magical illusions used up a great deal of energy. And Alea would soon exhaust herself if she tried changing the perceptions of everyone around her. He guessed that she would use non magical means for a disguise, and it was easier to blend in if she kept her general features.

"Can you keep an eye on them? And any other new female recruits that come in. From a distance, though. I don't want you interacting with them or getting too close. I don't want them to know you're watching them."

"I can. Is there a reason why?"

"There is, but I can't tell you."

"Okay. Is this the type of thing you ask your corps to do?"

"Sometimes."

"Doesn't sound too exciting."

"As I told Janco, ninety percent of this job is not exciting."

"Am I hoping to see them do something interesting?"

"Yes."

"And I'm to let you know."

"When you can."

"And what happens if I accidentally get too close?"

"Think about anything other than the reason you're that close. Think about one of your bo fights. Or visualize the moves for the Ranken Qua kata."

"That's a tricky one. I almost clunked myself on the head with that one. Are you going to explain what's going on later?"

"Yes."

"All right. I'm in."

After Maren left, his office seemed too quiet, but the thought of going to his empty suite held no appeal. Instead, he lit a number of candles to push back the encroaching darkness, opened Star's file, and read.

Her organization had been extensive. It included gambling, trading black market goods, theft, smuggling, espionage, and assassinations. He had thought her main business was located in Castletown, but when they raided the house, they only nabbed a dozen minor affiliates. Star and her upper echelon were long gone, along with any evidence that Valek could use to find out where they went. It was only a matter of time before he found her other hideout.

It was by pure chance that Star had been caught. She'd used Rand, Yelena's friend, and the Commander's ex-chef, to lure Yelena away from the camp when they had been traveling to Brazell's. But Rand felt guilty for the ruse and warned her. Valek never liked Rand, but after learning that Rand pushed Yelena out of the way and took an arrow to the heart for her, Valek had changed his mind about the man. He'd redeemed himself in the end.

By the time Valek had figured out what was going on, Yelena had killed both of Star's goons and was intent on killing Star. Valek had stopped her. Star had too much valuable information. Although, it appeared that Star wasn't going to divulge her secrets easily. That was okay, Valek liked a challenge.

A knock sounded on his door. Valek glanced at the window. Night had fallen and a few of the candles had burned out. How long had he been reading?

"Come in," he said, as his hand grasped the hilt of the cloud-kissed dagger sheathed on his belt.

The Commander entered. Valek about fell out of his chair when he tried to stand. The man avoided Valek's messy office at all costs. He claimed clutter made him nauseous.

"Sir?"

Ambrose carried a plate filled with steaming meat and potatoes, covered with a brown gravy. It smelled divine. "According to the kitchen staff, you missed dinner." He set it down on the desk and then sat on the edge of the chair as if to avoid touching anything.

"Uh, thank you." Valek settled back in his chair, but he was far from relaxed.

"I'd like to apologize for my earlier…outburst."

Oh no. Was the Commander already under Alea's influence? "You would?"

"The severity of my reaction was uncalled for. The business with Brazell and Mogkan has unsettled me. You are only doing your job. It makes sense to be extra careful, especially since Alea is in the castle."

Valek jumped to his feet. "You saw her? What happened?"

"I did not encounter her. However, foreign thoughts struck me from time to time this afternoon."

"Foreign thoughts?"

"Yes. There was the one insisting you are no longer trustworthy. Others that urged me to arrest you. And the ones compelling me to kill you were quite strong. I'm getting a sense this Alea does not like you."

"The feeling is mutual. Any other problems? Symptoms? Do you feel twitchy?"

The Commander lifted a brow. "Twitchy? No. Nor did I get the sense that Alea was digging for information."

"Is she targeting you at this moment? I might be able to find her."

"No. She has given up for now."

"I'll stay with you and—"

The Commander raised his hand. "I still believe your time is better spent hunting her down. However, I would like you to be close by while I'm asleep. I can ignore her requests while awake, but I'm afraid I won't be able to resist her while asleep."

That was a big admission for the Commander. "How close? Like big spoon close?" Valek joked.

The Commander didn't crack a smile. "On the couch in my suite is close enough."

"All right."

"Good. Any progress on the hunt?"

"I've a couple agents working on it. And now that we have confirmation that she's here, it'll take away some of the guess work."

"Good." He rose and glanced around the office. Valek was glad the light was dim. "This place is filthy. Get it cleaned."

"Yes, sir."

"I'll see you later." The Commander strode to the door. He paused at the threshold and turned. "And Valek?"

"Yes?"

"*I* would be the big spoon."

Valek laughed. "Anytime, sir."

Valek updated Kenda on the situation. "It's best to keep your distance from a magician. I want everyone to carry crossbows, blowpipes and darts filled with sleeping juice, and shields."

"Shields?" she asked.

"Some magicians can fling objects."

"But won't they be too obvious?"

"It doesn't matter. Alea already knows we know she's here."

"I'll remind our corps members of their training. And give the Commander's guards a refresher."

"Find me if anything unusual or strange happens." He told her where he would be sleeping until this was over.

"Is the Commander spooked?"

"No. I'd say rattled. Which is to be expected. He's always in control. For someone to take that away from him must have been…" Valek couldn't think of an appropriate word.

"Horrible," Kenda provided. "And he's probably going to be difficult to deal with as he recovers. There'll be mood swings, irritability, paranoia, and emotional withdraw."

Valek was impressed. "Do you have experience with this?"

"Some of our agents have the same issues after they return from an unsuccessful mission. And a few have it even when the mission is successful. Even though they're home, they can't shut that hyper-vigilance off. I've been learning to recognize the symptoms, so I don't assign a struggling agent a new mission too soon."

And this was another reason why he'd promoted Kenda. Valek just didn't have the emotional depth to address all his agents' needs. He could provide them with training, weapons, money, advice, but couldn't do more. Hell, he couldn't even manage his own emotions. "Does it take them long to recover?"

"Depends on the person. Some need a few days, others a few weeks or months. We've had a few retire early or transfer out of the corps due to it. I think the worst is when one of our agents dies. There's a ripple effect throughout the corps that extends beyond that person's friends and family."

And they had recently lost Sven, who everyone liked. "How's Sven's son, Adrik, doing with the training?"

"He has good and bad days. Same with Trevar. Sven might not have been Trevar's father, but the two of them bonded pretty quick. And Trevar's a right pain in the ass."

"Oh?"

"He's too smart for his own good. He learns new skills quickly but doesn't have the patience for repetition. And the trainer told me he disappeared today." She squinted at Valek. "Maybe you should talk to him."

"To scare him straight?"

"Something like that."

Valek laughed, thinking how Trevar hadn't been one bit intimidated when he had summoned him to his office. "Won't work. Once Trevar returns, start ambushing him. He'll learn real quick that he's not as ready as he thought."

"Ooohhh. I like." She sobered. "If he shows up."

"He will."

Kenda gave him a sharp look but didn't ask why he sounded so confident. "Where will you be before you join the Commander this evening?"

"I'll be around."

"That's vague."

"That's the point."

"Ah."

Valek walked slowly around the castle. He kept his senses open, hoping to encounter magic in use. Sometimes it was a light touch, like walking through a cobweb. Other times, it pressed on his skin like a wet towel, and moving through it required effort. If it was really strong, it could knock him off his feet, but that was rare. The King had almost killed Valek because he had thrown all his power at him when they had fought.

After he roamed through the entire castle without success, Valek headed to the Commander's suite. It was right across the corridor from Valek's, and the only way into that corridor was through a locked door normally guarded by two well-trained soldiers.

He rounded the corner. The four guards before the door turned and aimed their loaded crossbows at his chest. Valek stopped. He recognized all of them. However, their hard expressions didn't soften. He'd been searching for Alea's magic all night. Had he just found it?

CHAPTER 9

"Don't move," Millicent ordered.

Valek spread his hands out, showing he was unarmed. "Lieutenant Millicent, it's me."

"How do we know? You could be the magician in disguise."

He had purposely not released Alea's name. He wanted everyone to view her as *the magician*, the enemy. "I know your name along with Dagon's, Sora's, and Boaz's."

"You could have read Adviser Valek's memories."

While that was a good point in general, it didn't apply in his case. "A magician can't read my mind, I'm immune to magic."

They all relaxed. Now their weapons were aimed at the floor, he took his first full breath. But she raised a legitimate concern. How could the guards trust anyone? "Did you vet the Commander as well?"

Millicent ducked her head. "No, sir."

"The Commander had his key," Dagon said in their defense. "I've seen him fight, and while I can believe a magician might be disguised as him, I seriously doubt they could take his key away."

"In normal circumstances that makes sense, but this magician is clever. From now on, I'm going to accompany the Commander when he returns to his suite at night. This way, you can be sure it's him."

"But what if the magician is disguised as you?" Sora asked. "And she learns the answer to our questions by reading our minds?"

Impressed, he studied the woman. She had an oval face, and a faded scar marked her chin. "An excellent question. Too bad, I don't have a good answer for you. If we pick a password or use an object like the key to the door, the magician will discover that information from your minds. This is why they are so dangerous. You just need to trust your judgement. And please be careful who you aim at."

"Perhaps you should announce your presence to the guards before rounding the corner, sir," Dagon said. "We're on high alert and tend to get twitchy."

"Noted. Thank you."

The Commander was waiting for Valek in his living room. A glass of whiskey had already been poured. Valek sat down and sipped the liquid. Fire raced down his throat and burned in his stomach. A pleasant sensation to counteract his aching muscles. The cushions on the couch were soft, but not as comfortable as his bed.

"The guards made a number of interesting observations." Valek explained about the conundrum. "They really can't trust anyone but me. From now on, I'll escort you back to your suite at night."

"I think you're her primary target for now. Otherwise, she would have suggested I commit suicide or meet her in an unsecured location."

"Let's hope she stays focused on me."

"I see that tree branch hasn't rattled your confidence."

"No. It reminded me that just because I'm immune to magic, doesn't mean I'm invincible."

"You? Not invincible?" Ambrose pressed a hand to his chest in mock horror. "Say it isn't so."

Despite the danger, or rather, because of it, Valek established a routine as the days stretched without the Commander or anyone—that they knew of—being targeted by Alea. Valek guessed she was keeping a low profile while she waited for her team to arrive. And probably learning everything she could about the castle's security. That was what he'd be doing in her place.

Valek kept up his rounds, seeking magic three times a day. His daily soaks in the baths helped with his muscle aches. His headaches continued, though. While they weren't as severe as they were in the beginning, they were a daily occurrence, signaling that Valek needed to take a break, preferably a nap. At those times, Valek felt every one of his thirty-four years. When Medic Channa had removed his stitches, she warned that full recovery might take months or even a year.

Valek was in his office, massaging his temples to keep the throbbing in his head from escalating. It was day twenty of the warm season, and he still had no idea where Alea was hiding. Also, no epiphanies on how to trap eight magicians who were well aware they were walking into a trap. The solution eluded him even after two weeks of working on the problem.

Needing a change in scenery and some fresh air, he took a walk around the oddly shaped castle, designed by a young king overly fond of his toy blocks. The Commander hated it and would have destroyed it to build a functional, utilitarian, and spartan building, if it hadn't been a frivolous expense. The castle was perfectly usable, and the Commander was loathed to spend money on anything other than necessary infrastructure, the citizens of Ixia, and their needs. The walls of the castle would have to be crumbling in order for him to build a new head-quarters.

Valek rather liked the castle's unorthodox shape. The strange angles and roof configurations made for excellent climbing. He rolled his shoulders, testing his muscles. Some exercise might help clear his mind. Tweaks of pain shot across his back. Maybe not today.

The sun shone in the clear blue sky and the chilly air smelled of fresh earth. Valek ended up at the training yard in the northeast corner of the complex. Groups of soldiers sparred, practiced self-defense moves, or worked on their aim. Clangs of steel, curses, thuds of clashing bodies, and barks of laughter were music to his ears. Valek watched for a while. Ari and Janco worked with a lieutenant, teaching her how to fight with a bo staff.

They spotted him and eventually joined him at the fence.

"It's good to see you out and about, sir," Ari said.

"Yeah, you look better. No question mark," Janco said.

"Thank you."

"And it's good for them to see you, too." Ari inclined his head, indicating the other soldiers in the yard. "Rumors about you have not been kind."

"Let me guess. 'He's too old. We need fresh blood in the high ranks. He's too scared to come out and fight.' Sound about right?" Valek asked.

"Just about. Are you in any condition to fight?" Ari asked.

No. "It depends on who's asking."

"We're teaching Lieutenant Odell how to use a bo staff, and I thought a demonstration of its versatility would help her. And you."

Ah. More of a show that their leader doesn't have one foot in the grave. "All right. Who wants to spar me?"

"Your choice, sir." Ari said with a smile.

Ari's strength versus Janco's speed. At this point, he thought Odell would be enough of a challenge. "Janco."

"Woo hoo!" Janco bounced on the balls of his feet.

"This is a *demonstration*, Janco," Ari said. "Half speed or Odell won't learn anything."

"Pah."

"Next time, Janco," Valek said.

"Oh goody." He rubbed his hands together.

Valek peeled off his shirt without groaning or wincing—no need to show any weaknesses to the growing crowd. He climbed over the fence and Janco threw him a bo. Valek grabbed it, placing one hand approximately one foot and seven inches from the top and the other the same distance from the bottom of the staff. Basically, splitting it into thirds. Carved from cherry wood, the bo was an inch in diameter and the ends tapered to half an inch with a flat top and bottom. Swinging it around, he warmed up. Fire raced down his back as his muscles protested the motion.

"Whoa. That's—"

"Janco," Ari warned.

"Quite the bruise, sir."

"Shall we start?" Valek asked.

"I'm ready." Janco slid his feet into a fighting stance. He held his bo straight out and parallel to the ground. A defensive position.

With his bo underneath his right arm, and his left arm across his chest, Valek moved into an offensive position. Ari explained the significance of the stances to Odell. The young woman stared at Valek with large blue eyes.

"Begin," Ari said.

Valek performed a series of basic offensive strikes. Chin, temple, temple, ribs, head. Each move lacked his usual grace. His bruises limited his motion. Janco countered them all with ease.

Ari pointed out the various steps to Odell. "This is mostly a non-lethal weapon. The point is to knock your opponent unconscious so you can—"

"Hit and git!" Janco said, then he launched into a counteroffensive volley that was quicker than the first series. Valek managed to match it.

"There are only four killing moves," Ari said. "A direct smash to a person's windpipe, which will crush it and suffocate the person. An upward blow to the nose. It would break the cartilage and shove the pieces into the brain. A strike to the base of the skull and a head strike. But they only work if your bo is made from hard wood, and you have enough strength."

Janco increased the speed of his attack. "Hit hard and fast and your opponent won't last," he sang.

Valek blocked. Each impact with Janco's bo sent spikes of pain shooting through his arms and right into his temples. At least, his muscles had warmed, improving his flexibility enough to keep Janco from getting through his defenses.

Then Janco's ever present smile dropped, the glee in his gaze died and he focused on Valek with a grim determination. The fight went from friendly bout to a full out attack.

"Janco, slow down. That's not the point of this fight," Ari scolded.

If Janco heard him, he showed no signs. Now deadly serious, Janco mixed up his strikes, tested for weaknesses, and aimed for the neck. Valek barely blocked him, and he suspected he was fighting for his life. They circled as Valek tried to keep his distance, but it was only a matter of time before Janco beat him.

Valek sidestepped a lunge and magic brushed his back. Directly in front of him, Janco paused in confusion and Valek took advantage. He knocked the bo from Janco's hands, swept his feet out, and, when Janco landed, Valek pressed the end of his bo to his neck.

"Concede?" Valek asked.

"Yes! I don't—"

Valek spun and searched the faces of the crowd. Where was Alea? He spotted a flash of black hair and took off. By the time he pushed through the soldiers, she was gone.

When he returned, Janco sat on the ground. He rubbed his fingers along the scar on his right ear. "Was she trying to kill you or me?" he asked Valek.

"Both of us. You would have killed me, and the Commander would have killed you."

Ari lowered his voice. "Did you feel twitchy?"

"No. I was jacked on adrenaline. Even at half speed, I was fighting *Valek*. That gets into your head."

"I should have intervened, but I thought it would look bad," Ari said.

"You didn't know." Valek pulled Janco to his feet. "You've gotten better with the bo."

"Thanks. I'm sor—"

"Not your fault. We gave Alea an opportunity and she took it."

"She's going to be impossible to capture," Janco said.

Now that the fight was over, Valek's muscles trembled. He tightened them to stop the visible vibrations as he put his shirt on. "Come with me to the castle."

They said goodbye to the overwhelmed Lieutenant. All she could do was nod in response. Valek hoped Maren would take Odell under her wing.

As they walked toward the north entrance, Valek asked them, "What's the gossip?"

Janco signaled. *Everyone is mouth about the marriage.*

"You got a few words wrong, but that's impressive. This is talking." He demonstrated, touching his thumb to his index finger. "And this is magician." This time he raised his middle finger. "But let's not continue doing that here, someone might be watching. Anything else?"

Ari said, "The three main topics of conversation are the magician, your injury, and what happened to the Commander in MD-5."

"And don't forget the speculation that Valek killed Yelena." Janco added.

Ari frowned and signaled, *Be quiet!*

He was glad they were learning the signals so quickly. But he hadn't even thought about what the castle denizens would think when Yelena failed to return with the Commander.

Valek considered. "That's a good rumor to encourage. That way she'll be safer in Sitia, and we won't have to answer the question about why we let her leave." Huh. If he hadn't lost his mind and had arrested Yelena instead of thinking the Commander had wanted him to assassinate her right then, the Commander's order for her execution and her escape would have aided in the ruse.

When they entered the castle, Janco asked, "You want me to walk around the barracks and see if I feel twitchy? Maybe find Alea."

"No. In fact, stay in the castle and continue your lessons."

"But nothing is stopping her from being inside. What if I attack Ari in the middle of the night? Or attack someone else?"

"Then I *will* stop you," Ari said. "Partners remember?"

With a wave goodbye, they headed toward their suite. As soon as they were out of sight, Valek leaned against the wall and relaxed. The muscle tremors returned with a vengeance. He sank to the floor and endured waves of weakness as pain ringed his body.

When he could stand, he soaked in the hot water of the baths for a long time, before going to his suite. Even though it was the middle of the day, he collapsed into his bed.

❧

Expecting to be stiff, sore, and barely able to move when he woke up, Valek was surprised his muscles didn't scream when he sat up. For the first time since the accident, he felt good. Perhaps the fight had loosened and stretched his muscles.

The sun hovered over the western horizon. Energized, Valek fetched a plate of food and returned to his suite. After he ate, he lit two lanterns and entered his carving studio for the first time in seasons. Dust coated everything, but, then again, it was perpetually dusty. Grit crunched under his boots as he set the lanterns on the table.

He sorted through his piles of gray rocks, collected from the sea cliffs along the northern coast of MD-1. It was the location of the School of Night and Shadows, where he had learned the fine and dangerous art of assassination. And learned that carving helped focus his mind and soothed his soul. Thinking about his soul, he remembered the butterfly he had carved and how it had reminded him of Yelena. She'd admired it and he had turned it into a pendent and gifted it to her. He wondered if she still wore it or if she'd hidden it away so her new friends in Sitia didn't ask her about it. About him. A pang squeezed his chest. Had he lost her to the south?

One of the larger gray rocks called to him. It was long and narrow. He carried it to his table full of chisels and sat down.

Turning it around in his fingers, he let his mind drift. Thoughts of Yelena swirled as the emotions he tried so hard to suppress unfurled their wings and stretched, filling him with wonder, awe, and gratitude that the most amazing woman in the entire world loved him. He'd been worried the feelings would weaken him and had been the reason for his series of missteps. But he'd been wrong. They strengthened him. By acknowledging them and embracing them, he could do anything.

Yelena and Valek might have taken different paths, but they would be together again. And if her feelings had changed, Valek didn't know if he'd ever recover. Life would hold no appeal. But there was no sense wasting energy worrying about something he couldn't change. Best to focus on the next challenge.

Valek picked up his medium sized chisel and chipped away the rock that didn't belong, freeing the true shape that lurked within. Hours later and covered with a sheen of sweat and a coating of dust, he held a snake in his hands. Its body coiled as if around a small tree limb. Carefully, he polished it on the grinding wheel. The dull gray color disappeared in a cloud of dust as black streaked with silver emerged. A transformation that never failed to astound him.

For the snake's eyes, he scraped two small divots. Then he rummaged around in one of his drawers. He hardly ever added color to his statues, preferring the black and silver, but this one needed a pop. He found his pouch of small precious and semi-precious stones. Pouring them out onto his palm, he picked two tiny sapphires and glued them in for the snake's eyes. Perfect. Just like Yelena. He hand-polished the inside of the coils, and when it was finished, he thought she could wear it on her arm as a bracelet. If she desired. Yes, he knew he shouldn't worry, but knowing and doing were two different things.

Over the next several days, Valek spent all of his time in his studio. He carved several rocks of all sizes and shapes. During that time, he allowed his thoughts to drift. By the end of the third day, he had a plan on how to capture eight magicians. And a dozen statues littered his table.

"Don't worry," he said to them. "I'll find good homes for all of you."

~

A knock sounded, pulling Valek from his work. Annoyed at the intrusion—he only had five more days before the generals arrived and there were no signs of Alea—he wanted to ignore it.

But another knock, this one more insistent, rattled the wood. Valek unlocked the door, revealing a grinning Trevar on the other side.

"Hey, you look so much better," Trevar said.

"Thanks. Come in." His annoyance forgotten, Valek invited Trevar to sit opposite his desk. "Do you have anything to report?"

"I do. I found your girl."

"My girl?"

"Yeah. The one that doesn't fit. That doesn't belong. You said I'd know when it happens. Well, it happened."

Valek suppressed his excitement. "Please, continue."

"Okay. Well, I've been chatting and been friendly to everyone, working double shifts. Doing the dishes, running errands, cleaning chamber pots—I should get a bonus for that—and commiserating with my colleagues over said chamber pots. They accepted me rather easily. Either they are used to a lot of turnovers in their ranks, or I'm just that good." He grinned.

"The Commander insists his managers reward good work with promotions and transfers. That's why the menial jobs are usually staffed with new hires, who tend to be young."

That deflated some of Trevar's ego. "Oh. Well, during the last couple weeks, I met this one girl. She wore a housekeeping uniform, but no one can say if she's actually cleaned a room. I know not everyone in the castle is a hard worker and that people shirk their duties all the time, but there's something...*off* about her. It's more than just laziness."

"What's her name? Can you describe her?"

"Her name's Ada, I think. And she's...hard to describe. I didn't have much interaction with her. All I can think is black hair, usually in a bun. It's her...bearing that's most noticeable. As if she's important. Bristling whenever she's assigned a task." He shrugged.

"Have you attended the class on the art of observation?"

"Yes. I earned full marks! But her physical details just don't stick. Just like her name, I think it's Ada, but no one can say for sure. And we forget about her. She'll show up for a shift and we're all like, 'who are you?' and then it'll click. Weird."

It could be Alea. Her magic might keep people from remembering her. "Do you know where I can find her?"

"Yes. When I'm on kitchen duty and help serve dinner, she sits at the same table. Every time, I'm like, 'she looks familiar,' but I don't try too hard to figure out why. Well, I was finally able to figure out why."

"What was different?"

"She was distracted. Those two goons came into the dining room, and she was focused on them."

"Goons?"

"Yeah, the two newbies in our corps. They attract so much attention, there's no way they'll graduate and become spies."

Ah. Ari and Janco. Valek didn't bother to correct him. Trevar would discover their abilities all on his own. "Did she notice you?"

"No. No one, and I mean, *no one* looks at us. No eye contact, nothing. We set the plates in front of them and if they mutter a 'thank you,' it makes our day."

Someone rapped on the door, but before Valek could respond, Maren strolled into his office.

She carried her bo staff in her right hand.

"You have information?" he asked.

Maren glanced at Trevar. "Not in front of the snitch."

"Snitch?" Trevar's voice squeaked with outrage.

"Yeah, you're the kid that gave us the black market dealers' locations before the raids. Right?"

Valek was impressed by her memory. It had been dark and there were dozens of people there.

Trevar huffed in indignation. "I wasn't *snitching*, I was *spying*. It was my first mission for Valek."

"One of your corps?" She turned to him.

"In training. What did you find out?" Valek asked Maren.

"I found your girl."

Valek and Trevar exchanged a glance.

"I found her first," Trevar said, smirking.

Maren moved closer to Trevar as if she'd planned to rap Trevar on the head with her bo staff.

"Ignore him," Valek said before she could remove the smirk from his face. "Please report."

"You asked to keep an eye on the new recruits and the women from the visiting platoon. At first, no one really stood out. They were friendly, but distant. I get it. I'm not everyone's cup of sunshine."

Trevar covered a cough.

After a heartbeat, she continued. "But over time, I picked up on one lady. She didn't seem to belong to anyone. I'd see the diamonds on her uniform but couldn't remember if they were red or white. She didn't talk to anyone and just today, I saw her wearing a housekeeping uniform. Yet as soon as I thought it, she seemed to change into her soldier uniform just like a chameleon. Weird."

"What does she look like?"

"No clue. I might need glasses. Every time I looked at her face, it was blurry."

"Do you know where to find her?"

"Yeah, I figured out she's sleeping in the lieutenants' barracks on the first floor. The first cubby near the door. I was returning from a late shift and almost ran into her as she was leaving. I think I startled her, 'cause she hurried away."

All good news.

"Did we both find the magician?" Trevar asked.

"You did. And it's a game changer. However, you both need to stay as far away from her as possible. Maren, I want you to move into one of the bedrooms in the hexagon; and Trevar, you're to return to your lessons. Tell no one what you know, or you'll endanger them."

"And miss all the fun." Trevar pouted. "What if she gets close despite our efforts?"

"Recite kata moves in your head," Maren answered.

"In your case, go over all the hand signals you've learned. Both of you, move away if you can. Magicians have limits on their abilities."

"Thank fate for that," Trevar muttered.

"Distance is one of those limits," Valek continued. "The stronger ones can send an object hurling all the way across the room, while weaker ones can only push it a few feet."

"What about my duties?" Maren asked.

"I'll send temporary transfer papers to Major Shaw."

"Temporary?"

"I can always make it permanent," Valek said.

"I'll let you know."

Valek tucked his black hair into the hair net. Smoothing out the white tunic the kitchen staffers wore, he checked his reflection in the mirror. The bruises on his right cheek had faded into a grayish-green smudge, but he covered them with a bit of makeup just in case. He had also added a fake nose and thicker eyebrows.

The kitchen bustled with activity as the staff prepped for dinner. Valek helped where needed, stirring a creamy potato soup that smelled divine, and chopping carrots for a stew. When Rand, the head chef, had been transferred to MD-5, an interim chef had been appointed. The man hadn't been able to handle the pressure and quit. Sammy, Rand's fetch boy stepped into the chaos, fully expecting to be replaced when the Commander returned. It seemed Rand had taught the thirteen-year-old how to cook and prepare meals. The Commander had given Sammy a week to prove his skills. He rose to the challenge and was officially appointed head chef a few days ago.

When the dining room opened, Valek helped serve meals. A buffet or a serving line would be more efficient and less costly, but the Commander insisted the castle's staff and soldiers be served.

During the busiest time of the night, when almost every table was full, Alea entered the dining room. She wore a soldier's uniform with the Commander's colors. Her black hair had been pulled into a knot at the back of her head. With her darker skin and strong features, she did resemble Adviser Dema. But her gray eyes scanned the room with a cold appraisal, nothing like the warmth and kindness that emanated from Dema's brown eyes.

No one paid attention to her as Alea wove through the tables and sat at an empty one far in the back and close to the windows. The room was on the ground floor, so Valek guessed the window was her escape route should things go south.

He didn't bring her a plate, but he watched as another server set it in front of her. Alea didn't thank the woman, she merely ate in a quick and efficient manner. In the dining room, she was surrounded by her enemies and outnumbered. This was probably the most dangerous part of her day.

Valek fingered the blowpipe in his pocket. Darts filled with sleeping potion were tucked into his sleeve. She couldn't read his mind and, as long as he stayed out of sight, he'd be able to get a dart into her neck. Tempting, but he needed to mark the other seven magicians.

Instead, Valek followed Alea for the next three days and learned a number of things. She was a creature of habit, sticking to the same routine each day, which meant she was smart. Showing up at different places at different times, she would have been more noticeable. One of her daily stops was the armory; she'd swipe a couple daggers and head for the castle's storerooms.

Valek couldn't follow her down there. The rooms were all but abandoned and in an isolated section. He couldn't risk being discovered. But after she went to sleep for the night, he searched all the rooms and found her cache of weapons. Fourteen knives in total. He wondered if Alea used magic to keep the Arms Master from reporting the thefts.

It didn't take him long to figure out why she needed the knives. Many of her accomplices could move objects. Using magic to throw a knife was more accurate than aiming. Valek could easily guess who they planned to target. Not the generals nor the Commander, as they would control them with magic. Guards would be killed along with any of the generals' advisers not in league with them. No doubt, Valek would be their first victim.

CHAPTER 10

"The generals will be here in two days; do you have a plan to stop the magicians?" Ambrose asked during their nightly meeting.

"No comment." Valek relaxed on the couch. Even though he knew Alea probably wasn't a threat to the Commander, he still slept on it. Best to keep up appearances.

After a long pause, he asked, "Is there anything I can do?"

"Yes. The generals' retinues are to be housed in the barracks."

"Even the advisers?"

"Yes, everyone except family members."

"The generals will squawk."

"I don't care."

"You don't have to listen to them complain."

"Neither do you."

Ambrose grunted in amusement. "Anything else?"

"Yes. Only one adviser per general is allowed into the war room during your meetings. And no weapons allowed. I want everyone searched before they enter."

The Commander raised an eyebrow. "Except for me and you?"

"That goes without saying."

"All right. There won't be any meetings on the day the generals arrive. They'll need time to rest from their journeys."

The next morning, instead of following Alea, Valek put his plans into action. The door to the war room was normally locked when not in use, and then guarded when the Commander was in residence. Even though he was all about simplicity, functionality, and unpretentiousness, the Commander loved the tall and narrow stained-glass windows that striped three quarters of the round room, and would frequently work there. He also scheduled all meetings with the generals there.

Valek entered the war room and locked the door behind him. The early morning sunlight shone through the windows, spraying a prism of colors onto the walls. A large egg-shaped conference table occupied the center. Extra chairs with their backs up against the stone walls ringed the room.

Valek inspected the entire space, looking for places to hide weapons. He figured Alea's daggers would be hidden and secured underneath the table. At least, that was what he'd do. Then he studied the room, getting a sense of the colors and the shadows. The Commander always scheduled his meetings early in the morning. When he was confident he had the feel of the place, Valek spent the rest of the day collecting supplies.

It was trickier than he'd expected. How could he carry the items back to his suite without anyone noticing? Not wanting anyone to speculate on his actions, he ended up putting them into a pack and stashing it in a hidden corner outside the castle, where he could retrieve it under the cover of darkness.

After the Commander retired for the evening, Valek waited for him to fall asleep before he crossed over to his own suite. There, he changed into his sneak suit and went out onto the balcony. The cool night air bit through the thin, skin-tight material, but he needed flexibility rather than warmth.

High gray clouds skittered over the half-moon, blocking the light from time to time. Valek rolled his shoulders experimentally and stretched his arm muscles. Still tender, but at least they didn't ignite with pain. He climbed over the railing and, after finding the familiar hand and toe holds, descended the stone wall. Reaching the ground without trouble, Valek found the pack, slung it onto his back, and returned to his suite.

Pulling the heavy black curtains over his windows, Valek lit all the lanterns in the living room until the place blazed with light. His gaze immediately went to the left side of the couch, which Yelena had 'claimed.' A small pile of books she'd been reading rested on the end table along with an empty teacup. He wondered if he'd smell lavender if he sat in her spot. How he loved that scent. Perhaps he should buy a bottle of perfume and—

Valek huffed in annoyance. Focus. He cleared a space on the floor and then unloaded the pack, spreading the supplies out. Then he unrolled his scrim, which was made from gauze cloth. He'd used it a few years ago and it still looked good. Picking up a paint brush, he set to work. It took three hours, but he thought his efforts were adequate. He'd have to double check.

Leaving the scrim to dry, Valek searched for his box of wooden practice knives. He carried them to his carving room and spent the next couple hours altering them. Then he returned to Ambrose's suite in time to catch a few hours of sleep.

The Commander assigned Advisers Dema and Chelle to welcome the generals and get them and their retinues settled. According to Dema, Chelle turned into 'quite the tyrant' when they had both taken charge after Brazell was arrested. It made her a good choice, because she wasn't going to tolerate any pushback from the generals regarding the Commander's orders. Normally, the Commander would greet them, but Valek had advised against it.

After breakfast, Valek stopped in the war room. He hoped tomorrow would be equally sunny and the warm season's annual rains would hold off another couple of days. As expected, Valek found the daggers that Alea had stolen. She must have put them in place the previous night. Their sheaths were secured to the underside of the conference table. Glue? Or something else? It didn't really matter, as he'd figure it out later. Just in case Alea checked them again that night, he'd wait until right before the meeting to replace them.

Valek hurried to his suite and changed into his sneak suit and grabbed his pack. Then he climbed up the castle. There was a flat section of roof that was in a shadow most of the day and had a great view of the courtyard. No matter which gates the generals and their entourages entered, they'd go to the courtyard on the south side of the castle to be formally greeted and welcomed.

While he waited, he unpacked his knapsack, which held his black cloak for warmth, a spyglass, a water skin, and travel rations. He figured he'd be up here most of the day. Valek yawned and squirmed into a more comfortable position.

He looked through his spyglass. A foot long when closed, it was made of crystal and bronze and had three sections that slid out, increasing the length to three feet. A gift from the Commander, it was one of Valek's most prized possessions.

Scanning the edges of the courtyard, the southeast barracks, and the training yard, Valek searched for Alea. He found her along the fence, watching the bouts. No doubt waiting for her cohort to arrive with the generals.

The first general to arrive was General Hazal from MD-6.

The castle and Castletown were technically in MD-6, but he had no authority over them. Hazal brought two advisers and twenty soldiers. Rather modest overall, the general was the least demanding and the most pleasant.

Valek aimed his spyglass at the courtyard. Would Alea make eye contact or acknowledge her accomplice? Dema and Chelle approached the general and words were exchanged. It was easy to tell when the general learned of the change of accommodations for his advisers. Hazal straightened in surprise, and Alea's gaze darted to the left. A tall male adviser Valek didn't recognize was turned in her direction. They shared a look as she probably informed him about the trap. Gotcha.

Eventually, Dema led Hazal into the castle as Chelle escorted the rest to the barracks, where Major Granten would ensure everyone was settled. The top floor of the building had nice apartments for visiting officers. One apartment would house both of Hazal's advisers.

General Tesso of MD-4 arrived next. He brought four advisers and thirty soldiers. Anger blazed in his eyes when he learned of the Commander's orders. Three of his advisers glanced at each other in concern. The fourth, a woman, looked right at Alea.

The rest of the day played out mostly the same. Generals Kitvivan's, Dinno's, and Franis's initial reactions ranged from surprise to anger before they tried to intimidate or bully Chelle and Dema. When that didn't work, they tried to ignore them, which also failed. It was all very entertaining. Chenzo and Rasmussen accepted the new development with diplomacy and grace. In each case, Alea exposed her accomplice. All advisers. Not a surprise.

General Ute arrived last with only Adviser Kirwin accompanying her. A great choice. The older adviser had worked for Brazell before Mogkan arrived but had then been limited to balancing the budget. Kirwin had been helpful during the transition from Brazell to Ute. Ute had also brought ten soldiers, which was the smallest entourage. Kitvivan had the largest with fifty soldiers and five advisers.

In this case, Dema led both Ute and Kirwin to the castle. Kirwin could be trusted, and Valek suspected the Commander thought Ute would need his advice and companionship. While the Commander normally wouldn't show any favoritism, this exception was a warning to his generals.

Just the fact that none of the generals brought their spouses indicated they meant business and planned to team up to push for Ute's demotion. And for Valek's execution.

Valek had a busy night planned. As soon as Ambrose fell asleep, he went to his apartment, changed into his sneak suit, and climbed out of his window. A strong wind blew from the west, bringing the moist scent of rain. He climbed a series of walls, crossed roofs, and descended three stories to Ari and Janco's suite. He unlocked the shutters and pulled them wide before stepping inside the common room.

He waited, but neither man came out to investigate. Knowing better than to enter the room of a well-trained soldier in the middle of the night, Valek knocked into a chair, causing it to scrape the floor.

Two seconds later, Ari and Janco rushed from their bedrooms. Each held a knife. Once they spotted him, they charged. To them, he must resemble a man-shaped shadow.

"I'm in need of your assistance," he said before they could skewer him.

They both stopped but kept their weapons pointed at him.

"How do we know it's you?" Janco demanded.

"Ask me something no one knows but me."

"Ha! A magician can just read—"

"No, they can't. He's immune, remember?" Ari said.

"No, I don't remember. It's—what time is it? Why couldn't you just send a message at a decent time, like noon?"

"Who gave Janco his scar?" Ari asked.

"A man named Anders," Valek said.

They both relaxed and lowered their weapons.

"What do you need us to do?" Ari asked.

"Get dressed and wait for me outside the west entrance of the southeast barracks."

"Covert?" Janco asked, gesturing to the open window.

"Go through the castle. Just stay out of sight. Once you get there, don't think about staying out of sight. You're close enough to the south gate, pretend in your mind that you're working security at the gate."

"You're basically giving me permission to nap," Janco said. "'Cause that's what I'd be doing if I worked the night shift at the gate."

"Ignore him. We'll be there," Ari said.

Valek climbed out the window and Ari closed the shutters behind him. He descended to the ground and kept to the shadows as he crept toward the barracks. It was quiet and dark, but not pitch black. Lanterns burned in the stairwells. The shift change wouldn't take place for another two hours, but it wasn't unusual for people to walk through at different times. After all, nature called at all hours of the night.

All the visiting soldiers and advisers were housed in the south wing. Valek had considered that all the magicians might be together in one apartment, but that wouldn't be smart. They could mentally communicate so why risk being spotted all together?

Valek started with General Hazal's advisers. With only two of them, it should be the easiest. The apartments all had two bedrooms with two beds, a large common room with a couch, a couple arm chairs, tables, and a desk. Once inside, Valek considered the bedroom doors. Which one? He chose the one on the left and, as soon as he approached it, sensed magic and halted.

There was an invisible magical barrier around the door.

Pierce the bubble and wake the magician.

Valek paused. If the magician alerted the others, all his carefully laid plans would be ruined. What type of protection did the barrier provide? Did it alert the magician that someone lurked outside, or did it only activate if someone touched the door? Was it just attached to the door or was it seeking intruders. If it was the latter, he could go inside without alerting the magician. He could feel the magic, but he never knew its intention—a source of considerable frustration.

It was too risky to use the door, so Valek climbed outside, hoping the man didn't place a similar barrier outside his window. Most people didn't worry about intruders coming through their window when they were on the fourth floor, including his quarry.

Easing open the shutters, he stepped into the room. The magician appeared to be asleep. Valek stood in the darkest corner of the room, loaded a dart into his blowpipe, aimed for his neck, and blew. The dart hit the target.

The man's eyes flew open. "What the…" He glanced at the open window in confusion and pushed up to his elbow. "Is someone there?"

Magic brushed over Valek. The man struggled to sit up, but then the sleeping potion worked its magic, and he slumped over. Valek opened the door to the common room and then the one to the corridor. He returned to the bedroom and pulled the sleeping man over his shoulder and carried him to the west entrance.

Ari and Janco materialized from the shadows.

"Here." Valek transferred the magician to Ari. "Take him to the holding cells in the castle and come back here."

"Yes, sir."

"What about me?" Janco asked.

"You wait here, and I'll bring you a present."

"Oh goody."

General Chenzo's three advisers had sorted themselves into two sleeping in one bedroom and the magician in the other. He had also erected a magical barrier, but Valek repeated his actions without altering anyone. He carried the man to Janco and reiterated his instructions.

"Yeah, yeah. Got it."

Rasmussen also brought three advisers and Valek carried the third man to Ari, who had returned. Tesso's advisers slept two to a room. The magician hadn't put a protection on the door, but she'd erected a bubble around her bed.

She woke when the dart encountered her magic. It stopped in mid-air and then dropped to the ground with a plink. Sitting up, she glanced at her roommate, who was still asleep. Her magic brushed over Valek but didn't pause.

"Light," she said. The lantern blazed to life.

Thank fate her gaze was on the dart on the floor. Having no choice, he rushed her and jammed a dart into her neck. She struggled and various objects pelted his back before the potion took over and she fell asleep. It was only then that her roommate roused. Valek blew out the lantern before the woman could open her eyes.

"Farren? That you?" her roommate asked sleepily.

"Yeah, sorry," Valek said in a falsetto.

"S'okay." The roommate rolled over.

Valek sagged in relief, but still waited fifteen minutes before moving. He replaced the brush, book, and boot that the magician had thrown at him. Then he carried Farren to the west entrance.

Ari and Janco both waited for him.

Janco took the woman. "She's a little thing. Weighs almost nothing."

"She's powerful, though, and the last one," Valek said. "It's too dangerous to capture the others. Let's go back to the castle."

"That leaves four," Ari said as they walked through the shadows. "Three advisers and Alea. Can you handle them? Especially when they wake up and realize their accomplices are gone?"

"Yeah, how are you going to explain that?" Janco asked.

"I'm going to inform Major Granten they visited the infirmary in the middle of the night with a stomach bug and are still there recovering." Valek *tsked*. "Bad luck to have been served spoiled meat. It happens."

"Don't I know it. One time, I had this rancid meat pie and—"

"Janco," Ari interrupted. "Valek doesn't want to hear about your projectile vomiting."

Valek gave Ari a grateful smile.

They arrived at the castle's holding cells. Mostly used for temporary prisoners or for those waiting to be interrogated, as going through all the dungeon security was a lengthy process.

Each of the three magicians had their own cell. Janco laid the woman on the cot in the last one. Valek handed a bunch of darts to Ari and Janco.

"This is sleeping potion. I want you to prick our guests every six hours. Do not let them wake up. Understand?"

"Yes, sir," Ari said.

Janco scratched his ear. "Why not kill them now? Why risk them waking up unexpectedly?"

"I don't know if their deaths will automatically alert the others. I want their colleagues to wonder and worry about where they are."

"You don't think they'll believe the stomach bug excuse?"

"No, that's mostly for the generals."

"But won't the other magicians be alerted when they don't show up in the morning?"

Valek smiled. "Yes. But that'll be in the morning."

"You're hoping they won't have time to alter their plans?" Ari asked.

"Right. And I want you both to remain here and guard them. They're to stay locked up until *I* return. Make sure it's me. Don't release them to anyone else."

"Yes, sir," they said.

Valek hurried to accomplish the next task on his list. He woke Medic Channa and asked her to write Major Granten about the poor health of the four advisers.

"They're in my infirmary?" she asked.

"Oh, yes. They're sleeping and are *not* to be disturbed," he said.

"Okay. Now?"

"First light."

"All right, but you owe me."

"Thanks." Valek returned to his suite via the northeastern cornice and a few slippery roofs. He grabbed the scrim, his climbing ropes, his pack, and the wooden knives.

The only way into the war room was through the door, so Valek had to get there early enough so no one would see him enter. Once inside, he searched for another intruder in case Alea had the same idea. No one. Swapping the real daggers for the altered practice knives, he put the weapons into his pack. Then he climbed about two stories up the wall and slipped onto the rafters.

He unrolled the scrim and attached it to the brackets on the walls, just below the rafters. Brackets he had installed a few years ago when he'd first needed to use the scrim. However, that had been in the evening and the shadows and colors had been different than in the morning. He hoped his limited artistic talents matched the morning light.

The beauty of the scrim was it allowed only the people on the dark side to see through it. Because the sunlight would be coming from the stained-glass windows below Valek and the scrim, if anyone looked up during the meeting, they'd see nothing but the empty rafters he'd painted onto it. He hoped.

Valek put on his climbing harness and tied the rope to the main rafter just in case he had to drop into the meeting. In the meantime, he wrapped his cloak around him and found a comfortable spot to watch.

～

"…highly unusual. What is the Commander trying to pull?" General Franis's strident voice woke Valek from a light doze. He glanced down. Franis and Tesso had entered the war room.

"He's obviously unstable," Tesso said. "At least your adviser didn't get sick. I've three others, but I rely on Farren the most. And that medic wouldn't let me see her. Pulled rank on *me*. A general! Said only the Commander has authority over her."

Valek smiled at Tesso's outraged tone. But then he sobered. He was going to owe Medic Channa big time.

Dinno and Kitvivan entered together.

Kitvivan rounded on Franis. "Did you know Colonel Ute is here? What the hell, Franis? I thought you took care of the situation."

"I tried. She snuck out with Valek," Franis said.

"Valek," Tesso spat his name. "Stole all my Criollo. And destroyed the boxes that had just been delivered to my garrison! Thank fate Farren had some extra. She promised there would be more."

Generals Hazal, Chenzo, and Rasmussen had entered during Tesso's rant.

"Valek?" Rasmussen asked. "He's been busy in MD-5, when would he have time to go around stealing Criollo? My supply also went missing. Strange."

Kitvivan laughed without humor. "Come on, Ras. You can't be that naïve. He has his spies everywhere. They're working in the garrisons, in our manor houses. You can't trust anyone except your advisers. Bruse also said there'd be more Criollo."

"My Criollo disappeared as well, but I don't miss it," General Hazal said. "I don't know why, but I'm thinking clearer without it."

"Me, too," Chenzo said. "Nolten offered me more, but I stuck it in a drawer and forgot about it."

"Is Nolten sick?" Rasmussen asked Chenzo. "My adviser had to go to the infirmary last night."

"Yes, poor guy. The ones that got sick were all sitting at the same table in the soldiers' mess hall."

"You think Valek could have poisoned them?" Tesso asked.

"While that's something he would do, my adviser said there were seven of them at the table and only four got sick," Franis said.

Before anyone else could comment, Commander Ambrose and General Ute entered. All conversation ceased. The icy expression on the Commander's face didn't bode well for a pleasant meeting.

"Generals, please have a seat," the Commander said, taking his place at the end of the oval table while the others sat along the expanse—four on either side. Valek's seat next to the Commander remained empty. Dinno and Franis glanced at it with unease.

A light touch of magic brushed Valek's face.

"Where are our advisers?" Kitvivan asked, although it sounded more like a demand. "You said we could have one with us."

"They're waiting in the hall until I call for them," the Commander said.

"Why? Where's Valek? Is he busy searching our suites for Criollo?" Tesso asked.

"Valek wasn't invited. And neither are your advisers. Not yet. This is just between us. I'd like to introduce you to our newest general," the Commander said. "Please welcome General Ute."

The silence stretched. Ute tried to make eye contact with the others, but they stared at the Commander. She kept her expression neutral, but Valek noticed her death grip on the arms of her chair.

"Is something wrong?" the Commander asked.

"Yes," Tesso said. "We didn't discuss your selection. If you're going to promote a new general, you would naturally have consulted with us as we've been with you since the beginning. You've had a rough time of late, so aren't thinking clearly. Not giving us the courtesy to be a part of the process is one example. We all understand."

Everyone except Ute gave the Commander sympathetic and encouraging nods. Ute sat very still, as if caught in the jaws of a trap. Valek wondered if all the generals had voted to decide who would be the spokesman and Tesso was shafted or if he volunteered.

"And it can be easily fixed," Tesso continued with a generous tone. "There are plenty of talented candidates. I think we should nominate those we feel would be able to handle the job." He inclined his head toward Ute. "Colonel Ute can certainly be on the list. Once complied, we can discuss everyone's qualifications and vote."

The Commander leaned forward. The room held its breath. "When I promoted you to general, Tesso, did I consult with the other three generals at the time?"

Rasmussen, Franis, and Chenzo shook their heads.

"Did I consult with anyone when I promoted Dinno? Kitvivan?"

All nos.

"Then why would you expect me to consult you now?"

"You've been compromised and are not thinking clearly,"

Tesso said. "This is why you promoted us, Ambrose, to help you. Let us help."

The Commander paused for a long moment. "I agree, you've been most helpful in the past and I owe you an explanation of what happened in MD-5.

"Back in the middle of the hot season, Brazell sent me Criollo as a gift. I enjoyed the dessert and ate a piece at least three times a day. However, we later learned it's a Sitian drug that reduced my resistance to foreign thoughts and suggestions. Adviser Mogkan, a magician from Sitia, created a magical power ring so he could reach me from MD-5. He suggested I travel to MD-5, and as I drew closer, he was able to take complete control of me. Valek and his team rescued me and killed Mogkan. I woke from the compulsion, and I haven't eaten any Criollo since the middle of the cold season. I can assure you; I'm thinking clearly. Are you?"

Not sure how to react, they glanced at each other, looking for guidance. Magic pressed on Valek. Stronger this time.

"I can say that I am," Hazal said. "I haven't eaten any Criollo in two weeks, and it's made a difference."

"Oh, come on," Dinno said. "Mogkan's dead. There are no magicians trying to influence us. Without them, it's a harmless dessert."

"Is it?" Chenzo asked. "I'm feeling more like myself as well."

Magic filled the room as the door opened. Seven advisers entered, followed by Alea. She also wore an advisers' uniform. Ah, she sensed the generals might have had a change of heart. The advisers ringed the table. Then Valek's heart sank. The four magicians he'd captured last night had escaped. They stood with the others. Alea must have found and rescued them. He had betted she wouldn't have enough time and lost. Valek hoped Ari and Janco hadn't been harmed.

"I did not call for you," the Commander said mildly.

"It doesn't matter," Alea said. "You're no longer in charge."

"Is this a coup?" he asked in the same bland tone.

"Yes." She stared at him. "You will give control of Ixia to General Tesso."

"Now wait a moment," Kitvivan said. "Bruse, what is going on?"

"Shut up, old man," Bruse said. Kitvivan's mouth snapped shut and he clawed at his throat.

"You will give control of Ixia to General Tesso," Alea repeated.

"No," the Commander said.

"You *will*." Magic swelled and almost knocked Valek off the rafter.

The Commander stood. "No." Then he whipped out his knife and threw it at Alea in one swift motion. Surprised, she froze for half a second before she used her magic to push the knife off course, it whizzed by her ear, but a second knife pierced her shoulder from behind. Alea cried out and spun.

Everyone had forgotten about General Ute. None of the magicians controlled her, and they mistakenly thought she wasn't a threat. Valek celebrated.

"Kill the Commander," she ordered. "I want to see him bleed out like my brother, Kangom."

Ah, she was Mogkan's sister! That explained a number of things.

The magicians reached under the table and yanked out Valek's wooden knives. They were in the air, flying straight at the Commander before anyone realized there weren't any steel blades attached to the hilts. A few of the magicians were looking at their hands as blood beaded on their palms.

The Commander dodged a few of the knives, but the others pounded harmlessly on his chest. Well, he might have a few bruises.

"Farren, set him on fire," Alea ordered.

Flames erupted on the Commander's uniform.

CHAPTER 11

*V*alek cursed. Time to crash the meeting. He cut the scrim from the brackets, letting it float down. Too slow. Ambrose had dropped to the floor and rolled, but he couldn't smother the flames. Valek slid down his rope, pushing the scrim with his feet.

Everyone cried out when the fabric came down around their heads. A few advisers were knocked down, but Valek was focused on the lump that was Farren. Once he reached the ground, he tackled her and shoved his blade between her ribs. He hopped to his feet and raced to the Commander. Even though Farren was dead, the fire still burned. Valek used a part of the scrim to smother the flames.

Ute crawled out from under the cloth. She carried a pitcher of water, which she dumped onto the Commander. Between the two of them they extinguished the fire.

"Are you all right?" Valek asked, helping Ambrose to sit up.

Holes smoked, and a few angry burns marked his torso. The fabric of his uniform had a strange sheen. The Commander must have rubbed olive oil into the fibers to make it fire resistant. Valek shouldn't be surprised Ambrose had taken measures to protect himself.

"I'm fine. Worry about the magicians." He shooed Valek.

Valek only had to worry about one. The others should be sound asleep, because he'd rigged the wooden hilts with darts filled with sleeping potion. He lifted the scrim, but Alea was gone. Racing from the war room, Valek encountered no one. There should be four guards. With no one to ask which direction Alea went, he scanned the floor in both directions, looking for blood splatter. He found a couple drops and followed the trail.

It appeared she was heading to the castle's west exit. Hoping her injury slowed her down, Valek increased his speed. When he reached the hall to the double doors leading outside, he found the four guards that were supposed to be guarding the war room. They now blocked his way.

"No one must pass," they said in unison.

Valek considered. If he waited for the magic to wear off the four guards, Alea would be too far away. If he fought them, she'd escape for sure. He reached for his darts but there were none left. He'd given them all to Ari and Janco.

Well, there were other ways to exit the castle and plenty of windows. Valek turned around and raced to another room and then climbed out the window. Thankfully, the guards took her orders literally and remained behind. The blood was harder to spot on the dark ground outside, but there was only one place for her to go. The west gate. If she reached Castletown, she could blend in and disappear.

Valek questioned the guards at the gate. Did they see anyone? Hear anything? Of course not. He ran all the way to Castletown but didn't see her. Unless she stayed in the castle's complex? No. Her accomplices were caught. Her plans ruined. No way she'd stay.

A cracking crumbling noise sounded right above him. Valek

dove to the side without looking up. The top of a massive brick chimney slammed into the ground where he'd just been standing. Alea's parting shot.

The war room finally lived up to its name. Bodies littered the floor. Bits of ash floated in the smoky air that reeked of blood and burnt hair. The generals huddled in a clump as far from the prone forms as possible.

Ute remained by the Commander's side as Medic Channa rubbed a salve onto his burns. He'd taken off his uniform. Wearing only his sleeveless undershirt and boxers, he endured her ministrations.

"...good thing you keep your hair so short," Channa said. "Otherwise, it'd be gone. Your eyelashes and eyebrows will grow back eventually."

Valek knelt next to Farren and checked her pulse just in case he'd missed her heart. Her skin was cold. From this angle, Valek spotted pools of bright scarlet spreading from under each magician. Someone had killed the other six, saving Valek from the gruesome task. He glanced up and met the Commander's gaze.

"Generals," the Commander said. "We'll reconvene tomorrow morning."

The men bolted, almost tripping over the bodies in their rush to leave. Ute exchanged a glance with Channa before exiting.

"Valek?"

"Yes, sir?"

"Well done. Now go get some sleep, you look beat."

"Yes, sir." It was a good idea, except Valek had to find Ari and Janco.

General Ute waited for him in the hallway. "Thought you would want to know what happened while you were gone."

"I do. Tell me on the way?"

"Sure." She matched his quick pace. "After you left, I fetched the medic despite the Commander's insistence that he was fine. When we returned, the Commander stood over one of the magicians holding a bloody knife. Without warning, he bent over and stabbed the man right in the chest." Ute's hand briefly pressed over her heart. "The other generals were staring at him in horror, and I realized that man wasn't the first magician he'd killed. I'm shocked, too. It's one thing to know magicians are executed when captured in Ixia, but quite another thing to witness it."

"The Commander was making a point."

"Message received. Loud and clear. Although he didn't really need to. Just resisting the magicians' collective magic was impressive."

"That's why Mogkan and Brazell had to use the Criollo," Valek said. "They learned what I've known all along; the Commander is not only strong but stubborn as hell."

Valek reached the stairs leading to the holding cells and Ute followed him down.

"Where are we going?" she asked.

"To check on Ari and Janco." He explained.

"Oh my. I hope they're okay." She broke into a jog.

Valek chased after her. She rounded the corner and stopped in her tracks. "Oh." She covered her mouth with her hand.

With dread rising, Valek looked over her shoulder, bracing for the worse. Ari and Janco each sat in a cell, wearing nothing but their boxers. Laughter escaped Ute's fingers and Valek couldn't help joining her. Their expressions alone...priceless. Relief surged through him, sweeping away all the tension and worry that had collected since learning of Alea's plot. Light-headed, he leaned against the wall.

"Oh, sure. *You* can laugh," Janco said. "*You* didn't endure the absolute humiliation of being controlled by magic, forced to release the prisoners, and strip. Because of course that magician knew I had a set of lock picks hiding in my uniform." He gestured to a third cell where their uniforms had been heaped. Within sight, but out of reach.

"Magic sucks," Ari agreed.

"This one's on me," Valek said as he unlocked the cell doors. "I didn't expect Alea to figure it out so fast."

"I feel *much* better now." Janco's sarcasm thickened.

"No need to apologize if Alea's been captured," Ari said.

"Ah, about that…" He detailed the chase. "I'm pretty sure she won't return."

Janco groaned. "And the others?"

"Dead," Ute said.

"Good," Ari and Janco said in unison.

Valek unlocked the cell that held their clothing. They moved to retrieve them, but Ute was standing in the way.

"Uh, excuse us, General," Janco said.

She shook her head, then stepped back. "Sorry. I was admiring the view."

Janco smirked and rubbed a hand down his sculpted stomach. "Nice, eh?"

But Ute was staring at Ari's chest. "Very."

Despite the attack, the Commander was in high spirits that evening. He poured them both a generous glass of his expensive white brandy. And he wasn't wearing his uniform. Instead, he wore a flannel tunic over loose pajama pants. Valek guessed the soft fabric felt better against his burns.

The Commander settled in his seat. "What happened to Alea?"

Valek detailed her escape. "Bright side, I doubt she'll come to Ixia again."

"I would have preferred it if you'd killed her, but I understand. Alea is a powerful magician. I'm quite pleased that I was able to resist her. Alea's voice sounded in my head, but she had the other seven's magic. It felt like they were holding me underwater and if I didn't agree, didn't give up, I'd drown. I fought the magic and resisted. Nice to know I can. I should thank them for the peace of mind."

"Even though they set your uniform on fire?"

"It worked out."

"How are you feeling?"

"Tender. That salve soothed most of the pain, but in order to take it with me, I had to promise Medic Channa that I'd send for her if I have any trouble breathing."

"She probably wanted you to spend the night in the infirmary. You could have invited her to sleep on your comfy couch."

"I didn't know Alea's status at that time."

"Now you know. Should I send a message to Channa?"

"No. You still look exhausted. Did you rest this afternoon?" Ambrose didn't wait for a response. "Go to bed, Valek. I need you at your best for the meeting in the morning."

He groaned. "Is this a punishment because Alea escaped?"

"No. The generals need to know how to avoid this situation. How to spot a magician. And how to improve their security. We'll be visiting each Military District during the heating season. I want them ready for our inspection." He held his glass up, stopping Valek's reply. "Don't groan again. It was your idea."

"Definitely a punishment."

The meeting wasn't as tedious and frustrating as Valek had expected. The bodies had been collected, the floor scrubbed, and the entire war room cleaned. It smelled of soap and disinfectant. Best of all, it was quiet.

The generals sat around the table and listened to Valek's lecture on magicians. They didn't cry for his dismissal or press for his execution. All the bluster had been scared out of them. Their encounter with the magicians was a wakeup call to the dangers of magic. And just how close Alea had come to taking over Ixia.

General Ute was welcomed and praised for her quick actions during the attack. The generals didn't bicker with each other. Overall, the group had a renewed sense of unity. Of working together against a common enemy. Valek wondered how long it would last.

The Commander called for a break at lunch. Kenda carried the Commander's tray, but she gave Valek a pointed look that promised pain if he didn't explain what had been happening. When he was dismissed that afternoon, Valek stopped in his suite before heading to her office.

"Hello, stranger," she said when he entered. Despite her word choice, it wasn't a friendly greeting.

"I had to keep a low profile, so I didn't tip Alea off to what I planned," he said in his defense.

"I get that, but what about the other challenges we are dealing with? Were you just working on trapping Alea and her friends all this time?"

Actually, he had. Combine a concussion with a complex problem and the need for daily naps… He took a sculpture from his pocket and handed it to her. "I carved this for you."

"Bribery? You think that'll work?" She examined it, turning the thumb-sized dahlia atop a curved stem and leaves. "How did you know dahlias are my favorite flower?"

"You stop to sniff them every time you see one. Even if we're on a mission."

She huffed. "The detail is exquisite. But I'm still annoyed with you."

"I'd expect nothing less. And I did read through Star's file. We don't have enough evidence to put her on trial for murder."

"I thought so. Too bad."

"But *she* doesn't need to know that."

Kenda grinned. "I like the way you think."

An hour later, a knock sounded on Valek's office door. "Come in."

The door opened and two dungeon guards escorted Star to his desk. She stood straight despite the chains linking her wrists and ankles, looking down her sharp nose at him. Her long red hair was snarled with knots and muck splattered her prison gown. Dungeon funk—a fetid odor that clung to all the prisoners—emanated from her. Her gaze shone with defiance. Thin lips were already pressed together, as if she wanted Valek to know he'd get no information from her.

He didn't invite her to sit. "This won't take long, Star." Shuffling through a few papers in a file, he shut it with a snap and added it to a high pile of dossiers on the left side of his desk.

"This meeting is to inform you that you are being charged with murder. Your trial has been scheduled for the end of the cold season." Which was nine months away. Valek glanced at the guards. "You can take her back to her cell."

"Charged with murder?" Star asked. "*I* haven't killed anyone. Plus, you have *no evidence*. I've told you *nothing*."

"Oh, I know. You've been quite uncooperative." He rested his hand on the large pile. "However, your colleagues have been helpful. Very helpful. We have everything we need. Unless you wish to confess, you're irrelevant." And since she craved attention, Valek guessed that comment would produce the most damage.

"You've got nothing. My people are loyal." She sounded confident, but fear lurked in her gaze.

"If that will help you feel better, then you go ahead and believe it." He waved to the guards. "Take her away, she's stinking up my office."

She lurched closer to his desk. "I can't wait nine months. I'll go crazy. Look, I've information they don't have. Drop the murder charge and I'll tell you everything."

If he could trust her, it was a good deal. She'd still go to jail for a long time, but she wouldn't be executed. Except, he'd be an idiot to expect her to tell the truth. "I already know everything. But..." He leaned back as if considering. "We do need a new food taster, and it's a couple months before the next execution is scheduled..."

"I'll do it."

"It's dangerous."

"I don't care."

"All right, I'll check with the Commander. He doesn't like it when one of his loyal people are at risk, and since you'll be on death row eventually, it follows the Code of Behavior. I'll let you know."

This time Star didn't protest when the guards pulled her away. Valek would let her stew for a few days before starting her training.

That evening, the Commander messaged Valek to report to his office. When Valek entered the office, he looked up from his desk.

"Why are you surprised? You asked me to come," Valek said.

"I did. Why..." He sighed and rubbed his brow. "I never realized just how important eyebrows are in non-verbal communication."

Valek bit down on a chuckle as he sat down. "I'll lend you some makeup. You can draw eyebrows on until yours grow back."

"I'm not very artistic. Looking perpetually surprised might be better than appearing like a super villain."

"I'll stop by your suite in the mornings and help. However, I'm sure you didn't send for me to talk about your eyebrows."

"No. I wanted an update on your exploits, and what issues you're dealing with now the magicians have been taken care of."

The report wouldn't take long, since all his focus had been on Alea's plans. "Ari, Janco, and I believe, Maren are in training to join my corps."

"Believe?"

"She hasn't committed, but I think she will. Maren is hard to read, which is why I think she'd be an asset to my team."

"You've been relying on the captains since Brazell's. Are you hoping for them to be your seconds?"

"Yes. I know Janco can be annoying at times, but they're a powerful pair. In fact, I refer to them as the power twins. And I'd like Maren to join us as well."

The Commander gave him a shrewd look. "You're not thinking of retiring, are you?"

"No. I just think if something happens to me—like a chimney falls on my head—you'll need at least three people to replace me." Valek grinned.

"My, aren't we confident today." The Commander *tsked*. "Chimneys aside, what's the next challenge?"

He detailed his plan for Star. "It's the only way we'll find the rest of her organization."

"You're inviting a viper into our midst," the Commander said. "I'll have to watch her closely, or she might slip poison into my food."

"She won't. Star has created a successful business under your leadership. A new commander would be an unknown. Perhaps worse. Her sole focus is going to be escaping and rejoining her people."

"And you will facilitate that escape?"

"Eventually. There needs to be a few failed attempts before she believes she has escaped on her own and wasn't just allowed to escape," Valek said.

"I'm still going to watch her. And speaking of a new commander, who did you appoint?"

Ah, the Commander had figured out Valek wouldn't allow Brazell to be named the Commander's successor. Not when the change had been influenced by magic. "I switched it to General Franis because he's the youngest. Or was. Ute is younger."

"A good choice overall. But I've my eye on another. Time will tell."

"Not me. Please."

"Don't worry. You're not in the running." The Commander waited.

Valek suspected he wanted Valek to ask why not, but as long as he wasn't chosen, he was happy. "Thank fate."

When Star returned to his office three days later, Valek asked the guards to remove her manacles and invited her to sit down. The defiance in her gaze had been replaced by a shrewd look. No doubt already plotting her escape.

He told her all the same things he told Yelena nine months ago. It was a lifetime position, the training could be lethal, no days off, no spouse, no children, no payment for her services. Star would get a room in the castle to sleep but she had to report to the Commander to taste his meals three times a day. Star's gaze sharpened at learning she'd be free to move around the castle.

"And your first lesson starts now." He retrieved the goblet

he'd prepared and set it on the desk in front of Star. "Go on, take a sip."

Star sipped the drink. "Peach juice."

"Now take another sip and roll the liquid around your tongue before swallowing."

She did as instructed, and her eyebrows rose in surprise. "There are also honey and orange flavors."

"Correct. This time, gargle the juice."

Shrugging, she took a mouthful, gargled, and winced as she swallowed. "Spoiled, fermented oranges."

Valek couldn't help being impressed. Most tasters picked up the rotten flavor, but not the fermentation. "The peach juice is laced with a poison called Butterfly's Dust. The only way to detect that poison in a liquid is by gargling it. The foul taste is the poison."

"How much poison did I swallow?"

"Enough to kill you."

She jumped to her feet with a curse. "Is this a joke?"

"No, but don't worry, there's an antidote to Butterfly's Dust."

Sinking back down in relief, she scanned his desk. "Where is it?"

He opened a drawer and pulled out a glass vial filled with a white liquid. "This is the antidote. However, a dose only prevents the poison from killing you. It doesn't cure you. You'll need to visit me every morning for your dose. Skip a morning and you'll be dead by the next."

"Son of a bitch. You tricked me."

"No. I'm ensuring that you won't run away. That you'll report for duty every day. If you commit a crime or an act of treason, you'll be taken to the dungeon to wait for the poison to kill you. Symptoms are severe stomach cramps and nausea followed by uncontrollable vomiting. If your stomach starts to hurt, you're overdue for the antidote."

Actually, it was the "antidote"—a drug called White Fright—

that was in her peach juice. A handy concoction that took a day to work and did indeed cause those symptoms unless another dose was administered. Useful to put a person out of commission for a day. Star would live through the experience, but the longer she ingested White Fright, the harsher her withdrawal would be. As for Butterfly's Dust, it didn't exist.

Star stared at the vial of White Fright.

Valek picked it up. "This contains about two doses. I keep my full supply hidden. Even if you found it, it would eventually run out and you would die."

A knock sounded and Hildred, one of Valek's corps, entered. She wore a housekeeping uniform.

"Hildred will help you get settled," Valek said.

Star reluctantly pulled her attention from the vial.

When she reached Hildred, the agent wrinkled her nose and said, "We'll stop at the baths first."

Right after they left, Kenda entered. "Well?"

"She's smart and has a keen palate."

"Do you want to bet on when she runs away? I give her a week."

"That's too soon. I'll bet a month. Either way, keep an eye on her at all times."

"I've Hildred and Inrick on babysitting duties."

"And at night?"

"Star isn't getting her own room. She's sharing with Amensa."

Amensa was one of his agents. "You're housing her in the hexagon? Is that wise?"

"You know how the saying goes: keep your friends close, and your enemies closer. Besides, Amensa is a very light sleeper and wakes with a blade in each hand. Hard to sneak out when your roommate goes for the throat."

"I need Star alive. At least, until she gives us what we want."

"Oh, don't worry, Amensa hasn't killed anyone, but she'll

scare the crap out of Star, who will quickly learn to keep her ass in bed."

❧

Star's training occupied Valek for the next three weeks. The woman proved to be quick to learn and would play devil's advocate, finding work arounds to various tasting methods and the five S-steps—scan, sniff, sip, swirl, sample. Hildred reported that Star used her time off to familiarize herself with the castle's layout. One time, she even tried to pick the lock on Valek's office door. He had installed three very complex locks and only a few people had the skills to pick them. Yelena was one.

Working with Star was harder than Valek expected. It kept reminding him of Yelena. How her nose would crinkle when she tasted an off flavor, her quick intelligence and flashes of insights. With Yelena, it had been almost a collaborative effort. While with Star, Valek remained on edge as if they sparred.

At the end of each of the poison tasting sessions with Star, Valek's arms would ache to hold Yelena, wishing he'd told her he loved her sooner. Perhaps having more memories of them together would ease his loneliness. Or would it make it worse?

Star was officially declared the food taster at the end of the warm season. Just in time to be added to the list of people who would travel in the Commander's entourage. They would be leaving in a few days, and Valek still had a couple things left to do.

He found Ari and Janco in their suite. Janco sat on an armchair juggling three very sharp-looking knives. Ari was cleaning his broadsword.

"How's the training going?" he asked.

"Boring!" Janco said without looking away from the whirling weapons.

"It goes," Ari said noncommittally.

"Would you like to go on a mission?"

"Ow!" The daggers clattered to the floor and Janco sucked on his finger. "Geez, warn a guy first will ya."

"Of course," Ari answered. "What's the mission?"

Valek explained about the Commander's upcoming tour of all the garrisons and manor houses in Ixia. "We're going to test their defenses. They'll be informed in advance, making it a bit more challenging."

"Ho boy!" Janco bounded from his chair and bounced around the room. "Finally, a challenge! This is gonna be fun."

"How many agents are you bringing?" Ari asked.

"There will be six of us on the testing team. The other three are Maren, Hildred, and Inrick."

"Maren decided to join your corps?" Ari asked.

"Yes. I'm glad to have her."

"Good choices. I approve," Janco said.

"Thanks," Valek replied dryly. "I may have done this before."

"Yes, but this time"—Janco spread his arms wide—"This time you have us by your side. Big difference."

"I'm aware."

The Commander's entourage consisted of fifty soldiers of his elite squad for protection, Valek and his team of five agents, Star, and Adviser Dema. Valek, the Commander, and Dema rode horses, but the others walked. They headed west a few hours after dawn on day two of the heating season. General Rasmussen of MD-7 would be their first stop, and then Dinno in MD-8. They'd loop around mostly clockwise with a jig west to MD-4, then end at MD-5. That would give General Ute plenty of time to prepare.

"Are you sure you don't want us to scout the route?" Ari asked Valek.

"The new guys in the squad aren't very good," Janco added. "Plus, it's boring to do nothing but walk all day."

"Don't worry," Valek said. "I've a special job for you."

"Ooohhh. You say the sweetest things."

Valek explained what they needed to do.

Janco rubbed his hands together in glee. "Should we take bets?"

Valek left them to it as he spurred Onyx to the head of the column. He wasn't expecting trouble during this trip, but just in case the scouts missed something, Valek scanned for anything out of the ordinary. The trees were all dressed in bright green leaves and the underbrush provided plenty of hiding spots. Cloaks wouldn't be needed during the day unless it rained. During this time of the year, rainstorms would form over the Sunset Ocean and blow eastward, carrying the salty tang of the sea.

No matter how well-trained or physically fit everyone was, it was slow going. They had to stop while it was still daylight to set up camp. Major Granten and his soldiers handled all the construction and cooking. Only the Commander and Valek had their own tents, the rest shared. Star was assigned to Hildred's tent. The agent reported that Star never connected her to the housekeeper who showed her around on her first day.

Each night, Valek walked the perimeter after dinner. On the third night, a storm threatened. When Valek was halfway around the camp, big, fat, and cold raindrops splatted on his forehead. A couple at first and then more and more as the storm unleashed a torrent. Valek abandoned his task and hustled for his tent.

Hildred intercepted him. "Star's gone."

"She took the antidote?"

"Yes. She stole the bottle from your tent during dinner and headed southeast." Hildred put her hand up to protect her eyes from the rain. "Do you want me and Inrick to chase her down?"

"No need."

"Are you going to follow her, then? Find her accomplices?"

"No time right now. Don't worry, she'll be back."

"But that bottle has at least two months' worth of her antidote."

"It appears so."

Hildred groaned. "Are you always one step ahead of everyone?"

Valek grinned despite the rain pouring down his face. "Not always. Sometimes I'm two steps ahead."

"And so modest about it, too."

Star caught up to them the next afternoon. Hugging her stomach and retching, she begged for the antidote.

He handed her a pipette filled with White Fright. "Not a fan of spoiled goat's milk?"

She downed the liquid. When she caught her breath, she told him exactly what he could do with his goat's milk. It didn't sound pleasant.

"That's not nice." He filled up the pipette again. This time he squeezed the contents out onto the ground. Then did it a second time. "Whoops. That's a shame. I hope you'll have enough to last the trip."

This time she bit down on her nasty remark.

"You are now under tent arrest because of this stunt," he said. "When we stop for the night, you're only allowed to come out to taste the Commander's dinner."

Star's second escape happened three nights later. The entourage would reach General Rasmussen's manor house the next day.

When Valek seemed unconcerned, Hildred asked, "More goat's milk?"

"No. She's got the genuine antidote."

Hildred pursed her lips but didn't ask the question in her gaze. Instead, she scanned the camp. Valek waited.

"Ha!" she said. "Ari and Janco aren't here. Can scouts also track?"

"Yes. Although, they've been watching her so no need to track."

She deflated. "That's my job. Except, I haven't been doing it well."

"You're doing fine. I've been giving her some opportunities, and she knows you're watching her. While she has no clue of Ari and Janco's interest. Until now."

Ari appeared from the woods. He carried a screaming Star over his right shoulder. Her ankles had been manacled along with her wrists. They were fastened behind her back. Janco had his fingers in his ears.

"Should have brought a gag," Janco said when they reached Valek and Hildred.

"Where do you want her?" Ari asked.

Valek pointed to a tree trunk. "Secure her there for tonight."

Janco took the bottle of White Fright from his pocket. "She seemed really concerned that this didn't break." He pretended to fumble it and Star stopped yelling.

"Huh. Should have thought of that before. Here." He handed it to Valek.

In the morning, Valek squirted four doses of White Fright onto the ground, before giving Star her dose. "Your actions have consequences. No more sleeping in a tent. You'll spend every night secured outside unless we're at one of the manor houses or garrisons. Then you'll spend all your free time in a jail cell."

"How long?" she asked.

"Until I say so."

Testing the defenses of Rasmussen's manor house and garrison turned out to be a fun challenge. The team learned what worked and what didn't. They uncovered each of their strengths and weaknesses. Maren even learned the fine art of being a fake damsel-in-distress from Janco. They performed better together than he'd expected.

On the way north to MD-8, Valek gave Star another opportunity to escape, and she took it. Ari and Janco had orders to let her go further this time before capturing her.

They brought her back in the morning.

Valek dumped six doses onto the ground. "I don't know if this is going to last." He clucked his tongue. "All that effort to train you. What a waste of my time."

After that, Star stopped trying to escape. Either due to the punishments or because they were getting further and further away from Castletown.

His team spent the rest of the heating season and thirty-five days of the hot season testing defenses. It was equal parts exhilarating, exhausting, thrilling, boring, invigorating, and tedious.

MD-5 had been their last stop, and General Ute continued to impress the Commander. Overall, he was pleased with the results of the tour and energized despite the three-long months of travel.

Everyone whooped when they spotted the odd-shaped castle in the distance. Valek almost wept with joy when he reached his own bed. He face-planted and didn't move for twelve hours.

Three days later, he had the guards bring Star to his office in the afternoon. She'd been staying in the holding cells between tastings.

"Sit down, Star," he said.

She sat and glared at him, which she'd been doing ever since her third failed escape attempt. He'd made her sweat the last week of their trip, by scraping the bottom of the bottle for her antidote. Not that there had been any real danger of running out. White Fright was brewed from a common weed that grew throughout Ixia.

"You're getting your freedom back. If you try to escape again, you will become a permanent resident of the holding cells. Understand?"

"Yes."

"Good. You're dismissed."

She slammed the door when she left. Valek was curious what she'd try to do next. Hildred and Inrick would keep an eye on her.

He remembered Yelena's attempts. She'd picked the locks of his office to find his stash of White Fright. And she'd spent hours in the castle's library, seeking a book that might have the recipe for the antidote. Those had been in the early days. When Fourth Magician Irys Jewelrose offered to help her escape to Sitia, Yelena had refused. She had wanted to protect the Commander and stop Brazell and Mogkan at the cost of her own freedom.

He longed to breath in her scent. To have a conversation about something trivial, like what side of the bed she preferred to sleep on. Or her favorite season.

Yearning burned in his heart. But then it increased to a painful intensity and spread. Valek held out his arms. Had a magician set his clothes on fire? Sweat collected and dripped. An invisible force yanked on his heart. He pressed his hands over his sternum, but the pressure remained.

A cloud of bright light formed on the other side of his desk. It hovered in midair. The force pulled him to his feet and reeled him toward the center of the swirl. He squinted. Something inside...no, someone... "Yelena?"

Panic creased her face, and her green eyes were wide with fear. "Help," she cried.

CHAPTER 12

alek didn't hesitate. He stepped closer to the cloud of light and warped his arms around it. He pulled Yelena to his chest. "Anything, love," he whispered and allowed the force, allowed Yelena, to hide inside his heart.

The pressure of magic dug into his skin, twisting, and pushing to get to Yelena. He imagined his immunity. Imagined it resembling an impenetrable wall around them, protecting them from the onslaught. He poured every bit of strength into the imaginary stones and endured the attack all the while holding his love close.

Time blurred. The room spun. The attacker was in the Magician's Keep with Yelena. They were determined and strong. Valek proved stronger, and the assault eventually stopped. Relief, love, and gratitude pulsed in his heart before Yelena faded away. Suddenly bereft, he stumbled. His legs melted underneath him, and he collapsed to the floor.

He woke hours later. His office was pitch dark. Groaning, Valek sat up. Every muscle ached as if he'd fought an entire squad and lost every match. He staggered to his feet and fumbled to light a lantern. Once lit, he rubbed his hands over his face and smelled lavender.

Yelena! Somehow, she'd appeared in his office. Had needed his help. She was in trouble! He grabbed the lantern and raced through the castle, encountering no one. The corridors had the abandoned air of late night or very early morning. The guards at the entrance to his and the Commander's apartments blinked sleepily at him.

"What time is it?" he asked.

"About four hours into our shift, sir," Dagon answered. "Replacements should be coming soon."

The Commander wouldn't be up for another two hours. Valek debated waking him. Instead, he entered his suite and packed a bag. If he rode Onyx all the way to the Sitian Citadel, he could be there in two and a half days. He grabbed his Sitian clothing, his kit of disguises, a couple extra daggers, and two sets of lock picks.

His surge of energy sputtered and died. Valek staggered to the couch. Sunrise was in an hour; he'd just rest until then.

The bright sunlight woke him. It hung high in the sky. Valek cursed. When he stood, a wave of dizziness swelled. He couldn't remember the last time he ate or drank anything. Shouldering his pack, he stopped at the kitchen for a meal and to load up on travel rations. Then he headed to the Commander's office.

"Come in," the Commander said. "Ah, Valek. Where were you last night?" He eyed the pack.

"Yelena's in trouble, I'm going to the Citadel, I'll be back as soon as I can." The words rushed out in one breath.

"Hold on. How do you know she's in trouble or even at the Citadel?"

"She…visited me. Or her magic reached me from the Magician's Keep."

"But magic doesn't—"

"Apparently hers *does*."

"All right. What happened when you connected?"

"There was an attack." He explained it as best that he could. "Must have been a very powerful magician."

"Could it have been an exercise? Yelena is learning how to use her magic."

Could it? Valek considered. "No. Yelena was frightened and asked for help."

"All right. What about when the attack stopped? Was Yelena still scared?"

No. She'd been relieved and grateful. He sagged onto a chair. "I may have overreacted."

"May?" The Commander smiled. "Let's look at this logically. She's in the Magician's Keep and they're training her. They'd want her to be successful and they would protect her. Perhaps it was an exercise done during stressful, realistic, conditions, like some of our military exercises. I'm assuming by your reaction that she wasn't scared after you helped her. If she needed to be rescued, I'd think she would have let you know."

All valid points. Yet the desire to see her again—to know for sure that she was okay—thrummed in his veins.

"Plus, if she reached you once, she could do so again," the Commander continued.

True. All true. Suddenly exhausted, Valek wilted.

"I'd let you go if Star wasn't plotting something. You know she'll take advantage of your absence. Send a message to your agents in the Citadel to check on Yelena, for our peace of mind."

"Our?"

"Yes. Our."

Valek smiled. "You mean underneath all that ice you actually have a heart?"

"Surprising, I know. But it's top secret."

"As always, *all* your secrets are safe with me."

The Commander's gaze held weight, as if he tried to figure out what exactly Valek had meant.

Before he could question him, Valek saluted and left. He stopped in Kenda's office.

"Rough night?" she asked.

"I've had better." He explained what he needed.

"What type of information are you looking for? What she's doing? Who she's associating with? Her schedule?"

"None of those. I just need to know she's well. That no one is targeting her or harming her."

"And if there are people after her?"

Kill them all. He took a steadying breath. "Provide assistance."

"Yes, sir."

Valek returned to his suite to unpack. He considered the problem with Star. If Yelena called for help again, nothing would stop him from going to Sitia. Nothing. The Commander had made a good point about Star taking advantage— He paused as the solution to his problem materialized. Valek laughed.

"You're back," Kenda said. "The messenger just left."

"I've figured out a way to predict when Star will bolt again." Well, the Commander had.

"Do tell."

"I'll leave for a mission. She won't be able to resist the temptation."

"And this mission?"

"To wait for her to escape."

Kenda considered. "She has been practicing lock picking. The timing will have to be right, though. Too soon and she won't have the skills." She drummed her fingers on the table. "I'd give her ten days."

"What if we keep the antidote in your office? It would make sense because you'll have to give it to her while I'm gone."

"Then a week."

"All right. We can start dropping hints about my trip a few days before I supposedly leave."

"Where are you supposedly going?"

"Back to MD-5 to help General Ute with a problem."

It was business as usual for the next seven days, except for the wonderful day a message arrived that Yelena was well and appeared to be enjoying her time at the Magician's Keep. Valek rested his head in his hands as the crushing weight lifted from his shoulders, and he could finally draw a deep breath.

On the forty-seventh day of the hot season, Valek, Ari, Janco, and Maren mounted horses and headed east to MD-5. During the short ride from the castle complex, Valek learned a few things. One, Maren had never been on a horse before, and two, Janco's reflexes were far faster than Valek had expected. When Maren was bounced from her saddle, Janco managed to scoop her up before she hit the ground.

Once they were out of sight of the castle complex's wall, they turned south and looped back to the west. No doubt Star would head for Castletown. She'd need supplies and money. Valek had left a bottle of White Fright with Kenda to give Star her antidote each morning. It had enough to cover three weeks.

They took turns watching the west gate, while they camped in the Snake Forest. During the down time, Janco taught Maren how to ride a horse.

"…my heels *are* down, you dolt," Maren said. "My back *is* straight. Are you blind?"

"Grab the horse's mane if you're going to fall," Janco shouted. "It doesn't hurt the horse. I can't keep catching you. You're not light— Ow! What did you do that for?"

Valek tuned their bickering out. It was much quieter when Janco was on watch. That evening, Ari returned before the end of his shift.

"Star's on the move," Ari said. "She headed straight for Castletown like we figured. I trailed her to a house on the southern edge of town. Trevar's watching the place now."

Valek had assigned Trevar to Castletown for this exact scenario. The young man was very familiar with the city. "Is there a back entrance?"

"Not that I saw."

"All right, time to move."

While Janco and Maren took the horses to a stable in town, Valek followed Ari to the house. They joined Trevar. He'd been watching it from a shadow across the street.

Trevar gestured to the building. "That's an old smugglers' hideout." Then he pointed to a house at the end of the street, which was almost pressed up against the forest. "There's a tunnel to that house, which has a direct exit into the forest."

"Shouldn't you be there instead?" Ari asked in alarm.

"No need. Adrik is watching."

"Adrik? I don't remember assigning him to this mission," Valek said in his flat tone.

"This town is full of hidden entrances, tunnels, and fake fronts. I figured I'd need backup. And I did." He flashed Valek a grin.

"Next time, clear it with me first. *If* there is a next time."

Trevar's grin faded. "Yes, sir."

"Show Ari where the exit is. Then take Adrik and go to the Silver Stirrup Stables and tell Janco and Maren where we are. After that, go to the safe house."

Trevar sighed. "Yes, sir. This way, Ari. Try not to make any loud noises." Trevar moved deeper into the shadows.

Ari frowned but didn't move.

"Shouldn't you be following him?" Valek asked.

"Please. He's making enough of a racket; I know right where he is."

"That sounded like a Janco boast."

Ari grinned. "It's not boasting when it's true." Unlike Trevar, Ari melted into the shadows.

Valek focused on the building across the street. It was an unremarkable three-story structure that could pass for either a residence or a place of business. Like the others on the street, it stood alone. Lantern light peeked from the slits in the curtains on the ground floor windows, but otherwise, there wasn't any activity.

Janco suddenly appeared at Valek's elbow. "Do we need the puppy dogs on this mission?" he asked, referring to Trevar and Adrik.

"Yes. I want two watchers on each exit at all times. Besides, Trevar knew about the tunnel and back exit. He's been useful."

Janco harrumphed.

Star stayed at the house for two days before leaving with five others early on the third morning. They slipped out the back entrance and headed southwest through the Snake Forest. Janco had been on duty with Trevar. He sent the young man to alert Valek and the others while Janco followed Star's group.

Valek and Ari were in the safe house resting when Trevar, Adrik, and Maren arrived.

Clearly annoyed at being sent away, Trevar related the story. This was what they'd been waiting for.

"Trevar and Adrik, report back to Kenda," Valek ordered.

"Give her the address of the house, she'll know what to do. The rest of us will follow Star."

"But we can help," Trevar protested. "We're not—"

"Goons?" Ari supplied.

"Uh. No, no. It's just... We're quiet. Unobtrusive. Light on our feet. We..."

Valek waited.

Trevar sighed. "Yes, sir." He and Adrik grabbed their bags and left the safe house.

"Did he just call me fat?" Ari asked.

Maren laughed. "Oh, yes, he did."

"He's still young," Valek said. "Wait until he's learned how to fight. Then you can show him the error of his ways."

"Then he'll know you and Janco really are a couple of goons," Maren said.

"You're not helping," Valek mock growled.

"How about this? Ari can fight Trevar without a shirt on, that way he won't be accused of being fat. But you'll need to invite General Ute to watch the match; I hear she has a thing for the captain."

Ari turned bright red. "Shouldn't we be going?"

Amused, Valek thought about the growing rivalry between Trevar and Adrik, and Ari and Janco as they hurried to catch up. Newbies verses the old pros. He suppressed a chuckle. Calling Ari and Janco, who were twenty-six and twenty-eight, old was an exaggeration. However, they had more experience and skills than the two young bucks. They deserved more respect. After dealing with Star, Valek would set up a training exercise for all of them.

They followed Star's group to a small city in MD-7 named Crooked Nook. It sat just outside the northern edge of the Snake Forest. Not only did Star have a residence there, but offices and a warehouse full of black market goods. Janco hung out in the local pubs and discovered most of the town patrol were on her payroll. Lovely.

"Are we going to do a raid on these places?" Janco asked one night.

"Not yet. I want to see where else she goes," Valek replied.

Star then traveled west along the Snake Forest to Sectown in MD-7. Even though the town was half the size of Crooked Nook, her operation was similarly impressive.

"Wow," Janco said, returning from the pub. "She practically owns this entire place."

"It's quite the operation," Maren said. "Did you know all this was going on in this part of MD-7?" she asked Valek.

"No. I don't have enough agents to place in every single town in Ixia. I usually rely on the town patrol to alert me if there's any trouble."

"Well, there's the hole in the loop," Janco said. "All these little forgotten villages are close to the Sitian border. A perfect hiding spot for Star's operations."

The man wasn't wrong.

"It's a loophole," Maren corrected.

"That's what I said."

After Sectown, Star headed south with only one person. They crossed into Sitia late at night. She traveled to a small village in the Featherstone Clan's lands, close to the border, called Robin's Nest. The Citadel was only a few days southeast of their location. Valek could rent a horse and be with Yelena in three days. The temptation to let his companions finish the job dug its claws into his heart.

They changed into Sitian clothes and blended in with the citizens. It was an open secret that Robin's Nest was used as a staging area for black market goods and was a sanctuary for those who had escaped Ixia. The amount of people leaving Ixia had slowed to a trickle over the years since the Commander's takeover. And they were mostly magicians. But it appeared the route from Robin's Nest to Sectown was well traveled in both directions.

Janco returned from his nightly reconnaissance of the local taverns.

"What did you learn?" Valek asked.

"Their ale is terrible. They put a lot of pops in their brews. Yuck."

"It's hops," Ari said.

"Whatever. It's terrible."

"I meant about Star."

"Oh yeah, Star has an operation here as well. Mostly just buying goods, although there are a few assassins hanging out, looking for jobs."

Valek wondered if he would recognize any of them.

"And there's speculation that Star's sick," Janco added. "How much of her antidote did she steal?"

"Enough that she shouldn't be feeling any pain yet. Why do the locals think she's sick?"

"I think she visited the healer in town. Sounds like he's pretty powerful and busy. This place is filled with mostly criminals. I had a guy challenge me just because I looked at him. I think if you put a detailed tattoo of an owl in flight in the middle of your forehead, you should be used to people staring at it."

"You didn't—"

"No. That would have attracted too much attention. I apologized and bought the guy one of their yucky ales. *Pah.*"

Ari and Valek exchanged a look. Progress.

"Sounds like Star's trying to use magic to counteract the Butterfly's Dust poison," Maren said. "Will it work?"

No one knew about the Butterfly's Dust ruse except Valek and Yelena. And he planned to keep it that way. "It shouldn't." Unless the healer figured out the cause of her symptoms.

"Not exactly a ringing endorsement," Janco said.

"If the magic works, then Star will remain in Sitia because if she's found alive in Ixia, she'll be executed," Valek said.

"She's cocky," Ari said. "Maybe she's thinking we'll assume she's dead after the antidote runs out, and then she can return to Ixia without worry."

"Good point. Let's see what she does once her supply dwindles down to the point when she has to return to the castle for more."

"Who wants to bet she'll be too stubborn to return and dies here?" Janco asked.

"Not me," Ari said. "She's too smart. She'll go back to the castle and wait for another opportunity to escape."

And then there was a fourth scenario. That she survived the withdrawal symptoms of White Fright. Valek preferred that the magician heal her than for that fourth possibility to come to pass.

A day later, Star and her companion headed northeast. They traveled light and didn't take many breaks.

"I think she's in a panic," Janco said.

Valek hoped so. As they drew closer and closer to the castle, his confidence grew. They all celebrated when she surrendered at the west gate of the castle complex.

"That was so much fun!" Janco said in delight. "Our escapee returns home without us having to do a thing. And now we know all her hidey holes. Valek, you are a genius."

"Does it make up for being locked in a cell almost naked?" he asked.

"Yes! All is forgiven. You can stop angsting over it."

"Thanks."

"Now, now. No need to be sarcastic."

That night in the Commander's suite, Valek updated him on the fourteen-day mission.

"Star has no idea you were following her?" Ambrose asked.

"I'm pretty sure she didn't know."

"That's wonderful. Are you going to tell her?"

"No. It will be quite a shock if she escapes again and discovers her entire organization has been destroyed."

"Where is she now?"

"In the holding cells, where she will remain when not required to taste your meals."

"But you'll relent at some point."

"Of course. Otherwise, it wouldn't be any fun."

Ambrose just shook his head.

"I'm waiting for a few more agents to return from the field before we raid her places," Valek said.

"Don't worry about that. I'll send my troops," Ambrose said. "This is a city-wide problem and a squad of fifty soldiers makes more of a point than a small attack unit."

True. "Too bad you can't invade Robin's Nest."

"It's off limits to me. But your corps—"

"Can create some difficulty crossing the border."

"Exactly." Ambrose sipped his drink. "Do you want in on the action in Crooked Nook and Sectown?"

"No. Just make sure I get all the information they collect."

"I will. What's next on your to-do list?"

"I'm going to run some training exercises in the Snake Forest."

"Sounds like fun."

"Oh, it will be."

~

A gentle breeze shook the leaves of the Snake Forest, sweeping away the humidity for a little while. It carried the sweet scent of living green and bird song. Early morning sunlight flickered through the trees. It was only the third day of the cooling season, but the afternoon promised to be warm.

Valek scanned the faces of the two teams assembled around him. The old pro team of Ari, Janco, Maren, and Kimette—another soldier who recently joined Valek's corps. And the young buck team of Trevar, Adrik, Wilma, and Yegor.

"This is a simple exercise," Valek said. He pointed to a tent in a small clearing. "I will act as the Commander and be inside that tent. Your goal is to either kidnap me or protect me. If I'm kidnapped, the protection team turns into a rescue team. The exercise ends at dawn. If I'm still kidnapped, the protection team loses. If I'm in the tent at dawn the protection team wins. Then you'll switch sides, and we'll do this again. I've marked the boundary of the exercise zone with yellow ribbons. Neither team is allowed outside the zone. Questions?"

"What can we expect from you? How active will you be?" Ari asked.

"I'll stay in the tent so I don't give anything away. I will resist if possible and call for help. If there's a chance for me to escape, I'll take it."

"Will you be armed?" Trevar asked.

"Not for this drill. And you can't use weapons against each other. No knocking anyone unconscious, either. This is more of a mental exercise."

"Can we call to you to check that you're still in the tent?" Adrik asked.

"Yes. And you can also look inside if I don't reply."

"What about having one of us in there with you?" Wilma asked.

"No, the Commander would never allow that." Valek waited but there were no other questions. "All right, let's get started." Valek pulled a gold coin from his pocket and flicked it into the air. "Janco, call it."

"Diamond."

Valek caught the coin, flipped it over onto the back of his hand, and revealed it. The side with the map of Ixia on it was facing up. The other side had an image of Mother's Heart, the red diamond that funded the takeover.

"Ixia," Maren said to Janco. "Everyone knows to pick Ixia."

"Trevar, it's your choice. Protection or kidnapping?"

He consulted with his teammates. "Protection."

"All right. The kidnapping team must wait an hour for the protection team to get into place."

As Ari, Janco, Maren, and Kimette disappeared into the woods, Valek crawled into the tent. It was the one the Commander used. It had a few perks, like a cot with extra thick bedding and pillows. Valek's pack leaned against the center post. It contained everything he needed for the next two days.

Trevar squatted down and peered inside. "Any advice?"

"Remember what you learned in class."

"Thanks," he said dryly, then closed the flap.

Valek rummaged in his pack for a book. He stretched out on the cot and planned to spend the day reading. An occasional shout, shuffle of feet, or a call to confirm he remained inside the tent would interrupt him, but otherwise, he enjoyed his first day off in...forever.

The light started to fade and Valek debated if he should light the lantern. Suddenly, a ripping sound emanated from the back of the tent. Before he could stand, Ari and Janco rushed inside, grabbed his ankles, and yanked him to the ground. In what seemed like a rehearsed set of moves, they shoved a wad of something minty into his mouth, rolled him onto his stomach, and secured his hands and feet.

"Sorry, boss," Janco whispered before they dragged him through the hole in the tent.

Ari hefted him over his shoulder and then they took off at a jog. Valek lifted his head. None of the members of his protection team were in sight. He tried to struggle, but Ari had him in a tight grip. It wasn't long before he was dumped onto the ground.

"Awww, you brought us a present all wrapped up. How sweet," Maren said.

"Anyone see you?" Kimette asked.

"No," Janco said with a laugh. "They're out chasing rabbits."

"All of them?" Her tone was dubious.

"Yep. Lured the last puppy dog with a fake call for help. Adrik didn't bother checking with Valek before he raced off to the rescue." More laughter.

At least they were having fun.

"All right let's string him up," Maren said.

A rather alarming sentence. Valek tried to roll away.

"Oh, no you don't," Ari picked him up again.

They wrapped vines around his chest and under his arms, and then hauled him into the treetops. He'd be impressed if he wasn't worried about falling. They maneuvered him onto a sturdy limb of the tree, sitting him down with his back resting against a thick trunk. The vines around his wrists were cut. He struggled to break free, but they latched onto his arms and secured them to the trunk. A mercy, otherwise, it would become very painful leaning on them. Then they wrapped the vines around each of his legs so he couldn't move. Gagged and tied tight, he wasn't going anywhere.

"Sorry, boss," Janco said again. "This isn't going to be a pleasant night for you. We can't have you alerting the puppies, but we found you the perfect spot. Look." He pointed. The clearing was visible beyond the trees. "You can watch the puppies chase their tails when they discover you're gone. No need to thank me now."

"Janco," Ari warned.

"Just having a little fun."

"We'll come check on you from time to time if we can," Ari said. "Two blinks for yes, one for no. Understand?"

Valek blinked twice.

"Anything hurt?" Ari watched him closely.

The gag tasted like a wad of…spearmint leaves, and there seemed to be a vine wrapped around his head, securing it. Valek stretched his lips and cheeks, testing the gag. It didn't hurt, but it was damn uncomfortable. He squirmed. Or he tried, but nothing bit into his skin. He blinked once.

"Janco spent time we really didn't have picking the spearmint," Maren said. "He acts all tough, but he's really a—"

Janco held a hand up and they all went silent. "Time to go," Janco whispered.

They disappeared with just a slight rustle of leaves. Valek gazed at the tent with longing. His pack full of food and water was still inside. And instead of sleeping on the nice comfortable cot, he was tied to a tree. He could hope for a rescue, but the kidnapping team played it pretty smart. Good thing it was early enough in the season so it wouldn't get too cold tonight.

The protection team ran into the clearing, calling his name. With a cry of alarm, Trevar found the ripped fabric. Valek would have to replace the tent, or the Commander would squawk. The foursome argued and blamed each other before Adrik thought to check for tracks. The light was fading, so they'd better hurry.

Yegor found the boot prints Ari and Janco had left behind. Valek wondered if Ari and Janco were giving the puppy dogs a sporting chance, as the tracks led right to the base of Valek's tree. He yelled. Well, he tried. All that came out was a pathetic, muffled groan.

"Something happened here," Yegor said right below Valek. "Either Adviser Valek tried to escape, or they changed directions, going deeper into the forest."

Look up! Look up! Valek tried to lean forward. The vines had no give. None.

"Okay, let's think this through," Trevar said, taking charge. "Wilma, you scouted the area around the tent. Did you find any places that would be a good hiding spot?"

"A couple."

"All right. We stay in teams. Adrik and Yegor guard the tent in case Valek escapes on his own and returns. I'll go with Wilma to search those places."

"Do you want a lantern? There's one in the tent."

"No, they'll see us coming. The moon will be up soon, hopefully that will give us enough light. But light it so Valek can find the tent."

Valek approved of Trevar's orders.

"Take a long stick," Adrik said. "Valek's dressed in his black uniform. He could be tied to a log, and you could walk right by him in the darkness. Poke at every big shadow."

Another good idea. They dispersed. The lantern was lit and Valek had nothing to do except stare at the tiny flame and wonder why he thought this exercise would be fun. As the hours dragged on, Valek dozed on and off.

Janco visited him from time to time, ensuring he was well and bringing updates about the 'clueless puppy dogs.' He also apologized for the gag again.

"I hate those things." He shuddered. "My cousins decided to 'shut me up for good' once and ambushed me, hog-tied me, gaged me, and tossed me into a closet. My mother didn't find me for a day." The leaves shook again. "Bright side, spearmint is much better than dirty socks."

Sometime during the long night, Valek dreamed Yelena was in trouble. She shouted for his help. A large serpent chased her through a thick forest. Fear energized him and he suddenly had a sword in hand, but he couldn't cut the vines fast enough. They twined around his arms, legs, torso, and neck, yanking his sword from his hand. Ensnared and helpless, he watched as the snake caught up to Yelena, wove around her leg and bit her thigh. She screamed. He thrashed in his bindings but couldn't reach her.

Pain in his arms and shoulders woke him. His heart galloped in his chest and sweat soaked his uniform. Gasping around the now very soggy gag, Valek hoped the nightmare hadn't been real; hadn't been Yelena reaching for him to help. If so, he'd failed her. Dawn couldn't come soon enough.

When the first rays of sunlight lit the forest, it revealed the dispirited protection team sitting around the tent. Soon enough, Ari and the others materialized from the forest.

Trevar hopped to his feet. "Where's Valek? We couldn't find him anywhere within the exercise zone. You must have cheated."

"Cheated!" Janco reached for his sword, grabbing only air. "Why you, little, pipsqueak, upstart—I'm gonna make puppy dog shish kabobs out of all of you."

Ari put a meaty hand on his partner's shoulder. "That's enough, Janco."

"But, but, but," he spluttered.

"Not now."

"Promise?"

Ari turned to Trevar. "Walk us through what you found."

Trevar led them to the trail. "We lost him here. No signs of him in the forest in *any* direction."

"Are you sure?"

"Of course. We. Checked. *Every.* Direction."

Maren grabbed Janco around the waist, stopping him from punching Trevar. Valek would be amused but his muscles were cramping, and his bladder was about to burst.

"Even up? That's a direction," Ari said mildly.

Four faces peered up. All Valek could do was lift his

eyebrows when they spotted him. Four groans sounded in unison.

"Janco."

"On it." He climbed up and removed Valek's gag. Then cut the vines around his body. "You, okay?"

"I'm fine."

"Need help getting down?"

Probably, but Valek didn't want the young pups to feel worse than they did for failing to protect him. "No, thank you." Even though his muscles shook, and the lack of food and water made him lightheaded, Valek finally reached the ground.

He saw to his immediate needs and then gathered everyone around. "I think the biggest lesson of yesterday's exercise was to not forget to look up. I hide in the ceilings all the time because no one looks up. As agents, you need to think through all the possibilities."

"Yes, sir," they said.

Trevar hung his head and wouldn't meet Valek's gaze.

"All right, what else did you learn?"

They listed their errors. At least they recognized them. Ari added a few more to their list. When they were done, Valek grabbed his pack and led the two teams east to another tent a couple miles away.

"This is a new exercise area. The boundaries are marked with red ribbons. Again, no one is allowed outside the zone. Kidnappers give the protection team at least an hour to prepare."

Valek crawled into the tent. This one was his and not nearly as nice as the Commander's. He downed a water skin and ate a couple sticks of jerky. Then pushed up the sleeves of his uniform and inspected his arms. Raw abrasions stripped his skin. That had been quite the nightmare last night. He smoothed the material out and laid down on his bedroll.

Thoughts about Yelena swirled in his mind. Where was she?

What was she doing? Was she safe? He remembered their last night together. His body ached for her touch. All he wanted right now was to hold her again. And just like that, she was there in his heart. Yet, he saw her sitting in bed. Her brow was creased in concern as she stared at him.

You need help, love? he asked.

I need you. I need love. I need energy. I need you.

I can't come. It hurt to say those words. *You already have my love. But I can give you my strength.*

No! You'll be helpless for days!

Had they shared the nightmare from last night? At least she wasn't injured. Just exhausted. *I'll be fine. The power twins are with me. They'll protect me.* He peeked out the tent and, sure enough, they both stood nearby.

Good luck, love. Valek poured all his energy into his heart and pushed it toward her. There was a resistance, like he was trying to move a big boulder. Doubling his effort, he tried again, and it flowed from him and filled her heart. She smiled as the tired lines around her green eyes disappeared. Knowing that he'd helped rejuvenate her, Valek relaxed. Darkness rushed in.

CHAPTER 13

His eyelids were parted, allowing bright light to stab into his brain.

Medic Channa peered at him. "Ah, there you are." Then she checked his other eye. "I don't think it's due to the concussion."

His eyelids slammed closed as soon as she released them. He tried to open them. To move. To speak. But he had zero energy to do anything other than breathe.

"Tell me what happened," she ordered.

"He was fine yesterday morning," Ari said. "We checked on him at lunch and he was passed out. We couldn't rouse him. We thought the other team had used sleeping potion on him."

"Why?"

"We were doing an exercise. It made sense at the time. But they didn't use it, and we didn't find out until this morning."

"Is he allergic to spearmint?" Janco asked worriedly. "Did I kill him?"

Valek summoned a bit of strength. "No. I'm...okay."

"You don't look okay," Channa said.

"Tired. Gave...my all." And would have given Yelena more if he had it.

"What did he do before yesterday?"

Ari explained about tying him in the tree. "He climbed down on his own."

"That explains the welts." She pushed his sleeve up.

Valek couldn't stop her.

"Holy Snow Cats! Why didn't he say anything?" Janco cried.

"You had gagged him."

"Yes, but I asked every hour if he was okay. Two blinks for yes. He always blinked twice. Did I kill him?"

"My fault," Valek said.

Channa sat back on her heels. "Is there anything I can do?"

"Need sleep."

"Okay, we'll make a gurney and carry you."

"No! I...stay here." The last thing he needed was for everyone to see him so debilitated. The challenges would never end.

"Are you in pain?"

"No. Need Ari...Janco. Rest...can...go."

"Nice try, but I'm not leaving you. The three of us will stay here until you're recovered. Okay?"

"Okay."

It took him another day to gain enough strength to stand. By day four, he had the energy to hike to the castle with Ari, Janco, and Channa.

On the trip back, Valek asked Ari, "Was I kidnapped?"

"No. The pups never got close."

"That should help adjust their attitudes toward you."

"They want a rematch. They claimed you being injured was our fault and it wasn't a fair exercise."

"I'll have a chat with them."

"Oh no," Janco said. "We want that rematch. No one, and I mean *no one,* calls us cheaters and gets away with it."

Valek said, "Perhaps next time, I'll mix up the teams."

"Why, for the love of sand, would you do *that?*" Janco sounded mortified.

"Because sometimes puppy dogs need to learn how to behave from the big dogs."

"Big dogs! I like!" Janco barked and howled at the trees.

Ari sighed as his partner bounded through the woods. "I hope you know that if we don't get a rematch, those pups will go missing and you'll find them tied to the trees."

"Noted."

≈

"Medic Channa didn't give me all the details. She seemed perplexed about your relapse, but pleased with your recovery," the Commander said, by way of inviting Valek to explain.

All he wanted to do was crawl into his bed, but he owed Ambrose an explanation. He took a fortifying gulp of the fire whiskey before relating his disturbing dream and about helping Yelena.

"She must be a rather powerful magician to reach you from the Magician's Keep. But I'm worried about your immunity. I assumed it was permanent."

With nothing to do but recover over the last couple days, Valek had considered his immunity as well. "When she's with me, she's…in my heart." He tapped his chest. "It's hard to describe. But I think there must be a hole or an opening in my immunity that's just for her." He remembered telling her that she had slipped under his skin, invaded his blood, and seized his heart. Perhaps with that confession, he'd given her permission to bypass his immunity. To him, it really didn't matter why. He was so very glad that she could reach out to him, and he could provide aid.

"Let's hope that is indeed the case. In the meantime, I've some good news," Ambrose said.

"Oh?" Valek relaxed back.

"I sent a message to the Sitian Council requesting a meeting and they've agreed."

"But it's too dangerous for you to go."

"I know. I'm sending my ambassador."

"You have an ambassador?"

"I do now. I'm promoting my cousin Signe."

Ah, Signe. Valek had met her a few times over the years. She supposedly lived in MD-3, close to where Ambrose grew up. But in truth she was the Commander's alter ego. From time to time, the Commander allowed Signe to takeover his body. Valek wondered if the Commander realized that Valek knew about the Commander's alter ego. How could Valek not? But, then again, Ambrose had given him that measuring look when Valek said he kept his secrets.

"She'll need protection," Valek said. but his statement sounded more like an imploring, hopeful plea.

"It's too dangerous for you to go, but I know you'll go anyway." He smiled. "It's been almost a year since you last saw Yelena."

"What about you?"

"I'm going to hunt sand spiders in MD-8. I'm due for a vacation."

Only the Commander considered hunting the giant arachnids fun. "By yourself?"

"No. Everyone will think that you are with me, until I send you on a secret mission to MD-1. My father is coming along. He's traveling with Signe."

Valek liked the Commander's father very much. Caleb had been an integral part of the takeover but hadn't wanted to be a general or an adviser. He had returned to MD-3 to work the family's diamond mine instead, and to ensure the new safety protocols were being implemented in all the mining operations in Ixia.

"Who are you assigning to Signe's entourage?" Valek asked.

"Adviser Ilom and half my elite squad will escort her to Sitia. The other half will come with me to MD-3 because I know you'll squawk if they don't."

Ah, nice. Ilom wasn't often chosen to go on missions, but he was roughly the same height and build as Valek. He also had black hair. Bonus.

"I'm assuming you'll want to add a few of your corps to the group going to MD-3," Ambrose continued.

"I do, but for both groups. Ari and Janco are proving to be very useful. And they're friends with Yelena. When is the delegation leaving?"

"In three days."

Which meant in six days, he'd be reunited with Yelena.

"Ah, there's that smile," Ambrose said. "I've been missing it these last few seasons."

Then it dawned on Valek. "Did you arrange all this just for me?"

"Don't be ridiculous. I need to reassure the Sitian Council that the events in MD-5 have not affected the treaty. It's also a gesture of good will between our countries."

"Uh huh."

"Don't you have work to do? You're leaving in three days."

Three days was just about the right amount of time to get ready for the trip to Sitia. First, Valek visited Ilom. The adviser had a small office near the throne room.

"Adviser Valek, to what do I owe the pleasure?" he asked, but the glint in his eyes said he already knew.

Valek explained.

"Ha. I thought so. I never usually get picked for missions.

But I don't mind. I get to go to Sitia, and I'll be working under-cover as well. Exciting."

"You'll still get to sit in on all the meetings with the Sitians."

"Oh joy." Ilom's tone was sarcastic, but it didn't last long. He smiled. An easy-going man in his early forties, he had short, straight hair that just covered his ears. With a weak chin and a soft fat nose, Ilom frequently liked to give others the impression that he was an idiot. He claimed being underestimated gave him an advantage. Regardless, he knew all the intricacies of the trade treaty with Sitia and had a good deal of experience with diplomacy.

"Thanks."

His next stop was Ari and Janco's suite. Bonus that Maren was also there. Valek explained that the Commander was sending a delegation to Sitia.

"You're not going, right?" Janco asked. "They hate you there."

"No. I'm going to MD-8 with the Commander to hunt sand spiders."

Janco shuddered. "Those things are huge! And they're covered in sand. Double yikes."

"I need you and Ari to join the group going to Sitia. You'll be scouting for them. Maren, you and Kimette are going with the group heading to MD-8."

"Ooh, do we get to hunt spiders, too?" she asked, sounding just like Janco.

"Yes. Actually, everyone will. The spiders tend to overrun the beaches if they're not culled. Be careful you don't get bitten. They're venomous."

"Once we get to Sitia, what's our role?" Ari asked.

"You'll be part of the security team for the ambassador. But you'll have some free time."

They both grinned. No doubt looking forward to seeing Yelena again. Valek wanted to join them, but he needed to act sad that he was missing out.

Valek pulled out four of his statues. He handed Janco the snake bracelet. "Could you give this to Yelena for me? Let her know I'm thinking about her."

Janco took it solemnly. "Of course. It's beautiful."

"And I carved these for you." He handed a statue to Ari. "A horse, because you're strong and fast."

He gave another one to Janco. "A fox, because you're quick and clever."

The last statue went to Maren "A cat, because you're quiet and deadly."

They stared at their gifts in astonishment, then they thanked him. He waited, and Janco didn't disappoint him.

"Aww, you're a kitty cat," he teased Maren. "All purry and soft. Ow!"

"And I have claws."

In preparation for the trip, Valek cut his hair to match Ilom's length. Then he packed Sitian clothes, his kit of disguises, and plenty of hidden weapons. He'd blend in with the soldiers on the way south, then switch places with Ilom for the initial contact with the Sitians. That would be the time of greatest danger to Signe and Valek. Hopefully, no one would recognize them. Not even Ari and Janco.

When the Ixian delegation left in the morning, Valek sulked nearby. Adviser Ilom rode Onyx and the soldiers walked. Ambassador Signe sat on Diamond Whiskey—the strongest horse in the castle's stable. Signe had long, straight hair that used to be black but was now a dark gray. Wearing a tailored black adviser's uniform, she had real diamonds on her collar—a sign of her position as ambassador. The only family resemblance to Ambrose was her almond-shaped eyes and golden eye color.

Valek marveled at the transformation from the Commander into Signe. He'd call it magical, but Ambrose had no magical abilities. Unless turning into his alter ego was a one-trick power, meaning it was the only thing he could do. Most people with one-trick skills were unaware they even used magic. Since Valek was never with the Commander when he transformed into Signe, he'd no idea if magic was involved.

Once the Ambassador's entourage left the complex, Valek joined the other assembled group. Caleb looked uncomfortable on his horse. And sitting on the Commander's horse was… Well, Valek had no idea. Because the person wore a cloak with the hood up. The morning was chilly, and the Commander did occasionally put up his hood. Valek shouldered his pack and joined them.

He traveled with them for a few hours until the "Commander" paused next to Valek.

"Time for you to disappear," he said.

Valek glimpsed the man's face. His resemblance to Ambrose was striking.

"Another cousin?" Valek whispered.

"Twin brother." He winked. "Only when needed."

Ah. The Commander had found a doppelgänger. It appeared that Valek didn't know *all* of the Commander's secrets. However, if the Commander had switched places with his fake twin before, it *had* to be when Valek was traveling. No way he'd be fooled. The Commander's presence always held a weight that Valek felt deep in his heart.

Once Valek joined the Ambassador's retinue, the time it took to reach the Citadel in Sitia moved like the thickest syrup on the coldest day. The night before their official arrival, Valek just barely resisted the temptation to go find Yelena, despite the fact he couldn't sleep. Not at all.

A few hours before sunrise, he and Ilom switched tents and changed uniforms. Valek spent the next hour applying a fake nose, straightening his hair, and rubbing some grease into it to make it appear limp. The weak chin was the hardest to fabricate. Valek had to pad his cheeks to soften his jawline.

The first test of his disguise came with the sunrise. The soldiers bustled about, cooking breakfast, and breaking down the tents. No one said a word to him. Signe nodded when he joined her for the meal. She went over the agenda for the day. He half-listened as he watched Ilom blend in, helping the others pack their gear. Ilom's hair was tucked under a knit cap, and he wore glasses. No one looked at him twice.

When Valek approached Onyx to saddle him, the horse licked the side of his head and nudged his arm for treats. Guess he couldn't fool his horse. Or was it the smell of the treats in his pocket?

The Citadel's white marble walls shone in the morning sunlight. The high walls contained a small city inside along with the Magician's Keep. Once they neared the structure, Valek spotted green veins streaking the marble. The slick stone would be impossible to climb without a rope. Probably the reason it was chosen to safeguard Sitia's heart.

Signe and Valek led the procession through the north gate. With the soldiers following, they continued south down a long, curved road lined with factories and businesses. When they reached the mid-point of the Citadel, they turned left toward the southeast corner, where all the government buildings and officials resided.

The Council Hall was a square-shaped building and had multiple levels. Each level was smaller than the one below, so it resembled a multi-tiered cake. Valek gazed at the Magician's Keep that occupied the entire northeast corner of the Citadel.

Was Yelena inside? Perhaps sitting at a desk, listening to some magician lecturing about magic. Did she even know an Ixian delegation was visiting? It took all his strength to not turn Onyx, race over to the keep, and jump the gate.

Instead, he dismounted with Signe. Their horses were led to the stables, and they were invited inside the building.

Valek followed Ambassador Signe right into the heart of their enemies' lair. Well, *lair* might be a bit of an exaggeration. Might. He would see how this visit played out first.

A row of trumpets played a welcoming blast as the Ixians entered the great hall. The Commander would consider the music pretentious, but Valek thought the Commander deserved a little pomp. Of course, the Sitians had no idea the Ambassador was the Commander's alter ego.

As the Ixian delegation neared the line of people waiting for them, Valek scanned the room. The great hall was three stories tall and decorated with fifteen colorful banners. They hung between the long thin windows, which let in the bright after-noon sunlight. Overall, an impressive space and appropriate for receiving them.

All the members of the Sitian Council stood in a half-circle. Valek noted the eleven Sitian councilors, each representing one of the clans. They all wore formal silk robes with silver embroi-dery. The four master magicians, who governed all magicians, were hard to miss. They wore ceremonial robes and animal masks. Valek was already familiar with the hawk mask that Fourth Magician Irys Jewelrose wore.

And standing next to Irys— Yelena. Valek's heart jumped so hard in his chest, he swore it cracked his sternum. It thudded, demanding that he cross the room and sweep Yelena into his arms. *Now*, it thumped. It took all his will to keep his bland expression and to keep his feet in place. This was the closest he'd been to her in two-hundred and eighty-eight days—not that he was counting—and his soul ached with longing. Seeing her made it almost unbearable.

Since he couldn't break character, he drank in the sight of her. Yelena wore a pale-yellow apprentice robe with wide sleeves. A rather plain garment considering the others in the room, but it didn't matter. To him, she was the most beautiful person in the world, and she outshone all the others. His heart once again thumped its displeasure at his inactivity. *Later*, he promised it. He just needed to survive until later.

Yelena's attention was focused on Signe, and only Valek noticed the classic widening of her eyes and slight dropping of her jaw as she recognized the Commander. There was his clever fox. He wondered if her loyalties had changed in the last four and a half seasons. Would she inform the Sitian Council of the viper in their midst?

Her gaze then searched the rest of the Ambassador's entourage. She dismissed him immediately and moved on. Huh. He'd mixed feelings about that, but in the end, he was glad his disguise held up. No doubt she would recognize Ari and Janco among the soldiers.

Yelena fingered the lump on her chest under her robe as her gaze continued to sweep the delegation. He hoped she still wore the pendant he'd carved for her. Valek focused on the others in the room, counting guards, and noting the presence of a young blond man with a beard. An aide? A page? A magician? The blond scowled fiercely at the Ixians. Valek would have to discover his identity.

A tingling of magic brushed his skin and he turned, meeting Yelena's intense gaze. This time, her flash of recognition included a bit of triumph. Once again, his body demanded action, especially below the belt. Keeping his bored expression took every bit of self-control. He looked away, focusing on the political formalities.

After a few minutes, more magic pressed on him. This time

aimed at his heart. He briefly glanced at Yelena. *Later, love,* he promised with his gaze.

The introductions dragged on forever, but finally the meeting ended with refreshments. To keep his cover Valek stayed next to Signe, who chatted with Second Magician Bain Bloodgood. But Valek tracked Yelena's every movement. She headed toward Ari and Janco, but was waylaid by one of the councilors, who handed her a small scroll.

Once the man moved away, Yelena read the message in the scroll. She closed her eyes as if it was bad news. He longed to pull her close and find out who upset her so he could kill them. Drawing in a deep breath, he tried to calm the caveman living inside his body. Yelena was more than capable of protecting herself.

Yelena opened her eyes and shook her head as if to dismiss the news. She headed toward the Ixians and caught Signe's eye. *Ah, time for the true test.*

Bain stopped speaking and gestured Yelena closer. "Ambassador Signe, this is Apprentice Yelena Liana Zaltana."

Would she give the Commander away?

She shook Signe's hand in the Ixian greeting, then bowed in the Sitian way of salutation. Interesting.

Signe bowed in return. "I have heard much about you from my cousin. How are your studies progressing?" she asked in a pleasant soprano.

"Very well, thank you. Please extend my best wishes to Commander Ambrose."

It appeared Yelena planned to keep Signe's real identity a secret. At least, for now.

"I will," Signe said and then turned to Valek. "This is Adviser Ilom."

Valek extended a limp hand and muttered a polite hello. Her touch sent a shock of lightning up his arm, but he acted as if she was beneath him and glanced away. It about killed him, and it was a relief when Bain led them to meet another councilor. However, he kept an eye on her and was happy to see her talking to Ari and Janco.

Valek paid particular attention when Janco gave Yelena the snake bracelet he had carved for her. The captains hadn't been informed who they were really guarding. The fewer people who knew, the better. So Valek had given the bracelet to Janco to support the fiction that he had reluctantly stayed with the Commander.

Her face lit up over the gift and warmth spread through him. He'd carved a snake because her love would forever be coiled around his heart. And the sapphires for the snake's eyes were to remind her of him. Janco slipped the bracelet onto her arm. Jealousy flared briefly. His inner caveman wanted to thump his chest and grunt *mine*. Valek sighed. He hated the circumstances that kept them apart.

After the endless rounds of introductions and welcomes, Valek ceased to pay attention. Instead, his thoughts raced, planning the moment he could slip away from the Council Hall and find Yelena.

That moment came a couple hours before sunset. In the visitor's quarters, Valek removed his disguise and changed into the plain dark tunic and pants that the servants at the Magician's Keep all wore. His spies had reported that Yelena lived in the Keep's apprentice wing, so he headed in that direction.

Gaining entrance to the Keep was easier than he'd expected. Either it was due to arrogance that the magicians could handle any threat, or it was a false sense of security that no one would try to sneak in. The flow of people in and out of the gate stayed steady, and he just joined the others.

He'd memorized a map of the Keep before leaving Ixia and easily found the two apprentice wings. They faced each other like a set of parentheses. Yelena's unit was the last one on the left wing. The door was locked, and she didn't answer his knock, so he headed toward Irys Jewelrose's tower in the north-west corner of the Keep. Similar to the Commander's castle, the Keep had four tall towers in each corner.

As soon as he passed the bathhouse, he spotted Yelena in the pasture across from the stables. She groomed a beautiful copper-colored horse with a white blaze on her face and blue eyes. The young blond from the great hall stood next to her. And two armed guards waited nearby.

Who were they guarding? Yelena or the blond?

Valek stepped into the bathhouse's shadow to observe them. Yelena's tense posture and the sharp words she exchanged with the blond meant they were arguing. Was he a fellow student? Or an instructor? A friend? The blond gazed at Yelena with an intensity that wasn't friendly. Valek fingered the hilt of his knife.

Yelena finished grooming the horse and tossed the brushes and combs into a bucket. Then she led the horse into the stables. The guards followed her, abandoning the blond in the pasture. He stared after her for a few moments before striding away in another direction.

The sun hung low in the sky, deepening the shadows. Valek remained in place as he considered the implications of Yelena's guards. They could be there for any reason, so he decided to wait and ask her. Later.

After Yelena left the stables, she headed toward the bath-house, then went inside. Valek returned to her apartment, picked the lock, and entered. In the semi-darkness, he scanned the small living room and bedroom, seeking hiding places. If her guards were any good, they'd find him regardless. If they weren't, they'd only look in the obvious spots.

There was a couch, two chairs, and a table with some books and an interesting statue of some type of monkey on the top. Otherwise, it appeared that Yelena didn't spend a lot of time there.

When the key rasped in the door's lock, Valek stood on the back of the couch and reached for the dark wooden beams that crossed the ceiling. There was a gap between them and the roof they supported. Just enough that Valek could wedge his body on top of the beams.

The door swung wide and one of the guards entered. He did a cursory search, checking under the couch, bed, and in the armoire before declaring the rooms safe. Yelena came inside. She smelled of lavender soap and her hair was wet. She shut the windows, locking them before starting a fire in the hearth.

While her back was turned, Valek swung down from the rafters and eased to the floor without making a sound. Well, if he didn't count the thumping of his heart, which was so loud he worried her guards would rush in. Not wanting to scare her, he sat in one of the chairs and put his feet up on the table. Trying to appear calm, and not look like a love-sick idiot, he picked up the statue to examine it.

When the flames caught and crackled in the hearth, Valek said, "That's better."

She spun and studied him in surprise for a moment. "How did you—"

"Fool your guards? They're not very good. They forgot to check the ceiling for spiders." He grinned. That was his favorite place for both hiding and ambushing. No one ever looked up.

"This is dangerous," she said.

"I knew falling for you was dangerous, love."

"I meant coming to Sitia. Being here in the Magician's Keep with guards just outside my door." She gestured wildly.

If she thought to chase him away, she was in for another surprise. "It's only dangerous if they know I'm here. According to them, I'm just Ambassador Signe's lowly and dull-witted aide." No longer able to stand being apart, he stood and stretched his arms wide. "See, I'm not even armed." He tried to appear innocent, but all he really wanted was to hold her.

Instead of rushing to him, she asked, "Should I guess how many concealed weapons you have, or should I strip-search you?"

Ah, a challenge. Desire flared. "A strip-search is the only way to be absolutely certain."

She stepped toward him. Finally, she was pressed against him. In that moment, Valek was once again complete. All his worries about her feelings for him changing were erased as she proceeded to remove his clothing. She found most of his knives, darts, and even the short sword in his boot as they headed to her bed, but once she touched his skin, it ceased to be a game.

Her clothing soon joined his on the floor and they got reacquainted in a most intimate way.

It was late in the night before they lay tangled in each other's arms, exhausted but exhilarated. Valek wished time would stop. Wished they could live in this bubble of happiness forever.

"Thank you for the snake bracelet. It's beautiful," Yelena said.

"I was thinking about you when I carved it," he said. "I was wondering how you were fairing, what you were learning, who you were meeting, if you were safe." He paused. "Why the need for guards, love? Are you in danger? Is something going on?"

"Unfortunately, lots of somethings." She sighed. "The guards are for my protection. Sort of. There's a rogue magician turned serial killer who we're calling Ferde—it's short for Fer-de-lance, a venomous snake. He's been doing an ancient Efe ritual to bind a magician's soul to his body before he kills his victim. Once they're dead, their power flows into him, making him stronger. He has targeted eleven young women. His last victim, Tula, survived his torture, and we were protecting her. She was healing. Doing so well." Her voice hitched on a sob.

Valek pulled her closer. What a terrible beast. Another example of power corrupting. Why couldn't magicians be happy with the magic they already had?

"But Ferde murdered her and kidnapped her younger sister,

Opal." Yelena took in a deep breath, as if to steady her emotions. "Ferde has left us a message. He wants to exchange Opal for me. The last victim must be willing to go to him. Plus, Opal isn't a magician and I'm…I'm pretty powerful. Surprising, right?" She tried to joke.

"No, love. Not surprising. I knew you were extraordinary from the beginning." And Ferde was going to die.

"You're biased." Yelena swiped tears from her eyes. "Of course, I agreed to the exchange. The master magicians and the council have opposed it. Ferde can't be allowed to gain that much power, or he'll take over Sitia. They assigned guards to keep me safe, but also to keep me from doing something dangerous. Like escaping and searching for Opal on my own, which I did anyway. I was caught and Irys put a magical leash on me."

Valek tensed. Perhaps he should smuggle Yelena back to Ixia and away from all these horrible magicians.

Sensing his murderous mood, she rubbed his arm. "It's gone. We reached an understanding today and she agreed to let me help search for Opal. To keep me in the loop, instead of blocking me. In fact, we're going to the market tomorrow to talk to Fisk."

"Fisk?"

"A beggar boy I befriended. His gang of street rats is practically invisible. They see things no one else does, and we're hoping he has some information on Opal and Ferde's whereabouts."

"And you said it was dangerous for me," Valek grumped. "Good thing I'm here. You'll need backup that can't be influenced by magic."

Yelena turned to him. A mixture of hope and fear shone in her gaze. "How can you provide backup? You're supposed to be with the Ambassador."

He grinned. "Don't worry. I've got that covered. This is not the first time, nor will it be the last time, I've been in Sitia. Keeping tabs on our neighbors has always been one of my duties as security chief. Fun stuff."

"Until you're caught," she said, sourly.

"There's always that chance. Part of the allure, I suppose." He nuzzled her neck and then sighed with regret. "I better get back. It'll be dawn soon." He rolled out of bed and pulled on his pants. "Besides, I don't want to be here when your boyfriend arrives."

"Who?" She sat up.

"The blond that follows your every move with his lovesick eyes," Valek teased.

"Cahil?" She laughed, dismissing the blond. "He thought Janco was my heart mate. I think you should feel more jealousy toward my horse. She's the one who has stolen my heart."

Valek stilled as the amusement dropped from his face. Had he heard right?

"What's his name?"

"Her name is Kiki."

He shook his head. "Not the horse. The blond."

"Cahil."

That name should be attached to a dead man. "Cahil Ixia? The King's nephew? He's alive?" Had he missed one of the King's relatives? He thought he'd assassinated them all.

"I thought you knew," she said.

He hadn't known. But now—

"Valek, don't kill him," she pleaded.

"He's a threat to the Commander." And therefore, must die.

"He's my friend."

Valek's cold gaze met hers. Of course, Yelena had to find the one person in Sitia that she shouldn't be friends with. He relented. "The second he becomes more than a potential threat, he's dead."

She relaxed. "I'm glad the Commander is safe within Ixia's borders."

Even though she'd recognized Signe as the Commander, she wasn't going to say anything to him, keeping the Commander's secret. Valek admired her loyalty. "He's taking a vacation. He's the only person I know who thinks hunting sand spiders is relaxing."

"Aren't you worried he'll get stung?" She shuddered, just like Janco had. Those super-quick creatures were hard to kill.

"No. I still can't beat the Commander in a knife fight. His skills are more than adequate to handle a sand spider. Plotting royalty is another matter, though. I'll have to keep an eye on this Cahil." No wonder the man had scowled at the Ixian delegation.

"Valek, did you used to leave your carvings behind when you assassinated someone?"

He wondered where that question came from. "Have you been listening to Sitian rumors?"

She nodded. "But I don't necessarily believe all that I hear."

"Good. Although, I'm embarrassed to admit that one is true. I was young, cocky, and stupid, enjoying being known as the Death Artist. I even started leaving a carving before I began a job, letting my victim find it." Valek shook his head at the memory. "That nonsense almost got me killed, so I stopped it altogether."

Valek finished dressing. "I'll be at the market today in case anything happens."

He kissed Yelena and she clung to him for a moment. While he wished to stay more than anything, she was in danger, and he needed time to get into position. When she let go, he pointed his head toward the door where her guard waited.

As she distracted him, Valek peered out the window. Sure enough, the second guard heard their voices and was looping around. He climbed from the window. Thank fate she was on the ground floor and at the very end of the row.

Valek stopped by the rooms Adviser Ilom had been assigned; he was sharing them with Valek. Telling him he was 'on' for today, Valek changed into standard Sitian clothing of nondescript brown tunic and pants. He wore a warmer layer underneath the clothes, as it had grown cold overnight, and he didn't want to be encumbered with a cloak. Hurrying to the market, he hoped to find a good location to watch for Yelena and Irys. Dark clouds sealed the sky and threatened rain.

He pretended to shop and noticed a number of street rats helping customers. They carried packages and some negotiated prices with sellers. Almost everyone ignored them, and they took advantage of that invisibility. Not to steal, but to observe. To see who looked confused, so they could rush in and offer aid. Valek wondered if one of them was Fisk, Yelena's friend.

Yelena and Irys arrived in the market, joining the flow of shoppers. She wore her cloak, and Irys tried to blend in but there was no hiding her confident posture or her direct gaze. They bought a few items and a young boy, around nine years old, sidled up to Yelena and pulled on her sleeve.

They exchanged a few words and Yelena gave the boy a copper coin. Ah, this must be Fisk. He ducked his head when Irys spoke to him. Then he led them away from the market. Valek waited, scanning the crowd to see if anyone else took an interest in them. No one. *Good.* He hurried to catch up.

The boy cut through alleys and crossed courtyards, navigating the maze of buildings and factories with ease. They stopped at a plaza that had a large jade turtle in the middle. Intricate carvings decorated the creature's shell. It shot water from its mouth into a nearby pool. Valek would have loved to get a closer look at the markings, but he hung back, watching the trio.

They talked and gestured to a building on the opposite side, and Valek felt magic brush his skin. After fifteen minutes, they headed back to the market. He kept an eye out for followers, but no one paid any attention to them.

By the time he reached the market, it started to rain. Fisk gave Yelena a jaunty wave before melting into the chaos of the market vendors packing up or covering their goods. People rushed about, pulling hoods up over their heads. One woman bumped into Yelena. She slid a note into Yelena's cloak in one smooth motion while apologizing and dashing off. Not Ferde. But the lady could be working for him.

Valek debated following her. Thunder roared and the rain fell in sheets, soaking him. It was best to stay with Yelena; with this weather, it was too easy for someone to sneak up on her.

She parted ways with Irys, entering the Magician's Keep while Irys headed south. Yelena's guards had been waiting at the gate, and they followed her.

Valek hurried to reach her rooms first. He peeked through her bedroom window while her guards searched it. As soon as they left, he entered before they could get into position. When Yelena invited them inside, he almost jumped back out the window. Fortunately, they declined, citing some regulation. Thank fate.

He waited until she started a fire before coming out. Yelena stood in front of the small hearth, holding a piece of paper in her hands. She'd gone pale, and Valek hoped it was from the cold and not the note.

"What does the message say?" Valek asked.

She just gaped at him.

He plucked the paper from her hand. "She had some rudimentary skills. Probably a pickpocket hired to give you this note. Did you get a good look at her face?"

"No. Her hood covered most of her head."

Ah, too bad. Valek shrugged. He read the note and met Yelena's gaze. "Interesting development."

She gave him an incredulous look. As if to say, 'only you would think this interesting.'

"Seems the killer is one step ahead of the magicians," he said. "He knows they won't exchange you for Opal. So, he has taken matters into his own hands. How important is Opal's life to you?"

Ferde's note specified a location and a new date for the exchange. Three nights before the full moon, which was four days from now. Yelena's gaze turned distant and conflicted. Valek let her work through the possibilities. Tell the council about the change in plans and hope they could capture Ferde at the new location or go on her own. Well, not on her own. There was no way Valek would allow that. He'd tag along no matter what. Ari and Janco would provide backup.

She glanced at Valek with a sudden determination. "Her life is important. But capturing the killer is vital."

He agreed. "What do you need, love?"

CHAPTER 14

*Y*elena and Valek discussed various plans until late in the night. In the end, he would trail her to the meeting site and ambush Ferde when he appeared. Ari and Janco would keep far away so they didn't alert the magician but would be close enough if Valek and Yelena ran into trouble.

Valek returned to the Council Hall and collapsed into bed. Being with Yelena trumped sleep, but it had caught up to him.

Ilom roused him later the next afternoon. "Can you be me for dinner with the Sitians?"

"Sure. Why?"

"A couple of the councilors like to seek loopholes in everything and won't give up. They're exhausting and I've a horrible headache."

"Verbal acrobatics?"

"Yeah. Bring your sharpest wit."

Valek didn't mind standing in for the adviser. It was a good chance to see how Signe was getting on and to eat a delicious meal. Ilom hadn't been exaggerating; the Sitians liked to spar without swords. Signe kept up with the verbal battle with ease, seeming to relish the challenge. The best part, it never turned heated. No one appeared offended and there were no hurt feelings. A truly engaging discussion.

As dessert was being served, Bain Bloodgood's gaze turned inward. Valek had learned that meant he was communicating magically with another magician. A look of alarm crossed his face before he schooled his expression and excused himself from the table. Immediate worry for Yelena swirled in Valek's chest, which turned into a maelstrom when Ari appeared in the doorway. He caught Signe's eye and gestured.

Valek followed Signe into the hallway. Ari ignored Valek as they walked to a quiet corner.

"Sir, there's a situation that Captain Janco and I need to address," Ari said to Signe.

"What happened, Captain?" Signe asked.

"It appears Yelena Zaltana has been kidnapped."

Valek fisted his hands so hard his nails dug into his palms.

"Appears?" Signe asked with the same mild tone.

"She had two guards protecting her from an unknown aggressor. We were with her this afternoon, sparing, and doing self-defense training, and had parted ways. Except, Captain Janco had a…twitchy feeling, and we doubled back to check on her. Her guards had been knocked unconscious and she had disappeared."

Valek kept his bland expression, but inside he burned with rage.

"Did you alert the proper Sitian authorities?" she asked.

"Yes, we alerted the guards at the gate, and they passed the message along to the magicians."

"What more can you do? They have magicians and security people."

"The guards said a gardener wheeled a cart past them earlier and left the Citadel through the east gate. We suspect Yelena was in the burlap bag inside. At first light, we can track that cart and find Yelena."

"Aren't the Sitians able to do this as well?"

"They're sending search parties throughout the Citadel. They're convinced she hasn't left." Ari sucked in a breath in an obvious attempt to control his emotions. "They don't trust Janco's instincts. I do."

Signe met Valek's gaze for a moment. "Then you should proceed on your own. Keep me posted, Captain."

"Yes, sir." Ari dashed away.

"Don't get caught," Signe said to Valek before she returned to dinner.

Get caught? There was nothing he could do! Frantic with worry and livid that someone dared to kidnap Yelena, Valek prowled the streets of the Citadel, hoping Yelena would reach out to him through their connection. He'd gladly give all his energy to her again.

He went to the market to find Fisk. Perhaps the boy had seen or heard something. It was a slim chance, but he had nothing else to do. However, the market was closed. Valek followed the searches that had been dispatched from the keep. It was obvious they had no idea where Yelena had gone.

If she died… *No.* Not going there. Not now.

An hour before dawn, he found a spot to watch the east gate. Ari and Janco arrived at first light and left the Citadel. Valek followed them. They inspected the grass around the dirt road going east, then they followed the road.

After an eternity, they slowed and turned south onto a narrow path overgrown with weeds. Eventually, a small, abandoned farmhouse came into view. The barn had crumpled, and the fields had gone fallow. A small shed looked to be the only structure not on the verge of collapse.

It took all of Valek's willpower not to charge to the rescue. He waited as Ari and Janco made a loop around the structure.

The new locks shone in the sunlight—a bright contrast to the peeling paint and rusted hinges. *Hurry up!*

As if obeying Valek's mental command, Janco pressed his ear to the door, and signaled, *She's in here.* He yanked out his lock picks and unlocked the door. Then he stood back, and both men drew their swords.

On the count of three, Ari signaled. *One. Two. Three.*

They kicked the door open. Valek's heart stopped beating.

"Yelena are you all right?" Ari asked.

Janco went inside the shed. "Keys?" There was silence. "Guess I'll have to do it the hard way."

Valek crept to the shed's door and peered inside. Ari pointed his sword at some man. Ferde? Yelena's wrists were manacled and attached to a chain hanging from the ceiling. But she appeared to be uninjured. Valek almost staggered to the ground in relief.

Janco had his lock picks out, but Yelena shook her head. "I've got the situation under control. Go back to the Keep, I'll meet you there."

Janco stared at her in astonished silence.

Ari took her at her word. "Come on, she doesn't need our help." He sheathed his sword.

Janco recovered. He flashed a mischievous grin. "I'll bet you a copper that she'll be free in five minutes," he said to Ari.

Ari grunted in amusement. "A silver on ten minutes," he countered.

"I'll bet you both a gold coin that she kills him," Valek said from behind them. Surprised, they moved aside to let him enter. "The only way to take care of your problem. Right, love?"

"No killing," she said and gave him a pointed look. "I'll manage."

"He's my man. I'll handle this," a man said from behind Valek.

Valek cursed and spun. He'd been so distracted about Yelena

that he'd never heard the blond arrive. Cahil just stared at him for a moment. Ah yes, Valek had also forgotten he still wore his Ilom disguise.

Cahil entered the shed, which was way too small for six people. "Goel, stand down," he ordered.

Goel? Was that Ferde's real name? No. The man didn't have the red tattoos Yelena had told him about. Since it wasn't the rogue magician, Valek knew Ari and Janco could help Yelena if needed. Leaving the crowded shed, Valek circled around and hid behind it to listen.

"No," Goel said to Cahil. It was the only voice Valek didn't recognize.

"Goel, you were right about her. But this isn't the way to deal with her. Especially not with her two henchmen nearby. Release her," Cahil ordered.

"I don't take orders from you. Everyone else can pretend you're in charge. I won't," Goel said.

"Are *you* challenging my authority?" Cahil demanded.

"You don't have any authority with me," Goel shot back.

"How dare—"

"Gentlemen!" Yelena shouted. "You can fight it out later. Everyone leave. Now! My arms are killing me."

There was a rustle of movement and a door slammed shut.

"Where were we?" Yelena asked Goel.

"You can't expect me…"

"Forget about them. You have more to worry about in here than outside."

"You're not really in the position to be boasting."

"And you don't fully understand what it's like to go against a *magician*."

Ah, there's my love.

"You think I'm just some girl to be taught a lesson. That I should fear you. You're the one who needs the lesson."

Valek celebrated. Knowing Yelena could handle herself, he

found a better place to hide and watch. Ari and Janco waited for her by the dilapidated fence. Cahil had also hidden nearby.

He wondered if Goel was part of the "lots of somethings" Yelena had been dealing with since being in Sitia. Various grunts and noises emanated from the shed before Yelena exited ten minutes later.

Ari smiled as Janco slapped a silver coin into his huge hand.

"Your problem?" Ari asked Yelena.

"I left him hanging."

Yes!

"What took you so long?" Janco complained.

"I wanted to prove my point. Where's…ah, Adviser Ilom and Cahil?" She looked around the farmstead.

"Why the sudden concern for Ilom?" Janco asked with mock sincerity. "He's a grown man with surprising abilities. That stuffy old bore appeared out of nowhere, did a dead perfect impression of Valek's voice and disappeared as if by magic. The man's a genius! I should have known he would come along. Valek wouldn't miss all the fun."

The smile dropped from Ari's face. "Valek's going to get caught. Cahil made a beeline for the Citadel, probably to tell the council members about Valek."

Ah, so Cahil had pretended to rush back to the Citadel, only to loop around and hide. Interesting.

"Great disguise, though," Janco said. "He had us fooled."

"Cahil already suspected Valek was here," Yelena said.

That was new. He wondered what gave him away. Was it something he'd done or did Yelena tip him off? She tended to expose Valek's plans when defending him. And she had argued with Cahil earlier.

"I'm sure Valek can handle it," she said.

He could, but Signe wasn't going to be happy about it.

The three of them headed back to the Citadel. Valek waited behind to see what Cahil would do. Yelena might have told

Valek 'no killing,' but he'd seen the sick rot in Goel's gaze. Best to deal with the problem permanently.

Cahil waited until the others were out of sight before he entered the shed. Valek eased closer to listen.

"…disgrace to my unit," Cahil said.

"Your unit. That's a laugh," Goel said.

Valek thought about the comments Goel had made earlier. Sounded like there was some dissension in the ranks about who was really in charge. Valek hadn't left any of the royal family alive. Perhaps Cahil's people lied to him about his birthright? He would have been too young to remember his real parents.

The argument continued, but they both left the shed, crossing the field. Valek considered his options. He could attack them now and solve two problems. Except, there might be some push back from the Sitian authorities, and it might cause difficulties for Signe. No. He'd wait until the delegation left and then return to finish the job.

"Shut up. Just. Shut. The fuck. Up!" Cahil pulled his oversized sword from its sheath. "You've pledged your loyalty to me. Your life is mine, and I've decided you're no longer welcome in my unit." He plunged the blade into Goel's chest with one mighty thrust.

Goel staggered back with a look of astonishment. Cahil yanked the weapon out. Blood gushed and Goel collapsed. Impressed that Cahil had the wherewithal to murder a man, Valek approved the decision. Was this Cahil's first kill?

Cahil stared at the body. The red flush of his anger faded from his cheeks, and he swallowed a few times. His forehead creased. Would he get sick? Then Cahil cleaned the blood off his sword with a handful of grass and headed to the Citadel.

It would be interesting to see how the Sitians deal with Goel's murder. Valek took another route back and hoped to reach Ilom and Signe before the authorities. He found them in the suite of rooms assigned to the Ambassador.

Ilom stood. "What's going on? Why are you still in disguise? I've the morning shift."

"Did something happen to Yelena?" Signe asked.

"She's fine, but my cover is blown. I'm sorry Ilom, it's going to be a rough couple of days for you."

"Well, I wanted an adventure."

"That's the spirit, old man." He clapped him on the shoulder.

"You need to leave Sitia immediately," Signe ordered.

"I can't," Valek said. "They've a big problem here and I need to help them stop it. If not, it will eventually affect Ixia."

"How should I play this?" Signe asked.

"Indignant and angry. After all, Ilom is innocent of all accusations."

"Something no one has *ever* said of you, Valek."

He flashed her his cocky grin. Then he hurried to clean off his makeup and change into his soldier's uniform. Grabbing his pack, he removed all evidence that he shared the quarters with Ilom. The Ambassador's soldiers had been housed in one of the lower levels of the Council Hall. It was nicer than the barracks at the castle. A wing of bedrooms and a large common area had been earmarked for visiting guests not important enough for the nicer suites. There should be an empty room for him. He needed to create a new disguise. Perhaps a pair of glasses and a different nose.

As he crossed though the common area, Ari and Janco spotted him. They followed and practically manhandled him into their bedroom.

"Spill," Janco demanded.

"Are you crazy?" Ari asked. "You shouldn't be here."

"It's a good thing I am," Valek replied.

"What's going on?" Janco asked.

"I'm not sure what Goel was all about. He was one of Cahil's men and it sounded like he had a grudge against Yelena, but he's dead and no longer a concern."

"Did you kill him?" Ari asked.

"I planned to, but Cahil had the honor."

"What's that guy's deal?" Janco asked.

Valek had subtly asked the councilors at dinner last night about Cahil. "He's claiming to be the King of Ixia's nephew. He has a unit of special forces with him; they're soldiers from Ixia. Cahil wants to free us from the Commander's rule and become King, so he's been petitioning the Sitian Council to provide him with an army. They have no interest is starting a war with us. Also he accused Yelena of being an Ixian spy."

"That explains some of his behavior. We were sparring with Yelena, and he accused her of using magic to win bouts." Ari sounded offended on her behalf.

"He doesn't know how to handle that sword," Janco said. "It doesn't take magic to beat him. I did it in three moves with a bo staff."

"Do you think his unit lied to him so they could assassinate the Commander and set Cahil up as a puppet king?" Ari asked.

"It's possible. But we have a bigger problem than the Wannabe King."

"We do?" Janco's gaze lit up. "Do tell."

"There's a killer after Yelena." He explained about Ferde and the ritual he'd been performing. "Yelena would be the last soul he needs to gain a great deal of power. I'm going to need backup on this one."

Janco's glee faded into horror. "Wait. She's taking on this psycho magician on her own?"

"We'll be there," Valek said.

"He's as strong as a master magician and may have magician minions. I think having more than us as backup would be prudent," Janco said. "There are four *master* magicians in town. Don't you think *they* should handle this problem?"

"They can't hide who they are. Ferde has been dodging them this entire time. He'll sense when they're near and kill Opal."

"That explains why everyone was so frantic when Yelena went missing," Ari said. "They thought Ferde had her and would complete this Efe ritual."

"Have I said, 'magic sucks' recently?" Janco asked. "Because it does. Suck. Really bad."

"What do you need us to do?" Ari asked.

"I'm going to be at the meeting site. He won't sense me, but you'll need to follow at a distance. If we don't return by a certain time, you go get help."

"The same help that can't really help?" Janco asked. "That help?"

"It's not a good plan," Ari said.

"It's all I've got."

"It sucks." Janco certainly wasn't one to sugar coat anything.

"Attention!" a muffled voice called from the hallway.

Ari opened the door a crack.

"We need a protection detail, stat!" the same person yelled. "The Sitians are trying to arrest Adviser Ilom."

And so, it begins.

Ari and Janco exchanged a look before Ari pointed to the ground. "You better stay here."

"And miss all the fun?"

"You think getting arrested and executed is fun?" Ari growled.

Most people ignored Valek's cavalier attitude, but he'd upset Ari. "I don't. Sorry. I'll find an empty room and work on my new disguise."

"Good."

Ari and Janco hurried to join the detail that consisted of ten people. If the full complement of soldiers went, they'd trip over each other. Valek dutifully changed his appearance.

～

Ari and Janco didn't return until later that night. Valek was in the common area, slouched on one of the couches reading when they arrived. There were a few other soldiers hanging out. A foursome played cards on a nearby table. Pleased that the card players' gazes passed over him, Valek stood, stretched, and headed for his room. Ari and Janco fell in step behind him.

When they reached his room, Valek closed the door behind them. "Report."

"They arrested Adviser Ilom," Ari said.

"Genius move," Janco said.

"Who made the arrest?"

"First Magician Roze Featherstone, Cahil, and a security detail. They claim Ilom is you in disguise, but they're waiting to reveal him in front of the entire council. They also accused him of murdering Goel Ixia."

"So, they're pinning the murder on poor Ilom."

"They're having a trial tomorrow afternoon in the great hall to decide if formal charges will be filed. He's being detained here and guarded by Cahil's unit. Apparently, there are cells below ground level."

"You're not going to let the guy be executed, are you?" Janco asked.

"He won't be. How's Signe?"

"Ambassador Signe is livid. And I'm pretty sure it's not all directed at the Sitians," Janco said, giving him a pointed look.

Ambassador Signe was not invited to the fact-finding portion of the trial. Instead, she waited impatiently in a small side room next to the hall with five members of her protection detail, which included Valek. Ilom and his guards were also there. His hands had been manacled behind his back. He appeared tired and grumpy. Rough night? Or was it because four of Cahil's team held him at sword point? Valek guessed he should be flattered that the Wannabe King believed he needed four armed guards to keep Valek from escaping.

He recognized one member of Cahil's team. Captain Marrok was the only person to ever escape the Commander's dungeon. It was interesting that he worked for Cahil. Had he been one of the soldiers who had "rescued the king's nephew"? Valek had exchanged a glance with Signe when Marrok had entered with Ilom. Would the captain recognize either of them?

Eventually, the door to the great hall opened. Captain Marrok dragged poor Ilom in, followed by his guards. Signe marched in behind them followed by her detail. The decorations from the greeting ceremony had been removed. They had brought in a giant U-shaped table and a podium. Benches filled with people lined the walls. Valek spotted Yelena sitting on the edge of one of the benches. Her intense gaze fixed on Ilom's face. The podium faced the table and Cahil stood there with his arm out, as if he'd just made a grand sweeping gesture.

Roze Featherstone and the other three master magicians—Bain Bloodgood, Zitora Cowan, and Irys Jewelrose —sat at the bend of the table, while the leaders of the eleven clans sat along the straight sides. Six on one side, five on the other. The fifteen of them comprised the Sitian Council. Cozy.

Ambassador Signe was the first person to speak. "I demand an explanation. This is an act of war." Her tone was as frigid as the Northern Ice Pack.

"Cahil, I told you to release the Adviser until this matter was settled," Roze said. Fury flared in her amber eyes. Her rank of First Magician meant she was the most powerful magician in Sitia. Tall and with an athletic build, her midnight skin drank in the light. Not someone to get on your bad side. Her magic filled the room, pressing lightly on Valek's skin.

"And let him escape? No. Better to bring him here and

unmask him in front of everyone." Cahil strode to Ilom and yanked on his hair.

Valek would need to buy poor Ilom a bottle of his favorite bourbon for enduring what was coming next.

Ilom's head jerked down as he cried out in pain. Undaunted, Cahil pulled Ilom's nose then clawed at the flesh under his chin. Ilom yelped and blood welled from the scratches on his neck. Cahil stepped back in astonishment. It was worth all the trouble just to witness his reaction. The Wannabe King reached toward Ilom's face again, but Marrok grabbed him and held him.

"Release the Adviser," Roze ordered.

Ilom's manacles were removed as Cahil, his face red with rage, and his men were escorted from the room. The trial ended and Roze rushed to reassure the Ambassador and Ilom.

Valek didn't listen to the apologetic words. He met Yelena's relieved gaze. *See, love? And you were worried.*

Later that night, Valek snuck into the keep and was surprised that no guards watched Yelena's room. While it made it easier for him to visit, it concerned him. Yes, she'd handled herself brilliantly, but it never hurt to have a couple extra sets of eyes.

He still entered through her bedroom. When he opened the window and slipped inside, she sat up in bed and the snick of her switchblade sounded. Undaunted, he closed the shutters, shucked his boots, and joined her

"You need to leave. Too many people know you're here," she said.

"Not until we find the killer. And besides, the Commander ordered me to protect the Ambassador. I would be remiss in my duties if I left."

"What if she ordered you home?"

"The Commander's orders overrule all others."

"Valek, did you—"

He kissed her before she could ask him if he killed Goel. Tonight was not for talking or planning or problems. It was for them. It'd been a long separation, and he knew his time in Sitia neared an end. Yelena understood his need and tugged his shirt off. He smiled, delighted. All his worries melted away. Nothing was more important than the woman in his arms.

Unfortunately, reality intruded late into the night. Valek needed to be well away from the keep before dawn. Cahil wouldn't stop looking for him. He had to be extra careful.

He spent most of the next day keeping a low profile and getting ready for the exchange scheduled for that night. Yelena had told him about a new Sitian drug called Curare, which paralyzed a person but didn't kill them. According to her, it targeted a person's muscles but allowed their heart to beat and lungs to breathe. Ferde had used the drug on his victims and would probably be armed with darts full of it. Valek's extra layer of Sitian clothing over his sneak suit should help resist the needle of a dart, but he worried about Yelena.

Pulling a set of black clothing made from a special fabric from his pack, Valek grabbed his sewing kit and tried to alter the garments to fit Yelena. She'd be in the most danger tonight and it made sense for her to wear them.

Since it was easier to enter the Keep in the daylight, Valek crossed through the entrance in the late afternoon. Yelena wasn't in her room, so he searched for her. Riding her horse without a saddle, Yelena kept her balance as Kiki navigated the uneven ground with a smooth gait. The two of them moved as one. Yelena had said Kiki had captured her heart, and he was glad to see her riding with such confidence.

When they headed toward the stables, Valek returned to Yelena's room. Soon the sun would set, and they needed to finalize their plans for the rendezvous and exchange. Or rather the ambush. Ferde would die tonight.

Yelena arrived. No longer appearing confident, her brows were creased with worry.

"Here." He handed her the black turtleneck shirt and pants he'd altered, hoping it would give her some assurance. "They're made of a special fabric that will protect you from airborne darts from a blow gun, but it won't stop a dart if you get jabbed by one."

"These are great," she said, changing into them.

They hung loose on her small frame. She rolled up the sleeves and threaded a belt through the loops to keep the pants from falling to the floor. Adorable.

A brief smile touched Valek's lips. "They were mine. I'm not the best seamstress."

He watched as she packed. She stuffed various items into her bag, including a grapple, rope, and an apple, along with some things he didn't recognize.

"What's with the small brown egg?" he asked.

She grinned. "It's Theobroma."

That name meant nothing to him. He waited.

"Oh, right. It's Criollo. The Sitians call it Theobroma."

It took every bit of self-control for him not to tear into her pack and throw the egg into the fire. "Why do you have it? It's dangerous."

"It's an antidote of sorts for Curare."

He paused, letting her words sink in. "Of sorts?"

"It reverses the effects of Curare's paralysis, but it makes a person vulnerable to magical influence, which could be just as bad."

"How do you know all this?"

She pulled in a deep breath. "My father was the one who discovered that the sap from the curare vine can be used to dull pain. He sent some to the Sandseed Clan, but it was stolen by the Daviian Vermin and concentrated to cause paralysis."

Valek sorted through the new information in those

sentences. Yelena had found her family, and as much as he wanted to hear all about them, that could wait. "I thought the Daviian Plateau doesn't have a clan."

"Not legally. A bunch of Sandseeds broke off to form their own clan in the plateau. The Sandseeds refer to them as vermin. Ferde is one of those vermin."

"That explains the Curare. What about the Criollo?"

"My father also figured out it counteracts the paralysis. Esau is good with the plants growing in the Illiais jungle, discovering medicines and other useful ingredients."

"Why do the magicians even have Criollo?" The desire to tell her all about the recent trouble Criollo had caused in Ixia pushed up his throat. Unfortunately, they didn't have time for that conversation.

"In low doses, it helps new magicians who are learning how to communicate mind to mind. As with everything—"

"It can also be abused."

"Exactly. Hopefully, I won't have to use it." Yelena twisted her long black hair into a bun and used her lock picks to hold it in place. Then, she accessed the hole he'd created in the pants' pocket to strap her switchblade onto her thigh.

"Our plan is rather simple, but let's go over it again," Valek said.

They reviewed the sequence of actions for the night. The exchange with Ferde would be at a geological feature called Blood Rock in the Avibian Plains. Located southeast of the Citadel, the plains stretched over a large portion of Sitia and were home to the Sandseed Clan. They were a nomadic people who protected their homeland with a powerful magic that confused anyone who dared enter the plains without their permission. Thankfully, Yelena was considered a cousin of the clan and would be unaffected by the magic.

"I'm planning on taking Kiki with me," Yelena said.

He stared at her. Did she want the magicians to know she

was leaving? "Sneaking through both the Keep's and Citadel's gates without a large animal is hard enough, love," Valek said.

"I'll manage. Trust me."

He trusted her with his heart. In comparison, this was an easy thing to do.

"I'll take Kiki out to the plains and give you time to get through the Citadel's gate before heading toward the meeting site," she said. "Once Opal is out of harm's way and Ferde is visible, that's the sign to move in."

Valek nodded. "Count on it."

With only four hours until the rendezvous, Valek hurried back to the Council Hall, where Ari and Janco waited for him. He reviewed the plan with them, then grabbed his pack and headed out, trusting they would do their part.

Valek found a spot within sight of the Citadel's south gate. Four guards manned the archway. The oversized marble doors were never closed. Occasionally, barriers were erected to slow traffic through the gate. He guessed they'd close and lock them if the Citadel was ever under siege.

Yelena and Kiki approached the gate. The lack of the noisy *clip clop* of hooves on cobblestones meant Kiki wasn't wearing shoes. Smart. Suddenly fascinated with other things, all four guards turned their backs to Yelena and Kiki and didn't notice the horse and rider slip through. Another demonstration of her powerful magic. Amazing. He wondered if she had master level abilities. While he'd be happy for her, he knew if that turned out to be the case, she'd end up becoming a member of the council and would be too busy to spend time with Sitia's number one enemy.

Waiting a few minutes, Valek searched the shadows behind him for any signs of Ari and Janco, but they were well hidden.

They were to wait until Valek exited the Citadel before following him at a discrete distance. Since he was dressed as a Sitian citizen, he planned to walk through the gate as if on his way home after a day working in one of the factories. He donned his pack and sauntered toward the gate, hunching his shoulders a bit as if tired.

The guards barely looked at him. Only one man made eye contact. Nodding, the guard said, "Good night."

The words rang out. Much too loud for the distance between them. Valek thanked him and kept moving. As he cleared the gate, shadows rushed him.

CHAPTER 15

The ambush had been waiting on the opposite side of the gate. They had lurked in the shadows of the Citadel's walls and out of sight. Valek could appreciate the cleverness as he yanked his cloud-kissed dagger from its sheath and fought them off. But more and more ambushers appeared. Wary of his blade, they kept their distance for a while. No one drew a weapon, but they kept multiplying. Magic? No. The air wasn't sticky.

When the four guards at the gate joined the fight, they had sheer numbers on their side. Tackled from behind, he was slammed to the ground. His knife flew from his hand, and his wrists were secured in a heartbeat.

A cheer rose. "Got him!"

"Excellent job tracking him, Captain Marrok!"

"Woot! We caught the Scourge of Sitia! Let's hang 'im now."

Anger, more than fear pulsed in Valek's heart. Yelena would be unprotected. He needed to make them understand that she was in danger.

They yanked him to his feet, and he came face to face with the Wannabe King.

"Yelena—"

"Is going to be waiting a lifetime for you to show up to your little romantic rendezvous," Cahil said. "You've a date with a noose."

"She's in danger." Valek tried again.

"Not likely."

"She's meeting that killer. Going to sacrifice herself for Opal. He'll become too powerful if he succeeds with the ritual. You need to—"

Cahil punched him in the face. Valek rocked back, but stayed upright as pain ringed his head and blood filled his mouth.

"I don't need to do anything. Nothing. Except hang you, of course. This time First Magician won't ignore me. Let's go," he said to his unit.

Valek was dragged back into the Citadel and through the now empty streets. He searched for Ari and Janco, hoping they wouldn't try to rescue him, that they'd stick to the plan and follow Yelena.

During the trip, Valek waited for an opportunity to escape. Unfortunately, Cahil's people took no chances. And they didn't take him to the Council Hall, either. They cut through a couple dark alleys to a row of three-story homes. The older buildings were well cared for but in need of some renovations. Not the best neighborhood, but not the worst either. They accessed a back entrance of a house on the end of the row. Cahil's house?

Valek was led down a set of stairs into the basement. A bit of hope rose. There might be a better chance to escape from a home-made prison than the Council Hall's cells.

Someone lit a lantern. Hope died. A metal bunk had been secured to the far wall along with a set of two chains that ended in manacles. There were no windows. Cahil's people stripped Valek of his Sitian clothes and cut off his sneak suit. Dilana would be upset that he'd ruined another one, even though the seamstress should know by now to sew a couple extras for him.

It was better to think of Dilana's reaction rather than the fact that all his lock picks and weapons were now inaccessible. They allowed him to dress in a plain jumpsuit before they secured him, chaining his wrists and ankles to the wall. At least the chains were long enough that he could lie down on the small bunk, but that was as far as he could get.

Cahil's gaze scanned him from head to toe as he gloated. "The only reason you're not dead is because I need to play nice with the Sitian Council. But expect to swing by sundown."

"Please tell the council about Yelena," Valek said.

"The 'please' is new. Guess someone is finally realizing that you don't trick me without any consequences." He glanced at his unit, who all stood around him, crowding the small space. "Goel learned that lesson, too." He turned. "Let's go."

His unit dutifully followed him up the stairs. Except Captain Marrok. He lingered long enough to meet Valek's gaze. A question creased his brow.

"Yes," Valek said. "He killed Goel."

Marrok pressed his lips together but didn't look surprised. He grabbed the lantern and mounted the steps.

"I want four guards on this door," Cahil ordered. "And hourly checks that the manacles are still secured. This killer is not—"

The door banged shut, leaving Valek in darkness. Leaving him with nothing but the damp aroma of mold and his thoughts. They swirled and spiraled. He'd underestimated the Wannabe King. There was a real danger he would hang tomorrow. But it was not knowing what was happening with Yelena that plagued him the most. Had she captured Ferde and rescued Opal? Had she been captured? Killed? Utterly helpless, he could do nothing for her. Nothing.

Valek decided he'd prefer to be physically tortured than be left with nothing but his imagination. He searched for something, anything, within reach that he could use to pick the locks but found nothing.

The night dragged like no other in his life. Years spanned between the checks from Cahil's people. Sleep was impossible. Yelena's name thudded with every heartbeat. He tried reaching out to her through their special heart link.

Come on, love. Talk to me. I'm here. Take my energy, my strength, my life if you need it. He'd gladly go to the noose if it meant she lived.

Captain Marrok arrived for the twelfth check. Besides the lantern, he carried a water skin and a wooden bowl filled with… Valek had no idea. White and gelatinous, it resembled…oatmeal?

"I thought I ordered roast beef, potatoes, and candied carrots for my last meal," Valek said, sitting on the edge of the bunk.

Marrok grunted a half laugh before tossing the water skin to Valek. He set the bowl just within Valek's reach before backing up.

Valek raised an eyebrow. "Did you draw the short straw?" He squirted the lukewarm water into his dry mouth, sucking it down. It had been over twelve hours since he had anything to drink.

"I volunteered. Thought we could reminisce," Marrok said. "Except this time, we're on opposite sides of the bars. So to speak."

"Why aren't there bars?" Valek dipped a finger into the bowl and tasted…porridge? Surprisingly warm and sweet. His stomach growled. Between swallows, Valek asked, "Is Cahil afraid the council will set me free?"

"No. They're thrilled you've been caught and have demanded

Cahil turn you over to them. But they've been preoccupied and haven't followed up."

"The magician killer? Any news?" Valek didn't care that he sounded desperate for information.

"The kidnapped girl…Opal, returned late last night. She was hysterical and claimed a woman held her. No idea who, but Opal said she was forced to prick Yelena with a dart filled with Curare."

Ice filled his veins. "Yelena?"

"No sign of her."

Valek sagged against the wall and closed his eyes for a few seconds as he struggled with his emotions. The only thing keeping him from screaming was the fact she had her father's antidote-of-sorts to Curare. "What about the woman? Is she working with Ferde?"

"No idea. But the master magicians are assuming she is and are going to go search the plains once they have gathered enough information. It's a big place, and there's the Sandseeds' magic to contend with."

"Why are you telling me all this?"

"Unlike Cahil, I like and respect Yelena. Except her taste in men is appalling."

"Cute."

"But don't forget, I follow Cahil's orders."

"Why? He's an inexperienced brat that's going to get you all killed."

Marrok's expression turned bullish. "He's the heir to the throne of Ixia."

Valek laughed. "Save that line for Cahil. He's going to figure it out eventually. And when he does, you'll be the first one he turns on. Don't forget what happened to Goel."

"You should be more worried about yourself. Cahil has scheduled your execution at sunset. Very dramatic and, unfortunately for you, the location is very secret. We wouldn't want any of your people interfering."

"A private party?" Valek considered the implications. Less people would give him an advantage if he escaped. But if he didn't and the Sitian Council wasn't in attendance, they could claim Cahil turned rogue to avoid a war with Ixia. He met Marrok's gaze.

Marrok's smile was grim. "Exactly. Cahil might be inexperienced, but he's not stupid." He collected the empty bowl and water skin. Grabbing the lantern, he mounted the stairs.

"Captain?"

Marrok paused.

"If Yelena is killed by Ferde and he completes the ritual, he will have enough magic to counter all four master magicians and rule Sitia. You're going to need me to stop him. I'm the only person immune to magic."

He glanced back at Valek before disappearing up the stairs without a word. Darkness returned. Valek hoped he'd planted a seed of doubt. And even if he was hanged in the end, he'd die happy knowing he personally ripped Ferde's heart from his chest.

The hourly checks continued, but Valek wasn't given another meal. Instead, one unfortunate man carried a chamber pot down then turned his back so Valek could use it. Valek was tempted to throw the ceramic bowl at the guard, knocking him out, but he doubted the man had a key on him. Besides, he was about ready to explode.

When more than one person descended into his prison, Valek knew the time had come. He'd get only one opportunity to escape. Two people held each of his arms as the manacles around his wrists and ankles were unlocked.

He surged forward, jerking from their grip. Amid the cries of alarm, he lowered his shoulders and plowed through the others, making it to the stairs. Racing up them, he dove through the open door and landed among a group of surprised guards. He kicked and punched, getting in a few good strikes. Dodging and weaving, he tried to find a weak link to break through.

Except, there were just too many of them. One oversized man had a steel jaw and hard head, which he used to headbutt Valek. The pain reminded him of his concussion and stunned Valek long enough to be recaptured.

He cursed as his hands were yanked behind his back and secured. He glared at Cahil for a moment before slouching as if defeated, hoping they wouldn't think to tie his ankles and carry him to the noose.

"Well, that was a good test of our defenses," Cahil said. "Not as exciting as seeing you swing, but all in good time."

Valek glanced around at the crowd. A few people rubbed bruises and glowered at him. Marrok hung back. "You'll have to do better if Ferde takes control of Sitia."

"That's not going to happen."

"You're really good at denial. Aren't you, Wannabe King?"

Ignoring Valek, Cahil motioned to his guards. "Bring him."

Six people surrounded him. The ones behind him and beside him clamped onto his arms, neck, and shoulders. The two in front created a human barrier. It seemed extreme, but, unfortunately, it was quite effective.

Cahil led the little parade through the Citadel's alleys. Valek searched for someone, *anyone*, who might help him. But the few people they encountered took one look at the group and changed directions before Valek could call to them.

The sun dipped below the Citadel's walls as they reached a small, empty courtyard. The most distinguishing feature stood tall and sturdy, right in the center. The branches of the oak tree reached out and almost brushed the surrounding buildings.

Cahil removed a noose with a long rope from his pack. He threw the rope over one of the lower limbs and pulled it down, so the noose dangled in midair.

Valek's stomach climbed his throat as he realized they planned to strangle him and not break his neck. Cahil handed the end of the rope to Marrok. Then he gestured.

The people holding Valek dragged him over despite his efforts to break free. Once Cahil settled the noose around his neck, Valek froze as terror clenched his heart in its icy jaws. The guards holding him released their grip and stepped back. It was their first mistake.

Valek moved. He kicked high and hard, knocking as many people down as he could. Suddenly, Yelena filled his heart. Fatally injured, she had collapsed onto the ground, too over-whelmed by magic to heal her stomach wound. Strange visions of people and horses and the Avibian Plains zipped through his mind, as if Yelena's life was flashing before his eyes.

The noose tightened around his throat as Marrok pulled the rope, cutting off his air. He had fifteen seconds at most before he passed out. He'd run out of opportunities. This was the end.

Sorry, love. I don't think we're going to make it this time. Regret pulsed.

No! Stay alive. Think of something! Yelena yelled.

I'll stay if you will. Although he'd no idea how to accomplish that. But her agreement gave him a surge of energy. As the noose lifted him into the air, he hooked his legs around Cahil's neck.

Cahil yelled to Marrok as Valek shifted to put his heel on his chin to break the Wannabe King's neck. Marrok let go of the rope. Valek and Cahil thudded to the ground. He'd lost his grip on Cahil, and he still couldn't breathe. Then the guards around him staggered and collapsed to the ground. Shouts filled the courtyard followed by silence.

Black spots filled his vision. His throat burned and his lungs ached. Three black-clad figures leaned over him. A knife flashed and Valek braced for the pain. Except the blade sawed through the rope, and the pressure around his neck disappeared.

Valek filled his lungs. The air wheezed through his bruised throat. Two of the figurers helped him to his feet. The bindings around his wrist were severed and they led him away from the courtyard.

"Hurry," a woman said.

It took a few moments for his brain to connect the figures to his two agents assigned to the Citadel. And even more time to wonder who the third person was. It didn't matter. They'd saved his life.

He could only hope Yelena managed to survive as well.

They arrived at his safe house and entered through the alley. Once inside, the blackout curtains were pulled shut and lanterns lit. Valek collapsed onto the couch as his two agents pulled off their hoods.

The third kept their hood on but shook their head. "Disappear," Ambassador Signe ordered. "If you're caught again, it'll be impossible to rescue you. Understand?"

"Yes, sir." His voice rasped. It hurt to talk.

"Good." She turned to leave.

"Thank you," Valek said.

"Thank my cousin, Ambrose. He'd be displeased with me if you died. Frankly, I think death is the best cure for stupidity."

"Noted."

After she left, Valek thanked his agents, Brigi and Gabor. "How did you find me?"

"After Ambassador Signe alerted us to your capture, we just followed Cahil from the Council Hall. He tried to be stealthy, but…" Brigi shrugged.

"We found his house without trouble," Gabor said. "But the amount of people he had guarding the place made it impossible to get you out. We had to wait until they moved you. And wait for an opportunity to attack. Which was when all their focus was on you."

"And we only had seconds to act," Brigi added.

"Why did you endanger the Ambassador for this mission?" Valek asked.

"She insisted. And, damn, she has great aim and speed." Gabor mimed blowing multiple puffs with his blowpipe.

"You are extremely lucky on multiple accounts." Brigi unwound her long brown hair and combed her fingers through it. "First, that the Ambassador knew where this safe house is located. Second, that Cahil waited to hang you and chose a remote location. Third, that we had just enough sleeping juice for everyone. However, it wasn't enough to keep them down for long. The manhunt for you has probably started. I suggest you bunk with us until you can escape back to Ixia."

That was an excellent suggestion. However, he couldn't leave without finding Yelena and killing Ferde.

They helped him treat his wounds. With all the adrenaline of almost being hanged, Valek hadn't noticed any pain. Now, as Brigi cleaned and bandaged the raw abrasions on his neck and wrists, Valek gritted his teeth. Gabor made him a cup of tea and a bowl of soup laced with pain powder. His throat burned with each swallow, and not because of the temperature.

Valek raided the closet for a set of soft clothes to sleep in. Inspecting the other garments and disguises, he searched for inspiration. He'd need a damn good disguise if he was going to go out in public.

Gabor offered his bed to Valek, but he settled on the couch with the conviction he'd fall asleep instantly. Except, the images Yelena had sent him when he'd been trying to escape Cahil's noose resurfaced as soon as he closed his eyes. Now that he wasn't fighting for his life, Valek tried to slow the visions down so he could examine them. In one, an older woman who resembled Yelena clung for dear life to the upper branches of a tree. The limbs swung wildly in a storm. Either Yelena imagined her life would never be calm, or it was her mother.

The next flash was of Ari and Janco sitting next to a camp-fire and arguing. Surrounded by long grasses, they appeared to be camping in the Avibian Plains. No doubt lost due to the Sandseeds' magic.

Many visions of Kiki surfaced. The horse talked to Yelena, giving her advice: *Trust is peppermints. No stool in wild. Moon Man smart. Magic Lady.* Valek wondered if Yelena's magic allowed her to communicate with her horse. That would explain how they had been so in sync in the pasture.

Another mental image showed a woman brandishing a knife. Valek sat up in alarm. He recognized the gray-eyed magician. Alea. Had she been the one to capture Yelena? Was she working with Ferde? It made sense. Alea hated both him and Yelena for killing her brother, Mogkan. She wanted revenge. And the siblings had longed to rule Ixia and Sitia. What better way to achieve those goals than for one of your members to gain enough magic to conquer the Sitian Council and then Ixia? Same objective, different path. Valek added her to his list of people-he-must-kill.

Valek eventually laid back down. Not all the images were disturbing, and he clung to the one of Yelena climbing through a village in the tree canopy. Happy and relaxed, she laughed at the little monkeys that flew and swung through the branches with a nimble dexterity. He remembered the statue of one that he'd admired in her rooms at the Keep. It'd been well crafted with a bunch of colored stones. He wondered if he could do the same with his rocks. Finally, he drifted off to sleep.

The scent of fried eggs woke him...later. The curtains remained closed, but slivers of sunlight peeked through the gaps. He found Gabor crouched in front of the kitchen's small hearth.

"Breakfast?" Valek asked hopefully.

"Lunch."

He groaned. The morning had been wasted.

Gabor dumped the eggs on a plate and gestured for Valek to sit down at the table. "Eat."

"I am the boss," he grumbled as he sat.

"So the rumors claim. Personally, I think Kenda runs the show."

Valek would have responded, but he was too busy shoveling eggs into his mouth. Gabor added a cup of tea and buttered bread to the meal. When Valek finished eating, he leaned back.

"I've news," Gabor said. "Brigi works as a horse trainer in the council's stables. This morning, the master magicians mounted up with a full cavalry of armed guards to search for Yelena in the plains."

"At least they didn't waste the morning," Valek said.

Gabor smiled. "They didn't get far. Yelena and her horse were apparently on their way back to the Citadel."

Valek straightened. "Why didn't you start with that! Is she okay?"

His agent held up his hands in a placating gesture. "You needed to eat first. And, yes, it appears that she's fine. Her clothes were torn and covered with blood, but Brigi says she moved without wincing and just looked tired. Two captains from Signe's entourage caught up to her and then they parted ways. The men went to the Council Hall, and she entered the Magician's Keep."

Relief surged through his body, leaving him weak and light-headed. He rested his head in his hands for a moment.

Gabor laid a hand on his shoulder. "Now you can take the day to recover."

Except, he couldn't. Ferde, and perhaps Alea remained a threat. Although Yelena proved she could handle Alea on her own, they were still stronger together.

"I know what you're thinking. Brigi is watching the Keep and will let us know if Yelena leaves. Besides, Cahil and his thugs are out hunting for you."

"Will you stop being so logical?"

"Okay. Go ahead, throw on some lame disguise and rush to her rescue. Oh wait…she doesn't need to be rescued."

"Not helping. I'm a man of action."

"Clearly. How about I go check in with Brigi for any updates? Will that help?"

Actually, it would. "Thank you."

"Anything for you, boss."

"I'm your boss now? You were just treating me like a toddler."

"That's because you were *acting* like a toddler. Now, am I going to have to put you down for a nap or are you going to behave?"

Valek considered adding Gabor to his people-he-must-kill list.

Gabor correctly read Valek's cold expression. "Just kidding. Don't forget, I saved your life."

"You're lucky I'm unarmed."

"The weapons' closet is next to Brigi's room." Gabor grabbed his cape and headed out.

Most of the knives and lock picks the Wannabe King had taken from him were replaceable. However, he'd lost the cloud-kissed dagger he'd gotten from Sven—his agent who had died while working undercover. Even though he could probably purchase a new one at the Citadel's market, it wouldn't be the same.

Valek found the closet and tucked a few small daggers into

his clothing. The action improved his mood. Returning to the couch, he thought he'd shut his eyes for a moment.

A scrape of metal on metal woke Valek. On his feet with a knife in hand, he waited. Another *clank* sounded. He tracked it to the back door. Gabor and Brigi had keys and wouldn't need to pick the locks.

Valek waited until the door opened. Then he pulled it wide, grabbed an arm, and yanked the person inside. Dropping them onto the floor, Valek followed and pressed his blade on—

He cursed. "Did something happen? Were you followed?" he demanded.

"Hello to you, too," Janco said. "Can I get up now?"

Valek helped him to his feet and closed the door. "Talk. Now."

"Wow, you're jumpy. I guess it's the whole..." Janco motioned to his neck. "Almost getting hung thing."

"You talked to Ambassador Signe?"

"Yes." Janco straightened his tunic. He wore nondescript Sitian clothes and a pack, which he handed to Valek. "This is yours. We found it where you were jumped." He huffed. "And I'm insulted that you think anyone can follow me."

Glad to have his kit, Valek said, "Sorry, it was a knee jerk reaction."

"You're forgiven. Anyway, the Ambassador wanted me to update you."

"Come on in. Do you want some tea?" He set the bag on what he was starting to consider his couch.

"Love some."

They sat across from each other at the table as Janco filled him in on what happened. "We watched you get nabbed but couldn't do anything at the time. They had like, a million people. Maybe you shouldn't encourage that superman reputation of yours? Otherwise, they might have only brought a half dozen, which the three of us could—"

"Janco."

"Yeah, sorry. Then we had a dilemma. Follow Cahil and rescue you or follow Yelena as planned."

"I'm glad you followed Yelena. Thank you."

"Not that we did any good," Janco huffed. "By the time we reached the meeting site at that Blood Rock, no one was there. From the marks on the ground, it was obvious there had been three people. One ran off, another of them was dragged onto a wagon that was hitched to a horse. We figured that person was Yelena and we followed the tracks. They had to stop sometime. Except…" Janco shuddered and rubbed his arms. "We ended up spending the night and most of the next day going in circles. First time I've been lost since…" He scratched his ear as he thought about it. "Ever!"

"How did you get back to the Citadel?"

"Yelena's magic horse found us. What a beautiful mare. Sharp as a splinter." His good humor faded. "Yelena was cut up pretty bad. Good thing Ari packed some of Rand's glue and was able to seal the deeper wounds. Apparently, she had to use up her magic to repair a nasty stomach wound. I guess not *all* magic is bad. Don't tell Ari I said that!"

"I won't. Did she say what happened to her?"

"It was Alea who grabbed her! Claimed she wanted revenge for her brother's death. Ari and I wanted to go after her. Yelena stabbed her in order to escape and we figured she'd be easy to capture, but Yelena wouldn't let us. She's more worried about Ferde. Which makes sense. She beat Alea once, she could again."

"Did you tell Yelena about Alea's actions in Ixia?"

"No."

Curious. "Why not?"

"That's Ixian business. If we're going to be spies, we can't be blabbing. Not even to our friends. Now, if you tell us to tell her, that's different."

"Good to know. What else did you learn?"

"Alea is part of this Daviian Clan that are squatting on a plateau or something. Doesn't sound like they're good people, because Alea's cousin is Ferde and he's a part of their clan."

"They're working together?"

"Yelena says no. They're doing different things but with the same clichéd, power hungry, megalomaniac desire to eventually rule the world. *Bah.*"

Valek mulled over the information. He'd been right about Alea, but her relationship to Ferde put a new twist on things. "Any news about Ferde's location?"

"No. The master magicians are frantic. Something about the full moon tomorrow night being the dead in deadline."

He had a feeling that if Yelena discovered Ferde's location, she'd go after him alone. Considering how the master magicians hadn't been able to find the killer, Valek wouldn't trust them either.

"Thanks for the info. Anything else?"

"Yeah. You need to watch out for Captain Marrok. He's the one who figured out when and where to ambush you. Smart guy. So. *Don't.* Get. Caught. Or Ari will be upset."

"Ari, eh?"

"Underneath all those muscles lies a teddy bear. But don't tell him I said that, or he'll wallop me."

"Noted."

When Janco left, the safe house seemed overly quiet. Valek paced through the rooms, peered through the curtains, and considered Janco's report. When Brigi returned, he had a rudimentary plan.

"She hasn't left the Magician's Keep," she said. "Gabor will stay and watch this evening."

"I'll take the night shift," he said.

"Is that wise?"

"Probably not, but I need to be nearby in case Ferde attacks."

"Fair enough. There's a good view of the Keep's entrance

from the council's stables. There're always a couple hands there. At night, they mostly sleep on the hay bales, but are available for any emergencies."

"It's been a few years since I was a stable boy."

"I'm sure it'll come back to you."

He laughed. "Thanks, but I've a better disguise in mind."

"Better?"

"Oh, yes. This one will make me practically invisible."

Valek found Gabor in the shadows of the stables. Dressed in typical barn clothes and mud boots, he looked like he was taking a break from mucking out stalls.

"What in the world is that smell?" Gabor's nose crinkled.

"I rolled in a pile of horse manure," Valek said. He held his arms out. His clothing was stained and torn. Dirt streaked his face and he'd rubbed oil into his hair, so it hung in greasy clumps. "Well? Do I look like a beggar?"

"You certainly reek like one."

"Living on the streets is a tough life."

"Speaking from experience?"

"Yes. From an extensive undercover operation." At least this time he wore pants, and another layer of warm clothes underneath the rags. Skirts weren't as warm. "You can go back to the house."

"Brigi can relieve you in the morning."

"I'm staying here for the duration."

"I'll have her bring you breakfast."

"No, thanks. It might blow my cover. I'll scrounge like everyone else."

"Good luck."

Valek had noticed a group of beggars that hung around the Council Hall. At this time of the night, some of them slept on the steps leading up to the entrance. Others occupied nooks around the building, sleeping on dirty blankets. Valek found an open spot with a direct line of sight to the Keep's entrance.

When he sat on the lowest step, the man next to him grunted. "You're new. Where you been hanging?"

"Up near Moonlight Mane Stables."

"That explains the smell. Why you here?"

"The Stable Master caught me stealing food." Valek shrugged. "Nice enough not to press charges but told me to disappear."

"We don't steal here. And you share what you get, or you'll be run out."

"Got it."

"What's your name?"

"Kalek."

"Minel. You better not snore."

They shook hands.

Valek pretended to doze, but his gaze never left the Keep. Four pink columns supported the two-story high arches that framed the marble doors of the entrance. Unlike the Citadel, gates had been installed and they were currently closed.

His thoughts spiraled into a dark place. What if Ferde was hiding inside the Keep? It was probably the only place the master magicians didn't search. Was he stalking Yelena at this very moment? Or did he already have her and was preforming his vile ritual right now?

At least Valek's pile of worries kept him awake and alert. That, and the cold night air. It was almost the middle of the cooling season. Between the two, it was going to be a long night.

Sometime during the deep hours, a voice rang out. "Hey, you. Off the steps!"

One of the Council Hall's guards shooed the vagrants off the stairs. They shuffled away, melting into the shadows. Valek followed. The guard roused everyone from their nooks. Once they were all gone, the guard returned to the hall. It didn't take long for the beggars to go back to their spots and settle down. It happened two more times that night.

"Not the most restful place," Valek said to Minel.

"No, but it's a safe place. And a profitable place." He eyed Valek. "Not for you, though."

"Why not?"

"The generous citizens of the Citadel don't see the grime or the rags, but they notice smells and will be repulsed. There's a free bathhouse near the market, I'd suggest you pay them a visit."

"I'll consider it."

Minel grunted.

When the sky lightened, the vagrants woke. Many of them shuffled off behind the stables to relieve themselves in the piles of dirty straw and horse manure that had been mucked from the stalls.

Soon after dawn, the activity around both the Council Hall and Keep increased. The Keep's gates were opened and the staff entered, reporting for work. Minel handed Valek a stale heel of bread without a word. He stared at the generous gift. Why was it those with the least gave the most? Thank fate, there were no beggars in Ixia. The Commander took care of his people, giving them jobs and clothing. Even those who were physically or mentally unable to work were well cared for.

As the morning wore on, Valek played his part, holding out his hand and pleading for coins. Most people wrinkled their noses and ignored him. A few stopped and gave him a copper or two. One lady gave him a silver to get a bath. Valek kept one copper and handed the rest to Minel to distribute.

Minel grunted. "Maybe that stink is working for you."

It was getting close to lunch time when Valek spotted Yelena leaving the Keep. She had a determined expression. Heading west, she walked quickly. Valek was about to follow when another man left the Keep and sprinted after her. Ferde?

Valek was too far away to warn her.

CHAPTER 16

*Y*elena spun before the man reached her and yanked her bo staff free from its holder. He skidded to a stop, holding his hands out and away from the machete hanging from his belt. Muscular, but stocky with short black hair, the man was taller than Yelena. She said something to him and turned away. He grabbed her shoulder and spun her around.

Valek hurried to intervene.

"I know where you're going," the man said.

He slowed. Perhaps this wasn't Ferde.

"Bully for you." Yelena shrugged his hand off. "Then you know time is of the essence. Go back to the Keep." She resumed her walk.

"If I do, I'll tell the masters what you're doing." He trailed after her.

And just what was she doing? Going after Ferde on her own?

"Truly? You're not very good at telling," she said.

"This time I won't hesitate." The man kept pace.

Valek hung back. Close enough to overhear their conversation but not be noticed.

She stopped. "What do you want?"

"To come along."

"Why?"

"You'll need me," the man said.

"Considering how helpful you were in the jungle fourteen years ago, I think I'm better off on my own." She spat the words at him, surprising Valek with her vehemence.

But the man only cringed. And by the stubborn set of his shoulders, Valek knew Yelena's anger was not going to deter him.

"Either include me in your plans, or I'll follow you and ruin them."

"Fine. But let me warn you that you're going to have to let me inside your mind in order for you to get through Ferde's shield."

The man paled but nodded. They headed west.

As Valek suspected, Yelena planned to go after Ferde. But at least she wasn't on her own. She might hate the man with her, but she had accepted his help.

Valek followed them to the market. Yelena greeted a tall, lean man and left the stocky guy with him while she searched for someone. Valek found a spot to watch. Yelena approached a stand selling fabric. Her young friend...Fisk? Was helping a customer, but he finished quickly when he spotted Yelena. She talked to him and he flashed her a brilliant smile before racing off.

She returned to the two men and they waited together. Soon, a bunch of street rats gathered around them. Fisk's friends? Yelena appeared to be giving them instructions. The children nodded and scattered, disappearing down alleys. Fisk led Yelena and the stocky guy to another alley while the thin guy headed in a different direction.

Valek wished he could join them, but it was too risky. Instead, he kept close just in case she needed him. Although, he doubted she would. He marveled at her confident stride. It appeared she had a plan and she had made friends. Determined, intelligent, a truly remarkable person he was honored to know. Her time in Sitia had changed her for the better. Irys had been right to ask him to stay away for a year. Yelena had discovered her wings.

Her group stopped about half a block from a large courtyard. A magnificent white statue of fifteen horses running in a circle occupied the center. Words were exchanged and Yelena drew in a breath. Then she signaled Fisk. He barked like a dog.

Soon after, other barks echoed. And then Fisk's friends ran into and out of the courtyard, playing tag with loud joyful shouts and taunts. Yelena held Stocky's and Fisk's hands. The trio walked into the courtyard. Ah there must be a magical barrier around the courtyard and the kids were the distraction. Smart.

They paused next to the fountain. She released Fisk and he ran to join his friends. Then Stocky and Yelena headed to a house on the other side of the street, going around to the side. Valek assumed Ferde was inside that building. Once she picked the lock and they disappeared, he entered the courtyard. The magic slid around him as if he'd walked through a wall of water.

Valek searched for a hidden location nearby. He found an alcove that would work. Waiting was always the most difficult part of his job, and this time was no exception. He wondered how long he should wait. Yelena had proved to be quite capable of protecting herself, but Ferde had master level powers.

Trust me. Her words from four days ago echoed in his mind. She'd asked for his trust in handling the exchange for Opal, and she'd survived. He could wait a bit longer and not rush in there like some knight in shining armor.

Time stretched toward infinity. *Trust me, trust me, trust me,* he chanted under his breath.

Pain suddenly pierced his heart. He grabbed his chest and sank to the ground as fire burned inside him.

He concentrated, focusing on Yelena. *Trouble, love?*

I need your immunity to magic.

Yours. When she had asked for his strength, he'd pushed his energy directly toward her. This time, he imagined his immunity as a cloak. He lifted it from his shoulders and wrapped it around hers.

The effort cost him. He slumped but not in exhaustion. A strange sensation vibrated through his muscles. It was like a heavy blanket had been removed and now he could fly. He was untethered. Free.

His senses sharpened and he choked on the fetid stench of manure emanating from his clothes. Valek clambered to his feet, moving carefully so he didn't launch his body into the air. Then his immunity slammed back into him, knocking him to the ground.

Lying on the hard surface, he panted with the effort to breath under the pressure. Moving seemed impossible. He remained there as his strength slowly returned. When he'd recovered, he sat up.

From his position, he spotted the tall, thin man trotting across the courtyard with a wide grin on his face. He entered the building. A clear sign Yelena had stopped Ferde.

Way to go, love. But he couldn't celebrate for too long. Valek needed to move before the master magicians arrived with their soldiers.

He hurried back to the Council Hall and joined his new friends.

Minel sidled up to him. "Where've you been?" He sniffed. "Not bathing, unfortunately."

"Nature called."

"What? You too good to use the manure pile?"

"I've a shy bladder."

Minel laughed.

After a while, Yelena appeared. Her face was drawn, and dark smudges of exhaustion lined her eyes.

"Ah, that's one of the kind ones," Minel said as a couple beggars headed toward her.

Valek joined them.

"Sorry. I can't help you today," she called without slowing.

The others returned, but he followed.

Yelena turned. "I said—"

"Lovely lady, spare a copper?" Valek asked.

She peered at him with a bit of confusion. But when she met his gaze, recognition flared.

"Can't you spare a copper for the man who just saved your life?" Valek asked, guessing that was why she needed his immunity.

"I'm broke. I had to pay off the distraction. Those kids don't work cheap. What—"

"Unity fountain. A quarter hour." Valek returned to the steps.

"Any luck?" Minel asked.

"You were right." He dipped his hand into his pocket and removed all the Sitian coins he had on him, giving them to Minel. "She has a big heart."

Minel squinted at him. "Uh huh."

"I think I'll go take that bath now."

Instead, he headed to the Unity Fountain. It was a large jade sphere with holes that showed smaller and smaller spheres tucked inside. Water sprayed from eleven waterspouts around the statue. He found a doorway with a dark recess and removed a layer of rags, hoping to reduce the smell. Soon, Yelena entered the courtyard, she gazed at the fountain for a moment. He stepped from the shadows long enough to catch her eye.

She joined him and hugged him tight, trapping his arms. Then she released him.

"Thank you for helping me against Ferde," she said. "Now go home, before you get caught."

Valek smiled. "And miss all the fun? No, love. I'm going with you on your errand."

She rocked back in surprise that he'd guessed her next move. It made sense to him that once she dealt with Ferde, she'd need to finish her business with Alea.

"There's no way I can convince you to go to Ixia?" she asked.

"None."

"All right. Although I reserve the right to say, 'I told you so,' should you get captured," she said in a mock serious tone, but couldn't hide the relief that shone in her tired green eyes.

"Agreed." Valek would enjoy this mission for so many reasons. The best one, spending time with Yelena.

They arranged to meet at the edge of the Avibian Plains an hour after sunset. That gave him enough time to get washed, changed, put on a new disguise, gather a few supplies, including more Sitian coins, and grab his pack.

Brigi and Gabor both cautioned him to be extra careful when he'd updated them on his plans. There were still groups of soldiers out hunting for him in the Citadel. Plus, all the guards at the gates had been notified to keep an eye out for him. That presented his biggest challenge. Valek considered his options. He knew to avoid the south and east gates. The north gate was too far; he'd have to loop around the Citadel to reach the plains. That left the west gate.

When Valek reached the market, he paused as an idea struck him. He furrowed his brow in confusion and wandered through the stands selling goods. Picking up a few items, he shook his head and replaced them when the sellers started haggling. Soon enough, Yelena's little entrepreneur, Fisk, appeared.

"Kind sir, do you need some assistance?" he asked.

"I do. Can you provide me with a few helpers. I need a distraction."

Fisk crossed his arms. "I don't do anything illegal."

"You won't. Just a little commotion like you did earlier for my friend Yelena."

He squinted his light brown eyes. "Friend? Prove it."

"She wears a butterfly pendent that is black with silver streaks."

"She keeps that mostly hidden under her tunic. How do you know about it?"

Boy, this kid was definitely not a dupe. "I carved it for her. How do you know about it?" he countered.

Fisk smiled. "She fingers the lump whenever she's thinking. I asked her about it and she showed it to me. Okay, you're legit. How many helpers do you need?"

"Four should do it."

"It'll cost you two silvers."

"Agreed."

"Ha! I would have done it for one silver. You need to learn how to bargain."

Valek would have given him a gold if asked. The kid was delightful. No wonder Yelena liked him. "Noted for next time."

Fisk laughed and raced off to find three of his friends. When they assembled, Valek told them what he needed. Fisk gave Valek a shrewd look, but he grinned in anticipation.

"Sounds fun," the boy said. "I wanna be the tattler."

"You got it."

They headed to the west gate. Before the gate became visible, Valek paid Fisk and the boy hung back. Valek continued walking with the kids. Two boys and a girl who had dressed in their nicest clothes in order to work as helpers in the market. They still looked a bit shabby, but Valek found most adults didn't really look closely at children.

When they neared the gate, the girl grabbed his hand. "I'm so excited we're going to visit Grandmom!" she squealed.

The boys agreed. "She makes the best pie, doesn't she Dad?"

"She does indeed." Valek smiled indulgently at his "children." "Don't forget, your Uncle Vincent promised to take you fishing."

The guards asked a few standard questions, but one keen-eyed man asked Valek to come into the guardhouse for a safety check. No doubt wanting to pull on his nose and hair to test if he wore a disguise.

He gave the guard a puzzled look and signaled surreptitiously to Fisk. "But my children..."

"They'll be fine, we'll watch them for ya."

"Hey! Hey!" Fisk shouted, running toward the gate and waving his arms. "Hey!"

"What's that kid yelling about?"

"Hey! That man..." he puffed, "The one...everyone's looking for! Just robbed the bakery down the street!" He gestured wildly. "He grabbed a loaf of bread!"

Valek and his children were promptly forgotten as two of the guards took off in the indicated direction. He nodded a thanks at Fisk and continued through the gate. The children accompanied him outside of the Citadel to the south entrance, so they could return to the market.

However, before the kids could cross through, a group of soldiers exited followed by the Wannabe King riding on a brown horse. Valek yanked the children out of the way and hoped no one would bother to give them more than a glance. Thankfully, the unit was in a hurry, and Cahil didn't look back as they disappeared down the road toward the plains. The last time Valek had been here, they'd caught him. He shivered at how close he'd come to a repeat performance.

Once he ensured his helpers returned through the gate without trouble, Valek turned his focus on Cahil's plans. He doubted the Wannabe King had given up searching for him. Perhaps Cahil learned of the disturbance at the west gate and assumed Valek was on the move? Or was he hoping to set up an ambush before Valek arrived? But then, how did he know Valek was heading toward the plains and not returning to Ixia? Perhaps the trap was for Yelena, who would be coming this way in about an hour's time.

Regardless of who he planned to capture, where would he set his trap? Since Cahil wasn't related to the Sandseeds, he couldn't set it up inside the plains, so the best place would be at Valek and Yelena's rendezvous location. Party crashers. Lovely.

Valek could remain at the gate and warn Yelena, but he was dangerously exposed. Plus, she'd proved she could protect herself. It'd be fun to watch her take down the Wannabe King. He decided to find a good spot to watch the action. But before he did, he searched the ground by the Citadel's walls. Valek's pack had been left behind, but did one of his people take his cloud-kissed dagger— Ah. A gleam caught Valek's eye. Dried blood and dirt coated the weapon, but his weapon was undamaged. A good sign. He wiped the blade clean and tucked it away.

The road that traveled south dipped into a valley below the Citadel before snaking along the western edge of the plains. Valek stayed east of the road to avoid running into Cahil and his men and entered the plains. The Sandseed's magic pressed on him, but it wasn't hard enough to impede him. He crept westward through the tall grass and spotted the Wannabe King's soldiers. They hid on the other side of the road, but Cahil was nowhere to be seen.

Valek waited. Eventually the sky darkened and the sound of hoofbeats came from the north.

"Where do you think you're going?" Cahil's demand rang out over the quiet plains.

"That's not your concern," Yelena said.

Valek moved north. On the road, Yelena and Kiki faced Cahil on his horse. The Wannabe King's face was bright red.

"Not *my* concern? Not *my* concern?" He sputtered. "You're the heart mate of the most wanted criminal in Sitia. Your whereabouts are of the utmost concern to me. In fact, I'm going to personally see to it that I know exactly where you are at all times." He whistled.

His unit broke cover and fanned out behind Kiki. They all held blowpipes to their lips. That complicated things. Valek clamped down on a curse.

"What do you want?" she asked Cahil.

"Playing the simpleton to delay the inevitable, Yelena? I guess it has worked for you in the past. You certainly played me for a fool," he said with a flat tone. "Convincing me *and* First Magician that you weren't a spy, using your magic to make me trust you. I fell for it all."

"Cahil, I—"

"What *I* want is to kill Valek. Besides getting revenge for the murder of my family, I will be able to show the council my abilities and they will finally support me."

"You had Valek before and lost him. What makes you think you can kill him this time?" She asked.

"Your heart mate will exchange his life for yours."

True. *But touch her and die.*

"You're going to need more people to capture me."

You tell him, love.

"Truly? Take another look."

She glanced over her shoulder.

"The darts are treated with Curare," Cahil said. "An excellent Sitian weapon. You won't get far."

Unless she had the antidote-of-sorts, which was a game changer. Unease swirled in Valek's chest.

"Will you cooperate, or do I need to have you immobilized?" Cahil asked. The smug bastard.

Valek had had enough. He straightened and strode out to the road. Everyone gaped at him. Fun.

"That's an interesting choice, love," he said. "You'll need some time to think it over. In the meantime..." Valek held his arms away from his body as he approached Cahil. *See? I'm not armed.*

Cahil transferred the reins to his left hand and pulled his too-heavy sword from its sheath.

"Let's see if I have this right," Valek continued in a casual tone. "You want revenge for your family. Understandable. But you should know that the royal family is not *your* family. One thing I have learned over the years is to know my enemy. The royal bloodline ended the day the Commander took control of Ixia. I made sure of that."

"You lie!" Cahil urged his horse forward, lunging at Valek with his sword.

Valek side-stepped, avoiding being trampled. The sharp blade cut through air.

When Cahil turned his horse for another charge, Yelena said, "It makes sense. Valek wouldn't leave a job unfinished."

He pulled back on the bridle, stopping in disbelief. "Your love for him has damaged your senses."

"And your hunger for power has affected your intelligence. Your people are using you, yet you refuse to see the obvious."

Cahil shook his head. "I won't listen to any more lies. My people are loyal. They obey me or else they will be punished. Goel's death helped me to reinforce that lesson."

Yelena jerked back in surprise. "*You* killed Goel."

He smiled. "My soldiers have pledged their lives to me. I committed no crime." He brandished his sword. "Ready," he called to his unit. "Aim and—"

"Think about this before you gloat about *your* people, Cahil," Yelena said. "They look to Captain Marrok for approval before following your orders. They gave you a sword that was too heavy for you and failed to properly train you with it. You are supposed to be related to the King, who was a powerful magician. Why don't you have any magic?"

Nice, love. Valek met Marrok's wary gaze. *Sorry mate, but that's what you get for lying to Cahil all these years.*

"I—" Cahil hesitated.

Time to move. Valek took a running jump and joined Yelena on Kiki's back. The horse launched into the plains, and he wrapped his arms around her waist.

"Fire!" Cahil yelled.

A few darts whizzed past, but none struck either of them. If Cahil's people were smart, they would have aimed for Kiki—a much larger target. However, Valek and Yelena's comments had managed to rattle them.

Kiki flew through the grasses. He'd no idea what gait she used, but it was as if he sat between the wings of a bird. They rode for a few hours before Kiki slowed and stopped. It looked like they were in the middle of nowhere, but at least the full moon lit up the undulating landscape.

Yelena tried to inspect Kiki for injuries, but she snorted and moved away to graze. He studied Kiki with amazement. No sweat darkened her coat and it appeared she didn't need to be hobbled to stay nearby.

"That was close." Yelena shivered and pulled her cloak tighter.

"Not really," Valek said. He pulled her into a glorious hug. "We distracted his people so when Wannabe King gave the order, they didn't have time to aim."

The cold night air nipped on his exposed ears. Yelena glanced at his clothing, probably noting he didn't have a cloak. She raised an eyebrow. "I'll share yours." He grinned. "But first you need a fire, food, and some sleep."

She shook her head. "I need you." Grabbing his shirt, she pulled it up.

He tried to protest—she really needed to rest—but she was determined. And a determined Yelena was a formidable force. Plus, if he was being honest, he needed her just as much.

Together, they celebrated surviving, being alive, and safe. At this moment there was no past or future. They existed solely for each other.

∼

The morning sunlight woke Valek. Careful not to wake Yelena, he extricated his arms and legs. Although, it didn't matter, because she didn't stir with the motion nor when the cold air briefly touched her bare skin. The fight with Ferde must have exhausted her. He tucked the cloak tight around her, dressed, and scanned their surroundings. Nothing but grassland, rolling hills, and a sandy soil. Kiki grazed nearby.

Valek searched for firewood. No luck. Guess it would be cold tea and jerky for breakfast. Kiki nudged his shoulder. He spun around in surprise. How did she sneak up on him?

She snorted then glanced at her back before meeting his gaze. *Did she just...?* Another snort and she repeated the gesture. *She did.*

"You want me to get on?"

Clearly impatient with his stupidity, she pawed the ground. Okay then. He grabbed her mane and mounted. She took off at a canter, and within two strides switched to flying. Not long after, she stopped right next to a dead tree. It hadn't been big or thick, but it had fallen and broken into pieces that were perfectly sized for a campfire.

He met her intelligent gaze. "Janco called you a magic horse. I'm beginning to suspect he didn't exaggerate—a rarity. I'm glad you're with Yelena. Thank you."

She snuffled at his pockets.

"Ah, when we get back, I'll see what Yelena brought for you."

He gathered the wood in his arms, but mounting would be an issue. Kiki knelt and he marveled again. They returned in no time. Yelena hadn't moved. He found a couple peppermints in her pack and Kiki sucked them up.

Deciding to wait until later to build a fire, Valek organized their supplies. The sunshine warmed the air, driving off the morning chill. At one point, he may or may not have dozed. His breakfast of jerky hadn't really satisfied his grumbling stomach and he would have liked to offer Yelena something more nutritious. However, all he had was his knife. And he hadn't seen any game all day, but that didn't mean there wasn't any.

When in doubt, ask a local. Valek walked over to Kiki. She had ranged further from their campsite. She lifted her head when he approached.

Feeling a bit silly, he asked, "Are there any edible critters around?"

She signaled for him to hop on.

"All I have is my knife."

A snort.

"Okay, you're the boss." He mounted.

This time she took him to a dip in the landscape. It resembled a bowl made of clay. Except, small shrubs grew in it and on its walls. Dropping him off at the center of the bowl, Kiki gave him a significant look before leaving. Valek pulled his knife and waited. Not sure for what, as he couldn't see over the top of the bowl.

Squeals and grunts sounded just before a carpet of small creatures crested the lip and ran straight at him. About the size of a rabbit, they scurried on four legs like a ground hog. Panicked, they streamed passed his boots. Assuming they were edible, he stabbed one in what he hoped was its heart. Then skewered another.

Soon, the little herd disappeared, and Kiki returned. Magic horse, indeed. They returned to the campsite and Valek butchered the mystery creatures. Then he built a fire and cooked the meat. Yelena slept through it all, and he wouldn't wake her. She needed her strength for the coming fight.

Valek ate his portion and considered how they would find Alea. The Daviian Plateau was directly south of the Avibian Plains. A rather lifeless place, if he remembered from his history lessons. It was a quarter of the size of the plains, but still big enough that it would take weeks to search it all. Perhaps Kiki the Magic Horse would know where to go.

"Breakfast?" Yelena asked in a hopeful tone.

He turned. "Dinner. You've slept all day."

She sat up in alarm. "You should have woken me. What if Cahil finds us?"

"Doubtful with all this magic in the air." Valek peered into the sky, sensing the protective power. "Does it bother you?"

"No. I'm a distant cousin to the Sandseed Clan. If I came close to their village with the intent to harm them, I think the protection would attack me." She paused. "Either that or one of their Story Weavers would."

Valek considered the last time he was in the plains with Ziva Moon. They'd been confronted by several impressive Sandseed warriors. He'd like to avoid another encounter with them. "How long will it take us to reach the Daviian Plateau?"

"It depends on Kiki. If she decides to use her gust-of-wind gait, we could be there in a few hours."

"Gust-of-wind? Is that what you call it? I've never seen a horse run that fast before."

"She only does it when we're in the plains. Perhaps it's connected to the Sandseed's magic."

Valek shrugged. "Faster is better. The faster we can take care of Alea, the better." He purposely didn't tell her about his previous encounters with the magician. If Yelena knew that Alea had threatened the Commander, she would also know that Valek planned to assassinate Alea. Yelena had been living in Sitia long enough to know that Sitians preferred to capture their criminals even if they were dangerous renegades. And Yelena would probably get into trouble if she killed Alea. Valek was already the Scourge of Sitia. They should thank him for taking care of their problem.

He pulled the meat from the fire and handed the spit to Yelena. "Eat. You need your strength."

She sniffed it. "What is it?"

He laughed. "You're better off not knowing."

"Poisons?"

"You tell me," he teased.

She performed the five S-steps of food tasting. He loved that she hadn't forgotten. In essence, it was a survival skill. When she finished every last bite, they packed.

"Valek, after we deal with Alea, you must promise to return to Ixia."

He grinned. "Why would I do that? I'm beginning to enjoy the climate. I might build a summer home here."

"It's that cocky attitude that got you into trouble in the first place."

"No, love. It was you. If you hadn't gotten yourself captured by Goel, I wouldn't have tipped my hand to the Wannabe King."

"You didn't tip your hand. I'm afraid I did that when I was fighting with Cahil."

"Defending my honor again?" he asked, although he'd already suspected.

"Yes."

His heart warmed. "I know you love me, so you can stop proving it. I really don't care what the Wannabe King thinks of me."

"Valek, I'm sorry for believing you killed Goel."

He waved away her apology. "You would have been right. I went back to take care of him for you, but he had beaten me to it." Valek sobered. "The Wannabe King remains a problem."

Her gaze hardened and she nodded. "One that *I'll* deal with."

"Now who's cocky?"

She opened her mouth to retort, but he couldn't resist a kiss. He pulled back with a sigh. They needed—the sound of drumming hooves shattered the quiet.

Had the Wannabe King found them after all?

CHAPTER 17

*V*alek hid in the long grass as a horse seemed to materialize from the air. Not Cahil, thank fate. The stocky man who had gone with Yelena to fight Ferde sat on top. His green eyes were wide with fear.

"She's never done that before," he said.

"I call that Kiki's gust-of-wind gait." Yelena's tone was sharp with anger.

Valek crouched, preparing to strike.

"Is Rusalka a Sandseed horse?" Yelena asked.

Stocky nodded, and Valek launched from the grass. He tackled Stocky, knocking them both from the horse's back and onto the ground. Valek pulled the man's machete and held it to his throat.

"What are you doing here?" he demanded.

"Come. To find. Yelena," Stocky said between gasps.

"Why?"

"It's all right, Valek. He's my brother," Yelena said.

Brother? Valek moved the blade away but remained on top of him. They did have the same eye shape and color. However

Stocky had a square face, while Yelena's was oval and perfect. Their skin color was similar as well.

Stocky stared at him in horror. "Valek? You have no smell. No aura."

That made no sense. "Is he a simpleton?" Valek asked Yelena.

She grinned. "No." She pulled Valek off her brother. "His magic can sense a person's soul. Your immunity must be blocking his power." Yelena bent over Stocky and examined him, presumably searching for injuries. "Are you all right?"

He sat up and glanced nervously at Valek. "That depends."

"Don't worry about him, he's overprotective."

Valek harrumphed. "If you could keep out of trouble for one day, protecting you wouldn't be so instinctive." He rubbed his leg. It ached from where he'd hit the ground. "Or so painful."

Stocky recovered from his shock and stood.

"Why are you here?" Yelena asked her brother.

He looked at Valek then at the ground. "It was something Mother said."

She waited. Ah, she'd learned that tactic from him. Pride swelled in Valek's chest.

"She told me that you were lost again. And only the brother that had searched for you for fourteen years could find you."

"*How* did you find me?"

Stocky gestured a bit wildly at his horse. "Kiki had found Topaz in the plains, so I thought, since Rusalka was bred by the Sandseeds, I asked her to find Kiki. And… And…"

"She found us very fast." Yelena rubbed her arms.

Valek guessed Rusalka must be the name of Stocky's horse. Was Topaz another horse or someone Yelena knew?

"Why does Perl think I'm lost?" Yelena asked. "And why send you? You weren't any help the last time."

Perl must be their mother, but Valek wondered why Yelena was so angry at her brother. What had he done?

Stocky cringed with guilt. "I don't know why she sent me."

A rustle of movement sounded and a Sandseed warrior named Moon Man walked toward them. Valek tensed. The last time they'd met, when Valek was hunting the assassin who'd gone after Yelena, Moon Man had tested Valek's reflexes with a shower of sharp knives.

"A good guy," Yelena said, touching Valek's arm.

"This seems to be quite the meeting place," Valek muttered under his breath. But he held his ground as the big man came closer. This time, he was clothed in a pair of short pants. Scars on his arms and legs stood out against his dark skin. Moon Man's powerful build reminded Valek of Ari.

"No mysterious arrival? No coalescing from a sunray? Where's the paint?" Yelena's words dripped with sarcasm.

"It is no fun when you already know those tricks," Moon Man said. "Besides, Ghost would have killed me if I had suddenly appeared."

"Ghost?" she asked.

Moon Man pointed to Valek. "Kiki's name for him. It makes sense," he said. "To magical beings, we see the world through our magic. We see him with our eyes but cannot see him with our magic. So, he is like a ghost to us."

"Another relative?" Valek asked.

A broad smile stretched Moon Man's lips. "Yes, I am her mother's uncle's wife's third cousin."

"He's a Story Weaver, a magician of the Sandseed clan," Yelena explained. "And what are you doing here?"

Moon Man's playfulness faded from his face. "You are on *my* lands. I could ask you the same thing, but I already know why *you* have come. I came to make sure you keep your promise."

"What promise?" Stocky and Valek asked at the same time.

She waved the question away. "I will, but not now. We need—"

"I know what you intend to do. You will not succeed with that unless you untangle yourself," Moon Man said.

"Me? But I thought you said…" She stopped. "Why won't I succeed?"

Moon Man refused to answer.

"Do you have any more cryptic advice?" she asked in annoyance, but underneath, Valek sensed she cared for the man.

Moon Man held out his hands. One toward Stocky and the other to Yelena.

Valek huffed. "Looks like a family affair. I'll be close by if you need me, love." Meaning, he'd give her his energy or his immunity or anything else she asked for.

Stocky stepped forward and grabbed Moon Man's hand, shooting his sister a look of stubborn determination. The exact same expression Valek had seen on Yelena's beautiful face more times than he could count. However, he was smart enough not to voice that comment.

"Let's finish this," Stocky said, challenging her.

She grabbed Moon Man's hands and the magic that bloomed from the big man almost knocked Valek over. The three of them faded and disappeared.

Moon Man reappeared about half an hour later without Yelena or her brother.

"Where are they?" Valek asked.

"In the shadow world."

"Uh. Shouldn't you be there too?"

"Oh, I am. But I am also with you."

"Okay."

Moon Man smiled. "You are confused."

"There's been so much happening. And I'm not privy to all the information."

"Frustrating for a man who loves knowledge."

Valek wondered what all this was leading to. "Very. We

haven't had any time to talk about everything we need to discuss. I've no idea what she's been learning or doing in Sitia." And why was he telling this man?

"Or for her to learn of your adventures."

"She's dealing with a lot right now."

"Hmmm." Moon Man saw right through him. "I can help with some of your confusion. Yelena and her brother's relationship is twisted with guilt, fear, anger, sadness, pain, and loss. When Yelena was kidnapped, her brother watched it happen. Eight years old, he had been upset with her for not staying close to him—the Illiais Jungle is filled with dangers. Then, when Kangom carried her away, he was frozen in fear. Of course, an eight-year-old cannot fight a grown man. Especially not one with powerful magic. His guilt and shame over not acting caused his silence, and Yelena's family never knew what happened to her. She just disappeared."

"That's terrible. If they had known—"

"Yes. Which is why Yelena is angry with him. To atone for his inaction, her brother searched for her every day he was in the jungle. And then, she suddenly returned fourteen years later with tales of her life in Ixia, and his pain and guilt intensified into hatred. He thought she had been living a wonderful life, while his was wracked with guilt, shame, and pain. He had no life other than work. He sought to kill himself at one point. The horses call him Sad Man. Of course, Yelena and her brother have both made inaccurate assumptions about the other. It was time they untangled."

"With your help?"

"As their Story Weaver, it is my duty to aid them."

"Will it work?"

Moon Man grinned and gestured. Yelena and her brother stood nearby, staring at each other. "They have reached an understanding. And I will aid you as well, Ghost Warrior. The

Sandseeds will send you some soldiers to help you against the Daviian Vermin named Alea. Meet us at dawn."

"Where?"

"The horses know where to go."

"How?" He asked the air. Moon Man was already gone.

Valek went to join Yelena and her brother.

"How come they never schedule a New Beginnings feast when you really need to start over?" Yelena asked.

"That's okay. I don't dance," he said with a smile.

"You will."

Valek cleared his throat. "Touching as this is, we need to go. Your Story Weaver is providing us with some soldiers to aid against Alea's people. We're to rendezvous with them at dawn. I take it your brother…"

"Leif," Yelena provided.

"…is coming along?"

"Of course," Leif said.

"No," she said at the same time. "I don't want you to get hurt. Mother wouldn't like it."

"And I wouldn't be able to face her wrath if I didn't stay and help." Leif crossed his arms over his chest. His square jaw set into a stubborn line.

"Your mother sounds like a formidable woman," Valek said into the silence.

"You have no idea," Leif replied with a sigh.

"Well, if she's anything like Yelena, my deepest sympathies," Valek teased.

"Hey!"

Leif laughed and the tense moment dissipated.

Valek handed Leif his machete. "Do you know how to use it?"

"Of course. I chopped Yelena's bo into firewood," Leif joked.

"You took me by surprise. I didn't want to hurt you," she shot back.

Leif looked dubious.

"How about a rematch?" she asked.

"Anytime."

Valek stepped between them. "I'm beginning to wish that you were an only child, love. Can you both manage to focus on the task at hand without trying to catch up on fourteen years of sibling rivalry?"

"Yes," they said in unison, properly chastised.

"Good. Then, let's go."

"Where?" she asked.

"In keeping with his cryptic nature, all your Story Weaver said was, 'The horses know where to go.'" Valek shrugged. "It's certainly not a military strategy *I* would use, but I've learned that the south uses its own strategy. And, strangely enough, it works."

The horses did indeed know where to go. As the sun rose over the plains, they encountered a group of Sandseed soldiers on a rocky outcropping surrounded by tall grass. Valek counted. There were eighteen warriors dressed in leather armor and equipped with either scimitars or spears. They had painted red streaks on their faces and arms, creating a fierce countenance.

Valek and Yelena dismounted. Leif jumped off his horse, Rusalka. The two horses grazed as Yelena shivered in the cold morning air.

Moon Man greeted them. He had dressed like the others, but he was armed with his scimitar and a bo staff. Valek admired the carvings of animals and symbols in the black wood of the five-foot tall staff. They seemed to tell a story. And like his gray rocks, there was a hidden beauty inside the wood. The carvings revealed a gold-colored wood under the black surface.

"I sent a scout last night," Moon Man said. "He found the

blood-letting apparatus in the Void, just as Yelena described. Then he tracked the Daviian Vermin to a campsite about a mile east of that location. We are on the edge of the plains, about two miles north of that site."

Blood-letting apparatus? Valek wanted to ask Yelena for more details, but again, not the proper time. The rest was good news. "We'll wait until dark and launch a surprise attack," Valek said. That was the standard procedure.

"That will not work," Moon Man said. "The Vermin have a shield that will alert them to intruders. My scout could not get too close to their camp for fear of discovery." Moon Man scanned the horizon. "They have strong Warpers, who can hide their whereabouts from our magic."

"Warpers?" Leif asked.

Moon Man frowned. "Magicians. I refuse to call them Story Weavers, for they manipulate the threads for their own selfish desires."

Yelena glanced at the group of Sandseeds. "You don't plan to use your magic?"

"No."

"And you don't plan to take prisoners?"

"That is not the Sandseed way. The Vermin must be exterminated."

Valek liked the Sandseed way. "How are you going to prevent the Daviian Warpers from using their magic?"

A dangerous glint flashed in Moon Man's eyes. "We move the Void."

"What's a void?" Valek asked.

"It's a hole in the blanket of power," Yelena explained. "If a magician is inside a void, they can't use magic." She turned to Moon Man. "You can move it?"

"The blanket of power can be repositioned only with the utmost care. We will center the blanket's hole directly over the Vermin's camp, and then we will attack."

"When?" Valek asked.

"Now." Moon Man walked over to his soldiers.

"I'd hoped to use the Sandseeds as a distraction," Valek whispered to Yelena. "This will work. Once Alea is dead, we leave. This isn't our fight."

"I think capture and incarceration would be a harsher punishment for her," she said.

Valek studied her for a moment. If they could capture her, then he would refrain from killing the magician. "As you wish."

The group of Sandseed warriors shouted a war cry, then disappeared into the tall grass. Moon Man joined Yelena and Valek. "They will position themselves around the camp. The signal to attack will be when the Void is in place. You are to come with me." He glanced at the three of them. "You need weapons. Here."

He tossed his bo to Yelena. She caught it with her right hand.

"That is yours. A gift from Suekray."

"Who?" she asked.

"A horsewoman of our clan. She raised and trained Kiki. You must have made an impression on her. Her gifts are as rare as the snow. Your story is etched into it."

Yelena marveled at the weapon as she tested its weight. Moon Man handed Valek a scimitar. Nice. He admired the curved blade. It gleamed in the sunlight. Leif pulled his machete from its sheath.

"Let us go," Moon Man said.

Yelena took off her cloak and rummaged in her bag. When she finished, the three of them followed Moon Man into the tall grass and toward the Daviian camp.

Once there, they found a hiding spot behind a small bush. The cover was scant, due to the area's lack of rain. Somehow, the Sandseeds around them managed to blend into the barren landscape. Moon Man crouched in a slight depression.

Valek peered at the Daviian camp. There were a few people

around their tents and the campfire. Not many. He sensed a wall of magic and speculated that it was the Warpers' shield. As he waited for the signal, he wondered if he'd experience that unfettered feeling again once inside the Void. He'd still have his immunity, but there wouldn't be any magic to block. If so, would that lightness help or hinder his ability to fight?

The wall of magic dissipated. Moon Man stood as another war cry sounded. They jumped to their feet and followed the Sandseeds toward the camp. Yelena stopped and stared. What had she seen?

Valek followed her gaze. The camp had changed. Instead of a few people milling about, there stood over thirty. Instead of a handful of tents, there were now rows and rows of them. The magic shield had also been a powerful illusion, hiding the Davi- ian's real numbers. He admired the ruse even though it meant they were in trouble.

Despite the illusion, the Sandseed warriors didn't hesitate. They had the element of surprise and weren't about to retreat. Wading into the fray, they cut down anyone in their path. Leif followed along, hacking with his machete. He hadn't been lying, the man knew how to fight.

This wasn't going to be pretty. Valek shot Yelena a grim look. "Find Alea," he said. Then he hefted his weapon and joined the Sandseeds.

As Yelena stayed at the edges of the battle, Valek worked his way toward Leif. Blocking, dodging, ducking, and countering, he didn't waste time with fancy moves or to test an opponent's defenses like he would have if sparring with one of the Comman- der's soldiers. This was kill or be killed. The Daviians couldn't use their magic, but they knew how to swing their swords.

Shouts, screams, and curses rolled together into one loud cacophony. Blood spurted, coating his blade and staining his clothes. The smell of it fogged the air. It was brutal. The horrors of battle were the reason the Commander's rebellion used assassination, guile, and promises for a better life than outright war.

At one point, he spotted Yelena fighting with Alea. He shouted to Leif. When Yelena's brother looked over at Valek, he pointed to the women fighting. Leif nodded, and the two of them maneuvered through the crowd so they stood between the Daviians and the women, keeping the Warpers from helping Alea. From the brief glances he managed, Yelena held her own. Her bo staff countered Alea's short swords with ease.

Moon Man sprinted toward them. "Time to retreat," he called.

Valek ran over to Yelena. She stood above the now prone magician. "Next time," she said to Alea. "We'll finish this."

No, you won't, love. He couldn't leave Alea to come after Yelena or the Commander again.

Valek knelt beside Alea, picked up her knife, and said, "How fitting that I'm going to slice your throat the same way I sliced your brother's. This is what happens when you come after the people I love." He cut deep into her neck with one smooth move.

When Valek caught up to Yelena, he said, "We can't afford to play favorites."

They raced back toward the plains. The Daviians gave up the chase once they reached the border. However, they kept running until they arrived at the rocky outcropping where Kiki and Rusalka waited.

"No doubt they will move their camp farther into the plateau," Moon Man said. The effort of running had not winded him but sweat shone on his brow. "I will need to bring more soldiers. To have deceived my scout and me means their Warpers are more powerful than we suspected. I must consult with our clan's elders."

Moon Man inclined his head in farewell and disappeared into the tall grass.

"What now?" Leif asked.

Yelena met Valek's gaze. His heart lurched.

"You go home and so will I," she said to Leif.

Home. With him? Valek's heart thumped its approval.

"You're coming with me to the Keep?" Leif asked.

"I…" Her gaze stared into the distance.

Valek wished he could communicate with her mind to mind. Would he encourage her to return to Ixia? What about the execution order the Commander had signed? She'd changed so much, but she still had more to learn.

"I think you're afraid to go back to the Keep," Leif said.

Her attention snapped back. "What?"

"It will be much easier for you to stay away and not have to deal with being a Soulfinder, being a daughter, and being a sister."

Soulfinder? That was new.

"I'm not afraid. I tried to find a place in Sitia, but I keep getting pushed away. How many hints do I need? I'm not a glutton for punishment. And what if the council decides that being a Soulfinder makes me evil? And they burn me alive for violating their Ethical Code?"

Valek straightened. Not on his watch.

"You *are* afraid," Leif said.

"Am not."

"Are too."

"Am not."

"Then prove it," Leif challenged.

She opened her mouth, but then closed it. After a moment, she said, "I hate you."

Leif smiled. "The feeling is mutual." He paused for a moment. "Are you coming?"

"Not now. I'll think about it."

"If you don't come back to the Keep, then I'll be right. And every time you see me, I'll be insufferably smug."

"And how's that different from now?"

He laughed. "You've only had a small glimpse of how insufferable and annoying I can be. As the older brother, it's my birthright."

Leif mounted Rusalka and galloped away.

Valek and Yelena walked with Kiki toward the north. Toward Ixia. He held her hand, not sure if he should encourage her to return home with him or discourage her. In the end, he decided not to say anything. He would answer her questions, but she needed to make her own decision.

"Valek. What did you say to Alea?"

"I told her how her brother died."

She remained quiet. Was she mad that he'd killed Alea?

"We had no time to take Alea with us, love. I wasn't going to let her have another chance to hurt you."

"How do you always know when I need you?"

Valek gazed at her. "I know. It's a part of me like hunger or thirst. A need that must be met to survive."

"How do you do it? I can't connect my mind to yours with my magic. And you don't have magic. It should be impossible."

Valek thought of how she crawled into his heart whenever she needed him. He didn't care how it worked. He was just grateful it did. "Perhaps, when I feel your distress, I relax my guard and allow you to connect with me?"

"Perhaps. Have you ever done that for anyone else?"

"No, love. You're the only one who has caused me to do the oddest things. You have truly poisoned me."

She laughed. "Odd, eh?"

Yes, like sweeping her off her feet and ravishing her until the morning. "It's a good thing you can't read my mind, love."

"Oh, I know what you're thinking."

She stepped into his arms and dipped her hands into his pants. Then she raised an eyebrow.

"I can't. Hide. From you," Valek panted.

Kiki snorted and moved away, giving them some privacy.

~

Valek was in no hurry to rejoin Ambassador Signe's entourage. And Yelena hadn't decided what she wanted to do. So, instead of riding Kiki, they walked through the plains in a northerly direction.

"Tell me about meeting your family for the first time," Valek said one afternoon, as they relaxed on the sand eating lunch. The Sandseed clan had been leaving them small caches of food and water. Kiki found them all.

"I was terrified. Mogkan had suppressed my childhood memories. Six years gone. I had so many doubts. What if they're not my family? What if they hated me?" She gave him a wry smile. "The Zaltana Clan—my clan, lives in this wooden village up in the tree canopy of the Illiais Jungle. It's amazing. Living areas are connected by rope bridges, and it has multiple levels. My cousin, Nutty, learned how to climb before she could walk." Yelena laughed. But then she sobered. "When I first arrived, they brought me before the entire clan. I wanted to hide and then, when I thought it couldn't get any worse..." She winced at the memory. "It did. Leif, my only sibling, pushed to the front and told the entire clan that I had killed, that I reeked of blood."

"That bastard. Did you knock him out with your bo?" Valek asked.

"No. I was mortified and wanted to hide behind Irys. She defended me and chastised Leif. Said she reeked of blood as well. But I guess as Fourth Magician, she's allowed." Yelena huffed. "Leif's magic is unusual. He can smell a person's intentions and detect lies. It's useful for interrogating criminals, so he works with First Magician Roze Featherstone at the Magician's Keep."

"What do your parents do?"

"My father, Esau, enjoys experimenting with the jungle's bounty. He collects vines, leaves, fruits, plants; basically anything that grows in the jungle. He makes furniture with the vines, medicines and salves with the plants; and collects flower petals for my mother, Perl. She invents and distills perfumes from them. Apparently, when I was five, my favorite was her lavender perfume."

"Shocking." He deadpanned.

She swatted him on the arm. "I guess it's obvious I love the scent. The horses even call me Lavender Lady."

"And I'm Ghost. Do the horses have names for everyone?"

"I don't know about everyone. But they call Irys, Magic Lady; Cahil, Peppermint Man; Leif, Sad Man; Ari, Strong Man; and Janco, Rabbit."

"Just Rabbit?"

"Yes, Kiki says he's too fast for a man."

Valek laughed. "Moon Man must have been named by a horse."

"Actually, the horses do call him Moon Man."

"Do they talk to all magicians?"

"Ah, no. I have an affinity with animals. Mostly, I get an emotional vibe. Like if they're hungry or scared or nonplussed, useful for knowing if there's a predator nearby or an ambush. The horses are different. Along with their emotions, I also receive images and words. Not a lot of words. Two or three at most. Things like, go fast, bad smell, apple. Kiki loves her sweets."

Valek remembered the peppermints in Yelena's bag. "And you've become quite the rider."

"All because of Kiki." She frowned. "No, that's not entirely true. Cahil taught me how to ride, saddle, and groom a horse."

Valek stilled. "Why?"

"Apparently that's his job when he's not trying to get Sitia to invade Ixia. He is good with horses." Another scowl, this one fiercer.

"Is that how you met him?" Valek kept his tone neutral.

She sighed. "No. Leif thought I was an Ixian spy. When we traveled to the Keep so I could start my magic lessons with Irys, Cahil and his unit ambushed us. That's when I had an unfortunate encounter with Goel. In his small mind, I'd made a fool of him when I escaped Cahil's camp, and he'd plotted revenge." She paused, her gaze turning inward. "Cahil and I came to an agreement and traveled to the Keep together. However, when I arrived, instead of Irys greeting me, Roze Featherstone attacked me. Cahil had sent word that I was an Ixian spy and—"

"Attacked you how?"

"Magic. She tried to read my mind. My soul." Yelena grabbed his hand. "That's when I reached out to you. You gave me the strength to endure. To thwart her. She wasn't happy, but at least everyone knew I wasn't a spy." She squeezed his fingers. "Thank you."

"Anytime." Valek considered. "What a rocky start to your Sitian adventures. Did you have magic lessons with Irys? Have you discovered the extent of your powers?"

"Yes. Well, sort of."

"Sort of?"

"I figured out I'm good at mental communication with humans and animals. I can heal, but not like a normal healer. When I do it, the injury transfers to me and then I have to heal myself, which is really hard to do when in pain. I can't move objects or light fires. Not yet. Irys believes I may in time. And, well…I…might be a…Soulfinder…but I'm not so sure."

He remembered she'd mentioned being a Soulfinder when she argued with Leif. They were feared because they were very powerful and supposedly dangerous. "What exactly does a Soulfinder do?"

"I don't really know. All I do know is I have the ability to hold a soul."

"I'm going to need more than that, love."

"When Leif and I went to confront Ferde, he turned Leif against me. That's when he hacked my bo staff into splinters. After I sent Leif into a deep sleep, I caught up with Ferde just in time to see him kill Gelsi." Yelena paused as a shudder swept through her. "I saw her soul float from her body, and I acted on instinct, diving over her and inhaling her soul before Ferde could collect it and finish the Efe Ritual."

"Which would have been bad."

"Yes, really, *really* bad. Apparently, no magician in a very long time has been able to inhale a soul, which is why I might be a Soulfinder."

"What about Ferde? Is he a Soulfinder as well?"

"I don't think so. The ritual allowed him to collect souls. Gelsi's was the last one he needed. He tried to take it from me by using magic. At that point he had master level powers, and he was stronger than me. I came this close"—she held her index finger and thumb a tiny gap apart—"To caving in. But he made a mistake. He tried to entice me, showing my future life with freedom and joy and contentment."

Yelena took Valek's other hand. "When I'm with you, I have contentment and joy. I refused to join him and give him Gelsi, so he changed his attack. The pain was debilitating. I was finished. But then your immunity saved me, and I stopped him by spraying Curare into his face with my mother's invention for applying perfume."

"Sounds like you inherited your intelligence from your parents."

"They've both helped me so much."

"Did you kill Ferde?" he asked.

"No. I returned Gelsi's soul to her body, which revived her. Then I freed the eleven souls Ferde had stolen, taking almost all of his power. The master magicians will be able to detain him and keep him locked away."

Valek added Ferde to his people-I-will-kill list. In his vast experience, power-hungry people like Ferde were never satisfied. They constantly searched for a way to regain power. Death was the best cure for those people.

They continued walking and catching up over the next couple days. When they reached the edge of the plains, they switched to sleeping during the day and traveling at night. Skirting east of the Citadel, they continued north into the Featherstone Clan's lands. Valek estimated that by now, Signe and her retinue were on their way home to Ixia and he planned to catch up to them before they crossed the border. Yelena hadn't revealed her plans, and he didn't ask.

However, during that time, Valek told her about his adventures while they were separated.

Yelena chimed in from time to time:

"Ooh, I like the sound of General Ute."

"Why didn't you tell me about Alea?" And after he explained, "That's a lame excuse. You just didn't want me to make you promise not to kill her."

"You're training Ari, Janco, and Maren to be your seconds? Ha! Good luck with that!"

They had six wonderful days together, but Valek needed to update the Ambassador. The delegation was camped about half a day's walk from Ixia. Of course, Sitian spies were keeping a close eye on them. Valek did a loop and marked their locations, then he put on his Ilom disguise, because why not? He waited until the middle of the night before crossing into the encampment.

"Look who finally decided to show up," Ilom said sleepily when Valek entered his tent. "You missed all the fun, old chap."

"I'm sure you had enough fun for both of us," he said.

Ilom snorted. "Am I supposed to dress as a soldier now?"

"Just until we're in Ixia. After that you can be you."

"Gee, thanks."

At dawn, Valek visited Ambassador Signe's tent. She sat at a small table, eating breakfast. Valek received almost the same snarky greeting as from Ilom. At least she offered him some tea.

It didn't take long for her to turn serious. "Report."

Over the noise of the soldiers packing up the camp, Valek explained about Ferde and Alea. He also detailed the pending problems with the new Daviian Clan. "Both Ferde and Alea were part of that clan. If the Sandseeds don't exterminate them, they'll be going after the Sitian Council."

"I agree. We need to keep an eye on them."

"The Sitian Council should—"

"Should deal with their own problems. Unfortunately, they don't have the skills, and we'd rather fight an enemy with an Ethical Code than one who thinks killing twelve young women and stealing their magic is okay."

"I'll assign a couple of my agents to keep tabs on the Daviians."

"As long as they are discreet," Signe said. "While you were vacationing in the plains, Ixian relations with the council deteriorated. By the end of our visit, one of the councilors accused me of bringing you to Sitia to assassinate the members of the council."

"That makes no sense. If I were to assassinate the councilors, I wouldn't come with a delegation." Or would he?

"Regardless, we need to let tempers cool."

"The Sitians haven't discovered my network of safe houses yet, but I will warn them to be extra vigilant."

"Good. Did Yelena tell you her plans? Is she returning to Ixia?"

Valek stilled. "Why would she return to Ixia? The Commander signed an execution order if she's caught in our country."

"Interesting that she didn't tell you. Ambrose asked me to extend an offer to her."

"An offer?"

"To return to Ixia when she'd finished her magical training. In exchange, he will nullify the execution order."

The tent spun. Valek had to rest his head in his hands for so many reasons. He hadn't realized that order had dug its claws deep inside him. That when it released him, it would cause such a dizzying mixture of pain and relief. But he couldn't celebrate yet. Yelena had to agree, or the execution order would stand.

When he straightened, Signe was watching him with a semi-concerned expression. She sipped her tea.

One of the guards ducked his head into the tent. "Ambassador, there's a Yelena Zaltana here who wishes to see you."

"Let her in."

When Yelena entered, Signe dismissed Valek. He mouthed the word 'tonight' to her as he left. The camp was almost packed up. Valek would accompany them over the border just in case there was trouble, but then he could loop back and meet up with Yelena. He. Couldn't. Wait.

～

Yelena had found a small pocket of woods not far from where Signe's retinue had camped. Valek circled the clearing to ensure there weren't any spies lurking, then he joined her by the fire. The flames warmed his cold hands. They were already halfway through the cooling season.

"Forgot your cloak again?" she asked.

He smiled. "I like sharing yours."

It wasn't long before he joined her. They generated plenty of heat together.

The morning arrived too soon. Yelena burrowed deeper into the cloak, and before cold reality could sink in, Valek said, "Come with me."

She peered at him with regret. "I still have much to learn. And when I'm ready, I'll be the new liaison between Ixia and Sitia."

The claws started to dig into him, but he paused as her words registered. "What about the execution order?"

"Destroyed. Ripped up. As the Liaison, I'll be working in relations between the two countries and visiting frequently."

"That could lead to serious trouble," Valek teased. He wanted to shout for joy and jump up and down.

"You would be bored if it was any other way."

He laughed. "You're right. And so was my snake."

"Snake?"

He pulled Yelena's arm out and exposed her bracelet. "When I carved this, my thoughts were on you, love. Your life is like this snake's coils. No matter how many turns it makes, you'll end up back where you belong. With me." And he'd do everything in his power to make that happen.

THANK YOU

Thank you for reading *The Study of Magic.* If you like to stay updated on my books and any news, please sign up for my free email newsletter here:

http://www.mariavsnyder.com/news.php

(go all the way down to the bottom of the page)

I send my newsletter out to subscribers three to four times a year. It contains info about the books, my schedule and always something fun (like deleted scenes or a new short story or exclusive excerpts). No spam—ever!

Please feel free to spread the word about this book! Posting honest reviews are always welcome and word of mouth is the best way you can help an author keep writing the books you enjoy! And please don't be a stranger, stop on by and say hello. You can find me on the following social media sites:

- Facebook (https://www.facebook.com/mvsfans)
- Facebook Reading Group - Snyder's Soulfinders (https://www.facebook.com/groups/ SnydersSoulfinders)
- Goodreads (https://www.goodreads.com/ maria_v_snyder)
- Instagram (https://www.instagram.com/ mariavsnyderwrites)

ACKNOWLEDGMENTS

Once again, I have plenty of people to thank for helping me make this the best book possible. Most of them have been mentioned in many of my acknowledgments since they continue to support me and my writing career. A career that I'm still a bit surprised has worked out so well. Considering I failed spelling and grammar in elementary school, I had no clue that I'd eventually be writing for a living.

Eternal thanks to:

My creative team: Dema Harb, Joy Kenney, Martyna Kuklis, and Raphael Corkhill.

My editorial team: Nat Bejin, Elle Callow, Reema Crooks, Reilly Gahagan, Brittany Clevenger, Rodney Snyder, and Jenna Snyder.

My publicity team: The staff of Cupboard Maker Books, and Jeff Young.

My supportive friends: Christine Czachur, Judi Fleming, Kathy Flowers, Michelle Haring, Amy and Bruce Kaplan, Mindy Klasky, Brian Koscienski, Jenn Mason, Jeri Smith-Ready, Kristina Watson, and Nancy Yeager.

My loving family: Rodney, Luke, Jenna, Mom, Pop, Karen, Chris, Amy, and Kitty.

ABOUT MARIA V. SNYDER

When Maria V. Snyder was younger, she aspired to be a storm chaser in the American Midwest so she attended Pennsylvania State University and earned a Bachelor of Science degree in Meteorology. Much to her chagrin, forecasting the weather wasn't in her skill set so she spent a number of years as an environmental meteorologist, which is not exciting...at all. Bored at work, and needing a creative outlet, she started writing fantasy and science fiction stories. Twenty-four novels and two short story collections later, Maria's learned a thing or three about writing. She's been on the *New York Times* bestseller list, won a dozen awards, and has earned her Masters of Arts degree in Writing from Seton Hill University, where she is now a faculty member for their MFA program.

When she's not writing, she's either playing pickleball, skiing, traveling, taking pictures, or zonked out on the couch due to all of the above. Being a writer, though is a ton of fun. Where else can you take fencing lessons, learn how to ride a horse, study marital arts, learn how to pick a lock, take glass blowing classes and attend Astronomy Camp and call it research? Maria will be the first one to tell you it's not working as a meteorologist.

www.ingramcontent.com/pod-product-compliance
Lightning Source LLC
Chambersburg PA
CBHW060857210726

48293CB00006B/1840